Missouri Roughneck

Harryett Burden Hyde

Copyright © 2013 Harryett Hyde
Venture Galleries LLC
1220 Chateau Lane
Hideaway, Texas 75771

ISBN: 978-1-937569-57-0

Text: Harryett Burden Hyde
Editing/Design: Linda Greer Pirtle
Cover Design: Jutta Medina

Manufactured in the United States of America.

Missouri Roughneck is a work of fiction. Name, characters, places, and incidents are either the product of the author's imagination or are used fictitiously. Any resemblance to actual persons, living or dead, or events is entirely incidental.

To my precious children: Richard, his wife Jala, and their son Jackson. I love you more than words can ever say.

Chapter 1

May, 1930

"I ain't never been backed up so close that I couldn't con my way out; not if I set my mind to thinkin' on it for a minute or two." Had John Earl Terry's devious mind not been so clouded by the alcohol of the previous night's revel, he might well have reconsidered his boast.

"Damn!" his oath drowned in the clanging of chains and shackles as the man who only moments before lay wadded against the wall of Sheriff Jake Simms' boxcar turned jail responded to a definitive kick to his back by the toe of a spit-polished boot. Terry moaned, as much from the blow as from the residuum of the whiskey. In response to both, he made a strategic deposit atop the feet of his attacker.

The man towering above him wavered, the overpowering stench of urine mixed with the bodies of men and women confined for days within the jail made him want to gasp for air. And now this added insult. "You no account son of a bitch. If it weren't for sullying my wife's good name, I'd have blown your sorry carcass to hell last night."

"Take it easy, Lamar," urged the sheriff. "Soon as the judge hears his case, he's outta sight and outta mind."

The prisoner's eyes slowly focused on a glenurquhard plaid suit. "You listen to me." His voice echoed in the confines of the boxcar. "You ever come within a mile of my wife again, I'll kill you." Threat delivered, the considerable force of Lamar Tate tore through the old railroad car with the power of an Oklahoma twister.

"Got quite a knack for pickin' the wrong man's bed," teased Sheriff Simms as he began the task of releasing his prisoner.

John Earl responded to the lawman's reference to last evening's dalliance with Tate's much younger wife, Estelle, with a characteristic grin which underscored his handsome features. Waves of dark hair, a meticulously groomed mustache, and an irresistible charm had drawn women to him since his early teens, making them useful yet dispensable pawns in the advancement of whatever suited John Earl Terry. As for the jealous husband, perhaps Estelle Tate had been a poor choice. His mind traveled back to her bedroom and the person of Estelle Tate, a store-bought blonde whose vulgarity could not be offset even by the bank account of the President of Oklahoma Oil. She was a looker, all right, and as smooth outside the sheets as in.

"Hope she was worth it."

Rising unsteadily, John Earl replied, "For a woman of Estelle's talents to be wasted on an old man like Tate is nothin' short of a sin, let me tell you." He began a stretch, but the calliope inside his head put a stop to all but the most necessary of movements. "Worth it? Without a doubt. In fact, I highly recommend her, now that I won't be around to keep her company." He gave the lawman a knowing wink.

"Don't you get no rumors started, John Earl. Some of us can't afford to leave this town."

"Come on, Sheriff. With the reputation you've built here in Seminole, you can name your job and wage in any boom town in this state or any other. Now who but you could rig up such a gem of jail as we see here?" Terry gestured to the fifty odd men and women shackled in leg irons which protruded through holes in the wall and secured by a length of iron bar. "Why, you even give the ladies their own side. That's dignity, Sheriff Jake."

"You're damn right. I'd like to see any man take a town that jumped from nine to fifty thousand and do better." He added with another pat to his own back. "And that ain't countin' the fringes of the Field. That's exactly what happened here from July to August of '27."

"If I could find my hat, it'd be off to you, sir. You think ole Lamar would send it to me when he finds it under Estelle's bed?" asked John Earl.

Sheriff Jake nudged Terry toward the sliding doors. "You and your belongings are the least of my worries. Me and fourteen officers stand between law and chaos in Seminole, Oklahoma. I got all I can say grace over keepin' up with fights, knifins', and murders. If a husband can't keep reign on his own wife, it ain't my worry."

"Unless the man's runnin' the company that controls what is and ain't in this town."

The sheriff knew better than to reply. Terry was right. If the cuckold had been anyone other than Oklahoma Oil's top man, the sheriff would have told him to look for his next wife in the church house instead of a whore house. But, being that his position rested in the hands of those men securely deposited in the hip pocket of the wronged husband, his seeing to the disposal of yet another of Mrs. Tate's "friends" seemed little enough to do. The likes of Terry and Mrs. Tate were just two of the thousands in an assortment of prostitutes, thieves, and gamblers who descended upon Seminole's four square miles of iniquity known to some as Cancre Flats and to others as Bishop's Alley, attracted to the rapid exchange of cash of naive field hands and pompous millionaires like Tate who lacked the good sense to run their lives as well as they did their business.

Terry took one more look at Simms' grandiose accommodations before the onslaught of Okie sunshine temporarily blinded him. He drew in long breaths of what served as fresh air. The exhausts of generators and engines coupled with the burn off of excess gases from the rigs produced a coughing fit. As both lawman and prisoner walked onto Main Street, heading for the courtroom, Simms initiated a conversation more as friend than captor.

"You've pretty much sealed your fate in these parts. Dammit, John Earl, I can't help but say that I'll miss seein' you around. Not many men I can count on to help me in a saloon brawl."

Terry shrugged, "Don't shed no tears over me; I won't be standin' in none of Mr. Hoover's bread lines. You know that a man with as much experience on and around rigs as I have has an immunity to this Depression."

Agreeing with a nod, Simms did not fault the man's arrogance. While desperate farm boys and laid off factory workers queued to beg for jobs that didn't pay a dollar an hour, an oil field hand like a second driller could pull in upwards of fifteen to eighteen dollars a day. Of course, boom town prices being what they were, a four-bed hotel room going for about three dollars and fifty cents a night per man took a bite out of a pocketbook, especially if he forked over the extra buck for clean sheets.

Simms patted the man on his shoulder. "No, I 'm not gonna waste time sayin' prayers over you. You got just the right mix of confidence and silver tongue to get whatever you set your mind to."

Terry looked genuinely hurt, "You're forgettin' my good looks and fatal charm." He let out a resounding laugh.

The sheriff became serious, "Why don't you go wherever the hell is home?" Immediately Sheriff Jake realized his error. Terry's face took on an anger Simms had not believed possible in the usually genial John Earl.

In those split seconds, John Earl Terry traveled a decade back to his sixteenth year when he left Corsicana, Texas. That was the last time his old man or anyone else laid an unanswered hand on him. When his pa hit the liquor, no manner of reasoning could tame him; the mash did his thinking and his talking.

John Earl had been picking cotton on the Navarro County land left by his grandfather, a rich section of black dirt that supported Terry Senior, his wife, and the five children born to the blessed union. Far from wealthy, they at least owned their farm and paid their bills. What had him drinking that early, John Earl never knew, but the sight of his oldest child idling under a pecan tree when cotton needed picking sent him into a fit of belt-swinging rage. With one well-thrown punch, the son felled his father. Searching his old man's overalls, he pocketed the few dollars and caught a north bound Southern Pacific for whatever destination it was headed.

The accused arrived at the J. P.'s office in less than a minute. In order to expedite judicial proceedings, the Honorable Martin P. Hanson held court at a desk under a tree but a few feet from the jail. Reading from a stack of papers, the justice looked over his glasses to appraise the man before him.

"Says here, you done yourself proud, boy. Gamblin' with a marked deck, drunk and disorderly, creatin' a public disturbance, and destruction of private property of one Lamar Tate. How ya plead?"

John Earl looked to Simms. On all these accounts, he had been guilty at one time or another, but on the night in question, he was lily white.

"Guilty as charged," answered his proxy.

Leaning back in his chair and placing his fingertips together, the judge made his pronouncement. "It's come to the attention of this court that you have no visible means of makin' a livin', you bein' blacklisted by a major company and all. So I spect you'll be back to your gamblin' as soon as your sentence is up." Hanson feigned a moment of contemplation, though this decision, as many others had been rendered by the man who ran the town. Pointing his index finger at Terry, he sighed. "I'm gonna give you a break, boy. I want you out of Seminole within the hour, and if you show your face here again, the sheriff there's gonna be on you quicker than a fly on shit. You got that?"

"Yes, sir."

The gavel fell. "Case dismissed."

When John Earl Terry started toward the hotel to collect his things, Hanson and Simms watched him go.

"Hated to do that," bemoaned the Justice. "That piece of white trash has to be more trouble to Tate than she's worth."

Simms smiled. "Not to hear ole John Earl tell it."

The echo of their laughter followed Terry to the hotel where he hoped to retrieve his few belongings. To those unaccustomed to boom town living, the hotel in Seminole held all the charm of a New York tenement. In every direction, men were sleeping on any piece of furniture or consecutive feet of open space. Though the intensity of the boom was waning at the onset of 1930, those who first entered the town or those who could afford no better naturally migrated to the ill-christened Palace. If she had looked better in her heyday, there was no one who could recall just when that might have been. Dirt and tobacco stained wallpaper hung limply, sagging and tattered in a valiant struggle to cling to the lobby walls, as did the upholstery of the sparse chairs and sofas.

As for the rooms, their only furnishings were double beds, which at one time were rented in shifts to several occupants at any given time. Not that the men complained, most were too tired to care about how or with whom they slept.

Since the construction of a boarding house, a few more hotels, and the Company Camp for those fortunate enough to work for Oklahoma Oil, the overcrowding had eased, permitting a customer with sufficient cash or pull to rent a private room. Loading his meager wardrobe into some paper bags, Terry examined his broadcloth dress shirt which was ripped down the sleeve.

"There went a good ninety-five cents," he muttered.

His bill paid, Terry sauntered down the street like a man without a care, arriving at a boarding house where he often took meals and where his most prized possession, his Model A, roomed in the dilapidated garage of Edgar Means.

News traveled fast in Seminole, especially scandal. In anticipation of a hasty exit, the elderly Means was polishing the Model A one last time. "Sure sorry to see you leave, John Earl. It'll be like losin' a close friend." He referred to the car he liked to pass off as his own.

John Earl scoffed, "You and my old man. What he wouldn't give to drive around Navarro County in this baby." He caressed the fender as if it were Estelle Tate. "Someday I just may take her home and rub it in," a thought which occurred to him between big winnings in poker games and the big losses that inevitably followed. "The return of the prodigal will just have to wait until another streak of luck."

"Folks would say you were in pretty short supply of that right about now."

A lesser man might have agreed, but not John Earl. His spirits were never down, not for long at any rate. Already his mind was at work calculating the route and mileage to his next field.

"Where you figure on headin'?" Means quickly changed the subject.

"Word is the next big strike is due in East Texas."

"I figure oil field gossip runs second to the truth, but you got to know that the Van Field that come in last October don't have no jobs for a blacklisted man."

Although there was plenty of work in Van, a true boom, John Earl's only hope for employment, failed to materialize since the major companies secured the prime leases before independents.

The old man began to double over with laughter. "I guess you could hire on with Dad Joiner and Doc Lloyd." Means referred to the raising of money for what the geologists dismissed as total folly.

No oil existed in and around the town of Kilgore except in the dreams of the two men who were beating the bushes trying to build drilling capital.

To hear tell, the experts sized up Joiner and Lloyd's chances somewhere between slim and none.

Since that pretty much equaled his own, Terry stunned Means with a, "That's exactly where the hell I'm headed, and the next time you see me, you'll be laughing out the other side of your mouth cause I'll be runnin' this town."

"Ain't no oil down in Rusk or Greg counties, I'm tellin' ya."

In his own defense, "Don't appear as Joiner's agreein'."

"Joiner, hell, he's a con man from way back, takin' money from folks that got more dreams than good sense."

"Well, he ain't the only one. A man name of Skipper up at Longview is of a similar opinion."

"He one of them geo what's it fellers?"

John Earl winced, "Not exactly... sells real estate."

Between peals of laughter, the old man bolstered his argument, "And that in itself don't tell you nothin'? All that man's doin' is drummin' up business for hisself. Folks think there's oil, they'll be knockin' his door down to buy up land. Don't take no high powered education to figure that one out." Edgar Means took a longing look at the Model A. "The first two wells they drilled out there were dryer than bones, and the newest one spudded got as much chance as me dancin' high atop the Roosevelt Hotel in New Orleans. So when you're broke and ready to sell her, let me know."

Climbing into the automobile, Terry flashed the old man a grin. "Better resole them dancin' shoes, Edgar." And with that, he was off for Texas.

~~~~~

Miles of road and hours at the wheel transformed Oklahoma into the magnificence of an East Texas spring. The aromas of wildflowers mixed with the clean country air made John Earl a new man. As he predicted, signing on with a crew in Van posed little problem. Perhaps the job might have lasted a few more weeks before news of his blacklisting arrived had he and the farm boss not crossed.

"Hell couldn't be no hotter," murmured Terry as the Model A Phaethon migrated from one rut into another on a back road some one hundred miles East of Dallas. It was the first week in June, but the temperatures were already reaching the upper nineties. Increasing speed provided more of the dry, parching air, leading to a string of curses aimed at the farm boss, his hands twisting to a vice-like grip on the corrugated steering wheel substituting for the man's neck.

Tell me to climb a burnt out rig, not knowin' which piece of steel will hold your weight or send you to your maker. John Earl's refusal sparked a series of threats from the boss, a cross between a drill sergeant and his old man which prompted Terry to point out his distinct resemblance to the south end of a north bound horse.

Taking note of a clearing ahead, John Earl pushed in the clutch, for a quick turn into the drive of a hayseed dump labeled LaGuinn's Grocery, Gas and Feed. The building was as varied a structure as its sign boasted. What must have been the original framework peaked to an A-framed roof. Jutting from either side, two unequal flat roofed additions joined to achieve a segmented effect. On every available portion of wall, colorful metal signs advertised everything from cigarettes to soda pop. A single gas pump stood lone sentry under a weary, wooden porch, thus enabling drivers to park between it and the door to the country store.

The crunch of tires upon the gravel signaled an overall-clad farm boy who left his perch on an upturned R. C. Cola case. For Cale McCallister, spotting this type no longer proved difficult. A man of good size, deeply tanned, good clothes, a car, and callused hands reeked of oil field wages.

"I need to wet my whistle," stated the driver who wiped his forehead with a white handkerchief emblazoned as was the car's roof with the initials "JET."

"Coke Cola's in the box," pointed the square-jawed Cale as the two entered the limited respite from the heat granted by shelter and the moaning of ceiling fans. Cale ran his hands through a full head of sandy hair which set off his ruddy coloring. Once inside, the arrangement proved deceptive from what one expected by an initial outward viewing. The predominant portion of general mercantile counters and shelves gave way to a lower level to its right where a variety of feed and tack accounted for the smaller of the two expansions. The wooden floor creaked with their weight.

John Earl recognized the discrepancy of the floor plan immediately. "I mean a man's drink; the kind our Uncle Sam don't want us to have."

Behind the silver scroll-worked cash register, a gray-haired man of some sixty odd years leaned against a stool, enabling him to tower over the counter. A stained bibbed apron covered his clothing and his distended belly. From his lips hung a cigarette, the length of its ashes in direct defiance of gravity. Hoyt LaGuinn's thick eyebrows arched. A place like his offered no attraction to lawmen set on enforcing the statutes of Prohibition. Still, an ounce of prevention...

"Where you from, boy?" he questioned the thirsty patron, his tone and actions feigning disinterest.

"You call it. Left Corsicana at sixteen and Van this mornin'. Name's Terry, John Earl Terry."

"Hoyt LaGuinn. Work the field?"

"One kind or another; prefer oil though. The money's a sight better." All laughed, the charisma of John Earl Terry at work again. Indiscriminately John Earl moved the red and black checkers upon a table in whose top the unmistakable board was etched. The scent of pickles drew him to a bin where he raised the wooden lid and drank in the vinegar and dill.

"Like to take on the locals with a game now and then." The proprietor moved from behind the counter. "Keep her set up for any comers."

Reading his customers proved a harmless diversion for the storekeeper, and this one bore all the markings of a man who had worked for a living, not a citified lawman come to pry into the affairs of simple country folks out to make a dime or two off the government's interference.

As for John Earl, he too participated in the game and labeled the boy at the pump a rube just a bit younger than himself, the man behind the counter the type who had a good deal more money socked away than he let on, especially to his wife and kids.

My kind of folks, Terry said to himself, smiling inwardly at the prospects this unscheduled stop might bring.

Lady luck just keeps smilin' on me, guidin' me to the right spots and makin' sure I got all the necessary equipment. He patted his pants pocket to reassure himself that his ticket to a little unplanned cash remained safely inside.

"If you don't mind the shine, I can see to your thirst."

"Wouldn't be no country boy if I passed on some homemade brew."

Cale eased out the door, assured that all was square inside. Hoyt liked to put on a bold front, but years on his feet restricted his mobility and reflexes.

"Your boy?" Terry questioned as soon as Cale disappeared outside.

"In a manner of speakin'. He showed up here from Missouri a few weeks back lookin' for a fortune in the oil field, flat broke, and no experience except choppin' cotton. Wife and I took a shine to him. Our own boys moved off to Fort Worth to work at the meat packin' plant. Third boy took from us by them damned Germans."

His eyes glistened as they did each time he recalled the vision of his son abandoned on a foreign battlefield over a cause so far removed from the comprehension of an aging Texas father.

"I'm sorry to hear that."

"Millie and me went all the way up to Washington on the train to that big cemetery to see him buried military proper." He pointed toward the back of the store. "So when Cale showed up with nobody and no prospects, well, it gets lonely in that big old two story frame."

As Terry suspected, Hoyt pulled on a section of shelving to reveal a passageway into that most successful portion of the LaGuinn enterprise. Inside a makeshift bar and an assortment of mismatched chairs and tables lured a lucrative trade.

"I'll take care of this one, Willie," he told a black man setting up glasses behind the counter. "I'm about the only one makin' money outta this drought and Hooverism." He began to pour the drink. "Less it rains, the thirstier they get. "Besides," he poured a second for himself, "a body has the right to drink whenever he gets a notion." Saluting his lone customer, "It don't make no difference what a bunch of two-faced politicians up in Washington make into law. It was their thinkin' got our boy kilt over somethin' didn't concern nobody but them folks over there." He swallowed the drink defiantly.

Cale urged the cash register drawer into place, its subsequent grind and ring too familiar to warrant notice. His latest customer's purchase of a single gallon paid for in what appeared to be the man's last few coins reminded him of the times in which they lived and the hopelessness that drove him from a Missouri home toward his dream of a fortune working the oil fields. Cale's good nature afforded him a laugh at himself and his naiveté. When Willie Bacon left per Hoyt's instruction and entered the main part of the store, Cale addressed his new friend.

"Yep, Willie, I'm makin' a fortune in the oil business."

"'Cept you're pumpin' gas instead of oil."

The backwater Missouri town where Cale grew up would never have allowed this friendship between white and colored, much less understood the twenty-two year old Cale's almost fatherly respect for Willie Bacon. Past his fortieth birthday, Bacon farmed a small tract of land left by his grandfather, but times being what they were, he often worked off his bill at the store by cleaning up or tending bar.

A wistfulness crossed the younger man's face. "Looks like my plans of sendin' my sister and her husband money to buy back the farm is about as likely as your boy gettin' to go to that black college in Louisiana."

"Now don't you be thinkin' I done give up on that." Willie swept up some escaping feed near a stack of twenty-pound bags. "A man don't never know what the good Lord has waitin' 'round the next bend in life's road."

He shrugged. "Who's to say there's not fixin' to be a partin' of the dark clouds and a silver linin' just waitin' to bust out and shine on me and mine?"

The two returned to the back room to find Hoyt and the traveler pouring over some papers from John Earl's pocket. Cale seated himself next to Hoyt while Willie busied himself near enough to see and hear the goings on. As long as no customers could see, Hoyt treated Willie with as much regard as any man, but when folks stopped in, Willie knew exactly how far to extend himself in the company of whites in deference to Hoyt's generosity and his own safety.

"This here's these surrounding counties, of course," said Terry as he pointed on the crumpled map to the counties from Van Zandt over to Smith, north to Upshur, down to Gregg and Rusk detailed along with an intriguing code of symbols scattered with no discernible pattern. Try as he might, the rhyme or reason escaped Cale, though Hoyt's interest revealed his grasp of the perplexing figures.

"Now I know from field talk that Joiner and Lloyd spudded in on or about here, referring to a large "X.""

This information Cale recognized. Most folks from Dallas to Houston knew the names in John Earl's reference either in hope or in jest. For most of the Twenties, Columbus Marion Joiner, an aging wildcatter, had traipsed across East Texas proposing the existence of oil flowing in endless pools under their very feet. It required a particularly desperate or foolish listener to believe his tale, weighed against the seventeen dry holes drilled by independents and major companies alike in Rusk County, teamed with the damning geologists' reports based on the results of the most modern oil detecting machinery available.

Oh, he mustered a following of Depression-ridden farms and sweet-talked old ladies, enough to acquire some leases along with the aid of an old friend from the Oklahoma fields in the person of A. D. "Doc" Lloyd, whom Joiner heralded as a noted geologist but whose credentials, he thanked heaven, few thought to question. Battling hard luck, poor equipment, and a perpetual lack of funds, Joiner and Lloyd now found themselves on their third try at bringing in a well on the land of one Daisy Bradford located between Overton and Henderson.

"And ain't hit so much as a sign of oil," disputed Hoyt.

"Not yet," John Earl's eyes twinkled as he pushed forward. "You read these geological reports of Joiner's."

"How'd you come by these?" Hoyt's skepticism unchecked.

"From a wheel over in Van without the vision the good Lord give a Billy goat." A chuckle escaped. "Hell, he'll be askin' me to kick his ass all the way to Dallas when the boom hits and he's got nothin' to show but his own ignorance."

John Earl's remark drew no response with the entrance of what appeared to Terry as unlikely clientele. Dressed for his role as Brophy, Texas' lone banker, Clyde Russell wore his silver hair with the dignity born of wisdom. For nearly thirty-five years, he had dispensed sound financial advice to his patrons from the center of the town's business district of two city blocks facing one another, boasting Clyde's bank, a cafe, a general mercantile/Post Office, and several abandoned storefronts.

That Brophy maintained so much as a single enterprise bespoke of Clyde's skills, for if the populations of white and black in the outlying areas combined with the city folk, no more than three hundred or so residents might be scraped together.

With Hoyt's business facing the main road and as such removed from the city proper, two churches, a couple of gas pumps, and a three-roomed school completed the grand tour. Thus citizens depended on the surrounding towns of Longview, Kilgore, and Tyler for whatever demands could not be met, the joke being that folks had to leave town in order to be born or buried.

At his side, a woman barely five feet in height smoothed the skirt of a simple cotton house dress that clung sensuously to a body slender in form yet rounded at hip and breast.

John Earl could scarcely contain himself. Her every movement betrayed the unmistakable grace of a woman unaware of the effect of her beauty. Had he not lingered so long on her stylishly bobbed hair, he would have noticed a similar reaction in Cale.

As it were, Terry mistook the coy dip of the blonde woman's eyes as the necessary response of a gentlewoman to his all too eager gaze. He was about to initiate an introduction, when a boy of perhaps five bolted through the doorway.

"Momma, can I have a licorice? Please, can I?"

Elaine smiled down at her son. "Not now, Jake. Mrs. LaGuinn has worked awfully hard making you a fine supper. We wouldn't want to go spoiling it." Turning to the men, she said, "I'll see you gentlemen later," she promised as John Earl silently echoed his assurance that other meetings would follow.

"Let's go see if we can help Millie."

Her exit temporarily broke Terry's trance.

"What are you boys so all fired interested in?" questioned Clyde.

The necessary introductions and explanations dispensed, Clyde studied the map with professional intensity. "Old Malcom Crim's been pesterin' me to either invest or loan him the capital to drill on his mamma's place over on the Rusk/Gregg border."

"He's got some proof to back it up?" asked Cale.

Clyde beamed inwardly. Just the type of question a fledgling banker should ask. Unbeknownst even to his daughter, Russell intended to put the object of her affections to work at his bank. That was as soon as the boy put his intentions toward her into words. Practically from the day Cale McCallister hit town, he had seen the life stolen by the untimely death of her husband return in his only child. Now that they were attending church meetings and Brophy's meager offerings of social gatherings, tongues would wag as to how the school teacher and banker's daughter was marrying beneath her. Besides, a steady job and a chance to move up at the bank would keep the daughter and grandson upon which he doted close to home.

"Sure as hell does," snorted Hoyt. "A fifty-cent fortune teller over at Mineral Wells. Ain't that the way you generally decide on who's gettin' loans or not over to that bank of yours, Clyde? Call up that woman to read you some cards over the telephone?"

The two Brophyites shared a good laugh at the expense of Malcom Crim's encounter with and the stock shown in the predictions of a two-bit faker.

Undaunted, Terry switched his emphasis to the banker. *Lightening the old man's pockets by a few hundred, perhaps a thousand, would feather a nest, he thought, so's I could drill my own well. But with the entrance of a genuine banker, my plans are a changin' for the better. All I need do is convince these country hicks to back my venture. Lucky for them, it's the only business enterprise I ever tried to raise money for that I intend to see through to a successful end.*

"All joking aside, I am firmly convinced that the oil exists... maybe under this very store."

Only Willie remained outside the circle, though he passed the map at odd intervals to satisfy his own curiosities and keep up with a conversation growing more interesting by the minute.

The stranger continued, "We know that dry holes have been sunk to the east of Joiner and Lloyd's well. Takin' into consideration the other dusters over the years, and," he added none too sarcastically, "Crim's conviction about his farmland, I figure on oil flowin' in and around Brophy." Pointing to the shaded area, he tapped it lightly with a pencil and settled back in his chair to allow the audience sufficient time to grasp the impact and importance of his statements.

"I never been closer to a bigger pile of bullshit in my life," blurted the storekeeper.

From across the room, a voice firm in its delivery surprised even the man who insinuated himself into the white men's discussion.

"But there is oil in Brophy, Mr. Hoyt." All eyes riveted on a Willie caught off guard by uncharacteristic impertinence.

"What's that?"

"On my place, Sir."

The black man slowly breached the circle.

"Years ago, my grand pappy done drilt a water well, but they couldn't use the water none. The taste waz horrible bad. Didn't nobody drank from it, no matter how thirsty they got. Said the devil lived down that well hole. Me and some other boys opened it up on a dare when we waz little, and shore enough, there's oil in that water."

Terry counted Willie's words with equal merit with those of the fortune teller's until the first sparks of interest glowed in the eyes of Russell and LaGuinn. Seizing his opportunity, he determined to milk it for all it was worth. "You able to back this up?"

"I'll takes you all to see it right now."

"And you say you own this land out right?" Terry asked skeptically.

"Willie lives over at Freedman," Clyde explained. "It's not incorporated as such, but a good many black families can trace their land around there back to just after the War when Carpetbaggers helped freed slaves buy home sites. They worked hard and made their taxes. Though I hate to have to admit it, several of Willie's neighbors are mortgaged heavily now that money's as short as good crops in this damnable dry spell."

Terry drained his glass and announced, "I'm game."

LaGuinn Grocery, Gas and Feed closed early for the first time that anyone could remember, forfeiting the change-of-shift patronage from the Van Field and leaving an angry Millie LaGuinn and an equally confused Elaine Russell watching from the kitchen window.

With a turn of the NuGrape sign whose alternate sides broadcast the business' status, the five men donned hats and wedged themselves into the Phaethon for the mile and a quarter ride to Willie Bacon's farm.

Located just off the road and bounded by a creek which miraculously held water this late in the drought, the home place covered some twenty acres. A small, ramshackle house surrounded by barefoot children and an assortment of mongrel dogs greeted their arrival with a clamor of shouts and barks.

The scene bore all the markings of the effectiveness of the South's segregationist policies.

Arnolia appeared on the porch, a frightfully thin woman with a child balanced on her hip, in response to the car and the noise of her brood. The automobile sped past in a stream of dust to take out across the farm land for the back acres and left her with a mouthful of dirt for her troubles.

Bunch of white men out surveyin' us black folks like this waz their plantation again. Takin' me away from my chores, she estimated with contempt, unable to see her husband. "Ride on then," she urged on her way back into the stifling heat of the house. "I got no time to furnish no show to white men in their fancy cars. Got no use for the none of you, nor does any of mine."

She trudged further into the house without a thought to closing the door. Any breeze was welcomed regardless of whatever bugs came along with it. Life in general afforded her as little pity as the summer heat. Married at fifteen, a baby born before she got used to being sixteen, and more than she could stomach of being the lowest rung in the South's rigid caste, formed a hard crust around the woman's heart, solidified by the endless work of family, farm, and kissing the feet of town folks for the honor of doing work they deemed beneath them.

Only Willie could recall the beauty and the vibrancy of his child bride. Even Arnolia herself had lost touch with the woman asleep beneath the shell of anger and resentment. Arnolia Bacon was a cold woman, but rightfully so.

At Willie's instruction, John Earl braked the vehicle, and the men abandoned it, much to their mutual relief, for such close confines and the heat produced a most uncomfortable ride.

The further they went into the underbrush, John Earl doubted his decision to trade in his original hand. *This is turnin' out to be more of a wild goose chase than I thought.* Taking a look back at the profusely sweating Hoyt, *if we don't get to his place soon, I'll have to convince the man's widow to back this scheme. Still...widows are some of my most satisfied customers.* A few moments later, the lead man brought them to a halt near the ruins of what must have been many years before something akin to a house. Actually the structure's two rooms protected Willie's family from the brutality of the East Texas weather and their white neighbors for many years. Even after his wife's death and the wandering away of his seven other offspring, the old man lived in the original home place until his death at eighty-three. Little remained now except ancient boards leaning upon each other for support.

Kicking and pulling his way through a scrubby growth, Willie pointed to some rotting boards.

"We keeps it covered so no younguns nor animals falls in."

Cale bent down to help Willie remove the lumber only to unleash a vile stench and reveal a squirming mass of creatures unhappy to have their home disturbed, they being in sole possession of the only cool place south of Colorado. Pulling a frayed rope from inside the well, Willie offered the contents of its weathered bucket for inspection. Barely detectable were the bluish swirls of color. Hoyt ventured a taste, dipping his fingers into the cool liquid and pronouncing it bitter, determining a tell-tale odor.

"Let me see your matches, Mr. Hoyt."

In response to the request, Hoyt pulled a penny box of matches from the apron he had forgotten to remove in his haste to see the well. Striking it alongside the box, Willie dropped it into the bucket he had filled with dried grass and pine needles.

The dangling pail met with the sides of the well several times as the men, all on hands and knees, peered in with eyes intent upon the shrinking flames. As it reached the water level, a sudden and faintly detectable whoosh briefly spread atop the water. Looking from one to another, their expressions ranged from total surprise to the enormous white-toothed grin of the black man who knew better than to utter an, "I told you so," to four whites.

John Earl mustered the wherewithal to speak. "If there's enough down there for..." his voice trailed. "How much for your lease, Willie?"

Already John Earl had the land purchased and wells spouting gushers, sure that swindling the rights from a colored man would be the easiest dupe of his career.

"Can't rightfully say." His eyes pleaded to Hoyt for assistance.

"Slow down. There's a lot to be considered here," Clyde encouraged. "First we need a geologist."

A strident voiced Terry leaped to his feet. "And drive up the lease prices until we can't compete against the majors? Think, man. Do you want a repeat of Van? As it stands, we're all that's on to this. Now you let a soul get wind, and we've got speculators and oil scouts up to our respective asses all wantin' a piece of this mighty sweet deal. Pretty soon, we're out dollared and cheated of what we done discovered. That what you want?"

"He's right," Cale agreed. "If we buy up leases around here now, they're ours for a song." Turning to John Earl, "I don't have much of any money to invest, but I'm willin' to do anything, work any job, go anywhere to do this with you."

Clyde bristled at Cale's mention of leaving *as though he's got no obligations to keep him in Brophy. I've made some poor financial decisions in my day, and this will no doubt be the worst. But to keep Elaine and Jake happy and at home, it'll be money well spent. I'll pretend to be just as caught up in the euphoria as the rest, even if it means using the bank's resources and my own to prove it.*

"Don't go runnin' off," he soothed. "I can see to some lease money to cover your part and mine."

Suddenly picturing himself excluded, Hoyt demanded, "You ain't leavin' me out, not by no long shot."

With the afternoon heat taking its toll on his bulk, he suggested, "Let's us go back and get some real plans goin'. Drinks and supper's on me."

Bulging with fresh produce from Millie's garden and a heaping pile of homemade rolls whose yeasty aroma filled the entire house, the dining room table at the LaGuinn home bustled with the delights of a good meal and the excitement of oil fever. The hostess squeezed every available chair and a piano bench, piled with Sears catalogues for Jake, around the oak table. In light of the occasion, even Willie found himself with his feet under a white man's table, something about which Arnolia would later swear he lied.

"I'm still not sure I understand this leasin' business," Millie stated as she passed the Havilland pink rose bowl of snap beans.

"Well, it's a little like share croppin'," John Earl explained. "What we'll do is strike a deal with as many of the land owners as we can, as fast as we can. We agree on a number of years; let's say three for the sake of argument. In exchange, they get a yearly rental and roughly an eighth of the oil we hit."

"And if you don't strike no oil?" asked Millie.

"They made more money than they had before we came," answered Cale, a quick study in his new line of work.

"But there's a real danger of their crop cycles being disturbed," interjected Elaine.

"I'm afraid, my dear, that at today's prices a drought-stunted harvest is worth far less than the rent we plan on payin'," responded John Earl.

Taken aback by the familiarity of a man she had met only hours before, Elaine ducked her head less from the embarrassment by his endearment than from the emotions the man evoked. *Fright*, she told herself. *No, skepticism of a drifter taken into our bosom without so much as a clue to his identity and intentions.* It was then that the similarities between Terry, the man she did not trust, and Cale, the man to whom she wanted to give her life, struck her.

How can I fault John Earl, when I know little more about the man I love? But why do I have strong misgivings about this man and his promises to change our lives? And why do I feel prickles of excitement when his eyes...? Suddenly aware of the clamminess of her palms, Elaine began to fiercely wipe them on Millie's Sunday napkin, as if to erase evidence of her disquietude.

Unaware that Elaine heard nothing past his initial remark, he continued, "Besides, why drive yourself into an early grave farmin' when we're gonna hand them the money for no more effort than signin' their names and stickin' out their hands for profits?" Wiping traces of cream gravy with a Crown Derby napkin, he turned his attentions to more pressing matters. *There'll be time for more intimate conversations, Mrs. Crawford, and the subject,* he promised himself, *will not be oil.*

"You say you can draw me a pretty accurate map of who owns what?" he asked of Clyde.

Having loaned money to buy or against most of the property in the area, the banker possessed a familiarity that rivaled the County Clerk's.

"Done it." A map traced from Terry's original, but sectioned off to indicate ownership passed from hand to hand until it reached John Earl's. "Most of the land borderin' mine and south of town is black folks'. I know 'um all and them me."

"They all look up to Willie, and he can get the lot of them to go with us," added Clyde.

Terry concluded, *might just work to our advantage after all, havin' a black man as a partner.* "Who made these marks?" He pointed in reference to land jutting in other directions.

"I did," replied Clyde. "I held, and in most instances still hold, notes to these. There'll be a few stubborn old goats, but by and large, I believe we can pick up the leases for little or nothin' especially considerin' those with notes due. They most likely don't have the cash to make payments. Rather than see it come back to the bank, what choice do they have?"

"And if you foreclose, can we buy up what comes back?" Cale questioned.

"I don't see it comin' to that, but to answer you, it wouldn't be just real ethical not to let them know what we think is hidin' under their land," said Clyde.

That brief but honest addendum ran chills up Terry's back. *I thought, seein' that Hoyt runs a rural speakeasy, that I wouldn't have to run this deal by the books. This lookin' a foul of a gift horse can crimp my style of business operation. Well, they'll learn to see things my way,* he sighed inwardly.

Feeling as if he were being scrutinized at that moment, he turned and made eye contact with Elaine. A flush traveled across her face before she quickly left the room. *Yep, I've faced tougher and come out on top, exactly where I was meant to be,* he thought.

"Just how much land are we gonna need?" Hoyt remained the only one at the table; a piece of steak stabbed into the tines pointed at the map.

"I'm hopin' for a ten thousand acre block," responded Terry.

Cale whistled in awe of the amount and the task of securing the necessary funds for leasing. "But you said we'd be payin' fifty cents an acre! I never thought about fifty thousand of anything, much less dollars." He walked toward Terry. "We ain't got that kinda money, and you haven't even put pencil to paper on the drillin' expenses."

Such a large dose of reality stifled the spirits of all concerned, save John Earl. "I have some investors all lined up," he lied. "If we can raise the lease money, which we will try to buy for less than fifty cents, that's the top price, remember, I can handle the rest."

"And just what are we gonna do for wages?" Hoyt pointed to the banker, "Him and me ain't prospects for no drillin' hands, and if we hire out from under the majors, then they'll get wind of our find, and we'll be outta business before we get in."

"That's why Cale and me is headed to Seminole," answered John Earl.

Cale looked up in surprise at his revelation. Aware that he alone followed the logic, Terry explained. "These dyed in the wool East Texas farmers ain't about to lease an outhouse to two strangers. While Willie's courtin' his folks, Hoyt, you and Clyde call on the whites. And," he beamed, "me and Cale will be charmin' the pants off the best first driller to ever spud a well." His audience unimpressed by his last pronouncement, Terry continued. "The name's Bulldog Schneider. He will tip a few glasses, but that won't keep him from bringin' in a well. Course," he threw in as an afterthought, "once we have the leases, won't matter who the hell knows what we're up to."

"What's he doin' in Seminole?" Cale questioned from his seat on the mohair davenport that dominated the parlor.

"Supportin' the big shots at Oklahoma Oil and gettin' just his wage for his troubles."

"Hrmph, appears that's the dream of half the folks in the United States of America," piped Hoyt. "Why should any man with a lick of sense leave a sure thing to join up with a bunch of know nothings like us?"

John Earl rose, stretched, and lit a cigarette from the wooden smoking stand next to Hoyt's matching chair. From experience, he'd perfected the utilization of the carefully timed pause in a conversation to best enhance his position of dominance. "Not a thing for you to fret about, Hoyt. Just you leave it to ole John Earl." Placing the cigarette in the ashtray, he attempted to change the subject. "Suppose Millie has any more of that egg custard?"

"The crew?" Cale prompted.

With all the wisdom of a bear lashing back at its surrounding enemies, John Earl formed his crew, a regret he'd express to himself many times over in the next weeks. "You and me can roughneck."

"And me?" Willie's question bore the overtone of a demand.

"Don't no coloreds work a rig directly. There's plenty of odd jobs..."

"Oh, this one will, or you can count all the black leases out. This well is my one and only shot at makin' a decent livin' for my family. And if I can help along my friends, then that's all the better." There was more that Willie wanted to say including his knowledge that the white men were only allowing him inclusion because they wanted what he had and could provide. Not that he distrusted Hoyt or Clyde, because he knew them to be men of their word, something he suspected of Cale, though he normally required a longer period of time to pronounce any white man worthy of his trust. However, it had been his experience that the faster a white man like Terry talked to a black one, the deeper the latter needed to dig in his heels.

Patronizingly, John Earl put his arm around Willie's broad shoulder, "You can be whatever you want to be, besides first driller. That's for an experienced man, though I can't see why you'd want to put yourself out. Workin' a rig ain't no picnic, and a man's got no..."

"I ain't never knowed nothin' but hard work for another man's profits. No offense to you, Mr. Hoyt."

Hoyt nodded the lack of offense taken. He could appreciate Willie's point of view, familiar with the man's personal struggles and those of all blacks in East Texas.

"This is the only opportunity I gots to get the money to educate my children so they has a better life than me. And if we hits a dry hole, I gots experience to take somewhere else."

John Earl continued the pasted smile of a politician courting votes the rest of the evening as they wrote out leases by hand. After Willie left for home, John Earl found himself alone in the parlor. As he sat with his back to a window opening onto the porch, the now quiet room made him an unperceived third party to Elaine and Cale's conversation in the porch swing.

"I just don't know about all this, Cale. Things have moved just a little fast for my liking," said Elaine.

Cale removed his arm from around her shoulders, his voice pleading. "Don't you see, we have as much of our future ridin' on this as Willie."

"I'd hardly compare our situations."

"You've got to know that I love you." The tenderness with which she took his hand served as affirmation. "But an educated woman like yourself, with a boy to think of, what would she want with a man whose only prospects are for pumpin' gas the rest of his life?"

Before she could voice objections, Cale silenced her. "That's why we gotta gamble on this long shot, so you and Jake can have somebody to be proud of as a husband and a daddy."

His eyes following the awkward motions of Elaine Crawford's suitor, John Earl watched as they kissed. Less than his own six feet by a several inches and lacking enough meat on his bones or the cunning to wage a war for a woman's affection, Terry dismissed the import of the tender scene. He walked toward the stairs that led to the second floor bedrooms. *Six, seven months on the outside, till I'm in your heart and in your bed, Mrs. Crawford.* He flashed a knowing grin toward the LaGuinn porch.

Chapter 2

One week later

Side curtains flapping in the stale afternoon breeze, Hoyt bounced along the tree-lined drive leading to the Wallis house. Lingering scents of past deliveries battled with the dust of the road as the grocer turned lease hound practiced his spiel as nervously as though this were his first call until he pulled his 1929 Ford Station Wagon under a spreading pecan planted at least a half century before. Actually, between Clyde and him, the majority of the leases designated on their maps lay duly signed and secured in a bank vault drawer. This one, however, he purposefully delayed, dreading the property owner. Even an unprofessional leasing agent could smell that this transaction would be different from any of the others.

Throughout his life, Hoyt LaGuinn faced his share of vermin, human or otherwise, without demonstrating a semblance of fear. Previous encounters with knife-wielding drunkards and rabid coons be damned, this time Hoyt's hands shook. Slamming the wooden paneled door and heading around back to where the tailgate was suspended by covered chains, he reached into the cavity created in the wagon to retrieve his papers from a White Owl box pressed into service as a business case.

He expected it happened every single time he delivered here, though he couldn't quite dignify three times in ten years as a "regular stop" on his route. Out on the porch that covered the front of the house, Miss Wythel Sue Wallis emerged, toting the rifle that folks agreed must be glued to her hand, so seldom was one seen without the other.

Squinting behind, thick, wire-rimmed spectacles, Miss Wythel strained to discern the identity of her caller. Meeting with no more success than an outline of an overweight male, she screamed in a voice deeper and firmer than her ninety-five pound frame seemed capable of producing, "Get the hell off my land, or I'll blow you there myself."

"Hold on, Miss Wythel; it's me, Hoyt LaGuinn."

"I didn't order no groceries. I may be seventy-six years old, but my mind's as sharp as a tack."

The blue steeled barrel remained poised. To an unfamiliar observer, the aged woman on the porch might have been Belle Starr living out her latter years in East Texas seclusion. Clad in a man's work pants and shirt, her Western boots added just the right effect to suggest the resemblance.

"Times so hard you takin' to peddlin'?"

"No, ma'am, I come to offer you a proposition."

"Got no business with you nor nobody else. Now turn that contraption of yours around and high tail it back to that store."

If not for the Wallis place's strategic location, Hoyt would have done just that, but the spinster's land adjoined Willie's with only the creek separating the two. Fact was, the feisty old woman held title to five hundred acres of what John Earl determined to be the prime drilling spots. Left with no options, Hoyt dove in feet first.

"I, well my partners and me, want to drill for oil on your place." Unsure whether curiosity or greed motivated her to slowly lower the rifle, Hoyt muttered a "Thank you Lord."

"Oil... here?"

"Yes, ma'am. We believe it to be, but you got to sign papers to let us find out for sure."

"Come on in the house, then. I got to sit to think."

Hoyt followed her into the wide hall that ran the entire length of the house. An equal number of doors opened at exact intervals, facing each other to achieve the maximum amount of draw to cool the eight-room structure. Coupled with the shade trees, the Wallis house was the coolest site in Texas on a summer afternoon. Ushered into the parlor, he waited respectfully for his hostess to offer the privilege of a seat. Lace curtains, as ancient as the mistress, allowed sufficient light to observe the dust rise and fall when she sat. As she placed the rifle at the feet of a tattered rocker, she waved her hand toward a faded settee in invitation.

"How come I'm the last one you asked?"

Stunned by her knowledge, no rational reply came to mind.

Mistaking his silence for deceit, Miss Wythel snapped, "Even the hands that work my land been asked. Why, you paid some of them up to fifty cents an acre."

"Well, yes ma'am, but..."

"But the devil."

Her eyes bore through him, her speech slow and deliberate. "Wallis land's worth twice what colored land brings."

From his side pocket, Hoyt removed the checks Clyde provided for the venture. Removing the cap from his nickel-plated pen, he began to meet her asking price.

"Put it away," commanded the queen on her ragged throne. "I'll not let you drill on my land." With that she rose to lean on the rifle she employed rather than admit to herself that her arthritic limbs required a cane. The size of the woman coupled with the length of the barrel required that she bend, but only slightly enough to make the heirloom useful for the purpose she demanded.

When Hoyt heard the screen door's argument, he left straight for the store and the small safe concealed in the feed section. Spinning the Yale combination lock, he detected the tumblers' responses through the two-inch thickness of the door. From the safe he removed a cash drawer from between the double set of pigeonholes. With the contents in his pocket, Hoyt returned to the Wallis place as determination replaced his previous apprehension.

Wythel Sue Wallis awaited, undaunted, as Hoyt pulled the station wagon beside the porch where she sat in a swing gently rocking back and forth. No words were exchanged as the man hoisted his weight up the steps. Methodically he peeled off ten fifty-dollar bills, each of which he arranged in neat rows on the remainder of the swing. Offering her his pen, he watched as she wrote her name with a flawless, steady hand, won over by the awesome sight occupying the left side of the swing. Not until safely out of earshot did Hoyt release a triumphant yell.

While Clyde and Hoyt celebrated the culmination of their leasing operation, the newly-formed team of Terry and McCallister neared Oklahoma. As he tossed the butt of his Chesterfield out the window, John Earl decided it was time to do a little fishing. Reading people was a skill John Earl perfected to an art form whether in a poker game or a business deal. Instinct told him that Cale lacked the thirst for blood necessary to conduct business with real oil men. *His heart's way too soft*, Terry told himself after watching Cale leave the scraps of a roadside lunch for a mongrel. *Still every man's greedy; it's just a matter of identifying what he's greedy for.*

For some it's money, pure and simple, but for men like Cale, one with a double dose of conscience, it takes a cause. Now all I got to do is ferret out his cause; that'll tell me his weakness and let me hold the upper hand. John Earl Terry was an expert at doing just that.

"So, Hoyt tells me you come all the way from Missouri. How'd you settle on Brophy, not that it ain't the Garden of Eden relocated in Texas."

They both enjoyed Terry's humor.

Finally Cale shrugged.

"I guess it was the good Lord sent one of them guardian angels to guide me."

He shook his head in awe of his good fortune.

"See, my real folks both died when I was little. That's when my sister who was growed and married took me on to raise. We farmed a piece of rock hard land in the Missouri Boot Heel, till the country went to hell in a hand basket."

John Earl nodded in empathy.

"Not that my sister and her husband asked me to, but I seen that I was one more mouth to feed. While the land was theirs, I was a good hand and earned my keep. Now the bank owns the farm," his tone became bitter, "lettin' them work what's theirs by right for a slave wage."

"At least the bank didn't turn your family out."

"Now you'd think a man would be grateful for that, but not Jerry, my sister's husband. Not long after they foreclosed, he was sittin' over at the Corner Pig havin' hisself a barbecue pig sandwich, when he notices two men headed in kinda suspicious like. Somethin' told him they were robbin' the bank, but" Cale added in dismay of his brother-in-law's meager protest against the imposition of the bank, "he never missed a bite of that sandwich. And all he had to do was walk three or four doors down to the police station."

For a moment, Terry questioned his estimation of a man cursed with an over developed sense of integrity.

Cale looked toward the Oklahoma countryside. "That's the sort of man Winnie, Missouri, raises."

He turned quickly to the driver. "Not that I'm the least bit proud to say it raised me. You ever watched a man die, John Earl?"

Caught off guard, Terry could not decide on an appropriate lie before Cale continued his catharsis. "That whole town watched a man bleed to death. Jeb Stiles was his name, and even in Winnie, he was considered the meanest man to ever draw breath. You see, either end of town has an open saloon, the seedier being the Cairo. It was full of the lowest life ever born, the worst being Jeb Stiles. He'd cheat a man at poker even if he had the winning hand. If any of the witnesses was to be believed, Jeb provoked Joe Brown's oldest boy, Ed during a game of five card stud. Folks divided on just how good or bad a shot Ed was, cause he hit Jeb right in the small of the back." He pointed to a corresponding mark. "Right where it would cripple a man and produce the maximum of suffering. Course, Ed hadn't counted on the Doc."

"Saved his life?"

"A few of the boys toted him up the stairs none too gentle like to where Doc Prichert had his office, above the Show Me Theater. Ole Doc looked him over about as long as a body cares to sit in a hot outhouse before he picks up his bag and heads for the door. Stiles is screamin' and carryin' on about the Doc leavin' him. Doc tells him that a woman's havin' a baby, and that he ain't in no pain compared to hers."

"Maybe Doc knew he'd never get his fee out of Stiles."

"Maybe, but he could have made it up in admission. Somehow the news got to all of the county but to Stiles' kin. More people walked up those stairs to cuss him or just gawk than pays two bits to see the freaks in a travel show. Gamblers even took book on how long he could last."

"And how long was that?"

"He was there a good half a day when Jerry and me got there." Cale seemed genuinely ashamed, "and he died before we left."

"Son of a bitch got what was comin', I spect."

"Most folks would say, I guess. The way Doc Prichert saw it, too." He added incredulously, "There wasn't no babies born in the county that day or the next. Folks say he spent the time in a card came down at the Cairo. That's when I knew I couldn't be from that kinda place. I think a man has to do his level best toward what's right, not just what suits him at the time."

He brightened. "So, I saw on the Newsreel at the Show Me Theater about how they was discoverin' oil out here and how pay was high if a man wanted to work hard. Well, hard work and me's no strangers, so I started hoppin' freights." He laughed. "That's when that angel stepped in. I thought I was halfway to Oklahoma; instead I jumped off in Kilgore, Texas. There wasn't no more trains, so I started hitchin'. That's when Hoyt picked me up in that grocery wagon."

"Now you don't mean to tell me that you didn't leave any broken hearted females back in Missouri?" asked Terry teasingly.

A crimson blush captured his face as he stammered, "I didn't leave nobody in Winnie that means more to me than Elaine."

"If you don't mind me askin', how'd the two of you get so all fired serious in such a short time?"

Cale smiled in a wistful remembrance. "Hoyt sent me into town to get the mail. And there she was, talkin' to a tree."

"A what?"

Amused that for the first time Terry appeared interested in what he had to say, Cale leaned forward on the seat to push the driver good naturedly on the arm. "It just looked that way cause Jake was up in a live oak in their front yard. She was scoldin' the boy for all she was worth."

The glazed expression of a man miles and miles away slipped over his features. "There was just enough breeze to tug at her dress and muss her hair. I just couldn't help but stare."

As if he suddenly recalled that John Earl was in the car and privy to his most private thoughts, Cale experienced a capricious change in attitude. 'You heard me, Jake. Get down out of that tree,' she was sayin', but not like she was mad no more. She was scared plumb outta her mind. Jake had slipped and was danglin' just outta reach. So I grabbed him by the legs and let him fall in my arms. They both was cryin'. I didn't know what else to do; I just started on for the mail. On my way back, she musta been watchin', I guess. She called me over. Didn't even know my name. There was a brown bag of oatmeal cookies in her hand. We got to talkin'. The boy was fine, and if he wasn't already back in that tree, I'm a liar. That's when I suggested she have her husband nail up some boards for a tree house."

"What happened to the boy's pa?"

"I never asked her, but accordin' to Millie, and I'd bet a lease she knows, his car went off that bridge over the creek. Damnedest thing; no real why nor wherefore. Found him slumped over the steerin' wheel, dead."

"How long ago?"

"Seems Jake wasn't more than a baby. Clyde sent her off to Nacogdoches to live with his sister. It was there she decided on the teacher's college."

Unaware that he no longer held the man's attention, Cale rambled on about their courtship, how it blossomed as he built the tree house, and their plans for the future, now so dependent on the well."

Terry concentrated on Elaine Crawford.

A widow before she was used to bein' a wife. And you can bet Cale's never laid a hand on her. Well, this just gets easier and easier.

<p align="center">~~~~~~</p>

A few hours later, a dull sensation in the pit of his stomach abruptly sent Cale from his seat.

"Wake up, lazy butt," Terry was about to deliver another wakeup call with his fist. "We're here."

The wool cap covering his face fell into the Missourian's lap to reveal an incredible sight. As far as the land stretched, oil derricks dotted the landscape. Gawking as the Model A pulled through town, Cale's head jerked from one side to the other so as not to miss the wells.

The noise from their pumps made conversation between the driver and his passenger of sufficient difficulty as to forego any attempts. To Cale, no sweeter music had ever been composed, no words penned to describe the excitement of an oil town, no stench in comparison to that of drilling mud mixed with engine smoke with which he would become so intimate.

Everywhere people darted, men in oil-spattered work gear and women with money in their pockets and packages in their arms. Children on shiny bicycles wove between the traffic slowed to almost a standstill. In Seminole, there existed an oasis in the desert of unemployment and soup lines. Black liquid forced to the surface provided a verdant respite from the despair that lay just beyond its borders.

Had Cale chanced to look at his partner, he might well have noticed a tenseness as John Earl scanned the city for signs of Sheriff Simms or Lamar Tate. *It's a risk worth takin',* he assured himself. *I never been this close to my own well before. Hell, most likely never will again. What I need now is Bulldog. Besides,* he quickly turned his face from a former crew mate, *Estelle's probably been with half a dozen men since I been gone. Ole Lamar's done forgot about me and on the trail of some other boy who wanted a roll in the hay with his wife. Me, I'm old news.* The care with which he scanned the crowded streets betrayed his resolve. *Still, I better keep to the side streets; a man can never let down his guard if he wants to make sure he stays on top.* Turning onto the first of a series of well-tended gravel roads, the Model A passed rows of whitewashed, blue-trimmed duplexes, all exactly alike down to the clotheslines out back. Children representative of all sizes, enjoyed the carefree time of summer, and Cale found himself envious of their blissful ignorance of the sufferings of their counterparts selling pencils and fruit on city streets. Outside some of the homes, work crews painted or repaired, while others cut grass or planted trees.

"It's downright heaven," muttered Cale.

"Appears so to you, but I spect there's folks here who find a multitude of faults with the place."

"To a boy whose bedroom walls was covered over with newsprint to keep out the Missouri winter, this company camp's downright paradise."

"Hate to come home drunk around here," Terry joked. "It's all a man can do to pick one house from the rest stone sober."

"You sure your man will be home?"

"Will today; it's a holiday."

Searching his memory and drawing a blank, "None I know of," said Cale.

"Today's Founder's Day for Oklahoma Oil. No work for nobody after three. There'll be barbecue, games, and a dance with the company footin' the whole bill." John Earl cut the motor, recovered the dropped cap, and positioned it over his own face. "You watch for him while I catch forty winks."

"Now how's that make sense? You're the one knows him."

"Can't miss the son of a bitch."

Before long, Terry's snoring indicated that he'd be of no help in recognizing Bulldog Schneider.

Around three thirty a short, stocky man in overalls crossed the street. Broader than tall, his bowed legs appeared to be matched with the wrong body, thus producing a funny walk.

"Like a bulldog," Cale said aloud.

Focusing on the jowls that swayed with the man's gait, Cale's laughter awakened his partner.

A puffiness acquired from years of heavy drinking exaggerated Bulldog's features and accentuated the bags under his dark eyes. At fifty, the driller had experienced every aspect of oil production, beginning back in the cable days and bearing the burn scars of the time when the cast iron boiler used to power the cable rig built up too much pressure. Two men nearer the boiler than he died when it rained shrapnel. Bulldog caught the brunt of the steam across the back as he failed to make good his escape.

A few months of being laid up in the hospital, suffering through the torture they called care, left him unemployed with a family to support. Leaving his wife and kids with kin in Louisiana, Bulldog followed the booms. As most often occurred, a man secured a job through friends made during similar runs, and Bulldog knew them all, working Drop right in 1915, Mineral Wells in 1919, Desdemona in 1928, Osage Nation in 1922, and so many others that he'd lost track himself. Somewhere in between and four children later, his wife had her fill of a drop in husband. The eldest of their offspring, Norman, Jr., trailed a few paces behind the father he sought out after his stint in the Great War.

"Jumping out of the car, John Earl thrust his hand into the filthy offering of Bulldog Schneider.

"What the hell are you doin' here? You got a wish to die in your prime?" asked Bulldog.

By this time Cale stood at their side, the reference regarding Terry's demise fully understood as one of the selected escapades from John Earl's colorful past imparted to him between Brophy and Seminole.

"What Simms don't know won't hurt him none. Besides," he put his arm around Bulldog, "I'm here to make you a rich man." The oft employed smile crossed his face, and the slight twist of his head signaled Cale to follow the procedure meticulously outlined. Giving Cale time to lift a heavy crate from the Model A's rear set, John Earl sprang the trap. "I even brought along several friends for the celebration.

On cue Cale raised the lid, introducing a case of genuine Chicago, bootlegged whiskey.

How Terry procured it, Cale never questioned, a pattern developing in their relationship as much from Cale's naiveté as his unwillingness to admit that the profession he had entered would require the "bending" of ethics ingrained at the knees of his sister.

"You devil," Bulldog slapped the man's back. "Always a pleasure to entertain you and your friends. Let's go and get ourselves better acquainted."

Several cane-bottomed chairs and a tattered sofa furnished the living room of the company house occupied by Schneider and son. The familiar arched case of a radio sat atop a crate turned on its side to provide crude support.

"Every place just like this one?" questioned Cale of his host.

"All just alike, six rooms a piece." He returned from the kitchen with glasses in hand. "Course big shots like superintendents, geologists, and the like get a little nicer set up. As you pretty much can tell, workers use their own furniture, but the bills go direct to Oklahoma Oil."

A few shots downed and old times recounted, Bulldog relinquished his seat in favor of the son now cleaned of the drilling mud which previously caked his face. Christened Norman, Jr. by his mother and Pup by the proud father, the effects of life in Europe's trenches failed to mellow him. If anything the horrors witnessed reinforced his jocular, "live for today," spirit as did his freckled, baby-faced countenance. Thus, at age thirty, he avoided entanglements, especially those set by predatory females. Not that he discouraged their interest, on the contrary, Pup relished the chase, though careful to wrangle free of a woman's grasp just as she readied for the kill.

However, there was one great love of his life: baseball. Whenever an opportunity presented itself, he entered a game. Well-hewn muscles supported a frame inches above six feet. Uncle Sam shattered his vision of thrilling the crowds at Yankee Stadium, but he followed the Yanks and the game with a fervency. Pup busied himself with the radio which flooded the room with the sharp staccato of static and the occasional ear-piercing whines indicative of the search for the proper station. Settling back on the sofa, he propped his feet on a footstool and brushed away an errant strand of dark brown hair.

John Earl gave a disinterested wave of his hand. "Never listened much myself till Ruth showed everybody what it's all about."

He shook his head in disbelief.

"Sixty! Who'd of thought it?"

Cale relocated to the sofa where he and Pup alternated cheers and comments as the game progressed. Deep in thought, John Earl failed to regard Bulldog's return until the familiar tinkle of bottle against glass rim announced his presence.

"Mighty good stuff. How'd you get hold of it? Don't tell me you and Capone are the ones gonna make me rich?"

"Compliments of my partner, Mr. McCallister there, and three other boys back in Brophy tying down leases. Can't come courtin' the state's finest driller without somethin' to sweeten the pot."

Savoring the effects of the whiskey as it slid smoothly down his throat, Bulldog voiced his appreciation. "Mighty sweet indeed. Now tell me how I fit in your latest scheme." *I got no intentions of buying into any of Terry's shenanigans, but I got to envy the boy's confidence.* Though at this stage, the driller told himself, *good sense and what little I've picked up watchin' the mistakes and successes of folks have to count for something. Not that I'd tell him so; he just might get mad and pack his friends right back into that Model A.* He took another long drink. *That would be a terrible shame.*

John Earl detailed the events in Brophy, interrupted only by the irregular outbursts of the men on the sofa. "So, my backers, the wealthy merchant and the banker, authorized me to secure the finest crew available."

"Don't bullshit me. I've known you too long," tossing the Lloyd geological survey onto the wooden flooring. "This here survey is a sucker sheet, and I can't believe you're buying' into it. Hell, if there was oil there, the majors would of bought up that half the state by now."

Undeterred, John Earl countered, "And the oil in my partner's well? Lloyd and Joiner got no clue it exists, and they're drillin' to beat the band."

"Lloyd's a fraud, and Joiner's a washed up dreamer. But," he admitted reluctantly, "the water business peaks my interest. Not that I'm a sayin' that such a thing's possible. That water well can't be deep enough to hit nothin', and I ain't never heard of no seepage on that grand a scale."

"But suppose this is a field bigger than any ever discovered, and she's just havin' herself a fit to get out any way she can, even in a colored grand pappy's water well?"

The two remained deadlocked when the game ended, and Pup rose. "Dad and your friend are liable to be here all night. Why don't you and me go down to the barbecue?"

John Earl pushed for all he was worth. As long as he kept the talk and the whiskey coming, his first driller was as good as in Brophy. "Where's the excitement here, Bulldog? There's nothin' duller than workin' a sure thing."

"Now you're a hundred percent on that."

"Well, I haven't eaten in a while," he motioned to Cale, "and there's nothin' I can do to help out here," said Pup.

They left the men steeping in hot talk and tepid whiskey.

Outside, Cale asked, "John Earl gonna talk your pa into throwin' in with us?"

With a shrug of his muscular shoulders, Pup responded, "If the whiskey holds." Cale's expression registered surprise at Pup's disrespect. *Somehow it don't seem right for a son to own up to his father's faults. Back home, a man would go down fightin' for the honor of his family, even if as in Pup's case, the facts bare out.*

"See, the drunker he gets him, the better it'll sound. Why else you think he brought it?"

"Why are you lettin' John Earl do it?"

Exasperated at Cale's inability to grasp what he considered a rather obvious set of circumstances, Pup's tone took on the edge of impatience characteristic of a mother answering the one millionth question posed by her overly inquisitive child. "Cause I want to go."

"And leave all this?" Cale was stunned.

By now they had reached a brick structure larger than a high school gymnasium. Each side featured wooden shutters secured to the top of the wall with hooks to reveal screened windows that stretched within a few feet of the foundation. From inside a pervasive sense of gaiety filtered along with the sweet scent of barbecue sauce into the evening. A band playing country tunes amused dancers and top tappers alike while it served as a background to the horseshoe throwing, domino tables, women's gossip mills, and couples in parked cars at the recreation building's perimeter.

"This may seem like a lot to you and all them folks in there that ain't been nowhere there wasn't a derrick. Me, I been to Paris, France, and I seen how quality people live." His voice suddenly pleading with Cale to understand the intensity of his desire, "And I want that, too." With a defeated finality, "But you don't get it drillin' for no company. Sure they throw some crumbs to these ignorant fools," he gestured to encompass the crowd of revelers, "who see it as some sort of great reward for their hard work and devotion. So what happens when they're too old to work? The company don't give a damn then. You got no house, no job, and no money saved up." He quickly added, "And they just better not get themselves hurt, cause there may or may not be no job left when they get back. That is if they get back. You take a man hurt so bad he can't never work another day of his life. What comes of him? Besides," he became wistful, "A man ain't got nothin' if he don't have no dream." He pointed to a section of Oklahoma landscape that overlooked the camp. "See that house yonder? Belongs to the man that owns these folks."

Cale stated, "I thought it was a hotel."

Pup shook his head at the farm boy's remark. "Let me educate you some. With enough money, a man can buy his dreams, no matter how impossible they seem."

"What's yours?" Cale asked sincerely.

"Play profession baseball; but Uncle Sam seen to it I'm too old. The only way is for me to own the team. Then I can play whoever the hell I want; even me." They stopped just short of the entrance. "Anyway, a good driller can always find a job if your well's a duster."

Before Cale could reply, three attractive women descended. Taking Pup's arms, they drug him into the party amid hollow protests. Thus deserted, Cale spent an enjoyable night eating the company's barbecue, sampling the cooking skills of the camp's womenfolk, and dancing until the wee hours without a second thought to the goings on back at the house or wherever Pup and the girls took off to.

John Earl helped Bulldog to his bedroom where the driller passed out face first across the protesting bedsprings. As he bent to remove the man's boots, Terry reconsidered, the snoring indicative that the driller was long past caring. Checking the man's pockets, John Earl discovered fifty dollars.

"That'll about cover your share of the liquor, my friend. I salute your generosity." With that he proceeded to his car, course set for Cancre Flats. Patting the stake occupying his coat pocket, he relaxed his guard, "If luck holds, my mark should be waiting to be fleeced." The Model A jolted into gear.

Its "city limits" nudging against the northeastern portion of Seminole, crossing that imaginary line was to enter an entirely different world. Cancre Flats existed independently of the "good folks" of Seminole. All it desired of its neighbor were its oil crews and their wages from which every vice available took aim to separate the two. Churchgoers armed with the sword of right, demanded that Sheriff Simms obliterate the Flats, but the district's Philistine inhabitants stood entrenched. Thus warring factions grudgingly achieved a stalemate of sorts.

John Earl squinted to protect his eyes from the bright light and heavy, acrid smoke inside the Pearl Dance Hall. The scent of beer drew him toward the bar which he slapped before receipt of a brew. *This is a gem of an idea. Maybe I'll just build me one of these in Brophy in the not too distant future.* A fight broke out in the corner; it was regarded by most in the room as an inconvenience more than a threat. *Then again, maybe it ain't.* He shifted to allow a falling body to bounce off the bar. *Got to be a way with a lot less headaches to clear eighteen hundred dollars a night.*

Scanning the room, his eyes fell on a line of suckers of varying ages waiting to throw away their quarters for fifty-second dances. *The young boys I can see. There's been a time I was equally stupid or desperate for the excitement of the female. But the old codgers, what happened to wisdom traveling hand and hand with age?* A decidedly green farm boy seized his notice, as he staggered, ticket in hand, toward the mass of women waiting to dance. Just buying the ticket and making a pick used up a sizable chunk of the fifty seconds, and this boy was way too discriminating for his own pocketbook, having passed twice up and down the line.

John Earl's taunting fell upon deaf ears, "Just grab one, you fool. You ain't pickin' no wife."

A couple of sways with the music and one good whiff of dime-store cologne later, the dance ended. There he remained on the floor, too drunk to comprehend, as the woman returned to the line with her bosom padded with tickets she would redeem for a dime a piece at night's end.

As a glass flew by his head and shattered against the wall, John Earl ducked. Several seconds elapsed before his realization that it was not just an errant throw from another brawl. "Good to see ya, Darlin'."

An icy stare served as response.

Pulling the woman to him and bestowing a passionate kiss, he felt her body stiffen in defiance of his greeting. "You not still nursin' a grudge against Ole John Earl, are ya?"

"Don't know why I'm losin' money by givin' scum like you the time a day." Abruptly she turned, clogging across the wooden floor, pounding her heels in a rage.

Running behind at a safe distance lest she concealed anything else to hurl his way, Terry cajoled, "Inez, come on here. Sheriff Jake didn't give me space for no good-byes. Besides," he faced her now, "we never were much for talkin'." The first sign of softening, a reminiscent, pleasurable smile betrayed her. " I come back as soon as it was safe, didn't I? And where's the first place I stop?" His arms tightening around her waist forced the low-cut silk and crepe frock to reveal a hint of cleavage. "Why, to see my lucky lady." Their eyes met, and try as she might, Inez crumbled under the aura of John Earl Terry.

"Run get your money. We're off for some fun." Patting her affectionately across the rump, his eyes traveled the length of her body.

Inez is one of them females best appreciated from the rear, but she was at my side the night I won the largest pot of my life. Tonight I'm gonna need all the luck I can muster.

From the Pearl, the couple passed a string of establishments dedicated to satisfying a man's more basal urges. A few more dance halls fell in between the bawdy houses before they parked the A. Maneuvering through some chippies plying their trade on the line, John Earl guided Inez into the Paramount.

Catering to penny-ante gamblers intent on losing most, if not all, their pay, the casino boasted a roulette wheel imported from Chicago, though the shabbiness of its new home lent little credence to the claim. Alternating from five crap tables, the shouts and moans of winners and losers surged above the constant hum of the sporting men and hired women. Walking past a shell game, Terry pointed to the middle of the three, prompting the incensed player to select the first. With the exposure of the bead, indeed concealed under the middle shell, Terry shrugged. "Don't ignore a man on a roll, my friend." With that he left the man cursing himself and the crowd mocking.

"How much you got on you, Inez?"

"Ten dollars, I didn't have much of a night and it cut short."

Holding out his hand and performing some mental arithmetic, he calculated his stake at one hundred dollars, what with Bulldog's pocket money, Inez's take, and his own last cent. How he and Cale would finance a return trip warranted no concern. To fret over such a detail demonstrated a lack of self-confidence, something no one ever accused him of being short on.

"Run buy my chips in case any of Tate's boys should recognize me." Inez required no further instructions. She met him at a door to the left and behind a stage where girlie shows entertained at frequent intervals. A sharp rap on the door drew the response of a towering man who, taking one look at Terry, threw it open.

"Thought you wasn't welcome in Seminole no more?"

"I'm not," he grinned enormously.

Reserved for higher stakes players, the Paramount's back room sported three tables and a small bar. Scouting the table, he spied the last man necessary to make his Seminole trip a success.

Corbit Abernathy recognized Terry from similar encounters. With a wave of his cigar, he called the newcomer to his table. "Pull up a chair, boy, unless you got an appointment with a certain oil executive's wife." The room exploded in laugher.

"Why, I left her in your care. Don't tell me she's tired of you already?" The two men shook hands, after which Terry claimed the vacant seat next to Abernathy. "Have the rules changed since my rather hurried departure?"

"Not so's you'd notice," a professional player of sorts answered.

Joe Booth made his living in that room off men like Abernathy and those others who fancied themselves card players, like Bill Smith, a farmer whose dust bowl spouted more oil than he could account for; Jeb Stuart, a poor boy who married well; and Nobel Petersen, a drilling supplier.

"I got a hundred to my name," Terry declared.

"We'll start off easy on you," was Nobel's promise as he extended the newest player a cigar from a silver-plated case.

Inez drug a barstool behind and to the right of her date. From her vantage, both Abernathy's and Terry's hands fell into view. There she remained for five hours, discretely bumping Terry's chair at sporadic intervals in a code worked up beforehand.

All folded with the exception of John Earl and Abernathy when the signal alerted Terry of his upper hand. Calmly he deposited his bluff, in the form of all his remaining chips, in the table's center. John Earl, his original hundred substantially multiplied, placed his bet. The eyes of the other tables and those in closest proximity exercised all their skills in futile attempts to read the men locking heads over a pot now worth over ten thousand dollars.

"I'll need to send for more chips," searching unsuccessfully for a pen.

John Earl stayed his hand, "I don't want you inconvenienced none." He stalled for effect. "Say, you still got that extra rig?"

"You know I do; no contractor does business without two, least wise not in these parts."

"It ought to be an easy bet for you, then."

Small beads of perspiration popped onto Corbit's forehead. Inadvertently, he wiped them away with his dress shirt sleeve, cognizant that the loss of the rig would put a halt to half of his business as well as being a difficult piece of equipment to replace at any price.

"If your hand's as good as you're lettin' us believe, then you got nothin' to lose," baited his adversary.

Abernathy searched the men now packed around the circular table unable to conceive of any other way to save face.

A chorus of "ahs" reverberated in the confines of the Paramount's back room at the exposure of Corbit's two pairs, aces and queens, and John Earl's royal flush.

The winner whipped a blank paper and fountain pen from his pocket on which he scribbled his name and Hoyt's address. "Have the rig delivered here before the end of next week. I got me a lease just beggin' to be drilled."

A good many things could be said of Corbit Abernathy, the majority unfavorable, but the man knew how to lose with the grace of a Southern gentleman. "It'll be there in plenty of time. Treat her right, you hear; she's a lady."

"He don't know how to treat no lady," whined Inez promptly on cue. "You promised me a fine supper, and all I've gotten is a sore fanny from sittin' on this stool and enough card playin' to last me the rest of my natural life."

With a look of hurt and his most apologetic voice, John Earl patted Inez's knee. "You are so right, Darlin'. What else can

I do, gentlemen? You shall have your dinner, whatever your sweet, little heart desires."

Raking the chips into his hat, the couple departed, pausing long enough to convert the multicolored disks into folding, spendable cash. At as dead a run as Inez's one and a half inch heels would allow, they reached the A and sped off. Assured that no would-be robbers were giving chase, Inez sat back and lit a cigarette. "Do I get a share of that rig, or does our deal only cover cash?"

"Whatever treats you fair."

"Hmm...You're takin' that rig off to Texas, and dependable as you are, I might never lay eyes on you again. So, I believe I'll take four thousand and call it square."

"Done!" John Earl drove up to her boarding house where she shared a hotel-sized room with two other dancers from the Pearl.

"What are you doin'?" she asked as he killed the motor.

"Takin' you in so's you don't get knocked in the head."

"For a bodacious con man, you ain't got an ounce of common sense. Don't nobody know I got more than my ten dollars; now you, on the other hand..."

The motor was already humming. Inez followed his lights until they disappeared. "You're one hell of a man, John Earl." She patted the four thousand stuffed in her bra.

Unable to put a reign on a streak of flawless fortune, the Model A traveled as far to the opposite end of the social spectrum as Seminole, provided. The meager Model A pulled into the servant's entry of a majestic home set squarely on a manicured lawn. With the assurance of a resident, the late-night visitor walked confidently through the backyard and up to the window of the downstairs bedroom of the home's mistress.

Invitingly opened as if he were expected, Terry eased it wider to permit entrance to an azure boudoir. Sleeping seductively without covering in an effort to benefit from any breezes that might cool her room, Estelle Tate turned slightly, unaware of the intruder. Her platinum hair fell over the pillow with an effortless subtlety which reflected the moonlight that streamed through. The allure of French perfume urged him forward. Flawless breasts peaked from a gown as silken as the skin beneath it. John Earl could barely restrain himself as he stripped down to his undershirt and boxer shorts. Placing his hand over her mouth, he let his free hand slide under her gown.

The reactionary look of fear instantly left her at the recognition of the uninvited guest, as he slowly uncovered her mouth.

"You've got one hell of a nerve," she whispered in a raspy utterance that further heightened Terry's desire, "comin' here like this."

"You askin' me to leave?"

Wrapping her arms tightly around his neck, she whispered into his ear. He smiled. No further conversation was exchanged, and John Earl left her basically the way he found her, save for the look of contentment.

John Earl parked a full three blocks away and cut a trail to make a chased rabbit envious before arriving at Bulldog's backdoor. Cautiously, he eased through the rooms in a search for anyone awaiting the return of a big winner. In his bedroom, the driller lay in what appeared to be the exact posture.

Cale roused from a pile of quilts on the floor. "You talk him into it?"

"Don't you never worry about nothin' when John Earl's in charge. We'll be drillin' by the end of next week."

Cale drifted back to sleep, amid a vision of Elaine and Jake euphorically hugging and kissing him as a gusher sprayed them all with its liquid gold.

Chapter 3

"This is enough to make a preacher cuss," bemoaned John Earl. With them mattresses and suitcases strapped to the roof we look like a bunch of damned berry pickers in search of a crop."

"Come on, John Earl, pull over so I can open up another bottle. This here heat's got me dryer than a desert."

"Not five minutes ago, you swore off drinkin'," reminded the driver as he aimed for a chug hole.

Pup, his head resting on a pillow propped against the side of the Model A thrust forward.

"Just thought I'd let you know we was home."

A more pathetic load of men never crossed the threshold of the LaGuinn store. Wrung out or hung over, all with two-day growths of beards and road dust, they collapsed onto the feed bags or over the counter. Hoyt yanked Terry by the hair of the head, jerking him from off the counter, hissing into his face. "That's the hot shot driller you promised? He's a damn drunk!"

"But he cleans up nice." With that he headed to the room he and Cale shared and where they slept the better part of ten straight hours. "Make the introductions, Cale."

The LaGuinn living room soon resembled a hobo haven with scruffy men from end to end. Millie shook her head at Hoyt.

"I tell you, I ain't runnin' no boardin' house. Cale can stay on, but the rest of 'um are gone somewheres else when they wake up."

Hoyt searched his memory for the part of their agreement that obligated him to furnish free room and board for the crew.

"I'll talk to Clyde when he shows up. He's bound to have a rent house somewheres where the rest of them can sleep."

Doubtfully, Millie left him on the porch to try and prepare a meal. *Damn if I'm not right back where I started, cook and maid for a house full of dirt trackin' always hungry men.*

At dawn the men gathered at Willie's farm as the first driller took stock of his crew. *Two seasoned hands, a Missouri farm boy, two old men who think they can lend a hand after workin' a full day, and a colored. The good Lord himself wouldn't have put this plague on Pharaoh* he told himself. Though he would never admit it, even to himself, Bulldog reveled in the adventure of it all. As he told Cale on the road, "Wildcattin', bringin' in a well on virgin territory, that's the way for a man to win respect." With another glance at his crew, *Folks will sure be in awe of me, given the obstacles I got to overcome.*

In the dirt he drew a crude diagram of a derrick. "We'll build the derrick up to a hundred and twenty feet. Since money's tight, wood will have to do, but she's got to be put together right to bear the load inside." Pointing to a square at the apex, he scribbled "crown platform."

"The top of a rig ain't nothin' but a gigantic pulley system, the crown block restin' itself up here." He designated the area of reference. "Got a hoistin' drum and a hoistin' cable, and of course the blocks. Draw works sits next to our power generator. Guess you boys can tell right off how the cable runs over the crown block and attaches itself here."

The greenhorns hung on his every word. "I spect you all used a carpenter's drill? Well, that's all we'll be doin' with a bit that has more kick, since we got to send the pip down the hole. Top of the drillin' pipe's attached to this, it being the kelly; the bottom we fix to the drill collar about here."

"And this?" interrupted Cale.

"The collar's just a heavy joint. To it we're gonna add the bit," explained Pup.

"The Man Upstairs lookin' more favorable upon us than the Daisy Bradford, we'll spend most of our time on the drillin' floor addin' thirty-foot pipe lengths and mannin' the rotary table. Engine turns it, and it turns the bit. This bushin'," he indicated the square opening, "holds our kelly to the table. Once the power's set, the drill stem, the kelly, the bit, and the table all go ta spinnin'."

"Then how'd you two get so filthy in mud like you was when we got to Seminole?"

"That's the drillin mud. Just wouldn't work without it, what with the friction of drillin' apt to spark natural gas. Now the kelly here works another job, ya see. We got this here swivel for the kelly to hang from off the travelin' block. A rubber hose is connected to a gooseneck pipe."

Using his squatty fingers, he outlined the progression. "Loose end attaches to the top of this vertical pipe at the rig's corner, and finally to the mud hogs, circulatin' the pump which is gonna suck up our mud from the pit that's yet to be dug. Pressure sends her through the pipe and mud hose up top of our kelly. Next she heads downwards through the drillin' pipe till it catches up with the bit what's cuttin' up earth at a goodly rate of speed, and naturally gettin' mighty warm. So the mud cools it as it picks up the cuttings' of rock and forces it all back to us."

"And over us," Pup teased.

"Mr. Bulldog, how's that mud a goin' down while it's a goin' up, too?"

"Wasn't too clear on that was he, Willie B.?" Pup adopted the nickname for Bacon upon their introduction, likening him to a player in the Negro League he especially admired. "The mud comes out of the pipe, gravity and all considered, bein' confined in such a small spot, it works its way up the side till it reaches the surface."

"And keepin' the rest of the pipe cool?" asked Willie.

"Plus corks in gas, water, and we hope oil at the same time while it stops the well walls from collapsin'."

"Now boys, our crew is short a few hands, lessen we let loose of some money to work double tours." The last word he pronounced "towers" in oil field fashion.

It was Clyde who spoke up, "We've exhausted all our funds securing leases. That the way you see it, Hoyt?"

"Pretty much."

"Start with this," John Earl slapped his winnings on the ground less five hundred he tucked in the bureau for a rainy day or an easy mark. Smugly lauding over the banker, he crossed his arms, highly pleased with himself.

Eyes widened in astonishment.

"Where'd that come from less you been holdin' out on us?"

Ever assured, "Same place I got us a drillin' rig, a first class beauty if I must brag on myself." A rapt audience listened as John Earl retold the events of Cancre Flats, carefully omitting Inez's assistance.

"I'll be damned," swore the driller before bursting into laughter at the expense of Abernathy and the table of moneyed jackasses.

"She'll be here before the derrick's up unless this schoolmarm shuts up and lets us get to work."

Bulldog named himself farm boss and first driller, Pup as his second, and the rest of the men roughnecks, subject to change if a man couldn't pull his weight or necessity dictated otherwise. Willie's son Gabriel and two of his friends would pitch in when farm work allowed.

"John Earl, that wood delivered?"

"Had to send plum to Tyler, but she's promised."

"Then let's get started; this ain't no ladies' sewin' circle."

True to his word, the lumber dealer set the timber in symmetrical rows almost to the exact location pinpointed by Terry. The proximity of a limestone-bed road, a running creek for a water source, and Willie's mystical well eliminated any debate as to the site. The men and boys went to work assembling the rig where numbers splattered in red paint denoted special positions. With the three teenagers digging the cellar and mud pit, the men pounding timber, and even Hoyt hammering back to usability bent nails and trudging under the weight of water cans to the creek to replenish drinking water that literally evaporated in the June sun, the derrick took shape.

Willie spotted the approach of John Earl's gaming as he labored from the crown platform. A half dozen roustabouts of Abernathy's unloaded the rig. Beaming with the prowess of his accomplishment, John Earl sauntered around the truck to inspect his winnings. "She's been used some, but it just gives this girl some character."

He affectionately patted the rotary table.

"She's a damn beauty queen compared to that piece of shit over to the Daisy Bradford." Only Terry and the first driller could testify first hand of the poor boy operation in Rusk County, having paid a call as much to scout the competition's progress as to reassure themselves that others existed who shared their belief in East Texas's elusive oil. "That those boys reached two thousand six hundred feet, totals up to nothin' short of a miracle, considerin' the rusted pipe and ragtag machinery like a cotton gin boiler."

A few dollars apiece and the promise of a sampling of Hoyt's backroom merchandise sufficiently enticed the Okies to lend their hand to setting the machinery in place.

An anxious two days passed waiting for a welder from Bulldog's Desdemona days. Bulldog joined his men under the trees. "Pat McCoy's as good a welder as they got."

"So why doesn't some company snap him up?" questioned the always skeptical Clyde.

"Cause everything in a drillin' operation cries out for a welder from set up to pipin' oil out of the field. No welder, and the crew sits idle." He gestured to their stationary positions. "Welders can name their jobs; don't need no security when it's the companies that need them. With portable equipment like his, a dollar an hour ain't nothin'. Better be glad he owes me a favor. Left me to tell his intended that the weddin' was postponed due to him landin' a job fifty miles east. She pinned a note to his weddin' suit would make a sailor blush."

Pat piled out of the rig in knee-high boots and a pair of work gloves the size of gauntlets. On his belt a striker bounced in response to his stride to report his movements like the fabled belled cat. All about his khaki shirt and pants, pinpoint holes left by the hot iron thrown by the torch evidenced his profession. From his neck hung a pair of goggles. An offer of twenty-five cents an hour lured Gabriel to the dubious honor of assisting by carting, toting, and basically staying out of his way.

Preparations made and precise instructions given, McCoy donned a metal mask that covered his head. A double layer of clear and treated glasses protected his eyes from the glare of the torch. Before hitting the strike, Pat turned to Gabriel, "Now I'm tellin' ya, don't you be lookin' at what I'm a doin'. Even with them goggles I give ya, you'll be nursin' a case of welder's eye."

With no idea of what welder's eyes might be, he decided it worth avoiding, "Yes, suh, I ain't lookin' at nothin."

The striker ignited the oxygen-acetylene mixture and produced a glowing flame from the wand in his right hand. In his left, a metal rod touched the joint to which the rod blended. At the conclusion of each weld, Pat removed the helmet before dousing himself inside and out with creek water even at one point removing his clothing to sit waist high in the coolness.

"Combined heat of the torch and the day can dehydrate a man in little or no time," explained Bulldog when Hoyt grumbled over McCoy's repeated liberties at their expense.

Pup warned Cale as they constructed a shack for tools, "Now there's the reason you don't let nobody talk you into the weldin' trade. It's not just the heat; look at his chest. Years of them rays beatin' against a man burns and peels the skin plum off and the hair with it." He grinned knowingly. "Women set a lot in runnin' their fingers over a man's chest. Ain't that a favorite of Elaine's?"

Cale blushed a deeper shade of red than the one already attributed to the June heat.

"But on the other hand," Pup nudged his friend in the arm, "I hear a man at the torch a few years ain't frettin' over leavin' no babies behind. But I wouldn't expect a straight arrow like you to see that as an advantage, stickin' with the respectable brand of women as you do." He mused, "Now me and John Earl, there's a team of horses of a different color. Maybe the two of us better take up weldin'?"

June thirtieth of 1930 broke with a glorious sunrise peeking over the East Texas pines. The morning came as close to a holiday as Miss Wythel had observed since the last of her siblings passed on. For it, she selected the solitary dress that hung in the mahogany chifforobe. Boots protruding from her skirt, she picked up the rifle and set out for the rig about which her life now revolved. She and the rambling house were alive with the boarding crew.

By the time she crossed the creek bed, the entourage gathered on the drilling floor. Cale offered his arm, a gesture slapped away with the rifle barrel. To protect the children and themselves, John Earl had feigned an interest in the antique weapon and found it free of shells.

Principles in place, the photographer from Kilgore snapped pictures of the overalled roughnecks and roustabouts, the ladies in Sunday finery, and the spit-polished children. Then each family posed, Cale included in the photograph with Elaine, Clyde, and Little Jake.

Elaine smoothed her silk crepe, drop-waist dress and arranged its matching scarf so that the knot rested on her left shoulder.

Pushing Jake's cap away from his eyes, she explained, "I want my grandchildren to see everyone's face so they'll remember just what we looked like when we set out to put Brophy, Texas, in the history books." Inescapable pride was captured on the film later framed and hung in the Russell parlor.

The Bacon family took its turn on the drilling floor. Arnolia and the girls posed in identical hand-sewn dresses of flower-print feed sacks. Only the boys' patched trousers bespoke of their poverty, so skillful were Arnolias's hand-crafted creations.

A silent signal between Bulldog and John Earl sent the latter off the platform and over to his Model A while the farm boss passed tin drinking cups to the adults. Returning with one of the remaining whiskey bottles, he handed it to the man who most appreciated its content.

"Those of you who never spudded in before got no call to expect this." He began to pour small portions into each cup."

"This is real stuff," acknowledged Hoyt as he watched the bottle drain. "Which of you had this on reserve?"

"John Earl's doins'."

"Might have knowed."

The repetition of tin against tin lasted several seconds as all toasted the success of the well christened the Willie B #1, with Willie given the honor of breaking the bottle across the rotary table.

"Ladies," the boss announced with the flair of a radio professional, "if you will be so kind as to remove yourselves and the young folk, we'll commence to spuddin' her in."

An appropriate level of excitement accompanied the bustle of activity as onlookers and crew took their places. When Gabriel's check on the boiler's pressure suited him, Bulldog gave the order, "Let her go!"

Adrenaline pulsed.

John Earl, from his post as derrick man, stood ready to push the thirty-foot lengths of pipe toward the traveling block to which he would attach them. The rotary table began to turn which caused the drilling floor to quiver. A cacophonic tumult of clattering and humming rose above the cheers and clapping of the by-standers. The drillers poised over the table with their eyes on the spinning metal disk. Unseen, the pipe attached to the revolving bit pierced the soil to begin its journey into the bowels of the earth.

"You boys man that mud hog," shouted the boss man.

Off the platform, Cale and Willie followed instructions, as the hogs pumped in the ooze through the hose secured to the kelly.

"It's your job to make sure it's the right thickness and there's continual feed."

As novices, Willie and Cale's jobs were not as skilled nor technical, but they were nonetheless vital. Besides the mud and oiling of the machinery, the two would make countless trips to the creek to insure that the flow of water destined for the boilers was not impeded.

By dusk, the novelty of drilling settled into backbreaking toil. Roughnecking was a job for the young and agile. That Bulldog remained physically able to perform his duties spoke highly of his tenacity and determination. When he grumbled and swore at the crew, his cramped muscles and stiff back did the talking.

An occasional nip from a flask concealed under the overall bib dulled the aches and contributed to his longevity.

"Used to," father reminisced to son, "wildcatters sniffed out oil pools relyin' on a man's nose for oil and a good dose of luck. Nowadays, the college boys and their sciences rule, placing stock in things like anticlines or structural traps like them salt domes or faults. So here we are, wildcatting where them experts say their can't be no traps. I can just hear the conversations of the scoffers."

"No more than's been said about the Daisy Bradford #1, #2, or now #3."

"Yep, must have killed Joiner and Lloyd to have to abandon them first two sites. Just served to fuel up the supply of damnin' evidence."

"How far you think they are?"

"Last word, nearin' three thousand feet and no Woodbine sand in sight."

Pup's dejection showed. If the miracle sand, which marked a trail of faults and pools from North Central Texas across the borders into Arkansas and Louisiana could not be detected, a well was a guaranteed duster in the opinions of majors and independents alike.

As the kelly neared the level of the rotary table, Bulldog pulled a Van Buren watch from his pocket. Noting the time, he waved to signal a cessation of power. The roughnecks hoisted the kelly and released it from the pipe. Settling the kelly in its rat hole where it would remain until needed, John Earl ventured onto his monkey board to guide a new section of pipe to the traveling block. The hard working block lowered the pipe where Bulldog and Pup waited to receive it. Using a massive wrench-like device, they inserted the new length of pipe between the drill collar and the retrieved kelly.

"Three minutes," the first driller and his second shook their heads. "At this rate Jake will be old enough to work this rig before it's brought in."

Leaving the well at the end of a particularly draining day, Pup announced, "I ain't workin' tomorrow. Folks in town are all anxious over the Fourth celebration, and I bet they can use a genuine veteran to lift a glass for."

Cale's countenance brightened, "Elaine's been worryin' me for days about it." He appealed to Bulldog, "She says it's a real good time. What do you say?"

Contemplating the pros and cons, the farm boss surveyed his crew. "You've worked damn hard and shaped up to be a fair lot, considerin' the most of you didn't know your ass from a hole in the ground. What the hell?"

The boys began to whistle and holler.

"But," he demanded, I expect to see you all here at sunup on the fifth, sober as judges and with no complaints about no headaches."

<hr>

The morning of the Fourth started early for the hostess. Pushing away errant strands of blonde hair for the countless time, Elaine continued chopping up the sweet pickles she had canned the previous summer. *One whole glorious day with Cale,* she thought while guiding the slices into a crockery bowl already filled with potatoes, mayonnaise, mustard, and eggs. *The Willie B. has certainly made what little time we have together all the more special.* She chided herself for the selfishness she felt. *Here he is trying his hardest to bring in a well so that we can get married, and I'm upset because he's trying to get it accomplished as fast as possible.*

"Elaine, I smell something burning!" Clyde entered from the parlor.

"Oh, Lord, my chicken!" Yanking a potholder from a nail by the stove, she lifted the huge, iron skillet.

"Let me help you with that. A man can't afford to lose his Fourth of July chicken."

"And what makes you think this is yours?" Suddenly afraid of what he might do, she begged, "Daddy, don't you dare bid on my box lunch."

Clyde was enjoying himself immensely. "Why, I will die of embarrassment when nobody offers a bid for my daughter's lunch. Just trying to save our reputations."

The daughter slapped playfully at his arm. "You know perfectly well that Cale will bid on my lunch, and Lord help anyone who gets in his way. Now," she pushed him toward the door, "you promised to go get Miss Wythel, and you better shake a leg."

"I wonder if Cale knows what kind of a nagging woman you are."

"He hasn't a clue, and don't you tell him, either." She kissed him on the cheek as she ushered him out the door.

"Men and kitchens," she shook her head trying to decide what to do next. The sound of the front door announced reinforcements.

"We're here," Millie called.

Elaine rushed into the parlor. "Where's Cale?" her disappointment evident.

"I sent him into Kilgore to the ice house. You said you wanted ice cream," reminded Millie.

"I know, I know."

"Well, you don't know I invited Vernell Spires to match up with our Mr. Terry."

In disbelief, "You didn't. That girl's as shy as they come. What could she possibly have in common with John Earl?" asked Elaine.

"She don't have to talk; he can say enough for the both of them," said Millie jokingly yet quite seriously.

While the women put the finishing touches on lunch, Hoyt sat on the wicker sofa newly moved onto the front porch to provide extra seating for the children's parade and the fireworks to follow. Wondering just how much he was losing in sales, he watched John Earl pull up under the live oak that bore Jake's tree house.

Precisely on cue, Vernell Spire, a mousy woman in wire-framed spectacles rounded the side of the house. "Damn," he said, "Millie's at it again."

By the time Terry could park the car and get out, Vernell occupied the top of the steps. Indiscreetly hidden behind her, a crepe paper covered shoe box which sported the appropriate colors of the day and two American flags in its lid stuck out like a sheep in a goat pen.

John Earl also noted the grinning Miss Spires and her lunch. As was the custom, the eligible young women of Brophy would each prepare a decorated boxed lunch to be auctioned by the mayor. Supposedly, no one knew the name of a particular owner; however, a good deal of cheating assured those interested parties of purchasing the correct lunches, thus granting them the pleasures of their contents and the companies of the ladies who prepared them. Under his breath, Terry vowed, "Before I spend a dime on that one, I'd rather starve."

Millie rushed out the door, rescuing Hoyt from the humiliation of the obvious bit of matchmaking. Taking Vernell by her skinny arm, and John Earl by his, she directed them to the sawhorse table set up on the lawn. Hoyt could only imagine the conversation and welcomed Elaine's pleas for help in seeing that everyone was ready for the trip downtown. She placed in his hand a shoe box covered in solid blue with silver stars and topped by a large red bow.

"Don't tell Cale this one is mine," she hinted. "I want you to carry it so that no one thinks we've cheated when he bids on this lunch."

Hoyt grunted. "All this foolishness. Why everybody can't eat with who they want is beyond the realm of good sense."

It seemed every citizen of Brophy and a few imports stood outside the houses or had already reached the auction stand in front of Clyde's bank. Patriotic bunting draped the few business still winning their private battles against the failing economy and the drought. Already rows of decorated boxes filled the tables to display the artistic accomplishments of the single ladies and for the bachelors to examine in hopes of finding the one his sweetheart described.

As mayor, Clyde called for quiet and asked the single women whose boxes were to be placed on the auction block to stand together. "A lovelier crop of females I've never seen," he boasted. The crowd clapped and cheered as the girls in their best summer frocks eagerly anticipated the sale and the pleasant evening it was sure to bring. For those without a beau, fantasy of the unknown led to giggles and faces hidden behind funeral parlor paper fans.

Standing on the toes of her shoes, Elaine scanned the crowd in a vain attempt to locate Cale. *He's had more than enough time to get to Kilgore and back,* she told herself. *If only I could get word to Daddy so my lunch will be bid last.*

A keen sense of observation, so John Earl found, often proved to be the key to making luck run in a man's favor. Even from the distance which separated him from Elaine, he could detect the agitation she sought to disguise. His eyes traveled her body, lingering on the folds of the georgette crepe, and watching the swell of her chest as it rose and fell with a rapidity that convinced him Elaine deserved a man capable of appreciating her finer qualities. *So Cale's late. Well, John Earl, it's time you showed this little lady some attention.* A hand upon his shoulder pivoted him toward the single obstacle that blocked his path to Elaine Crawford.

Breathlessly, McCallister sought answers, "Has he started yet?"

"Just about to. Where you been?"

"Kilgore to the ice house; the girls wanted to make ice cream. So then I had to store the stuff. That and folks lined up at the ice house, and the manager shorthanded." Cale searched the cluster of women for his lady. "Damn!"

Feigning a sympathetic interest, "What's the matter now?" John Earl asked.

"Elaine didn't get to tell me how she decorated her box."

"That all?"

Judging from Cale's expression, his partner's lack of concern over a situation bordering on life and death was doing little more than adding to his exasperation.

"Don't get your bowels in no uproar. I," with enormous pride, "just so happened to eye a box lunch on the porch of the Russell residence this very morning, and," he motioned with his head, "your would-be daddy-in-law is about to put it up for sale."

The flag-studded box belonging to Vernell Spires rested in Clyde's hands. "I'll open the bidding at a quarter. Who'll give me thirty cents?"

"Fifty cents," boomed John Earl.

Vernell's heart leapt. *Millie promised to set me up with that handsome Mr. Terry, but I never dreamed he'd really be interested in me. Now Elaine won't be the only girl with a good-looking out-of-towner paying court.*

Jerking violently at the cotton sleeve of Terry's shirt, Cale snarled, "Just what do you think you're doin'?"

With equal vehemence his arm dislodged, "Didn't you see that girl beat with the ugly stick have her lunch go for a dollar? What do you want, Elaine to think she ain't worth more than a bargain price when that girl fetched a full dollar?"

Cale's anger faded, convinced yet again by John Earl's logic. "Sixty cents."

It was Elaine's turn to be shocked when she recognized the voice and saw his hand go up in the air. Her mind tore in all directions. *Is he crazy?* She stomped her foot, gesturing as best she could with her hands and expression.

"How high are we goin'?" Cale asked.

"Better go at least better than a dollar," warned John Earl, "or you could sing out a big price. Now, that'll really impress her in front of her friends."

"A dollar and a quarter!"

The audience responded with whistles and cheers, all save Elaine Crawford whose mouth gaped.

"Anybody willin' to raise that?" the auctioneer queried. The lack of response prompted, "Sold to Cale McCallister for the sum of one dollar and twenty-five cents for the school building fund." As per tradition, Clyde opened the lid to reveal the name of its owner. "Looks like your lady for the day is," he read with disbelief, "Vernell Spires?"

With the exception of John Earl, the shock of all who knew of Cale and Elaine's involvement, and all of Brophy fell privy to the business of every citizen young and old, proved genuine. Cale found himself staggering toward Clyde to pay his money and claim his date, unable to meet Elaine's eyes. Seething with jealousy and anger directed at Hoyt, Elaine awaited the sale of her lunch. When it did come up very near the end of the auction, several men vied for the few remaining ladies.

"Some fella's gonna see stars in his eyes tonight," baited Clyde. "What say we start with fifty cents?"

Delayin' one purchase raises the price, but it also gives a man a much better chance of knowin' the lady. Such a strategy promised a more delightful prospect to Sam Windham. *With only four ladies left, and two of them known to be matched up, I like my chances of spendin' the day with Brophy's most desirable widow.* With Cale out of the picture, he placed his bet that the box about to be sold by her father had to be Elaine's. "One dollar."

"Two," called John Earl.

Somewhat irritated that he would have to spend more, but feeling Elaine worth the exorbitant sum, he heard himself bid, "Two fifty."

"Three."

The crowd began to find itself actively participating with cheers of, "Higher!"

Not to be outdone, Sam took in a heaving breath, "Four."

Temporarily forgetting the despair of losing Cale's company, Elaine discovered her pulse had escalated to a giddy rate.

"Let's us put a stop to this right now," Terry proclaimed, quieting the crowd. Ever the showman, he approached Clyde, pulling a roll of bills from his pocket. Peeling off twenty-five dollars in Lincoln portraits, he placed them dramatically atop the starred box. "Twenty-five dollars for the school fund."

His gesture impressed everyone. Even dyed in the wool skeptics who distrusted anyone with a mere sapling for a family tree, viewed John Earl Terry in a different light. A fool, sure enough for putting stock in the existence of East Texas oil, but a man willing to put up twenty-five dollars for the school had to garner a certain amount of admiration.

Untying the ribbon, Clyde provided the information for which the crowd clamored, "Mrs. Elaine Crawford."

The crowd's affections accompanied the lady to the table. Betrayed by her own vanity, Elaine basked in the spotlight. Clyde placed his daughter's hand into John Earl's, unwittingly imitating a father of the bride. As the two filtered through the bystanders to accept their accolades, Clyde brought the auction to an anti-climactic conclusion. Pushing aside well-wishers, Cale slowed the man who had so stylishly stolen his girl.

In anticipation, John Earl defended his actions. "Did you want her with a man you can trust or a son of a bitch with designs on your lady?"

Mistaken in the assumption that Terry considered himself the former of the two, Cale fell back begrudgingly to join an equally despondent Vernell. The admiration continued as John Earl and Elaine walked back to her home with the twenty-five dollar box irreverently tucked under his right arm. Only in the confines of the Russell yard did the opportunity arise for them to acknowledge one another.

"I don't quite know what to think," she confessed. Such was the only accurate assessment she could offer. From their initial encounter, a single smile from the man placing two wooden folding chairs under an elm on a more isolated side of the lawn placed her aboard an emotional carousel ride. She hopped from the horses of fear, distrust, awe, gratitude, and friendship during each encounter, avoiding the stationary, two-seater in a childlike innocence of the heretofore foreign experience of lust. Elaine's inability to accurately recognize her own desire lay buried under the stifling code of Sunday School mores which denied capability for the existence of love for one man and a driving, reckless passion for another.

With a sweeping gesture to rival Sir Walter Raleigh, Terry offered her a seat, "For you, madam."

A formally delivered, "Thank you, sir."

"I hope you don't mind spendin' your day with me," he apologized. With the humility of a sinner on the mourner's bench, he explained. "This here mix up is all my doins'." Purposefully avoiding the eyes he believed to be brimming with denial, "You see, I told Cale to buy Miss Spires, lunch." Eyes still down, he felt the anticipated recoil his confession should inspire. "When he came up all upset cause he didn't get time to find out which box was yours, I tried to help him out by tellin' him about the box I seen on your porch this mornin'." Allowing his eyes to meet hers, he pleaded, "How was I supposta know that it was hers and not yours, it bein' on your porch and all?"

Transfixed by lashes envied by every woman alive, Elaine peered into what she believed to be his soul. Involuntarily a hand covered her mouth to stifle an escaping giggle that soon erupted into an hilarious exchange between them as they pointed out the absurdities of the events leading to their present situation. The arrival of the older generation sent Elaine to her feet. "I've got to set the iced tea and see to my company."

Gently urging her back into the chair, "Not today. You can't expect a man to donate twenty-five dollars just to see you waitin' on everyone else?" The slightest of motions marked his progression up her arm and coaxed her into a submission that would last the entire afternoon. She busied herself opening the lunch and arranging it on a small table John Earl removed from the porch. An afternoon of meaningless conversation ensued, amid patriotic tunes furnished by a radio and the intoxicating scent of Elaine's rose garden.

Poised on one arm slightly below and to her left, John Earl listened to Elaine's concerns for the children in her class and her gratitude for the supplies his donation would mean to the students. Cautiously working his way upward, intent upon kissing her, Jake's bounding around the corner of the house spoiled the moment.

"Mamma, it's time to go to the parade!"

Under his breath, Terry cursed the kid's timing.

Elaine, already on her feet, began to clean up their mess. "I'm on my way; you have everything?" Elaine was torn between her child and a desire for this time in the company of John Earl not to end. *This is ridiculous*, she berated herself. *I'm in love with Cale; John Earl is just... just being nice to me.* Yet she heard herself ask as awkwardly as a Sadie Hawkins schoolgirl, "Are you going to the children's parade?"

Pleased with the progress of the afternoon, "Couldn't pass up a chance to see this fine young man in action," he mussed the boy's hair affectionately.

As they joined the rest, Pup informed them, "Your daddy's gone to take Jake." The big kid ever close to the surface, he admitted with a degree of disappointment, "He wouldn't let me take him."

"Don't be offended," Elaine felt pangs of guilt rising from her stomach as Cale broke John Earl's spell. "He and his grandpa don't let much get between them."

Cal's eyes bore into Elaine.

Eager to set things right, she took Cale's hand possessively, but addressed Vernell, "I hope you didn't mind this little mix up." Turning her attention to Cale, "John Earl explained how he mistook Vernell's box for mine; isn't it just the funniest thing?"

Narrating the events from Terry's perspective to the rest of the family, soon everyone enjoyed a good laugh at Cale's expense.

"Here comes the real entertainment," Miss Wythel hobbled toward the street.

"All of this is so wonderful for her," Elaine sighed. "Even if the well never comes in, it has for her already." John Earl and Vernell forgotten, Elaine and Cale waved with parental pride as the parade made its progression in front of the Russell home.

An assortment of children and conveyances festooned with flags and streamers glided down Brophy's main street. Oldsters pulled youngsters in red wagons, some rusted a few shades away from the original fire engine luster. Tricycles and scooters both store bought and homemade from scrap lumber and apple crates drew the admiration of the hometown folks. A small contingency of pedal-powered cars marked the end of the parade, including Jake in his red Dodge racer with nickel plated hub caps.

As fireworks began to explode high above, the scent of burned powder filled the night. Appropriately timed "oohs" barely died away before the surge of another Roman candle incited another. Sparkler waving children riding in circles and the singing of "The Star Spangled Banner" officially ended the Fourth.

Unobserved by the captivated onlookers, John Earl stood back, taking the opportunity for a smoke and an assessment of the day. *Twenty-five dollars well spent. If I play this hand right, she'll be the first and only Mrs. John Earl Terry.* As he patted himself on the back, even his grandiose imagination could not have conjured the new hand being dealt by an unknown ally about to descend on the serenity of Brophy.

Chapter 4

Mid July, 1930

"It sure beats choppin' cotton." Ever since Mr. Robach the Kilgore druggist give me this job stockin', waitin' on customers, and generally helpin' him run the store, I been havin' the time of my life."

But carrying out his duties as delivery boy, now there was an unbridled pleasure for a boy of sixteen. *No doubt about it, I'd work for free just to drive this '29 Packard, even though most of my trips take me on these back roads. Still, I can't exactly get back to the store without takin' her downtown.* Bobby Lee practiced driving with one hand and tipping his cap to a now imaginary beauty, the kind he liked to spot outside Kilgore proper, who was unaware of the owner of so magnificent an automobile.

A sight only to be compared with that which put a halt to Balaam's ass appeared out of nowhere. Pushing the brakes until he almost stood, the Packard spun to face the roadside, narrowly missing the woman who seconds before stood smack dab in the middle of the highway frantically waving her arms.

Grabbing the handles of two brown fiber suitcases whose leather straps hung loosely, she broke into a run toward the car to peer into the window which now faced her direction. She was the kind of woman who demanded your notice. In the lemon-colored dress, a checkered pattern of black squares floated. A frilly jabot draped too snugly for any semblance of prudence. Though smudged by the effects of the afternoon's merciless sun, the remaining paint on her face rivaled that of any movie star.

Mesmerized by her appearance and bombarded by Woolworth's bottom of the line perfume, Bobby Lee did little other than nod in response to the rapid fire voice that pleaded with him to take her to Brophy.

Suitcase deposited, she tugged at a pair of black patent leather heels with polka-dotted quarters, throwing the spiked heels to the floorboard. Massaging her feet she declared, "Hell's bells, my dogs hurt. I been walkin' for hours from the train depot and tryin' to thumb a ride from the self-righteous Samaritans you got livin' here."

His eyes fell upon the exposed legs covered by genuine silk stockings and a wide runner progressing to places he dared not consider. Turning his attention back to the road, he pushed the accelerator further down. *Mr. Robach's warned me not to allow passengers to benefit from his gas.* His mind darted from the road back to the shapely legs. *I know I risked it for them cheerleaders, but this is different.* A twist of the woman's body sent the hem higher. *Oh, this is real different. What if Momma gets wind of this?* The wrath of the druggist paled in comparison. *I got to get rid of this woman the first opportunity that presents itself.*

"Anyways," he concentrated again on her relentless conversation backed with an incessant popping of chewing gum, "I'll pay you five dollars to take me to him," she said.

Even the vision of his mother at her worst could not offset the lure of extra wages. "You got yourself a deal, ma'am."

As the LaGuinn store crept into view, Bobby Lee promised, "If he's in Brophy, it's known about in there."

She smiled sweetly, "Will a Coca Cola do you? It won't come outta the five."

"Can't say as I'd refuse."

A seriousness yet unwitnessed crossed her face. "Hell's bells, is it always so damn hot here?" She threw off the close-fitting hat adorned with an elongated feather.

"Only in the daytime."

She sneered, "Ain't that just the way my luck's been runnin' with timin'?"

No more than a few minutes elapsed until she returned with soft drinks in hand. Thrusting one toward her chauffeur, she wasted little time. "You know where they're drillin' that wildman, wildcat, wild somethin'' well?"

"You mean on Miss Daisy Bradford's land?"

"Hell's bells, now that woman told me Willis," she griped, readying herself to reenter and give the clerk what for.

"Oh that's no real well. They're not doing nothin' but wastin' sweat and money." Bending forward to start the engine, he vowed, "But you want to go, that's where we'll head; it ain't far."

The woman sat back to enjoy the ride, wiggling her toes and keeping the boy nodding acknowledgments to the drone of her conversation.

~~~~~~

Arriving with a brimming lunch basket, Elaine cautioned her son, "Don't go too far down the creek." Listening to the now familiar noises of the pumps and boilers of the rig, she prayed, "Please Lord, let it be here." Elaine opened her eyes to the tiny form of Miss Wythel crossing the planks Pup placed to serve as a path over the creek bed. Using the rifle butt at regular intervals, she steadied herself until she reached her destination. Thinking of the once lonely woman whose life now held purpose, Elaine raised her head to heaven, "For all of us."

As always, Miss Wythel set about to help as best she could in preparing lunch, talking openly, enjoying the pleasure of the younger woman she had begun to appreciate as the daughter she never had. The unexpected approach of the Packard claimed their attention as did the emergence of its female passenger.

"Don't you run off till I know he's here," she commanded her driver.

"No danger in that; you still owe me my five."

"Hell's bells, you'll get your money." Raising her head slowly to absorb each detail of her first glimpse of a drilling operation, she allowed the magnitude of its height to enthrall her. Vainly she tried to identify the man she sought. Then, spying the young woman and the old harpy dressed in men's clothing, she ventured toward them.

Back in the Packard, the druggist's employee appreciated this new viewpoint. Aching feet and one heel worn slightly lower than its mate created a seductive sway of the passenger's hips as she crossed the arid grass toward the shade trees. *I can dream about her from now until the day I die and go to my grave a contented man.*

"'Scuse me, ladies; I'm lookin' for a man."

"Well, ain't none of these interested in no floozy. These here is respectable gentlemen."

Whether from downright ignorance of the old woman's allusion to her character or from absolute determination, she plowed on, again straining to define the features of the oblivious men scurrying about the rig. She spoke without addressing either in particular. "Is Cale McCallister up there?" she pointed to the derrick.

Astonished by her knowledge of any of their men, Miss Wythel bristled as she closed a protective gap between Elaine and the harlot. Deterred by Elaine's hand upon the rifle now aimed at the mass of red curls, the younger woman stepped beside her despite an ominous churning at work beneath the gingham dress.

"What connection have you with Mr. McCallister? Are you his sister?"

The woman in yellow turned, beaming with pride, "Of course not. He's my fiancée." She extended her hand. "I'm Mavis Osborne."

A whirlpool within Elaine's mind spun unchecked with questions, scenarios, and foreboding. Unaware of the impact of her introduction, Mavis shook her hand steadily until its owner jerked free to wipe it reflexively. "Is he here, or did that woman at the store send me on a wild goose chase?"

Elaine nodded an affirmation.

"Cale!" the redhead began to scream in a strident voice, as she covered the expanse separating her from the Willie B. #1 as swiftly as her shoes and skirt allowed. Now impossible to overlook, the mass of yellow, red, and black caught the attention of first one man and then the other. On his monkey board, John Earl leaned on the pipe just attached, anticipating what undoubtedly must prove to be a wildly amusing encounter for the unassuming McCallister and a woman of such unbelievable contrast. For this he required a better view and headed for the drilling floor.

Pup, distracted by Mavis' outcry, allowed the block to slip from his grasp. It swung to the left at the precise moment Cale rose from lubricating the rotary table and caught sight of Mavis. Though Pup and the Bulldog shouted to alert him, only the piercing whines of Mavis Osborne elicited a response. In the path of the swaying pipe, stood a thunderstruck Cale.

I figured she'd know we was through. Why, I ain't even written and sure never dreamed she'd leave Winnie, he told himself. The whines grew louder as she neared. *How did she find me?*

Suddenly cognizant of the pipe, John Earl dove to avert it to a sufficient degree that the full brunt of its force was stayed and greatly reduced the severity of the blow dealt Cale's back. Face first and arms extended, Cale fell to the drilling floor.

The clouds of a nightmarish haze slowly cleared to Elaine's face. Cale fought to move against an invisible foe which pinned him to the ground. Then Elaine's face became distorted by undulating colors until all around him bore a reddish yellow tint. He tried to call her name, but the dissonance emitted from the form looming above him drown his own voice in a deluge of tears.

"Mavis?"

"Oh, Cale, you're alive!" she hurled herself upon him.

In a gesture of self preservation, the injured man raised his arms which sent a pain so acute that it emptied his head of all save its intensity. Thankfully the reactionary groans propelled the sobbing woman to her feet in a profusion of apologies. When he next awoke, his disorientation had increased.

"Where am I?" he asked.

"At the hospital in Kilgore," she answered in all too familiar a banter from which she so seldom came up for air. "That sweet little druggist boy that give me a lift to Brophy in the first place drove us up here. Of course, I did have to pay him two more dollars, that added to the five I already owed, and he was goin' this way anyhow, the little horse's behind." She stopped as excitement replaced concern, "We was in a Packard. Wouldn't folks back home just die to see us drivin' up in one of those?" She squeezed his leg, "Oh Cale, it was like drivin' on air. I'm so sorry you couldn't remember enough to enjoy it; guess you was ridin' your own air, so to speak."

Somehow Mavis' enthusiasm over the joyride eluded him.

"Where," he caught himself before saying her name. "Where's everyone else?"

"They're all outside, but I wouldn't leave you, no not for a minute. It's like I told them, I'm the closest thing you got to kin around here. You'd have been so proud of me. I says, 'I am his fiancée, and you all ain't stoppin' me from holdin' the ailin' hand of the man I love.'"

Wincing at the impact her revelation must have had upon Elaine, Cale sighed.

"Oh sweetie, I know you're hurtin', but the doc says you only got a broke wrist, you bein' in a coma's what worried us all. And now that you've woke up, that's not nothin' no more."

If only I could go back to that coma, he brooded, *then maybe I could wake up again and have Elaine standin' there. Elaine, what you must think of me?*

In the sparsely furnished waiting room, Millie and the crew, minus Hoyt and Gabriel, waited with Elaine for news. The women occupied the only chairs, while the men sat on the floor or braced themselves against the wall. Elaine could not take a firm hold on her sanity. Worried over Cale's condition, confused about Mavis' sudden appearance, furious that her claim on Cale might not be based in fact. *And why didn't I push her out of the way to be at Cale's bedside? After all, I'm the one he's really going to marry... or am I?* The more she thought about this woman, the more convinced she became that Mavis Osborne could in no way attract Cale. *She's so common, so vulgar. Still, she has the shape of a screen star... but Cale isn't the kind of man that... who are you fooling?* She took stock of her own trim but hardly voluptuous form. *All men can muster some interest in a woman with her figure.* Removing a handkerchief from her bag, she wiped away the tears trickling down her face.

Finally Miss Wythel could watch Elaine's suffering no further. "Why don't you march yourself right in there and tell her you're Cale's intended?"

Looking up Elaine replied, "I have no right; there's no ring on my finger, nothing official, nothing but his promise." She turned to Millie, "Are you sure he never mentioned her or gave you any sort of hint that someone was waitin' back in Missouri?"

"Honey, I'm real certain. The only one he ever wrote was his sister. The only woman I heard him speak of was you. He loves you; I'd bet Hoyt's last dime."

"Which is why I say we pull her outta there by that henna treated hair of hers. It ain't natural for anyone to have hair that red."

"No, Miss Wythel, we're not confronting her. I want Cale to tell her, if... if he wants. Now you hear me, all of you. I don't want her to know a thing about Cale and me, not one thing about the two of us. Don't tell her now; don't tell her ever."

She can't expect no promise on that account from me, Terry told himself. His heart swelled, *Ain't this just a kick in the ass. There's no easier woman to woo than one with a busted heart. And here I am just waitin' to pick up the pieces.* He looked toward the treatment room. *You old skunk. Catchin' a woman like that will just have to raise you a notch in my book. But, now we've got to work a man short. Can't you get nothin' right?*

Clyde Russell 's reply to Elaine's request was a silent prayer. *Please let that son of a bitch live so that I can shoot him myself. He had no right to toy with my daughter and to make an innocent boy believe he could be the daddy he never knew.* His head dropped in shame. *Not that I'm not partly to blame.*

Somehow I should have made her listen. You can't trust a drifter, cause there's always a past that crops up when it's not expected. He looked at John Earl. *And he's another one we don't know squat about. He's probably wanted in every state. Comin' up with six thousand dollars outta thin air. No honest man comes by that kind of money overnight.*

"Mr. McAllister has regained consciousness, and a few of you may go in now." The nurse wrinkled her nose at the men whose collective bodies outdid the pervasive ether. Her eyes lingering on Willie, "It would certainly be wise if you all returned home; your friend is out of danger."

As the woman in starched white exited, her instructions were ignored. The door eased open at Millie's touch, thus allowing them to file into the cramped quarters. Only Elaine stayed behind on the pretext of seeing to Jake, unable to face Cale and the woman that had so disrupted their lives.

The room was large enough for a metal-legged examining table upon which Cale lay and a single chair. An entire wall accommodated metal cabinetry whose opaque glass bore a red cross. Contained inside, cotton medicine bottles and doctor's essentials stared out to scare the patients as they awaited treatment. Cale dared not ask about Elaine. *I've got to explain this to her, he thought. But not with everyone around, and not till I've sent Mavis back to Missouri.*

Hoyt burst in the door. "They've cored woodbine!" his eyes bulged as he dropped his breathless body onto the table. Mavis lurched forward to prevent the crushing of Cale's legs by Hoyt's expansive rear end.

"Reese says it's salted," scoffed Bulldog, irked at Hoyt's disregard for Cale's condition and his attempt to stir up an already addled crew with a con man's ploy. "I know for a fact that the Daisy Bradford's first man, Laster, ain't nowheres near the forecasted five thousand one hundred feet where woodbine's at." Well circulated round the Tyler, Henderson, and Kilgore areas by Donald Reese, a scout for Sinclair, was the accusation of Laster's feeble attempt to boost lease sales by faking a core sample. "Gettin' a genuine coring from a promising well in some other part of the country is as easy as buying cigarettes. Put your money down, and it's yours. Only a fool falls for the driller's con of leavin' in plain view the samplin' at the site for anyone to pick up." The first driller crossed his arms defiantly. "This is all we need," he decided. "And your," his mind turned to Cale, "stupidity has cost us three quarters of a day's work, not countin' the time you're laid up. Damn, stupid bunch of inexperienced..."

Having caught the better portion of his breath, Hoyt cut back at Bulldog. "I' ain't talkin' bout Reese. Shell Oil's done buyin' leases up for two dollars and fifty cents an acre over in Rusk County, all on the quiet. Some ole boy named of Cheesman's doin' it. Word's out that Shell tested one of Laster's cores to be legit."

Even Cale joined in the raucous that followed. If the Daisy Bradford could hit, the Willie B. could follow her in.

John Earl stood at the door. "We're waistin' time; let's get the pressure rebuilt."

"Millie, we're droppin' you and Elaine off in town. The two of you borrow cars. We'll aim the lights of as many as we can get at the rig so's we can drill all night," ordered the farm boss.

Millie left in a shot, the others in quick succession, leaving Mavis and Cale alone once again. Groggily, Cale sat up amid Mavis' ardent protests. "I've got to get to the rig; they can't work no shorter than we do."

"They left us with no car, and there's the doctor to see first," said Mavis.

Defeated, Cale sent Mavis to fetch the doctor. Staring out the window, he saw only a vision of Elaine blotting the reality of the Kilgore township. *There's not but one thing to be done. Mavis has got to be told. Then I'll beg Elaine's forgiveness.* His spirits finally rose. *She loves me. And with a little pamperin' and coaxin', she'll forgive me.* He reclaimed the table.

As he turned in response to the creaking of the door, Mavis anticipated his question. "He's settin' some boy's leg, but he give strict orders that you stay flat of your back till he says different." She deposited herself upon the table. With palms down on either side of Cale, she leaned forward and kissed him.

A momentary spark rekindled. "Say Nubbin, how'd you find me way out here? Did Bethel hire one of her detectives out of them crime magazines she's so crazy about?"

Mavis slapped playfully at his shoulder, "No, silly. Did that blow knock out all your memory? You've been sendin' your sister money regular enough."

Cale chided himself. *Of course, Sara. Damn, her big mouth.*

"Momma and me guessed you was just too busy to write," she fished.

"You see for yourself. They're out there tonight, and we've been at it since dawn," explained Cale.

"Is there gonna be time to visit the preacher?" Mavis rose and peered out the window, dreading his reaction too much to face him. In her heart she knew the answer. *How much time would it have taken to write three words on a postcard? He's changed; I can see it. Those old feelins' are gone forever.*

Cale stammered, muttering about time and his commitment to the crew.

Tears welled up and slowly streamed down her cheeks. "I can't go back to Winnie."

"Sure you can." Cale joined her at the window. The image reflected in the pane frightened him. This was a vulnerable woman before him, a Mavis he'd never known. "Bethel will get over you takin' a little vacation from the cafe. She's forgiven you worse."

Mavis' red curls shook violently. "I can't," she pivoted, covering her face with his chest. Clinched fists battered. "You and me made a baby, Cale McCallister, and I ain't goin' home to carry that shame alone."

This time it was his own image that frightened him.

~~~~~~

August 1930

Constrained within the womb of the earth for centuries, the penetrating bit of the Daisy Bradford III was about to precipitate the delivery of a pool of oil spanning one hundred forty thousand acres. The mother had concealed her secret long enough, weary of baffling those who sought to rob her of her bounty and weathering adamant declarations of the naysayers who denied its existence.

Gradually, the rush of expectation swelled. Leases once ridiculed acquired new ownership at slightly higher prices, and the undercurrent of hope reached across the state to summon others to a Mecca where worshippers awaited the arrival of their economic savior.

Encouraged by the omen of woodbine at the Daisy Bradford, the Willie B.'s crew toiled with a renewed passion, accomplishing the impossible by reaching a depth of one thousand five hundred feet. Were it not for the stability of Hoyt's store and Clyde's bank and the women who saw to their needs, the entire operation would have collapsed. The LaGuinn store fed and clothed them, while the ladies cooked, nursed, and supported their spirits when depression beset by fatigue and reality claimed their souls.

The plaster cast on Cale's wrist retained none of its original pallor. Caked over with drilling mud, he tapped against it, inquiring of the doctor on his last visit, "Don't know if she wouldn't heal faster with this mud mendin' the bone. This accident has cost me two days off the job." It was a partial truth. On the first day he rested; on the second he married Mavis.

As he and Hoyt watched their wives bustle about the kitchen, Cale remarked. "If Mavis ain't the happiest woman alive, she sure puts on a hell of a show, talkin' on like she does about the baby and how much she loves me. Now she's caterin' to Miss Wythel like she was the Queen of Sheba by waitin' on her hand and foot just like she slaved for Bethel Osborne all these years."

Hoyt lit a cigarette before assuming the posture of a sage. "Women in the family way got that nestin' instinct about 'um, boy. Millie was the same way each time. They got to get themselves set in with a place and someone to sympathize with their complaints." He shook his head. "A man won't do. No sir," he bent over slightly, a sly grin on his stubbled face. "It's their way of gettin' revenge for what's been done to 'um."

Not that Cale wanted to be the center of his wife's world. Elaine Crawford occupied the majority of his thoughts. The morning he broke the news to her about Mavis and the baby constantly replayed in his mind.

Elaine and Millie stayed on the site the night of the accident, as per Bulldog's instructions to keep the lights on the rig. The doctor tied them up at the hospital for something he called observation. It was just as well; he had been too sick over his impending fatherhood to care about the rig. The next morning they rang up Bobby Lee, only too willing to make another five as soon as he could contrive a plausible excuse for his boss.

They hit Brophy before noon. Depositing Mavis with Millie, he walked to the bank and summoned Clyde from the teller's cage he occupied when his only employee went home to lunch. Clyde shut down the bank, not that there was any business lost. No one had money to put in, and he sure wasn't in the mood to loan any. The banker hadn't bothered to reply to Cale's request for a word in private, just locked the door and headed to his office.

Had Cale the talents of the Mineral Wells fortune teller, he would have run as fast as he could manage. The banker looked sternly at the man who had plunged his daughter into the depression that gripped her following the death of Jake's father. "You've got nerve wantin' to explain yourself to me."

Grasping the leather arms of the chair, Cale began. "We was sweethearts back in Winnie where she and her momma run the only cafe." His narration culminated with the news that prevented him from exorcising the woman from his life. "So I need your permission to talk to Elaine; I owe her that much," his voice trailed. There was nothing left to say.

"You never owed her a damned thing but honesty right from the get go." Cale cringed at the vehemence of his sentiments. "So you go tell her and be done with it. She can't start to heal as long as the wound's festerin'."

Waiting at the front door for the key that would usher him from the bank, Cale paused.

The last words Clyde would speak on the matter for the rest of their association left Cale in more pain than if the father of the woman he loved had beaten him senseless. "I respect you for doin' right by Mavis; plenty of men wouldn't have done the same in your place."

Elaine sat on the porch, snapping beans into a crockery bowl. She never stopped her chore during the entirety of the conversation. Only the fierceness with which she popped the beans betrayed her anger and hurt.

"How's your wrist?"

He lifted the cast, "Doc says it'll be a few weeks before it's mended."

Pop. Pop. She discarded a rejected bean into a wash tub of snapped ends and shriveled beans.

"Elaine, I've got to tell you somethin' that's gonna hurt, and that's somethin' I wouldn't do for nothin' in this world."

"So she was telling the truth?"

"Yes."

He wanted to throw the bowl into the yard as much to hold her in his arms as to quiet the infernal snapping that resounded like gunshots throbbing inside his head.

"I never knew anyone like you," he pleaded, "and when I did, well, I decided that you and Jake were what I wanted, but..."

"You seem to have neglected to inform Miss Osborne of your little change of heart."

"She's expectin'." He blurted the news more bluntly than practiced, making it cold and impersonal. "And I can't deny what's mine."

The bitterness that distorted Elaine's features haunted him. Never observed prior to the moment, they reappeared often enough, always reminding him the ultimate responsibility for the unhappiness in her life rested with him.

"Don't feel obliged to explain this to my son; I'll make your excuses. Kindly follow whatever story I decide to tell to make you less of a heel than you are. The boy's already lost one daddy, and I think he's a bit young to know that a baby can come before the ink's dried on its parents' marriage paper."

And so he left without really leaving her. He turned too quickly to observe the tears of heartache disguised by the fury of the snapping.

Millie waited up in the kitchen a few nights after the wedding. Sitting at the oilcloth covered table, her gray hair mashed close to her head in pin curls, she offered him a glass of cold lemonade. The dehydrating effects of a day at the rig often drove him downstairs during the night, and he appreciated the drink as much as the company, since he didn't prefer his own anymore.

"It's none of your business now what happens in Elaine's life, so I'm tellin' you this so's you got some time to get used to the idea and your place in the matter."

Cale hung his head, focusing on the lemon seed that bobbed in his glass. *So, she's leaving town,* he surmised. *Can't say it's not for the best of all concerned.*

"And it's for certain it ain't your place to go commentin' on the man who's takin' your place. Anything from you won't be seen as nothin' but sour grapes."

"Takin' my place?"

"John Earl's payin' her court, and she ain't asked him to leave."

With that Millie retired. He sat on the porch for another hour until he was sufficiently drained of mental and physical strength. Returning to the bedroom, *why can't I feel something for the woman I married? Resentment, anger, sympathy, even the love I had for her. It's like I'm dead inside.* Easing himself into the bed he had made, he set his resolve. *Millie's right; I got no call in Elaine's life. Mavis has seen to that.*

Mavis bided her time. *I thought waitin' on the cantankerous folks at the cafe had taught me to deal with every kind, but these Texas folks are sure different.*

Without turning over Mavis asked, "Why don't none of your friends like me? Did you tell things on me before I came to jade them?"

As had become their custom of late, for her to speak and Cale to merely listen disinterestedly, she expected no reply, regardless of what subject had the floor.

"It's because of the baby, ain't it?" she blurted. "They think I'm a tramp or that it belongs to somebody else and that you're just a good enough man to take on someone else's leavins'."

She felt the back against hers stiffen as he defended his friends. "Now that just ain't so. You don't see none of them shovin' the Good Book in our faces so's they can rub our noses in it. And just who out of all of 'um is a sacrificial lamb of purity and piousness?"

It was Cale's turn to answer his own question.

"Don't Millie and Hoyt sell illegal liquor and Bulldog drink up his share and half the state's? And John Earl, the Good Lord Hisself has to work double tours to keep him wrote up in The Book of Life."

"But Elaine's a lamb."

She struggled to leave the bed. "She's so damn perfect. Hell's bells, they'll be puttin' statues of her in churches." Mavis began to whine in utter frustration. "I'd like her and me to be friends; she's the only girl close to my age I met."

Elaine's wishes regarding the truth, as related by Millie, stayed the words he most wanted to say that could send Mavis from his life forever and Elaine into his arms. You'll just have to give them all time; nobody can make things change for you but you."

Inwardly, *that's all I need, the two of them bosom buddies.*

As Mavis trudged to the bathroom, she set her resolve. *I'm gonna woo these Brophyites to my corner, so help me.*

Beginning with Miss Wythel and Millie, Mavis performed chores at both houses. While Millie worked the store, Mavis cleaned, cooked, washed, anything and everything to please.

As Millie explained to Elaine, "Even as pregnant as she is, the woman can do the work of two men around the store. Why, she can tally rows of figures in her head and barter a deal from the farmers better than Hoyt ever has. I never dreamed I'd say this, but I don't know what we'd do without her, the store and me is bein' wrung dry to feed, clothe, and salary all of us."

Millie sighed. "That girl and her mouth is in nonstop motion."

In one of the few dresses she could still button, Mavis appeared at the Russell house intent on killing two birds with one stone. Eager to learn all she could about the oil business, she quickly exhausted the meager resources in Brophy.

Her call on Elaine Crawford was a request to be driven to Kilgore to visit what served as a lending library. At first appalled by the woman's gall, Elaine berated herself as Mavis accepted a seat in the parlor.

This woman is totally ignorant of my history with her husband. Besides, what possible excuse can I give for turning down such an admirable request?

On the road to Kilgore and back, Elaine listened as Mavis narrated tales of the people in Winnie, often lacing them with appropriate voices and gestures. "...It musta been two minutes before closin' and there's Ben Milan, he's perched up there on the eighth stool, both cheeks lappin' over the side, sayin' 'This here soups' cold.'"

"What do you expect this time a night? I says."

"'I expect you to serve hot soup the way God intended...hot.'"

"So I take it back to the kitchen. Any fool would have knowed somethin' weren't right when I come back so quick like. But Ben ain't just any fool. He puts the spoon up to his mouth, and the likes of cussin' you never heard."

"How did you get it that hot so fast?"

Mavis smiled triumphantly, "Hell's bells, I didn't heat nothin' but the dippin' end of the spoon, but that sucker was red when I put it in the bowl."

Laughter and tears caused the driver to pull the car off to the side. When she finally gained control. "Mavis, you are a radio program come to life."

The woman possessed a rare openness which somehow drew Elaine; her bluntness both surprised and amused the prudent school teacher. Thus, with each encounter, the wall Elaine erected between herself and the woman who cost her Cale McCallister began to crumble.

Both women now delivered lunch to the crew. Carrying the heavy basket between them, the girls chatted, unaware that their conduct prompted notice of the crew.

John Earl wiped his hands on a bandanna as dirty as his hands. "Beats the hell outta me." Referring to the irony of the friendship. "What gets to me most, Cale, is Elaine really likes her. Guess there's just no understandin' women. Now take us, for example," his thumb pointed to Cale and back. "You rob me the way she did Elaine, why I'd whip your ass every time I got the chance. And look at 'um," he waved the bandanna toward a shade tree where the women were spreading quilts and sharing Jake's latest antic.

"Elaine's a wonderful woman; I can't believe there's anyone with that kind of forgivin' nature," Cale agreed.

"That's why I'm gonna marry her."

John Earl leaped from the rig before Cale could respond. He prayed that Elaine would recognize him for the rogue he was. *You deserve better, so much better. He'll hurt you,* he paused in shame, *just like I did. The difference is, he won't regret doin' it.* Despite his misgivings, the romance prospered, and Mr. and Mrs. McCallister held ringside tickets.

Chapter 5

Squinting from the pitiless sun, Clyde nodded respectfully at the two chaw bacons whittling from the wooden bench between the bank and the post office/general store.

One winked at his companion in preparation for a good time at Clyde's expense.

"It sets a man to worryin' when he can dress better than his banker." He referenced the tattered overalls and slouch hat traded for his business suit.

"Maybe he needs a loan?"

The second slapped his knee, caught up in his own levity, which escaped both Clyde and the other occupant of the bench.

"He'd just throw it down that hole."

He spat a stream of tobacco juice for emphasis.

"Good money a goin' for bad, I'd say. Better hurry that gusher up, Clyde. I'm plannin' on christenin' my new grand youngun with the oil ya'll find. I spect there'll be just enough for the job."

The verity of the codger's words still rang in his ears as the derrick loomed in view. *It's all been for naught,* he told himself, *and this latest news ought to shut her down for good.*

Practiced to a point of precision, the crew repeated the task that habitually occurred when the Willie B. penetrated another two hundred or so feet of the East Texas strata. Pup manned the enormous wrench in place around the pipe. From the draw works, the suspended kelly awaited its release from the newly exposed drill pipe. When several yanks from Pup failed to separate the two, Cale lent his strength to force the two apart and released a spray of mud over men and machinery.

Bulldog deposited the kelly in its rat hole where it would remain until all the pipe from within the well had been removed, the bit replaced, and the pipes refitted. The boys considered a recall of the thribbles, three joints of thirty-foot pipe lengths, in less than two hours of the repetition a blessing. Once unscrewed, John Earl guided the thribbles against the derrick and released the traveling block to claim yet another section of metal accompanied by the pervasive mud.

Clyde shouted at Gabriel over the incessant roar of the boiler, "Shut her down."

"Suh?"

"I said, shut her down."

"But Mr. Clyde, Mr. Bulldog's the man what give that order. I can't do nothin' what he don't say." Exasperated, Clyde stormed to the platform to repeat himself to the driller.

"What the hell's wrong with you?" Bulldog demanded, peeved at Clyde's insistence and the waste of time it would produce. As he turned to argue his point, another spurt of the sticky, ooze sprayed his face, the stench penetrating his nostrils. He scraped his eyes with the backs of soiled gloves.

"I'm tellin' you there's no use; we got no more money for pipe."

Muted by Clyde's revelation, he grudgingly waved to Gabriel, who began the steps to shut down the rig. Unable to hear the conversation, but judging from the grimace of the first driller, the boys slowly joined the two below the platform. The sun cast a checkerboard shadow across the men and the land that magnified the derrick into an odious, unconquerable presence.

His news recounted for the crew, Clyde summed up, "So we got no more ready cash, and I just can't work out any more creative means of producin' more, short of jeopardizin' the bank."

"I can mortgage the farm," proposed Willie.

Hoyt's reaction spoke for the others. "Nobody can let ya do that. The land's all you got to support your family. Besides, who's gonna loan you money anyways with no hope of it bein' paid back? Farmland, even good as yours, just ain't worth nothin'."

John Earl threw down a cigarette he crushed in frustration. "You all got to promise never to ask how I get this money." The ominous inflection with which he seized control and dictated his terms cowered them all into silent assent.

"I may be gone upwards of three or four days. Anybody comes around, we're showin' no signs of woodbine nor the Austin Chalk." He quickly added, "But don't volunteer no information; make 'um pull it out of you like there's somethin' to hide. Don't waste no time while I'm gone, neither. Be cuttin' more wood cause we're gonna use it."

The rest of the instructions went directly to Clyde. "Order the pipe so it'll be here when I get through."

"But I told you..."

John Earl cut him short by thrusting his index finger in Clyde's face. "And I told you to order the damn pipe. The money's comin'."

The acrimonious glare of Terry's eyes bore into the banker. He was not alone in his assumption that a further challenge to John Earl would unleash some manner of physical retaliation. Pup and Cale, already on their feet to avert the anticipated reaction, eased back as Clyde acquiesced.

With Terry on his way to Miss Wythel's where he now stored his gear, Cale looked at Bulldog. "What do you suppose he's gonna do?"

The farm boss shook his head. "I don't know, but whatever he's up to, it's crookeder than a dog's hind leg, and we're the better off for not knowin'."

"He's gonna land us all in the jailhouse," predicted Willie.

Hoyt rose, leaving the crew with an imparting of his wisdom. "I say we call it a night, and that you younger boys get to cuttin' that wood tomorrow. John Earl's a slick one. Whatever's up that sleeve of his will be done smart like." Meeting the skeptics head on, he dared them to refute his argument. "Got us this far, ain't he?" With that Hoyt ambled to the delivery wagon.

For the second time in five minutes, John Earl checked the seemingly motionless hands on his timepiece. The outside of the estimated span long since passed, he squinted tightly to search the small pine break that separated him from the Daisy Bradford III. A snapping of twigs and the rustle of dead needles sent him behind a tree that concealed him from what he now believed would be someone with designs on his throat.

Instead, a barefoot boy bounded toward the spot where a lifetime of residence in the area instinctively told him was where he had left the man for whom he now found himself gainfully employed. Just spreading its first rays, the sun shared just enough of its light to allow the man in hiding to feel secure about the boy' solitary status. Frantically, the boy turned his head from side to side, a faint jingle of his overall clasps evident in the stillness. The man in hiding sighed with a relief encouraged by the rusted pail dangling at the boy's side.

"Good work, boy."

John Earl's praise sent the boy into the air and the pail crashing to the ground. Now he faced the direction of the voice that he hoped had at least scared the freckles off his face, according to his granny a surefire cure. The absence of the hateful freckles would surely help to make up for the shame of the warm trickle now traveling down his pant's legs.

"Let's see what ya got."

Holding the ashy substance in his hands, the man's eyes dug into those of the boy. "You sure you went to the right spot?"

"I told you, Mr. Hoover, that I done been to that well a bunch with my pa. He's been pitchin' in when he's able like other farmers here about so's that well can make us all millionaires; that's what Dad Joiner says is gonna happen. I fetched water for the crew." He straightened with pride, "I'm as good a hand as there is, and I know a corin' when I see it."

Beaming, John Earl withdrew five bills from his pocket which he counted off in an aggrandized fashion. He'd picked this boy off a creek bank, finding him drowning worms and eager to answer a multitude of questions as long as Terry continued to lose nickel bets at rock skipping. Convincing the kid that he was a duly deputized representative of Tom Mix and his Wonder Horse Tony, Terry swore the ten year-old to secrecy about the mission that required him to sneak out of the bedroom he shared with his two brothers and remove a core sample from the Daisy Bradford III.

John Earl shook the excited lad's hand before extracting a solemn oath. "If I am to be able to return to send you on further secret raids, you must never tell a livin' soul of what transpired here this evenin', nor even acknowledge me if we pass on the street."

"Oh, you can count on me, Mr. Hoover. Will you tell Tom Mix how good I done?"

"Of course, I wouldn't be a bit surprised if he didn't send you a letter with an autographed picture, or," he gestured to an imaginary wide screen, "that this little adventure don't appear in the movie theater someday while you're a watchin' a Saturday serial."

"Wow! Thanks."

Terry watched the boy scamper home and congratulated himself on the second phase of this newest scheme. Hurrying to the car, he wheeled it toward Tyler as he mulled over his progress. *Let's see, after a day of finagling with Depression starved East Texans, I got three thousand acres of new leases for the sock money. These fifteen cent an acre purchases leave just enough workin' capital to bring the plan to fruition, and with just the right players, the game can be won.* He patted the leases in the brown paper bag at his side. *Just the right amount of inflated worth, not way more than the goin' rate, but just enough to look interestin'. By the time I'm through playin' with you fellas, you'll be kin folks with solid gold.*

〰〰〰〰〰

"**Q**uit your playin' at games, chile."

This time the frail girl leaped at the command of her mother.

"Miriam, you ain't through with that shirt, not by no long shot."

The edge on Arnolia's voice foretold of what would await if she chose not to obey, and sent the child of six on a search of the galvanized washtub for the shirt just discarded. Plunging it back into the soapy liquid that filled a second tub, she withdrew the garment and proceeded to rub it against the five truss back of the washboard. When her work pleased Arnolia, it left the confines of the rinse water for the metal-framed wringer attached to the rinse tub. Miriam longed for her mother's chore, ignorant of the brute strength required to force wet clothing through the double rollers, imagining instead that wringing was the easier job.

Wiping the sweat from her forehead with the bottom of her apron, Arnolia Bacon caught sight of her husband displaying all the signs of a whipped dog as he trudged toward the house. *He ain't been home in two days. That was when he hit the last lick of work in these fields. Got him and Gabriel both at that damned hole in the ground.* Her resentment rose to surpass the heat of the wash boiler she'd set on fire only a few minutes before.

As Willie came within hearing, "I hope you're too tired to lift your feet, cause I sure am. All the farm chores restin' direct on my shoulders, besides the house work of raisin' your five youngest. What with cookin' their meals, washin' their dishes and clothes." She put both hands in the air, palms out to stay off words she supplied for him. "Oh, but you don't care none to hear that I takes to the fields earlier in the mornin' and stays later than before with my hands around a hoe handle in a losin' battle to chop the weeds from around that drought-stunted cotton, puttin' baby Elizabeth under a tree with Tamara as nurse. I's scared to turn my back with her barely five. Only cause it's Monday's keepin' me from bein' there today. Course, Jeremiah, God bless him, twelve year old and the man of this house. Wish you could have seen your boy. Left at dawn, two molasses cans in tow for food and water to last the day."

She cranked the wringer as if it were Willie's neck. "And for what? Cotton not gonna bring nothin', but that won't matter none. No suh, we's all gonna starve this winter unless I can find the time or the help to put up vegetables from that garden."

Tamara ran and jumped into Willie's open arms, and smothered her father with kisses. He still held her when he bent over to kiss his wife.

Pulling away, Arnolia continued to vent her frustrations. "What brings you around to see us?"

Willie placed Tamara on the ground and started up the sagging, wooden steps, too exhausted to endure yet another of his wife's tirades.

"You too good to answer me back? Life with them white folks sure done give you airs."

Stopping at the opened door of the house, Willie closed his eyes in an appeal for strength. "I ain't got the time to fight with you. I'm sleepin' a few hours and goin' back to relieve Gabriel so's he can come home for the same."

"You," she leaned upon the word, "got no time? Well, excuse me, Mr. Bacon. What with all the relaxin' I does all day, I plumb forgot about workin' folks' troubles."

Ignoring the last remark, Willie entered the house, avoiding the mattress upon which the three girls slept, crossing into the center of a room cluttered by a table and four benches, a sofa made from old bedsprings severed by an ax and placed on a handmade wooden frame, some cane-bottomed chairs, and the sidestepped mattress. Toward the back of the same room, the cook stove, sink, and pump lined the wall.

Above them rows of shelves contained the dishes that were not sitting in the sink awaiting washing. The sink exemplified the ingenuity with which the Bacon household made do, consisting of a hole punched in the bottom of a dishpan to which a funnel had been attached to a hose hooked beneath to run through a missing plank in the floor. Reaching under the gingham material tacked to the top of the shelf to conceal its contents, Willie removed a glass into which he pumped some water.

Standing in the doorway, Arnolia demanded, "When are you gonna give this up? We got no crop, no food, and no hope less you and Gabriel get back to help us." She flung herself onto the bench and buried her face in her hands.

"It's not that I am callused to your sufferin', but you just refuse to believe in what this well is gonna be for us." He scanned the room. "I'm tired, too. Tired of straw stuffed under bed sheets to fill the gaps in the floor in winter, tired of my girls wearin' shoes with soles nothin' more than cardboard, tired of every stitch of clothin' bearin' a patch or hole and comin' from discards of white people or flour sacks." As he occupied the rest of the bench and placed his arms around his sobbing wife, Willie tried yet again to explain. "You're right as rain, Nolia. We got nothin', nothin' but the slimmest of chances. But we gotta take it, else these children gonna work like slaves the rest of their lives. I want 'um to go to college like I never got to do, and..."

"You're the one that's the slave. Ain't no white men never gone partners with a black one what the black didn't end up with the shortest end of the stick. They is usin' you, and you lettin' 'um."

She looked him in the eye, her tone now pleading, "If you brings in that well, you won't never live to spend that money. White folks, won't let us live no good life."

Willie stood, anger rising, "They ain't reneged on their word so far. You not gettin' what you need at the store from Miz Millie free as a bird?"

True enough, each list she sent came back filled; however, years of mistreatment of her race by whites could not be dismissed. "And someday they'll come callin' with the sheriff and a book of unpaid bills run up," she prophesied. "Then they'll get our land," which she emphasized, "includes your precious oil well."

"You're wrong, woman." Throwing aside whatever stood in his way, he stormed toward their bedroom, throwing aside whatever stood in his way.

Arnolia heard the springs groan. Rising, she blotted her eyes and returned to the washing with the shallow comfort of knowing she was right.

∞∞∞∞∞∞

"Just about right." Ten o'clock saw John Earl waiting in his parked Model A and helped himself to a long drink of whiskey. Checking once again for passers-by, he gargled a bit before swallowing the liquor. "Forgive me," he begged aloud as he splashed the whiskey on his khaki work clothes until he assured himself that the aroma of good liquor would be inescapable. Tucking the folded leases in his back pockets and picking up the pail, he left for the confines of the Smith County Courthouse. Once inside, he passed over the waxed, hardwood floors and climbed a flight of stairs recently swept by the black man employed to keep the place in some semblance of cleanliness. As he passed Terry, the odor of liquor inspired him to partake of a deep whiff in hopes of gaining some benefit.

Hands upon the wooden banister whose paint disappeared long before his arrival, Terry climbed to the second story. A quick survey of the numerous doors halved by frosted glasses neatly lettered with black inscriptions denoting their various tenants led John Earl to the appropriate entrance. Placing his hand upon the knob, he fell in, barely able to prevent himself from sprawling onto the flooring. His unexpected entrance and a slurred, "Son of a bitch," reverberated within the office to the notice of its occupants.

Stumbling toward three men occupying half of the six armless walnut office chairs lined against one wall, Terry leaned much closer toward them than necessary, questioning far too loudly, "This here the place I file oil leases?"

The men reeled, hampered by the thickness of the slat-backed chairs and their proximity to the wall. Before any could answer, the drunken man released a whiskey soured belch that spread through the office with fatal speed.

A curt voice from a prim little woman in her fifties freed the repulsed men from further onslaught. "Perhaps I can be of some assistance?"

John Earl smiled broadly as he made a couple of attempts before removing his hat. *You are too good to be true. Every boy's nightmare, an opinionated Aunt Polly transplanted to East Texas and ready to spew more information than necessary to convince folks of her own importance.* Gray hair in close set waves, framed a pale, wrinkled countenance as unpleasant as her demeanor. Lips pursed tightly in disapproval, she lightly tapped one black oxford whose stacked heels and styleless construction bespoke of her no nonsense personality.

"You wish to file some mineral leases?"

"Hell no, this ain't for no minerals. This is for oil."

"Sir," she snapped, unable to conceal her aversion for the ignorance of the drunken lout before her. "Oil is included within mineral rights." She extended her hand. "May I examine your leases?"

"You can examine whatever I got," he winked. From the corner of his eye, John Earl reassured himself of the collective interests of the men. Exaggerating each movement, he withdrew the papers, handing them to the woman, bowing as he placed them in her hand.

"It will take a bit of time. Please be seated," she gestured toward the row of chairs.

"Take all the time you need. I got nothin' but time now that my well's sure to come in." He positioned himself between two of the members of his audience, allowing the pail to clang to the floor in full view of all. "Nothin' but time to count them barrels. Yes sir!"

Able to contain himself no longer, David B. Carmichael peered into the bucket. "Mind if I take a look?" The question was rhetorical, as his hand already clasped the handle.

"You know a good core when you see it?"

"Forgive me." He withdrew a card from inside the suit coat that draped the back of his chair due to the already stifling heat. "I represent Oklahoma Oil."

Feigning surprise, John Earl baited his hook. "Well, Mister Oklahoma Oil expert, what do you think?"

His enthusiasm evident, Carmichael bent over the pail resting in his lap. "Where did you say you spudded this well?"

"Don't recall as I said." He slapped Carmichael on the arm with a force that pushed him into the man at his opposite arm. "Hell, I ain't that drunk. Wouldn't do for information like that to get out too quick. I ain't told nobody about this core." Addressing another, "Say, you got a cigarette?"

The object of Terry's question replied as he offered a smoke, "You takin' on any partners? My wife's momma died a few months ago and left her a little nest egg..." his voice trailed in shame of his own greed.

John Earl turned toward the least interested of the three men who occupied himself by cleaning his wire-framed glasses. "Ain't that the way? When you're cryin' for help, don't nobody give a damn, but when your ship's come in, they all want to jump on board." He returned to the questioner, "I got all the leases I need to keep me busy and my pockets full. These here," he pointed toward the inner office into which the county employee had disappeared, "is some that border my well. I just bought 'um to help out my neighbors."

No one's generosity extends that far, Carmichael thought. Still his instinct as a fledgling oil scout told him that this drunk could be the key to his success with Oklahoma Oil. Since his arrival, he had discovered little to report to the home office. Oh, the Daisy Bradford showed promise but generated little excitement, reinforcing his view of his present assignment as a virtual exile, a banishment unearned but awarded nonetheless on the merits of inexperience.

Tyler being the only town of any size, oil scouts working for the majors and independents alike set up offices there to await news of any magnitude concerning the Daisy Bradford. No one really expected it to hit; however, a few dollars and the least valuable employees could be risked. The oil business, after all, was based on the taking of chances. Thus Carmichael and his counterparts often passed time at the courthouse on the lookout for selling or trading of leases, especially those near spudded wells, which would indicate the eminence of a strike. The scout excused himself, hurried down the stairs and opened doors until he located a vacant office with a telephone.

Picking up the receiver, he tapped the hook and placed his call to the office of the President of Oklahoma Oil.

"Gimme Tate," he barked at the seasoned secretary and Tate's right arm.

"He's busy, Mr. Carmichael. His 'wife's' in there now." She lingered far longer than necessary on her reference to Estelle Tate.

"This is important." Nervously he paced the area afforded him by the cord. *That rube upstairs is a fool, coming into town with his core.* He looked toward the ceiling carved with rosettes. "Thank you. Thank you." *Yes indeed. This is my big chance to show Old Man Tate that I am one first class oil scout. Sending me to Texas to keep an eye on Joiner and Laster was a long shot, but this, getting in on the start of a field that nobody else knows has hit the woodbine. I can buy this whole damn county for a song and a dance. That'll show Tate.*

"Lamar Tate here."

"Mr. Tate, it's Carmichael."

"What do you want, boy? I'm a busy man." The exasperation pervading his speech had its origin from the encounter with the shapely woman exposing an alluring amount of leg. Carmichael merely provided an avenue to vent his anger.

Estelle Tate was about to victimize yet another hapless male, this time without even laying eyes on him. Having been summoned by the king himself to his throne room, the beautiful Mrs. Tate who spent the past twenty minutes listening to her husband's lambasting, welcomed the interruption to collect her thoughts. *All this over an itsy bitsy party. So what if it got a little outta hand. When I find the weasel who snitched the minute Lamar hit town, they'll wish they never learned to talk.* Estelle had only to look into the outer office for the source. She lit a cigarette encased in a long, ivory holder. A contented smile appeared as she recalled the young man with whom she spent the evening and most of the following morning. She sighed. *But you can't hold a candle to John Earl.* The sound of Lamar's fist pounding his massive desk shot her into reality.

"What kind of an idiot are you, calling me when you don't even know where the hell that well is?"

Seized by the accuracy of his employer's estimation of his intelligence, Carmichael's confidence waned to leave him a mass of jumbled thoughts and stuttering speech. "But, it has to be the one at... at Brophy."

"Can't you read a map? Brophy's no more in Smith County than I am."

"But... but,"

"But nothin', you listen to me, boy, and you listen good. Don't you write a draft on this company without more to go on than a salted core sample. My God, that's the oldest trick in the book, buying a promising coring from a producing well and passing it off as the coring from a worthless one."

At any other time, news like Carmichael's would have sent him into a frenzy of speculation, perhaps leading him to the field to buy the leases himself, and take the kinds of chances that shot his company to the top of all the majors in the southwest. Today, he had other distractions, and he continued firing questions at the costliest gamble of his life.

In Tyler, Carmichael rubbed his fingers across the marred top of the desk upon which he sat. *If the old man needs more proof, by golly, I'll see to it. Before that fool sobers up, I'll have those leases.* Taking the stairs two at a time, he opened the door just as the clerk slapped the leases into John Earl's outstretched hands.

"You have wasted my time," she snapped. "Not a single one of these acres is in Smith County."

John Earl slapped his forehead with an opened palm. "You mean I come all the way from Brophy for nothin'?"

So, he's let it slip. It is the Brophy well. Such an affirmation confirmed the scout's suspicions and determination.

Having reached the peak of her endurance, Aunt Polly placed her left hand on her hip and waved the right index finger in Terry's face. "I'm up to my elbows in papers and gnats, but none of them is as annoying as you. You're just too plain drunk to know where you are. Sober yourself up and take these to the proper courthouse." With a pristine flounce, she left the four men stunned by her diatribe.

John Earl threw up his hands. "Guess the lady has spoke her piece."

The heretofore silent member of the quartet spoke up. He was a short fellow constantly wiping perspiration from the bald crown of his head. A milquetoast sort, he epitomized the henpecked male devoid of backbone or opinion. "I believe I can offer a solution to your dilemma." He smiled nervously. "If you would allow me to take these leases off your hands, then you could," he searched for a euphemism, "you could return to your earlier pursuits."

Puzzled, John Earl queried, "What use are they to you?"

"Allow me to make an introduction. My name is Percival Armstead," a hand unaccustomed to a proper day's work met Terry's. "I'm a professor of geology at the University in Austin. Between terms, I, as you might express it, moonlight a bit," a flush quickly traveled from his neck to his crown, "for Sinclair." Suddenly aware that he possessed the floor, his confidence waned further.

"I have completed a body of research concerning this area and its intriguing geological formations. You are aware of the existence of the Overton Anticline?" Receiving no affirmations and sensing the lack of sophistication of the majority of his audience, he proceeded. "Well, in actuality it is a faulted anticline, undoubtedly trapping an immense amount of oil."

Terry slapped the professor's back, "It didn't take me no fancy title to learn that." Stumbling back to the chair, John Earl bent his head against the wall, clasping both sides of his head in an attempt to prevent the room from spinning.

The geologist followed.

"Therefore, I am keenly interested in your discovery and am in the position to offer you," he paused in contemplation, "thirty cents per acre."

Bending over with exaggerated laughter, the lease holder dabbed his eyes with a kerchief, loudly blowing his nose with a sound sufficient to guide a ship safely through the fog.

Taken aback by what he deemed not only a fair but a lucrative offer, Armstead sputtered, "Now if you believe anyone exists ready to offer more for unauthenticated leases..."

From across the room, the bespectacled man interrupted, "I'd give forty."

Simultaneously, the trio rotated to assure that what was heard was true.

"Ridiculous," scoffed the professor, "what verification have you that these leases are adjacent to this well that may or may not even exist?"

"You callin' me a liar?" John Earl bristled as if preparing to defend his honor.

Carmichael defused the offended Terry with his suggestion.

"With a little sweet talk, we might persuade our congenial hostess to place a call to the other courthouse."

"She looks like your type, Professor," quipped Terry. "I don't think she's taken much of a shine to me."

The professor straightened his tie and strode toward the door. A faint knock produced the clerk. Soon evident was an amiability which resulted in the leases returning to her possession.

The subsequent passage of the better portion of an hour sped by as each of the three speculators vied for the leases. John Earl, who had at this point identified himself as the Brophy storekeeper, lest his reputation at Oklahoma Oil have trickled down to such a low ranking employee as an oil scout, feigned an appropriate confusion.

Alternating between a desire to keep the leases and a loyalty to the most generous bidder, he vacated the room for a nip of refreshment in order to let the men simmer. As he listened through the door, a heated argument filtered through the transom into the hallway. Clearly each intended to purchase the rights for whatever price Mr. LaGuinn demanded. John Earl's reentry trailed that of the clerk.

"Gentlemen, the well in Brophy is situated on the land of a Negro named Willie Bacon. According to a partnership agreement, Mr. Hoyt LaGuinn is listed along with a venerable banker, one Clyde Russell. Other associates are out-of-towners unknown to Miss..." She coughed over the near disclosure of her counterpart. Should the divulgence of such legalities become common knowledge, it would most certainly have meant both their jobs.

The professor pressed for further verification. "Then there is such a well?"

"Most definitely."

"And these leases are adjacent?" coaxed the Oklahoma scout.

"No sir, not directly; however, they are no more than a few miles north and east," she answered. Then in anticipation of his next inquiry, she added, "All the leases in adjacency were purchased by Mr. LaGuinn, Mr. Russell, or Willie Bacon."

Under his breath, the husband about to disturb the nest egg asked more to himself than those about him, "Now who'd sell to a colored?"

"Why, his own kind, of course," responded the clerk. "The area near Brophy abounds with freedmen's lands."

"But can we be sure this man is LaGuinn?" mused Carmichael.

Sensing his cue, John Earl purposefully flung himself at the door to announce his return.

Carmichael rushed to his side. "I'll go one dollar and fifty cents an acre, but that's all I can manage without the written authorization of Mr. Lamar Tate, President of Oklahoma Oil."

John Earl grabbed the man's hand with both of his own. "She's a done deal," he pronounced.

The ardent protests of the losers fell on deaf ears, each pleading his case only to leave the office amid harsh epitaphs directed at Mr. LaGuinn's parentage.

An attorney procured from a courtroom drew up the transfers once the clerk affixed notarization, John Earl accepted the bank drafts.

David Carmichael flew to his hotel room with the knowledge that he had engineered a significant coup, a euphoria that lasted long enough for Lamar Tate to fire him and insure Carmichael of his inclusion on the industry's blacklist.

A cooling off period of four days found Tate in a more forgiving nature when Carmichael presented the leases. The news from the Daisy Bradford grew more promising each day, but not sufficient enough to salvage Carmichael's position as a scout. Tate inserted the documents in his desk drawer and locked them out of sight and mind, as was the young man now demoted to a subordinate position at the East Texas outpost.

A trip to the First National Bank netted a passer-by a glimpse of a teller counting off twenty-three hundred dollars in one hundred dollar bills to a rather malodorous customer. His request that the remaining twenty-two hundred be dispatched to Brophy's financial institution granted, John Earl stepped across the street to the city's finest department store, or so the marquee boasted.

The merchandise was passable, though hardly on a scale of a man who over the past few days had secured such a tidy profit. Purchasing a blue pencil-striped suit of cashmere, he passed the time necessitated to perform the desired alteration by selecting a present for Elaine.

"Now this is my first choice," he told the salesgirl as he held up a provocative satin gown. *But no lady like Elaine is gonna' accept such a personal item from any man short of a husband.* He settled for a uniquely set brooch of sterling silver that looped to form a perfect bow. The diamonds were imitations, though they caught the light with an engaging sparkle. A bracelet of the same design completed the set for which Terry considered his investment of eight dollars well worth the price.

Returning to the men's section, he donned his new clothing after requesting the disposal of the old. Before John Earl could reach the jewelry counter to claim the gift-wrapped baubles, the man who sold him the suit had disappeared with the liquor-doused shirt and trousers, thankful for the relief.

Well on his way out of town, John Earl did a bit of mental arithmetic. *If I don't tarry too long here, I can make it by to see Elaine at a respectable hour.* Slamming on the brakes of the Model A, Terry jumped out at a farm house. The barking of a dog eager to defend the homestead summoned a bespectacled farmer from his radio.

"Shut up, Nellie," a command that sent the German shepherd under the house. "You didn't miss it far, Mr. Terry."

"I make it a point to be a man of my word."

Emerging to join the farmer on the porch, Professor Percival Armstead chimed in with a decidedly different accent. "I hope a buck and a half was fine enough."

John Earl was peeling bills from the wad previously at home in the pocket of his new suit pants.

"Hell, I'd of been tickled with a dollar." After handing each man one hundred dollars, he mused, "Don't seem right somehow not to give that old biddy a few dollars. She was better than both of you."

All laughed in agreement as the farmer taunted his friend. "Oh she got her share, all right. Ole Clarence had to take her to lunch to make that Longview call."

Returning to his portrayal of the geology professor he sadly informed them, "Such a pity that Sinclair has summoned me for more noble pursuits."

John Earl left the men recruited from the line of down and outs hunting day labor. *Always happy to benefit the less fortunate*, he told himself on the way back to Brophy, *and all it cost me was a couple of hundred and some new get ups. Not bad for all concerned.* Wishing for the wasted whiskey to keep him company on the road, he settled back against the upholstery. *Damn, I'm good*, and he punched the pedal closer to the floorboard.

Undisturbed by the length of Terry's absence, those in Brophy welcomed the respite from the drilling. Millie delighted in Hoyt's return to the store, and those thirsty for the back room elixir echoed her sentiments. Much to Arnolia's surprise, Pup and Cale spent the better part of the time with Willie in their fields, leaving Gabriel and his friends to cut wood. Returning home, Cale found his wife missing and instructions for him to bring the wagon to Elaine's.

The floral pattern of the seamless tapestry rug which covered the majority of the Russell parlor lay concealed by mounds of clothing. Atop the Beckwith piano stool, boxes as yet unopened were stacked. The walnut covering for the keyboard doubled as a display area for booties of assorted sizes and colors.

"Daddy, don't you be popping in, now. Mavis is trying on these clothes."

Clyde entertained no such notions, having voluntarily positioned himself on the cretonne pads of his white reed rocker, after aiming the radio speaker as near the front window as possible. *When Elaine and Mavis get together, the room becomes decidedly smaller. I hope she's gone before 'Amos and Andy,'*

"The lighting's better in here." Elaine referred to the five frosted globes of the parlor's ceiling fixture that fell a full three feet and spread an even glow throughout the room.

Hesitantly, Mavis left Elaine's bedroom, for the first time in her life self conscious of her appearance. Clad in a waterproof nursing bra and an elastic maternity corset, the attached garters flapped with each unsteady step.

"I can't wear this thing."

Patting her distended belly, Elaine teased, "I don't see what other choice you have." As she examined Mavis for the first time in such a revealing mode, Elaine skeptically prodded, "Are you sure this baby is due November first? You're awfully big."

Mavis groaned as she lowered herself awkwardly onto a velvet hassock situated at the hearth. "Hell's bells, what's there to lie about now? Anybody knows us won't be able to count to nine before I call out a domino."

Ordinarily the prudent Elaine would have blushed at such a tawdry remark, but when it came from Mavis, such utterances shed their vulgarities for an aura of comedy. She kneeled in front of her despondent friend. "That's not what I meant at all; you know that."

She reached up and adjusted the button on the nursing flap. "All I'm saying is that I don't see how you can go until November at this rate. I think you've miscounted."

Red curls and garters shook. "No, I'm sure. Mamma was gone to Memphis to see Uncle Bert at the Methodist Hospital. He had the prostrate troubles."

"Prostate."

"Uh huh, pretty common in them old codgers. And me and Cale was at the house smoochin' and feelin' around." Her eyes grew distant in memory. 'I don't know how it all come up and out, but it did."

Mavis noticed Elaine's bowed head. "I know you think I'm just the cheapest kind of girl, but that was the only time before or since."

Shocked, Elaine's eyes jerked upwards.

"Well, he's never to home what with the drillin', and if he is," she ran her hands over her abdomen, "who can think of romance with this starin' him in the face?"

Elaine turned and busied herself with her old maternity dresses to hide eyes filling with angry tears.

Do I pity Mavis or myself more for what we've lost? Cale owes her so much more. If he married her, he has a duty to his wife, not some misguided sense of loyalty to what will never be.

She stacked the booties in Mavis's suitcase. *I don't know why this should surprise me; I saw it coming in ever so many ways, brushing her hand away at the movies, ignoring her when we're at the well.*

Not one to dwell in despondency, Mavis struggled to stand, "Now show me how to tie myself into this contraption. I need all the help I can get to hold this load up."

"The lacers at both sides of the corset lift the baby up." As she tightened each side, Mavis nodded her understanding. "Suck in while I hook these eyes in the back."

In exhaling the mother-to-be looked over her shoulder. 'I can't thank you enough for lettin' me borrow all this. The money I had saved up will cover the doctor and the hospital, but that's all. And even if I didn't mind askin' Millie for the material, I'd sew my fingers together tryin' to make anything."

She raised a gingham dress over her head. "Waitressin' don't leave no time for sewin', and momma and me done well enough to get ready-to-wear."

"Does your mother know about the baby?"

"No, not yet. She just knows we're married. With Bethel, one thing at a time's better."

"Don't put it off," advised Elaine as she stood back. "I'm going to let the hem out."

Giggles erupted over the obvious height disparity.

"Now, I always like flashin' a lot of leg to the men folk," she wiggled her toes. "With this heat, there's sure a reason to show as much as you can."

As the girls completed their fashion show, John Earl braked the Model A under the live oak. Rising to meet him at the top of the porch steps, Clyde looked questioningly at the wanderer, mindful of their last encounter and the vow to which all had sworn.

Without so much as a greeting, John Earl held the transfer slip at each top corner directly at Clyde's eye level. "Will that cover it?" he demanded.

"There abouts," was the incredulous reply.

"Is the pipe here?"

"Arrived this mornin'." Clyde stepped in front of Terry as he walked toward the front door. "No men allowed. The hens have a party going. You see where I've been sent."

The younger man smiled. "A man's home is his castle unless the queen says otherwise. Say, ain't it time for 'Amos and Andy'?"

"Oh," Clyde bustled toward his set just as the familiar music announced the show.

"Elaine, it's John Earl. Can a man bust up this secret society lodge meetin'?"

A scurrying of footsteps preceded the opening of the door. Unknown to him, the women were working their magic on Elaine by tidying her hair and clothes for the unexpected caller. Though the intensity of her love for Cale still dominated her heart, John Earl's attentions excited her as no man before. The man was a smooth talker, a charmer with just the right allure of danger that drew a woman unaccustomed to his worldliness like a moth rushing headlong into a flame.

Greeting her with a friendly peck on the cheek, he apologized for the lateness of the hour, explaining its necessity with an abridged accounting of the success of his venture outside Brophy and his procurement of the funds to restart the drilling.

"Cale said you'd do it," Mavis cheered with a newly discovered energy.

"Somebody talkin' about me?" Cale stuck his head in the door. Waddling over, his enthusiastic wife took his face in her hands and planted an unappreciated kiss from which Cale fought for an escape. Undeterred, she pressed on with her bubbling account of John Earl's news.

Crossing to the settee upon which their hero and his lady sat, Cale shook his hand. "You're a one man wonder."

"That's what I keep tellin Elaine, but she don't listen hard enough."

Unable to meet the eyes of either, Elaine looked down at her hands in a gesture only Mavis mistook for shyness.

"I plumb forgot," Terry dove into his coat pocket for the gift box. "Bought my favorite lady a little present."

Speechless, Elaine tore away at the wrapping with a childlike delight.

Mavis came to her side which pushed Elaine and John Earl closer as she insinuated a spot on the already crowded settee. "Hurry, this is better than Christmas."

Lifting the lid, both women gasped in unison. Waving her husband closer, she urged in a high-pitched summons, "Come here, hon, and see what he's brought. It's just darlin'."

Cale remained on the hassock with eyes fixed upon Elaine's elated face, watching as her benefactor pinned the brooch to her checked house dress and slipped the bracelet on her arm.

Jealousy and anger collided. *How can she let herself be bought by some dime store trinkets?* Watching Elaine put her arms around Terry's neck and the ensuing passion of their kiss gnawed at his soul rendering him oblivious to anything except the length of their embrace.

"I said," she twitched his nose to awaken him from his trance, "for you to help me load up this stuff so we can leave these two lovebirds to their business."

Cale glared at Mavis with a vengeance that puzzled his wife. She shrugged, "If you're not a mind to leave, it's no matter to me." She occupied herself gathering the clothing tossed across the room.

"I'll help you, little mother," volunteered Elaine, a spiteful stare aimed at Cale finding its mark and speaking her thoughts.

Lighting a cigarette and deposited the spent match in the metallic stand, John Earl threw one arm across the back of the settee. "You girls rob the Sears and Roebuck delivery boy while I was gone?"

A light exchange followed between the women and Terry until the grocery wagon was loaded. No one acknowledged Cale's silence which loomed well after he and Mavis climbed into bed.

Chapter 6

September 1930

*A*ll considered, things have gone pretty good, too good. Here it is the first week in September, and the bit's penetrated to about three thousand feet with only some minor irritations like a patch job on a boiler or days taken off to shore up more wood. Runnin' out of money for the pipe's been the biggest hitch, but, Bulldog smiled, *John Earl handled that with his own brand of magic.*

A quick check of Terry's car by the farm boss produced the battered pail emptied of all but a few shavings, enough for a seasoned driller to recognize the coring. *It didn't take much to guess the source, but my hat's off to you, boy. I wish I knew how you got a hold of it. Yes, sir, we were overdue for this one. But this time it'll have to be me instead of John Earl to get us out.*

And so he tried for most of four days to retrieve the broken pipe which severed halfway down the bore hole of the Willie B. Over and over he replayed the fateful afternoon when the pipe snapped, unable to determine any possible way he could have avoided the calamity. Sometimes it just happens; you run afoul of the lady's smilin' face.

The upper portions of the pipe removed and stacked, Hoyt was dispatched to purchase the fishing lure which Bulldog repeatedly guided into the bore hole during numerous attempts to latch onto the disconnected pipe. Taking a disgusted look at the lure, he followed the cylindrical shaped device to its tapered point.

Kicking the apex to remove a shroud of mud and exposing its teeth, Bulldog examined the blunt end, which attached to the upper pipe section, in hopes of discovering some error in workmanship to explain his inability to force the tapered end within the broken pipe to create a vice-like grip with its teeth.

His fears confirmed, he resigned himself to failure and joined his crew under the trees.

"Boys, we got one more shot before we skid the derrick someplace else and start over."

An outpouring of sighs and expletives ensued.

"I had Clyde do some checkin' for me after the second day. You greenhorns ain't familiar with the tool we need; it's called a wall hook."

"How come you didn't get us one when we was settin' up?" griped a miffed Hoyt at what appeared to be a costly oversight.

"Bad luck, Hoyt. No crew wants to see one on a regular basis. More you look at it, the more apt you are to have to use it."

"Bullshit."

Ignoring Hoyt, "Tell the boys what you got wind of, Clyde."

"The crew over at the Daisy Bradford located a wall hook from Laster himself back in '29. That's how he ended up with Joiner and Lloyd in the first place; they went to where he was drilling on another well over at Waskom."

"But to make a long story short." urged Pup.

Clyde took the hint. "We might be able to talk them out of it, that is if it's still around."

Pup was on his feet, "Get her gassed up, John Earl."

Terry looked from one to another. "I spect I better sit this one out; I wouldn't know a wall hook from a shoe hook." He covered his reluctance to come in contact with anyone outside the Brophy area so close on the heels of a scam. "This sounds like one of them father and son trips to me."

Pup accepted the keys to Hoyt's wagon. "Come on, Dad. We're wastin' daylight."

As the pair drove by the store, Pup sounded the horn at Mavis who was finishing a sweep of the entry and waved as she reentered.

"Thank you, Mrs. Newton." The proprietor's wife watched as the mother of six passed through the labyrinth of merchandise toward the door. Addressing Mavis, "It was all I could do to take that fifty-nine cents for the Fletcher's Castoria from her."

"I swear, if it were your call, this store would be outta business. Better not let Hoyt hear you talkin' that way. You know what he said about extendin' credit."

Millie gave an appreciative nod. "Where would I be without you to keep me straight? And the customers have taken quite a shine to you, too. You give them just the right mix of attention and suggestion. You even charmed the horns off that old billy goat Jesse Witherspoon. Why in ten years, he's never bought more than a two ounce box of Beech-Nut at one time. Now you got him samplin' different brands and into a pair of new overalls cause you say they make him look younger." She watched as Mavis completed a pyramid of toilet papers. "What are you up to now?"

Mavis stepped back to survey her handiwork. "The cheap White Rose is on the bottom, and the more expensive Silk

Velvet's an easy reach. A skinflint after the White Rose will bring down the house."

Millie sighed. *Just how will I manage without Mavis when the baby comes? And judging from her progress, that baby will be better than a month old by the November first date she's broadcastin'.*

A traveler in a white shirt and bow tie claimed notice. Though disinterested in the goods offered for sale, he scoured the store in search of something. Millie's suspicions of the stranger instinctively moved her closer to the Ranger repeater Hoyt kept under the counter.

Unaware of Millie's fears, Mavis left her display to greet the customer.

"What can we do for you today, Sir?"

"I'm looking for Hoyt LaGuinn."

"Sorry as I can be, but he's out at the well."

As always, Mavis could not control her tongue and proceeded to talk the man's arm off. "You know we, that is my husband Cale, Mr. LaGuinn, and several others are gonna strike oil any day now."

The dizzy rate at which the redhead spoke drove the man past the limits of proper decorum as she rambled on about the well, forcing him to break in as she paused for a breath. "When do you expect him?"

"I'm not right sure, but you can ask Millie." She pointed toward the counter. "That's Miz LaGuinn, yonder."

His bewilderment showed.

A troubled exchange of expressions between the women drew Mavis away from the stranger. As she moved toward Millie and the rifle, she inquired, "Somethin' wrong? Millie is Hoyt's wife, and I, well, I am like their daughter because my husband works here, well, he did before they all started to drill and..."

With annoyance evident, "Hoyt LaGuinn, about thirty, dark hair and eyes, mustache, lean build, maybe an inch or so taller than I am?"

Between giggles and full grown belly laughs that forced her to clasp hands under the baby, Mavis contradicted, "Mister, somebody sold you a lengthy bill of goods. Hoyt LaGuinn is plannin' on actin' as this youngun's granddaddy."

"I've got to hear that one, Mavis." Cale and John Earl had arrived unnoticed. "You been tellin' the customers some of them dirty jokes?" asked John Earl.

Recognition of the familiar voice spun the stranger toward it. Pointing repeatedly he informed the startled women, "That's Hoyt LaGuinn."

Trapped, John Earl's will to survive told him to run, but his rogue's instinct willed him to play out the cards he'd been dealt.

"Mr. Carmichael," Terry cried in his most amiable, "welcome to the next oil boom."

Being made the fool atop his unceremonious demotion compelled the otherwise passive Carmichael towards the limits of his emotions.

He demanded, "Just who the hell are you, really?"

Crossing to the pop box, John Earl withdrew an R. C. Cola, nonchalantly popping the lid with the built in bottle opener and offering the cold drink to his nemesis.

'Let me buy you a drink."

An unexpected swing of the scout's arm sent the bottle crashing to the plank floor where glass and the carbonated liquid traveled in all directions. "I want to know who you are and what game you're playing."

As he eased his way to the counter and the concealed rifle, Cale motioned for the women to leave. *I don't know which of your enemies has finally caught up with you, but this time, you're gonna need more than quick wit and good looks to come out on top* mused Cale.

"Oh, now Carmichael, a man sittin' on a million dollars can't go broadcastin' his real name. Why, there might have been lease thieves in that office."

"There sure as hell was, and you were it."

Lunging forward, the impact hurled John Earl to the ground in a mass of fists and punches. Scrambling to his feet, Terry grasped the smaller man by the arm and swung him toward a stack of Silver Quill growing mash feed sacks.

"Listen here, you got no call to carry on so. Them leases is worth a fortune as soon as we strike."

Heaving against the feed, Carmichael managed, "You all but cost me my job. Tate's taken away my authorization to use everything except the telephone and cut my salary by half till I pay for those leases."

When his eyes fell upon a steel mill file carelessly discarded when the last sack of mash had been split, the hopelessly outclassed scout sought to equalize the differences in size and ability.

Unaware of its existence, John Earl hovered above his downed opponent, vainly seeking to talk Carmichael out of what would be the beating of his life, feeling he owed the boy as much.

A single motion swept up the file and plunged his body forward. His eyes now fixed on the honed apex, Terry's left hand controlled his opponent's right while his own right hand pushed back the man's head. Able to maneuver the file toward Carmichael, the force of the more muscular fighter sent the sharpened point across the left cheek of the smaller. Carmichael's sheer will to survive propelled Terry backward at the cost of control of the weapon. Despite the painful stream of red, the scout straddled John Earl like a colossus prepared to plunge the file into the neck of the man at whose hand he had suffered.

Cold steel of the Ranger at the back of his head stayed the attacker's hand. "You can throw that thing over by the counter."

With no response forthcoming, Cale methodically closed one eye as a loud click announcing his intent to fire. "Want yourself dead more than him?"

As the file landed against the main counter, the store became a cavern echoing the hollow sound of metal against wood. Waving the barrel toward the entrance, Cale stepped in front of Carmichael. "Now get the hell out of Brophy."
Picking up his hat, he turned to speak but was silenced by the finality of Cale's declaration.

"And if you're thinkin' to call in the law, there's two witnesses to one says you tried your damned level best to murder this man."

Carmichael arched his shoulders then straightened his dirt-streaked shirt and tie in an effort to regain some semblance of composure. He spent the entirety of his trip back to Tyler and many a stolen moment in weeks to come creating scenarios in which he would make the swindler pay through the nose. It would be through Lamar Tate that he would learn the identity and history of John Earl Terry and his means of revenge. Stumbling out the door, he drove back to Smith County.

Without regard for the man struggling to his feet, Cale returned the rifle to its home.

"I owe you for that one."

Cale searched his partner's face for some clue of what Elaine could see, some element of good he'd overlooked. Cale loathed both his partner and himself. *He's nothin' but the kind of low life I left home to get away from. And I'm sinkin' in the same filth.* In his own defense, *But it happened so gradual like. Not askin' no questions, takin' money like he just found it layin' on the ground somewheres, till here I stand, waist deep in the muck that is John Earl Terry.*

He stole a look at the man grinning with pride in his accomplishment. *Am I any better to have helped him cheat this man and who knows how many others? Why am I sellin' my soul to this devil?* A picture of the derrick loomed in answer to his question. For one chance in hell of hittin' a gusher. The magnitude of how far he'd fallen rushed a wave of nausea throughout his body.

Aloud, he said, "You don't owe me a damned thing!"

The unexpected vehemence of the response momentarily humbled Terry. "But you saved my life," he quietly stated under the mistaken assumption that Cale required an admission of such from him.

Cale turned and slammed his fist onto the counter with a force that rattled even the metal bins of crackers and candies.

"You stole that man's money sure as I'm livin', and it ain't no use to deny it."

"And you," he emphasized the last word, "spent it on pipe."

Terry leaned across the counter that separated them, narrowing the chasm until they were almost one in the same man. "Where do you think the money comes from to keep this wildcat goin'? You think rigs appear out of the kindness of somebody's heart like donations at them prayer meetins' you like to frequent?"

Cale drew back, but Terry caught him by the arm. "Oh, you and the rest think you got no dirt on your hands as long as Ole John Earl does the connin'. Well, let me set you straight, just so's there's no further outbreaks of holier than thouness on your part. Yeah, I fleeced that fool, but he at least got some leases to show for it. Who knows? They might pay off. That's a hell of a lot more than I can say for the man that furnished us our rig. But he was a growed man, and anyone who sits down to play cards ought to be on the watch or face the consequences."

Cale's knees weakened along with his resolve.

Relaxing his grip as the knowledge that his hold on Cale extended beyond the physical, John Earl watched him leave the store.

He'll come around, Terry promised himself. *They all do. If a man wants to succeed in the oil business, he has to throw down his scruples and wallow in the drillin' mud with everyone else. It's a cut-throat business; he might as well get used to it early on.* Terry began the process of returning the store to its usual ordered clutter.

Cale had to escape. *I'm gettin' Mavis, and we're goin' back to Winnie.* A vice tightened around his throat precipitating a battle that raged, maddening that part of him that saw the wrong in what he was doing but was unable to surpass the grimness of reality or the lure of wealth.

Go back to what, a life on another man's land or one in Bethel's employ, countin' the days till she dies and leaves Mavis the cafe? Visions of a vengeful Bethel scribbling wildly gave him reason to ridicule himself further. *It'd be just like her to write Mavis off for leavin' her in the lurch and gettin' herself pregnant to boot. And what about Sarah? Ain't they dependin' on what little I can send them just to get by?*

The heat of reality seared him with shame and futility like a branding iron as a reminder of the man he had become.

〰〰〰〰〰

As Cale grappled with himself, the Schneiders stopped on what substituted for a rise at the midpoint between Henderson and Overton. They were on the nine hundred and seventy-five acres of land belonging to Mrs. Daisy Bradford, but an errant turn left them confused. Following the derrick as the crow flew proved impossible on the winding roads designed to pass each house. But persistence and a few directions from the locals brought them this far.

"There she sits, beckonin' like a lighthouse drawin' the lost ships to a port of prosperity from the seas of despair," announced Pup.

Some four hundred feet away from the rig, remnants of the Daisy Bradford #2 loomed as a silent legacy to the perdition of broken pipe and a contrast to the hope of the third well spudded on the Bradford farm. Since 1925, Dad Joiner and Mrs. Bradford shared the dream of an oil-soaked East Texas, entering into a business agreement that most chalked up to a victimized woman flattered into a no-win deal by a down-and-out oil man.

"So Joiner's another buddy of yours?"

The father reminisced, "Met Columbus Marion Joiner in Oklahoma years ago where his near miss of the Seminole Field made him a legend to folly. Two hundred feet deeper, and he, not Lamar Tate, would have been the big man in Seminole. But that's Joiner's life story, a little deeper, a bit more luck, a few miles over."

The man about which they spoke sauntered into view. "Seems like sixty odd years of "almosts" has took its toll." Pup referred to the fact that Joiner walked stooped at the waist.

"That's from the rheumatic fever, but it ain't kept that silver-haired wildcatter from sweet talkin' landed widows into believin' in his dreams."

Joiner now stood beside his partner, A. D. "Doc" Lloyd. "Them two make quite a pair. Need a gin scale to weigh Lloyd; he must be better than three hundred."

"The man's got to be seventy-three, four," the father added, "and he's passed himself off as everythin' from a veterinarian to a barker for Doctor Alonzo Durham's Great Medicine Show. Now folks think he's a noted geologist, and they're placin' their hopes and dreams on a man who abandoned his Christian name of Joseph I. Dunham and six times swore to love, honor, and cherish. Somehow it don't seem right."

"Don't seem to be keepin' folks away none." Pup referred to the endless queue of cars lining the road to the Daisy Bradford #3. As the Schneiders left their delivery wagon and walked down the rise, they passed through a collection of farmers, families and business-suited city folk from whom they overheard that Laster had reamed the well on the fifth of September by using an experimental tool for a drill-stem test.

Father looked to son, "See how them leases is flyin'? And you can bet the price is inchin' up with every exchange."

Bulldog approached Laster, a curly-headed driller high on the euphoria of the test results, who listened with empathy to the tale of broken pipe. Running his fingers through the disheveled blonde mass before replacing his hat, he took the Schneiders to the abandoned well. "She was give to us," The three easily lifted the ten foot pipe with the assistance of the third man's twenty years of roughneck strength behind them. "So, I'm passin' it on to you."

As Pup tied red bandannas to the protruding ends of the pipe, Bulldog pressed, "None of Lloyd and Joiner's brand of bullshit; how close are you, really?"

A seriousness replaced the joviality of before, "Not more than a month if we can get the casing on time. How about ya'll?"

"If I'm any kind of fisherman, we'll be about that far behind you." He winked, "Less if you strike."

With Laster's prophecy fresh on his mind, early the next morning Bulldog guided the wall hook down the bore hole of the Willie B. A few hours later he had it, having twisted the device inside the length of the lost pipe. Cheers went up from the crew that by day's end returned to the routine of drilling.

~~~~~

October 4, 1930

At daybreak a small crowd representative of the true believers and the diehard critics gathered a respectable distance from the well to await the test that could spell riches or ruin for the Brophy crew. Separated by the barrier of race, the Black land owners fell to their knees in prayer with the reverend of the New Jerusalem Church.

White on-lookers divided their attention between the goings on at the rig floor and the prayer vigil. Whenever an emphatic "Amen" rose from the supplicants, all heads pivoted toward those beseeching Jesus to save them from their earthly hell of poverty and injustice, only to return to the rig to offer supplications of their own.

To the crew, the crowd offered few distractions, such being the intensity of the test. Through some finagling by Bulldog, the experimental tool used on the Daisy Bradford found itself attached to their drill stem. Easing the tool to the bottom of the bore, it opened to receive an influx of mud and water.

On their hands and knees, the men bent over the hole in their own posture of prayer, though only the first and second driller and John Earl actually possessed first-hand knowledge of what they sought.

When a swift lifting of his head sent him into a spiral of dizziness, Cale fell backward, 'It's gas!" Slipping on the mud-soaked drilling floor, he fell onto his back in a scramble to get away.

"She's gonna blow us sky high!"

By now the impact of Cale's erroneous omen struck home with the seasoned oil men.

"Get her up," ordered the farm boss.

Joint by joint the pipe removal eked along at a snail's pace. Straining to contain their delirium but unwilling to excite the others, the three offered no encouragement. The discovery of gas strengthened their hope; oil must be near. With each reappearing length Pup and Bulldog scrutinized the encapsulating mud, as did John Earl when he handled the discarded pipe.

Nearing the three thousand three hundred foot mark, the driller scraped away the mud from the exposed pipe. Gently applying cleaner water, he threw his arms around his son.

"We got the woodbine!"

The men alternated with congratulatory cheers and hugs that puzzled those at the perimeter who expected, to their disappointment, a gusher. Confidence bolstered to assurance, the driller called for the removal of the testing tool. Before the sample could be removed, a gentle vibration of the platform grew in intensity until the crew grasped for the derrick or machinery as they poured from the rig. Back in Brophy the windows of the houses shook, and pictures went askew. From the hole, gas forced mud and oil halfway up the derrick.

"What's it mean, Bulldog?" demanded Cale desperately seeking reassurance from what he assumed to be a precursor of disaster.

Swinging his Missouri roughneck like a ten-cent dancer, his voice rang with an unbridled glee. "Means there's oil down there, but we got to go further to bring her in. She's a comin', though, she's a comin'."

John Earl stared toward Miss Wythel's home from which the old woman came, repeatedly screaming the same curse. Reaching their sides, she collapsed in a breathless gasp, "She hit."

Receiving little more than inquiries about her health, she pulled Bulldog toward her. "She hit," the aged woman repeated.

Patting her hands, the driller kindly spoke, "No ma'am, not yet, but it was the first sign. Give me a few more weeks, and I'll have you an oil well."

Of all things, Miss Wythel abhorred being patronized as a feeble-minded old woman. Mustering all her remaining strength, she spewed at Bulldog, "Not the Willie B., you jackass, the Daisy Bradford. She come in last evenin'; it's on the radio."

It was Bulldog's turn to collapse. Forced to Miss Wythel's front porch by the onslaught of rain that would deluge East Texas for the fall of 1930, the "family" remained at the Willie B; the curious and the professional rushed to the Daisy Bradford.

A conservative estimate placed them along side five thousand scrambling for positions on a road jammed with cars, trapped on a one-lane path. Within the throng, leases changed ownership at speculative prices, while entrepreneurs on a small scale hawked cots, refreshments, and transportation. On the once arid land, mud began to transform East Texas into a quagmire.

At Miss Wythel's the prized copy of the Longview newspaper passed from reader to reader who scrutinized the headlines and articles about the strike. "Six thousand eight hundred barrels a day," Bulldog pushed the paper toward Clyde. "Nothing but speculator fodder."

"Maybe we should name this baby Daisy?" the mother-to-be posed.

Pup scoffed, "Why name it after someone else's success when you'll have one of your own?"

Ever practical, the banker represented the lone doomsayer. "She's not in yet, and we're low on funds again. With prices bound to skyrocket, how much more can it cost us to bring her in, Bulldog?"

Prepared for Clyde's inevitably disheartening attitude, the driller jumped in with both feet. "I want to drill a few hundred further."

"And risk a gusher we might not be able to control? I'm not for that," John Earl's view was emphatic.

Bulldog countered, "We're a good deal of distance from the Daisy Bradford, and judgin' from the survey..."

"You think I ain't studied them surveys? Hell, I'm the one chose this damn site."

Cale listened to the argument, unsure of which to believe. All that was certain was the dream so close to his grasp. To let it slip through their fingers now..."Go half," he heard himself say.

"What do you know?" growled Terry.

Coming to the defense of her husband, Mavis lunged verbally at Terry.

"Enough to say we got to go as deep as the Daisy Bradford. The odds got to be played here." Adding for emphasis, "Ain't you the big gambler? Where's your spirit of adventure all of a sudden?"

Elaine's hand tightening around his ended the discussion, and Bulldog seized the opportunity to break the uneasy silence that ensued. "To answer Clyde's question, we don't need a red cent. We got drill pipe, and a call to any equipment company will get us casing on credit if we agree to purchase for our next few wells exclusively from them."

Cale savored the sound. *Our next few wells. It all seems so unbelievable. More wells, more money, an endless supply. Why, I can own half of Missouri in a year's time.* He glanced at his wife wildly chatting to Millie and Elaine about what she'd buy for the baby when the well came in. *I'm gonna have the best for my son. My boy won't never pull a cotton sack nor hoe a field; not my boy.*

The farm boss won, and at his insistence the Willie B.'s bore hole lengthened to that of the Daisy Bradford. The crew began the task of casing the well with the seamless pipe to prevent a collapse of the well's walls. As a further reinforcement, the boys forced concrete between the walls and the casing. True to the driller's promise, oil field suppliers beat paths to their door to offer lines of credit without so much as a signature. Folks from all over streamed into the area, mostly toward Kilgore, in hopes of capturing a piece of the boom.

Battling the intermittent rain and fatigue, the boys sat on the drilling floor for a breather when a group of thirty odd black men and teenagers approached. Willie jumped from the platform and greeted their callers with handshakes before engaging in a private conversation with Ezekiel Mims of the New Jerusalem flock. Hurrying back to the rig, Willie presented their cause. "They wants to go to work."

"Them and half of America," spouted Pup.

"No suh, free work," Willie explained to the questioning crew. "The Reverent Mims, that'd be him in the front here, says the sooner we hits oil, the better it'll be for all us black folks sittin' atop it. So they's willin' to work for nuttin' to get sumptin' a piece down the road."

"Totin' pipe, feedin' boilers, and choppin' wood?" queried the farm boss.

Willie nodded, "Whatever the boss man says."

Bulldog smiled broadly. *The Reverend is right,* he told himself, *the quicker the better. Haven't done so bad with a green crew so far.* Without so much as a word of consultation, "Divide into two crews, adults and boys mixed. Send one home till after supper, and we can try to work a double tour tonight."

Willie was on his way when Bulldog shouted after him, "Tell 'um they won't regret it."

"Yes suh," was a cheer.

For almost two weeks, the Willie B.'s boilers labored at sixteen hour days setting the casing and inserting the plug at the bottom of the hole. About noon, the boss announced, "I want you all to go home to rest up. If the Reverend Mims' prayers hold weight, the Willie B. will be comin' in, and we're gonna need all the strength we can muster to cap it."

Alone and taking a final walk around his rig, Bulldog checked the Christmas tree whose valves would regulate the pressure of the oil and gas and a series of storage tanks built with the aid of his newest crew. *This is what I've stored up a lifetime of experience for. And I never really believed it till now. In a few hours, I'm bringin' in my own wildcat well.* He turned around and spread his arms into the air, "My well," he shouted, savoring the sound and the beauty of the rig as he took a long drink from his flask. "Here's to you," he saluted.

Days had passed since John Earl and Elaine spent time alone, something he intended to remedy as soon as the well hit. Driving toward the school, Terry wrestled with unfamiliar emotions. *I went after her for Clyde's money. That it came all wrapped up with a pretty bow didn't hurt none. But I'll be damned if she ain't chippin' away at my resolve against permanent attachments. A woman like her sure never crossed my path. College educated, sensitive, unselfish, can't describe the Estelle Tate's of this world with them words.* Whether the capability existed for him to truly love her or any woman never occurred to John Earl. *Only detour down the road of happiness is that boy.* He gripped the wheel as he made the last turn. *I tried my best to make friends with Jake, but he don't want no part of me.* Thinking back on his own childhood, *Guess I just don't know how to be no daddy. Sure as hell got nothin' to blueprint by. Nope, man like me don't need no kids, and she's apt to want more. We'll just have to make sure that don't happen.*

He parked near the now bulging school. Even Brophy experienced the influx of boom seekers. Naturally, some came with families to house and educate. Unprepared for the barrage, Kilgore and its surrounding areas filled quickly, resulting in overflows as far out as Brophy.

In response to the familiar engine, Elaine's face appeared at the window.

"Recess class," she announced to her exuberant pupils. Mrs. Crawford, unusually nice for a teacher in their estimations, endeared herself to them even further with this added freedom and secured for herself a nomination for sainthood.

John Earl watched as the overall and feed sack clad youngsters bounded out of the building and raced each other for the two swings suspended from an ancient elm. *This boom's gonna build you kids a real school, one you'll be proud of, the kind that big city newspapers and magazines come to write about.* A ragged boy caught his eye as he pushed a smaller child out of the swing. As the boy pulled high in the air, the holes in the soles of his shoes shone. Momentarily Terry saw himself. *This money's gonna make me a man can't nobody look down on. And God help anybody gets in my way to seein' that it's so.*

Elaine peered into the window of the car. As he leaned through to kiss his girl, she pulled away.

"John Earl, you're shameless... the children."

A woman immune to the pleasures of my advances, another new experience introduced by Elaine Crawford. Real ladies, I guess, think they have to play at bein' coy. But you, my lady, leave me to wonderin' if you ain't just plain cold. He reassured himself. *Once we're married, I'll set you straight.* He gave her his full attention.

"What are you doing in town? Answering her own question with dread, "Something's gone wrong at the well."

"No, darlin', all's right with the world Bulldog give us time to rest up before we drill through the plug. I come by to make sure you show up to see us bring her in."

"I can't do that; there's school."

"Oh, Mrs. Crawford, in Doc Terry's expert opinion, you look a might peaked."

"Lie about being sick?" Such a deception appalled her. "I could never... besides half the town knows about..."

"Hell Elaine," his forcefulness frightened her, sending her back from the window. "You don't need the job now and sure won't once the well begins pumpin'. Here's the most important day of my life, and you're actin' skittish about a white lie. Besides, with the money I'm gonna make, I can tell people what they ought to think." Suddenly aware of his cruel edge, he softened. "I'm sorry as I can be, darlin'. All this work and no sleep's got me out of sorts. I just want you with me when my well hits, that's all. You're everything I been workin' for." He flashed a smile that cajoled her with the charms she was powerless to combat.

As he pulled from the curb, she waved shyly, lest the children spice their suppers with tales of the teacher's conduct. *So it's come down to tomorrow...and I'm still no closer to a decision than I was the day we hit the woodbine.* The scene replayed often enough as she lay in bed, causing a disturbing urge that left her sweaty and ashamed of what she felt stirring within.

John Earl drug her behind the tool house where the ardor of his kisses and the battle to stay his caressing hands left her breathless. As his lips traveled down her neck, John Earl whispered, "I want you to marry me the very day the well comes in."

Only Gabriel's embarrassed presence in search of a wrench freed her from a response, though he pressed for an answer at every turn. *All my instincts rage against this, and Daddy certainly makes no secret of his displeasure over it all. Dear, sweet Daddy. You still believe Cale and I belong together.* She sighed. *Why can't life ever be the fantasies we dream up in our minds?*

Claiming the hand bell that summoned the children back inside, the fantasies aroused by John Earl rushed to the forefront before being driven back by self reproach. *And what have dreams ever brought me but heartache and disappointment? Maybe some of us aren't ever meant for happily ever afters.*

The Lord was a popular fellow in East Texas, privy to deals, demands, and the despondent on a regular basis.

"Thank you, God, Willie praised at finding Arnolia out in the fields. "I ain't got no strength for another fight with Jacob's angel." Their last remained freshly etched in his memory.

"And now, Mr. Uppity, you gots the Reverent and them others slavin' for them white men at no pay whilst their farms waste away like ours. Hope you're mighty proud of yourself, Willie Bacon."

What if she's right? Willie asked himself as he fell back onto the mattress. *What if it brings us more troubles than we ever seen?* The small but persistent voice answered, *But what if there's a gusher?* Behind closed eyes a house, a fine house, appeared with five bedrooms and the plumbing inside. One just like it set on every farm whose lease they owned. The kids all sat at full tables, dressed for school in store-bought clothes that fit them right. In his dream he allowed for a new Arnolia, a contented woman with hired help and a sweet disposition brought on by an easy life and money in her pocketbook. As always occurred in his reveries, he drove the children to town in a brand new Cadillac to a brick school furnished by the free-flow of oil. *I can trust them men; they's all decent, honorable gentlemen. Well, exceptin' that John Earl. That man don't even trust hisself. They won't be doin' us wrong, not them white men. It's time in this world that me and mine be treated fair. Arnolia's gonna see.*

Did the oil that lurked beneath really possess the powers to set the world to right for them all? Could it truly be an elixir of life capable of surmounting the individual difficulties of the entire region under which it flowed?

Mavis McCallister believed. *I know that Cale's gonna love me like at home. Whatever happened between Winnie and here to turn him against me, the oil's gonna wash it way.*

What Mavis, what they all failed to realize was that the object of their collective desires dictated as a cruel master, controlling fates at its own whims, spewing lives into arbitrary directions as far flung as the pressure built over thousands of years of entrapment beneath the surface willed.

His boots deposited on the back stoop, Cale pulled himself up the stairs and stripped down to his nainsook undershirt before sitting down on the edge of the bed, too tired to remove his socks.

Mavis waddled in without speaking as she eased herself to the floor where she began to pull them off her husband's feet.

"You don't need to be doin' that."

"But I don't mind." She looked up, and their eyes met. "I love you," she said with a sincerity so touching that it warmed Cale for the first time since her untimely arrival. He helped Mavis to her feet and patted the side of the bed.

She does love me, and I've been the worst kind of heel. Showed her no affection, treatin' her like I wish she'd just disappear. Worst of all, dreamin' of another woman all the while. As he tenderly took her hand, Mavis burst into tears.

"Is it the baby?" cried Cale in alarm.

Red curls shook, "Not the way you think." She looked at him through her tears. "I wish there weren't no baby."

"But..."

"This baby's tore us apart by not lettin' me be a real wife to you." She searched the pocket of her dress for a handkerchief. "I'm not blamin' you. No man alive could get romantic over this freckled whale. I just...I just want it to be like it was back home", she pleaded. "When you was happy to see me and wanted to sit in the balcony of the picture show and smooch."

Her voice trailed.

Pulling her as closely as the baby would allow, "I love you and our baby, and I ain't been no kind of husband not to see you been hurtin' all on my account. Things will be better; I promise. Startin' tomorrow everything's gonna change."

Chapter 7

Word of mouth spawned by Mavis McCallister rivaled any telegraph or telephone. By inviting the scattered patrons of the LaGuinn store and ringing up a few more, the news spread. The crew, piquant with desire to see what the day would hold, dribbled in before daylight.

They sat at the round pedestal table that dominated Miss Wythel's kitchen, enjoying the aromas of sizzling pork and brewing coffee. All six of the burners atop her enameled range spouted blue flames as a hearty breakfast neared completion.

"Will we have time to clean this up before the gusher?" moaned Mavis.

"I don't want to miss it scrubbin' no dishes."

Pup bent over her shoulder to steal a slice of the fried tenderloin from whose juices Mavis stirred a pan of red eye gravy.

"Listen, it'll take us longer to bail and swab that well than it will for you to birth this baby elephant."

Leaving her gravy, she followed Pup, her speech playful, but its words seriously uncharacteristic. "Don't you talk like that; it's bad luck."

"Not as bad as unpluggin' a well after fightin' a gravy fire." He pointed to the unattended pan.

Acrid smoke rising from the stove sent Mavis hurrying back to her concoction of grease and coffee. As she ran, Pup pretended to grab for a stabilizing hold. "Feel that earth shake? The well's comin' in without us."

The boys discussed the day's procedure over fried eggs, homemade biscuits, and the tenderloin with a renewed expectation. Sun up would not come quickly enough to allow the day to begin and their fortune to be won or lost. As the women cleared the dishes, Pup walked down the broad hallway for a smoke on the porch. Miss Wythel adamantly opposed to the practice within the confines of her home. Stepping out the door, he stopped cold, "Shit fire! Get out here, boys."

"Now I know how Travis felt lookin' out of the damn Alamo," quipped John Earl. "There must be five hundred of 'um."

Dotting the landscape on the opposite side of the creek, a crowd of folks and vehicles vied for position to witness the strike. Composed of farm families on the nearest thing to vacation they had ever experienced, a smattering of scouts, geologists, and speculators milled around offering expert opinions that ranged from a spectacular strike to a dry hole.

Patchwork quilts colored the grass, despite the muddy conditions wrought by the almost daily rains, contributing to the Sunday picnic atmosphere of the on-lookers undaunted by the blaring of car horns and the squeals of children unsure of the reason but nonetheless thankful for the day's diversion. Tucked away in its amen corner, the New Jerusalem saints kept their prayerful vigil.

"Let's give 'um a show, boys," urged Pup as he threw his cigarette butt across the yard.

A rousing cheer went up as the rotary table turned to pierce the concrete seal deep within the core. The breaking of the seal necessitated the seemingly endless process of bailing. By insertion of the elongated bailing tube, mud and water were repeatedly removed, trying the patience of crew and audience.

A few of the more skeptical made ready to abandon the site since no gusher rose from the derrick's heights, but they were forced to remain by the impossibility of moving automobiles through the entanglement of people and cars on the single road of mud leading to the Willie B. Resigned to their fate, they capitalized on the opportunity to spread their view of impending failure to those within earshot.

Staying behind afforded the ladies a better view, until waves of anxiousness prompted Millie or Elaine to attempt treks to the well for any sort of information. Following one such venture, an infuriated Millie returned. "Do you know there's some shyster up there sellin' outta the tailgate of his truck? Got Coke Colas for a quarter a piece."

"My Lord," exclaimed Mavis, "we got to get to the store and load up, Millie. We can pull in a pretty penny."

Elaine grabbed in time to nab a goodly portion of dress tail. "You're not going anywhere in this crowd. Besides, you're liable to miss something."

"What the hell is takin' them so long?" Miss Wythel demanded.

"It's all the muck; kind of weights down the oil sand. Takin' off the heavy coverin' makes the oil want to escape," answered a disappointed Mavis.

"Like releasin' a pressure cooker?"

"More like when I loosen up this maternity corset at night."

Breakfast became lunch, and still the hours drug on. By four o'clock, Bulldog satisfied himself that he had bailed as much as humanly possible. Every muscle ached, and despair began to settle in over all concerned.

A pool circulated with chances offered on the time the well would come in.   On the fringe of the excitement, David Carmichael, caught between a rock and a hard place as to where his loyalties lay, leaned against his car. *If this well comes in, and I do think the possibility is remote at best, I could become Old Man Tate's golden boy for securing the closest leases not held by the Brophy partners. If she's a duster, I can witness the sweetest kind of revenge on that son of a bitch who scarred me for life.* Rubbing the evidence of his fight with John Earl, Carmichael could not honestly decide which side of the coin he hoped would land on top.

"What's he doin' now?" Cale asked of Pup.

Only those closest to the platform saw the elder Schneider outfitting a new tool to a steel cable. Dropped into the hole, the swabbing effect of its tight fit, coupled with a vacuum created as the opened end retracted with its removal from the hole, hopefully would suction the oil to the surface.

With the sunset swiftly robbing them of light, Bulldog motioned to Gabriel.

"Shut her down; show's over for today." The driller threw down his gloves. "I let everybody down, son."

Pup was about to reply when the two noticed Gabriel in the midst of picnickers spreading their evening meal. A spirited discussion ensued which ended with the men heading for their trucks and cars. Suddenly lights began to shine from the vehicles parked around the well, and hands went up in protective motions.

"We can give you a couple more hours," came a voice from behind the lights.

From the house, the lights emblazoned the derrick in a picture postcard fashion. Mavis stood, her back cramped from sitting, and stepped off to walk about the yard to enjoy the cool breeze and the view of the well. Millie, Elaine, and Miss Wythel remained, locked in a game of cards. Having foregone supper in lieu of a bout of indigestion, Mavis decided to fix herself a sandwich, more from boredom than hunger, and to take another McCoy's tablet.

It drew her attention to the rig. Whether a sound or intuition, she never knew, but it could not be ignored. Rushing back through the house in the semi darkness, she alerted the card players, "Girls, there's somethin' goin' on over to the well."

Cards hit the table. "I'll get a lantern; don't you leave before I get back." Leaning on the rifle, Ms. Wythel hobbled away.

"What's happening?" questioned Elaine.

"Hell's bells, I don't know what it is; it's just different," responded Mavis.

Millie's complaints went unheeded as the eldest reappeared with an eight inch cylinder carried by a metal handle whose beam shined from the opposite side. "I gave up a good hand for a feelin' of yours?"

On the drilling floor, the nothing began an ascent from its centuries old burial. A faint sound like the flowing of the creek sent Pup's ear to the bore hole on the completion of a swabbing. *I just can't be sure with the background noises.* Embarrassed by the foolish reaction to his own wishful thinking, he scrambled to his feet, muttering excuses to explain his action.

Not so easily dismissed, his father assumed the position so recently abandoned by the son. Leaping to his feet, his shouts and animation attracted the notice of everyone. "Get down here, Terry; she's gonna blow!"

Motivated by the death of a roughneck thrown from such a position high above the drilling floor, John Earl shinnied at a record pace down a ladder built along the side of the derrick. *I've come too far, risked too much to be blowed half way back to Corsicana* he thought.

By the time John Earl reached the ground, the tapped gas sweeping to the surface rivaled a freight train with all the stops pulled. A deafening rumble and the quaking earth drove observers from the site. A small child, veteran of a Texas twister, lay crying in the back of the Ford his daddy floored in reverse, assured of the return of the tornado and the imminence of his death. The child screamed for his mother who was frantically searching for the rest of her brood lost in the panic. Only the truly brave held fast, ignoring the pandemonium around them, fixed on the shivering rig.

Catching up with Cale, John Earl locked him in an embrace. "We did it, partner," screamed Cale.

"Hot damn, didn't I tell you she was there? Didn't I?" yelled Terry.

Each sobbed on the shoulder of his partner as the oil shot up through the derrick like Fourth of July fireworks before falling to the ground. The ladies were helping Miss Wythel off the plank bridge when the earth beneath them shuddered. Eyes drawn toward the rig's apex, they witnessed the first surge of the liquefied manna that would transform their lives.

"Oh, I hope the men got away," moaned Millie.

"Sure they got away; don't Bulldog know everythin?" reassured Mavis. "Hurry up now."

"Go on," urged Miss Wythel. "This here's close enough for an old woman. Got my protection," she patted the rifle.

"Only if you're sure," said Mavis.

"Sure as I'm gonna have me a bigger bank account than Daisy Bradford."

Millie and Elaine took Mavis' arms to travel a perilous course dodging cars and people stampeding for cover from the oil and mud that saturated all within its reach. The girls were covered when they reached the derrick, each fighting the tears and oil that hampered her vision.

From behind an arm reached around Elaine's waist. Before she could react, his mouth was on hers, sliding, then battling toward her lips only to slip yet another direction in the coating that removed any distinction between the New Jerusalem saints and those outside their flock. Only the voice betrayed his identity.

"Everybody's gonna remember the name of John Earl Terry; won't nobody forget." Elaine could only nod her affirmation between the effects of his embrace. Lifting her in the air, he spun until they were drunk with the joy that surrounded them, and they glided to the ground in the ooze like giddy skaters attempting to gain a footing but preferring the repeated falls into each other's arms.

Millie discovered Hoyt and Clyde slapping each other's back in congratulatory gestures. They were laughing so loudly that they held reign over the cacophony around them.

"Where to Madame LaGuinn, London, Paris, Athens?" asked her elated husband.

Gasping in disbelief at her husband's suggestion that her dream of seeing Europe might come true, "Oh, Hoyt, you're takin' me cross the ocean?"

"Hell, no woman, on a trip across Texas. You ain't gettin' me on no water with nothin' betwixt me and the deep but a boat bottom."

A smile disturbed the oil-smeared face, "Of course, Europe. The LaGuinns gonna show them old time rich folks just the kind of class East Texas oil money can buy." He pulled his wife close to him to kiss her now blackened hair and whispered, "I promised to give you the world when we married; thanks for waitin' me out to make good on my word."

"I love you, you old coot."

Hoyt pushed his wife's face back in righteous indignation. "That's rich , old coot from now on."

As if the ebony rain hadn't sufficiently covered him, Pup Schneider sat on the ground bathing himself in oil. "Now I can buy me a baseball team," he shouted, in cries drowned by the roar of the gusher. At regular intervals he flopped on his back to wallow in its mire, a child in a mud puddle relishing each moment before parental discovery.

His father's strong grasp pulled him to his feet. "Round 'um up, boy; I want my share in a tank."

Suddenly aware of the wisdom of his words, Pup raced to get help to contain the well lest any more of his money lay wasted on the ground.

Arnolia Bacon held the dress on which she sewed yet another patch closer to the light. A stubborn refusal to condone the goings on at the rig kept her and the girls at home. "After all," she informed Willie, "I'm the one what has work to do to keep a man afloat on a sea of worthless dreams." Staring down at the dress, she thought *Just another way of usin' somethin' up or makin' do. Damn you Willie Bacon.*

Watching the flame in the lantern flicker, she grabbed just in time to prevent it from crashing to the floor and burning what little they had. Blowing out the flame, the room plunged into darkness fed only by a full moon.

"It's da moon, Mamma," Tamara latched onto her legs, preventing her mother from standing. She pushed the screaming child away and crawled the space toward the basket that held a miraculously sleeping Elizabeth before allowing Tamara solace in her lap. "Miriam, get in here quick!"

"You gots to come out; there's a uncommon light over the well," came the terrified voice. "I done seed Jesus comin' with his angels." The threat of a mother's hand brought Miriam inside where the female members of the Bacon family huddled in the corner, one child awaiting the rapture, her mother and sister the angel of death.

As Arnolia rocked her babies in the darkness, she pictured herself at Willie's funeral so assured was she that her man had been killed in the explosion that rocked the earth. *Why couldn't you pay me no mind? You done left me all alone, no husband, no crops to sell.* She began to cry uncontrollably. She wanted to run to the white folks that robbed her and the children, but all she could do was sit and allow the hatred to swell. Unaware of the passage of time, she too drifted off into a troubled sleep.

A force snapped her back and forth. She awakened to a form blended into the shadows and propelled herself backward.

"Sweet mercy, save us all."

"Mamma, it's Gabriel." He scooped up his wailing sister in a gesture which frightened the child all the more. "Mamma, we's rich folks now."

As he groped in the dimness of the matches and lantern, his mother slowly absorbed the reality of what occurred. From the lantern held over her, the dried oil reflected the flickering flame as he laughed at her incredulous expression. "You got no worries now; come up to the rig and see." He pulled his mother to her feet.

The anguish of the night's events and the burdens of a lifetime lifted burst forth in sobbing waves.

"What you cryin' for? Don't you know what this means?" he scolded.

"You the one that don't really understand, and thank heavens for that. It means my babies don't never have to eat cabbage no more."

Frantic by now, Mavis combed the well site in search of Cale, yelling his name, hampered by the blinding spray and a belly that obliterated her feet and made footing more treacherous in the ooze. She leaned up against the wagon used to haul wood from the tree line, as exhaustion left her powerless to prevent a gradual easing to the ground. The warm ooze traveling down her legs meant nothing mixed as it was with the oil and slime. Several minutes later, she spotted Cale and vainly attempted to pull herself up.

Summoned by Mavis' cries, Cale joined her on the ground to kiss her between releases of euphoric Rebel yells. On and on he prattled as if immune to the novelty of his wife's first extended period of silence.

"Come on, Bulldogs' a motionin' for me." Placing one hand behind her back, Cale sought to lift Mavis to her feet. A low moan protested his insistent action.

"What's the matter?"

Through a face masked with oil, her eyes pleaded. Rolling onto her back, the moan escalated into an anguished outcry.

"Get Millie and Elaine; I'm havin' this baby right here and now." Torn with indecision, Cale started for help, reconsidered, and stood over his wife in a helpless stupor.

"Hell's bells, get goin'."

Half sliding, half running, he reached the rig where Bulldog, Pup, and Willie had begun the process of controlling the well.

"Took your sweet time gettin' here," barked the farm boss. "We still ain't found John Earl; you seen him?"

"I tell you, he's sellin' leases," advised the son.

"Get to work, McCallister. Hell, this thing could quit as fast as she hit."

"You don't really mean that?"

The driller hadn't meant to spoil the moment for anyone, least of all for Willie, so he covered the truth. "Ain't you lurnt when I'm a jokin'? You gonna be wipin' your butt with twenty dollar bills, but oil on the ground don't sell."

From the corner of his eyes, Cale spotted Millie and Hoyt. Without so much as a word to the boys, he broke tail and ran.

"Millie, Millie, the baby's comin'; you got to help her!"

Momentarily the work on the rig floor ceased. Only Bulldog's calmer head held reign.

"Less either of you delivered a baby, there ain't nothin' you're gonna do that's anywhere near to helpin' Mavis. Gettin' the cap on the Willie B.'s where you can be the most good. Damn that John Earl, if he don't have the knack for slippin' out when you need him most."

In all the confusion, John Earl and Elaine disappeared into the crowd. Carrying her to his car, he deposited her on the hood and leaned forward. "I'm takin' you to the J. P. right now, and there won't be no arguin' the fact."

"Dressed like this?"

"Just like a female," he shook his head. Then reconsidering their appearances he relented. "Guess we don't resemble your typical bride and groom at that."

"I can pack a bag in a flash after I clean up some." That her indecision suddenly subsided the delirium of the moment provided only partial explanation. No surer of her feelings than before, John Earl nonetheless filled the void in her life rent by Cale's obligation to Mavis and their child. Somehow the gusher underscored a loneliness, a desire to have a man with whom to share an experience for which few could claim a kinship. The Willie B. released an impetuousness in them all, urging Elaine to embark upon the untried, plunging her headlong into what would ultimately take her to the brink of hell.

Scrubbed free of oil, Elaine threw the last of her clothing into the suitcase. As she closed the lid, she continued humming the fox-trot "It's a Happy Old World after All." *Let's see,* referring again to a scribbled list of chores. *I have my gown, slippers.* She drew a line through the name of a neighbor with whose son Jake was spending the night. *I'm sure Daddy can pick him up in the morning sometime.* A grimace appeared. *Daddy.* She flew into the parlor and unlatched the fold out table from its closed position of her mahogany writing desk. On a sheet of sky blue stationery, she jotted him a quick note of her whereabouts and that of his grandson. Placing the note atop the radio, *I'm so glad I don't have to face him. The way he makes no secret about his dislike of John Earl and me, he'd be sure to try and talk me out of this.*

Positioning her bag near the door, *I can't think about Daddy, now.* She consulted the full length mirror. I'm glad I bought this when Mavis and I went to her last appointment. She fastened the three rows of double buttons that began below the waist of her black velveteen jacket. Its pocket bore a handkerchief that picked up the color of the braiding that trimmed the blazer's lapel and sleeves. Adjusting the silken flower on her left lapel, I guess this will just have to do for a wedding corsage. The pleats of her white skirt flared as she spun to check the single point seams of her stockings. With a black hat tugged into place, she toyed with its white brim, folding it back from her forehead in the latest fashion.

Married in black, she repeated the old cliché, *and you'll wish yourself back. I'll just have to be sure and take off this blazer before the ceremony.* In keeping with the omen, she took her vows with the jacket in place.

Whistled strains of "Here Comes the Bride" filtered through the house. "I put your bag in the Ford, my lady." Elaine barely had time to hold her hat in place as he swept her into his arms and carried her to the car. "Your chariot awaits."

Butterflies swarmed within the rotund stomach of the grocery man turned oil tycoon as he backed his delivery wagon as closely as possible to where Mavis lay upon the blackened ground wrenching Millie's and Cale's hands at the onset of each contraction. As Mavis cried out, Hoyt turned away. *I'm gonna be sick right here.*

Reaching from the front seat, Millie plucked empty bushel baskets and debris from the back. An old portion of a tarp wadded into a pillow she shoved under Mavis' head.

"There's not room but for one of us in the back," she shouted to the dumbstruck father-to-be, "and I'm the cooler head."

Amid Mavis' protests, Cale allowed Millie to climb into the rear as Hoyt fastened the gate. Assuming Millie's previous position, he never saw the road as he traveled bent over the seat.

With his head protruding from the window, Hoyt screamed and gestured repeatedly. "Get the hell out of my way; woman's havin' a baby here."

A form stepped from nowhere to block his path and send the wagon into a brake-locking spin which tossed the women across the wagon's back.

Rifle in hand, Miss Wythel pushed herself into the passenger side, "You're not a leavin' without me. When I heard there was a woman havin' a baby at the well, I knew it had to be Mavis." She peered over the seat. "You and that kid got the damnedest timin'."

As Mavis answered with another contraction, Hoyt slammed the shift into gear and sped toward Kilgore. Hampered by the lack of lighting, the contractions, at Millie's estimation, were erratic at best. One would follow on the heels of another, to disappear for what seemed to be as much as five minutes. Hoyt's capricious route of back road short cuts placed them at the Kilgore Hospital in record time with Cale bounding from the grocery wagon before it pulled into a parking slot.

He returned with an oak veneer wheel chair raised on its two larger wheels as the smaller back wheels pivoted wildly from the speed of travel. Under the small sign filled with colored neon, the expectant mother and her motley entourage entered the emergency door announced by Mavis' screams, Hoyt's curses, and Miss Wythel's, "Let me drive the damn thing before you sling her out."

A pristine nurse in a uniform so crisply starched that it crackled with her every movement, briefly glanced from the chart which she promptly returned as she offered without looking further at the people before her so obviously unschooled in the proper decorum of a hospital. "You people will need to make use of the entrance around back."

Had the seriousness of the moment not robbed him of all humor, Cale McCallister might well have appreciated the amusement of the nurse's mistaken appraisal, a source of future laughter for all involved as the tale of the strike and the race to maternity became legendary entertainment. Cale never tired of describing the oil-covered group, smelling to high heaven of sweat and the rig, and the crusty old woman aiming her rifle at Florence Nightingale.

His emotions strained, Cale savagely slapped the most recently selected chart from the hands of the startled nurse thus sending its metal encasement clanging against the wall. "Dammit, woman, can't you see my wife's havin' a baby right in front of you?" Further angered by the cold stare and her gesture toward the rear entrance, Cale grabbed from a box a tissue which he dragged down his cheek to expose a streak of white skin to the now contrite nurse. "Does this make you any happier to help us?"

"You will need to fill out these general information forms," she stammered. Hesitantly she urged the paper and pencil toward the younger of the two men, now cognizant of the old woman and her rifle. "I assume you have no doctor engaged."

It was Hoyt who hoisted Cale's fallen battle flag. "Now you listen here, Missy, you done assumed yourself right out of a job. We ain't no Depression driven crop followers, and this here filth you're seein' says we can buy this hospital and everything in it."

By this time a small contingency of hospital employees gathered in response to the commotion. Providence placed Mavis' doctor in residence. Recognizing her, he barked orders to those nearest and sped her down the corridor.

Abandoned, the four looked questioningly. Miss Wythel bent forward on the rifle butt, "I guess we sit and wait; seems the lot of us done a good deal of that as of late."

Trudging into the waiting area, they collapsed into the discomfort of furnishings scattered about the tiny enclosure. Seven chairs, their padding long departed, lined the walls. A scarred table held an ashtray and several magazines whose tattered covers disguised their identities. Anesthetized by the odorous ether, they sat in silence broken by intermittent reports on Mavis' progress.

"Mrs. McCallister's contractions are continuing, her progress is apparent but gradual. If I were to venture a guess, the baby might arrive by noon."

With the doctor's exit, Cale began to pace. "Does it always take this long, Millie?"

"Well, all women's different when it comes to these things. Some's just luckier than others. But don't worry' things are gonna be fine. Why, Sybil Watkins stayed in labor near to two days, and..." Instantly aware that she had said the wrong thing, she quickly corrected, "but that woman just likes to hear herself talk. Ain't a shred of truth to what comes outta her mouth."

"Two days!" Cale faced his thoughts and a wall lined with pictures of fat, happy babies. *I can't go two whole days with Mavis in there and me not knowin' what's happenin'.* He sat back down and threw his head against the wall for support, a tell-tale reminder of his presence permanently affixed.

"I still couldn't get nobody at Elaine's, so I woke up Elsie. She's sendin' Fred over to the house to get us some clothes." At his wife's urging, Hoyt walked to the hotel to reserve a room with a bath where, starting with Cale, they cleaned up in preparation for the duration of the vigil.

In the labor room, a languid Mavis drifted into consciousness with each contraction. Whenever the gas eased in potency, she rallied in a drugged stupor and mumbled what she believe to be shouts, "Damn you men and your prostrate troubles; it's what's got me in this mess. I hate you all." She swung her legs over the bed, only to receive a scolding from the shocked nurse for her efforts.

"Hell's bells, I'm tired of this; goin' home," she vowed. "I'll come back tomorrow when I'm all rested up." The throws of another pain forced her back. "How long have I been here?" she moaned. With no answer forthcoming, she scanned the room for the barbaric nurse, suddenly aware of a new source of anguish between her legs. She screamed in response to the gloved probing. "I'll kill you with my bare hands."

"I see the head," she announced matter-of-factly to her would-be attacker before exiting the labor room and returning with the doctor and a second nurse.

Mavis fought the cone pressed against her face and the sense of motion as they wheeled her into the delivery room. Bright lights beamed as the doctor set to work. "I'm pushin' as hard as I can," she argued upon ripping the cone away." She was almost in a sitting position, thrust forward by the shoulders of now unseen nurses. A heated blade ripped her body with a sensation so dolorous that her nails raked into her palms. The ensuing reaction carried down the hall toward the room where the family waited.

Springing to his feet, Cale tore toward his wife and burst through the double silver doors at the moment the physician drew his newborn daughter into the sterile luminance. Awestruck by the scene played before him, his mouth gaped. A red, writhing mass wailing from the doctor's slap passed from him to his nurse in preparation to cut the cord that protruded from Mavis in a way he dared not imagine.

"She's a healthy girl, Mavis, with all the necessary parts." Patting the new mother's arm, he sensed her thoughts. "The next one will be easier; first babies are always hard."

"Never again," she muttered before falling to sleep.

Unable to remove his eyes from the baby, Cale required several nudges and finally a hearty punch on the arm to initiate a response.

"Really, Mr. McCallister, this is against every hospital rule."

As she ushered him toward the door, Mavis bent forward as if reliving the nightmare.

The second nurse shook her head at her colleague. "A complainer all along." To Mavis, "All over now, Dearie," she patronized.

As the doctor rushed to Mavis' side, Cale held his ground while the doctor probed and prodded Mavis in unspeakable ways.

"Well, it looks like that second baby I told you about is coming quicker than any of us expected."

"I ain't havin' no more babies, I said!"

Moments later the scene replayed, identical to the last detail. "Another girl."

Two babies...the well in at last...Mavis' piercing cries... Cale's head began to spin. When he awoke in the waiting area, his head in Millie's lap as she fanned him with a funeral parlor palm, Hoyt, Bulldog, and Pup adjourned their impromptu business discussion to tease and congratulate only to be pushed aside by Miss Wythel. "Hope you're proud," she snapped. "Made a damn fool of yourself, runnin' in there a faintin' like a belle with the vapors." A deep-set, "Humph," preceded the reclaiming of her chair.

"Mavis?" he questioned.

"Just fine, Honey. She wants to see you when you're up to it."

"Mavis lying in the hospital bed waitin' for me to feel up to seein' her," he leaned heavily on the last word as ashamed of his behavior as Miss Wythel.

Addressing Millie, "Fine husband I turned out to be."

"At least you was there when it counted," she cajoled.

With her assistance, Cale reclaimed his unsteady feet and allowed Millie to direct him toward Mavis' room. Clad in a hospital gown, her curls drooping limply onto a pallid face, to Cale she never appeared more lovely. The door creaked as Millie eased into the corridor.

"Two for one," Mavis smiled in a vain search for his approval of the unexpected baby, still unsure of his true feelings toward the first. "Nothin' like a bargain; never could pass one up."

Cale leaned over and kissed her with the fervency of their courtship. "They're beautiful."

Mavis wiped the tears that slowly descended his cheeks and her own. "You're a lousy liar, always have been. They're red, ugly, and look like Bethel at the end of the day."

She listened with disbelief at his recounting of the delivery. Each time she tried to laugh, her hands rushed instinctively to her diminished abdomen to ease the discomfort.

Cale pulled a chair to her bedside and clasped her hand. "I know the first one's Earline, but what will we call the extra one?"

As though she planned a second daughter, Mavis spoke without hesitation, "Pearline."

Drawing back as if to escape the horror, Cale released her hand. "That's the awfulest name I ever heard of."

Taking hold of his shirt, she yanked him to her with the strength of a madwoman. Glaring into Cale's face, she spoke with deliberateness, "All you done is start them babies, and enjoyed every minute of it, at that. I been to hell and back, Cale McCallister, which entitles me to name those twins whatever I damn well please." She released the grip, allowing him to ease back into the chair.

The birth certificates registered a set of female twins weighing nearly six pounds each. "Bethel Earline and Pearline Elaine," Cale read to Hoyt from the foot-printed documents. His eyes and voice pleaded. "I sure hope they grow up pretty bein' their names is ugly as sin."

The whereabouts of John Earl and Elaine remained a mystery to those at the hospital and of great concern to the bride's father who sat with the Reverend and the best shots from New Jerusalem guarding the well against intruders who might ignite it in their careless curiosity or steal the now priceless equipment the Brophy partners wanted used on the Willie B. II.

At an hour when decent folks had slept for hours, John Earl pressed the release of a miniature gate. Secured to its fence, a sign designating the gabled residence as that of Henry Jackson Whistler, Justice of the Peace, rattled as the gate closed. His arm tightly wrapped around Elaine's waist, lest she slip away, John Earl all but ran up the scattered pieces of broken brick which served as a path, literally dragging his bride to the altar. When no response to repeated knocking was forthcoming, the perspective groom vaulted the fence and proceeded to honk the horn.

Mortified, the bride begged, "John Earl, you'll wake the whole town."

Overhead the scraping of a window suspended both urgings. "What's all the ruckus?"

John Earl called up to a bald man in his nightshirt, "We want to get married." Winking at Elaine, he watched the man speak over his shoulder into the darkened room. An overhead light bounced off the slick head of the Justice.

"Down in a minute."

Such late night interruptions often roused the Whistlers. An inconvenience of his duly elected position, the romanticism of impromptu weddings still touched Lou Dean, his wife of thirty years. Shedding her long-sleeved muslin nightgown in favor of an overlapping work dress she kept ready for just such a happenstance, Lou Dean adjusted the strands of iron gray that escaped the elastic of her boudoir cap and shoved her feet into a worn pair of slippers. She was already welcoming the couple when Henry plodded down the stairs, his nightshirt stuffed hastily into his trousers.

In a coffee klatch later that morning, Lou Dean told her neighbor, "A handsome couple. The woman was an elegant lady, dressed real nice, but a tad shy. Course, most all our brides are fidgety; an elopement is a such an adventure. Now, her young man, my, my, he talked enough for the two of them, and so very good looking with that dark mustache and hair and a smile that would melt stone. I swear he could be the next Valentino if he had a mind to."

Before the ceremony, the Justice felt an obligation to discuss the seriousness of the step about to be taken. As he spoke, Lou Dean watched the woman who virtually fought eye contact with her intended. If Justice Whistler noticed her hesitation, he ignored it and gestured to the fireplace where he acknowledged the ceremony to be his two hundred and thirteenth. On cue, Lou Dean scurried to a Queen Anne cabinet which held a phonograph. Almost on tip toes, she lifted the lid, simultaneously turning the crank. The needle in place, a scratchy rendition of the wedding march began.

"You can join hands," prompted the Justice.

Before offering her hand, Elaine wiped the palm across her skirt, unable to prevent its clamminess from startling the groom. Hesitantly she smiled as a stab of doubt took hold.

I can run back to that all-night cafe, call Daddy, and her mind rushed. Jake, how could I have left you like that? I don't even know if Daddy can get you. What kind of mother am I? Her eyes met John Earl's. What kind of woman am I to run off and marry a man I hardly know, who won't even speak of his family or his life growing up?

"To join Elaine Russell Crawford and John Earl Terry in the bonds of holy matrimony."

Bonded for life, sweet thing. John Earl peered down in pleasure at what he mistook for coyness. *And with the well money and all those leases just waiting' to pay off, John Earl is sitting on the street named Easy. Let my old man eat his words. I am somebody now, and a banker's daughter for a wife will back it up.* "To love, honor, and cherish, as long as ye both shall live. Shall live," he repeated.

The repetition prodded Elaine into blurting a quivering, "I will," in a voice she did not recognize. Tilting her head slightly, she realized that Cale stood next to her, holding her hands, and promising to care for her in sickness and in health, forsaking all others...Mavis's chatter began, deafening, throbbing within her head until Elaine wanted to scream for an end to her prattling about Cale's baby. She now appeared from behind Cale, stroking her belly and finally taking a possessive hold of his arm. Tears streamed down the bride's face.

"I now pronounce you man and wife. It's customary to kiss her now, son."

Placing his hands on her face, John Earl drew her head upward for a gentle kiss. *This won't be so bad, he assured himself. I ain't my old man, and she,* he drank in his bride appreciatively, *won't turn out to be no broken, haggard woman like Momma.*

Aloud, "I'll take care of you, always; there ain't nothin' in the world you won't have," he whispered, and at that moment, even for a few weeks to come, he succeeded in pulling off the biggest con of his career on himself.

Mr. and Mrs. John Earl Terry left the home of Justice Whistler bound for a diner in Kilgore where they could have a late meal. For Elaine the remainder of her wedding night passed in the same haze. Their stop at a cafe teeming with men anxious to find employment or leases at the nation's newest boom proved brief. When John Earl appraised the rowdies through the windows of the diner, he apologized to the oddly silent woman at his side.

"It's no place for a lady at this hour, and before long, neither will most of this town. There's men who follows the booms that's wholesome, family types, but there's a goodly number who'll work all day, drink and gamble all night. You'll see it soon enough; booms bring fightin' and killin' so often folks begin not to pay notice."

John Earl paused in contemplation of the change his life had taken. *I used to be right along with 'um.* He began to twist the slender gold band from the set he often employed as a ruse to satisfy moral desk clerks. Already the circle cut into his finger, leaving a reminder of the stranglehold a piece of metal could put on a man's life.

"Will Brophy have to change?"

He patted her hand. "Not if we take a hold of the situations from the get go, settin' up city ordinances and takin' a firm hand to the riff raff that tries to stake claim." As a form of reassurance, "Five will get you ten Kilgore bears the brunt, bein' a more established town and all."

The sky opened up to release more of the rain. He started the engine, "Better get over to the hotel, if there's any rooms left."

~~~~~~

Back at the Willie B. the man whose name it bore sat just inside the tool house, wrapped in an old Army blanket to ward off the night chill. Across his lap lay a loaded gun that awaited any intruders. In the distance, the sounds of chattering girls filtered through the stillness, preceding the beam from a lantern. Placing his weapon out of reach, he walked out to greet the family he had all but deserted.

Imitating a radio announcer, Gabriel ran ahead of his mother and siblings. "An' here he is folks, the richest black man in Texas, Mister William Bartholomew Bacon." The girls clapped gleefully, enjoying the game and the opportunity to stay up so far past their bedtimes. "Tell us, Suh, exactly what make of automobile are you buyin' for your oldest boy what done worked hisself half to death stokin' them boilers yonder?"

"He'll' be gettin' one soon as his momma's sittin' in a fine home." Looking toward his wife, he detected the signs of happiness he thought forever lost. Turning his attention to the interviewer, "Course, my boy won't be keepin' that car you mentioned less he gets hisself registered up at the Prairie View College where he'll be doin' his family proud."

A tearful Arnolia threw her arms around Willie's neck. "I'm so sorry; I didn't have no faith in you."

Consoling her, Willie motioned for Gabriel to take his sisters and Jeremiah, who had spent the day at the well, back home.

"You never done wrong by me, nor my babies, but I still dealt you the miseries," Arnolia said contritely.

"It don't matter no more, cause we got a heap of livin' to do startin' right now." Leading his wife into the tool house, the extent of his guard duty included the equipment within the shed and a very neglected wife.

~~~~~~

Elaine Terry stirred from the commotion in the hall of Kilgore's only respectable hotel. Waking in such unfamiliar surroundings momentarily startled her. Barely able to move from the weight of John Earl's leg on her thigh and his arm draped over her chest, Elaine's eyes traveled the room she really saw for the first time.

It's no more than a closet. There's not even a bath or a wardrobe, nothing but this bed and a chest of drawers. She almost laughed aloud. *And John Earl had to bribe the clerk for this?*

Elaine blushed, suddenly aware of her nakedness and the scattering of clothing upon the floor reminiscent of the urgency of their desires the previous evening. A shudder traveled the length of a body awakened to sensations never experienced. As he pushed the door to their honeymoon suite closed, John Earl's mouth was on her, moving down her neck while he tore at her dress and forced her onto the bed. Consumed by a passion so foreign, she allowed him to take control, permitting his caresses and kisses free reign to transport her to an ecstasy she wanted, demanded throughout the night.

An increasingly loud exchange in the corridor roused the bridegroom who began to explore his wife's body until the voices became distinct.

"I tell you what's the truth, Cale, them's the two prettiest girls I ever laid eyes on." Gasping, Elaine motioned for her husband to peer into the hallway. Elaine was appalled. *Everyone deserved a little celebration,* she told herself, *but for Hoyt and Cale to come into Kilgore and spend the night with... with women?*

As he eased open the door, its advanced age betrayed him.

Recognizing their partner, Hoyt chided, "We been wonderin' where the hell you got off to."

He joined them in the hall. "Get her capped?"

"No thanks to you."

"I had other business."

Hoyt grinned, "You dog, you. Takin' off like that you missed all the real excitement."

"Had plenty enough of my own to please me."

"Come on over to the hospital and see the two best lookin' females in Texas." With all the pride of a new grandfather, Hoyt pulled Terry halfway down the hall before calling back to Cale. "Go get his shirt."

Before John Earl could protest, Cale swung open the door to a mortified Elaine who sat up in bed with the sheet held high. Cale bristled, overwhelmed with loathing for John Earl. His actions revealed his thoughts of disgust and disappointment. Extending his arm, he slapped an opened palm against the door, shaking his head and causing the woman to jump at its impact.

"Cale, it's not what you think at all."

"I'll stay out here." Hoyt's voice drifted.

Terry slipped back into the room when Cale's outburst assured him that the full impact of the night's events produced the desired effect upon his wife's former sweetheart. Only John Earl appreciated the awkwardness of the situation.

"I see you've met my wife."

He took the few steps toward the bed. "Yep, me and Elaine tied the knot last night," He put his arms around her possessively and kissed her hard. Gloating he added, "Tied it real tight."

"Mavis will be tickled." Cale turned his face toward the door.

Elaine's heart ached.

Oh, Cale, I wanted to tell you more gently. A voice deep within assumed control. *Why?* This voice that guided her to the situation in which she now found herself abruptly pushed aside compassion. *Isn't this the man that ruined your life? And now you're makin' excuses for starting a life?* Mustering the courage to search his face, Elaine saw only anguish. *He still loves me.* She wanted to cry out for an end to the terrible charade. *This is all a mistake, Cale,* she wanted to scream. *You're the man who's supposed to be with me, not...not anyone else.*

"I got to get back to the hospital," the intruder fought to excuse himself.

"The hospital?" questioned Terry. "Who got hurt?"

Cale began to smile. "Mavis had the baby, well she had two."

"Twins?"

"Yeah, and she named one for Elaine."

The innocence of Mavis' sentiment made the irony all the more bitter. Elaine began to cry. *How can I be such a hypocrite, acting like Mavis' friend when I can't get her husband out of my heart?*

"Now, Darlin', what's got you to cryin'?"

"It's all so sweet," she lied.

Hoyt's banging on the door sent Cale into the hall.

Inches ahead of her husband's attempt to detain her, Elaine jumped from the bed.

"Get back in here; I'm not through with you."

Half dressed, Elaine continued all but throwing on her clothes. "I want to see the babies." She did, but the thought of herself in John Earl's bed after the scene with Cale drove her toward the door all the faster. "Aren't you coming, too?"

"You tryin' to run my life already?" he teased. "I'm gonna sleep in. You go ahead. I got a feelin' we'll be seein' them babies till we're sick of 'um.

"Nobody can get sick of babies."

"You can if they both talk like their momma."

The sound of her laughter filtered down the hall, joined by John Earl's bass as he recalled the look on Cale's face. Counting his chips, he declared himself the big winner. *I hate to leave a man broke, Cale old buddy, but damn, you asked for it, tryin' to play in the big time. You'll get to see her, just enough to make you ache over what ain't never gonna be. Damn, I love to win.!*

Chapter 8

February 1931

In the months since the Willie B. and the Daisy Bradford II robbed the earth of its liquid treasure, the world focused its attention on East Texas and the immense riches that must lie untapped beneath her soil.

Shortly after the Brophy strike, the Rusk County well of Arkansas oilman, H. L. Hunt, came in to the tune of three thousand barrels a day. By December's end, the words of the fortune teller bore out when Ed Bateman's crew drilling on the Crim land some thirteen miles north of the Bradford brought in the Lou Della Crim I at twenty-two thousand.

Oil fever spread at an epidemic rate. By January twelfth, the Lantrop I claimed the proffered ten thousand dollar prize from the Gregg County Chamber of Commerce as the first producing well within ten miles of the city of Longview. Everyone wanted his or her share of the bounty, if not by oil, then by any enterprise capable of pullin in an oil field dollar. As with the businessman charging ten cents for the use of his latrine, it made little difference by what means.

Descended upon by the major oil producers like Oklahoma Oil, Humble, Sinclair, and Shell with their geological teams and infinite budgets, acreage in the five counties determined to be atop the estimated one hundred forty thousand acres of the East Texas Field escalated in value. Parcels in Gregg, Upshur, Rusk, Smith, and Cherokee counties once unsellable now leased for thousands of dollars per acre. Every possible stretch large enough to contain a derrick attracted lease hounds.

Capital flowed as freely as the oil which allowed operations with outlays of less than twenty-five thousand dollars to bring in wells with incalculable profits. What required the crews of the original wells months to accomplish, the round-the-clock, experienced teams spudded and capped in weeks for fear that the pool beneath would soon be drained. Once the underground pressure of a pool became altered by an existing well, the available oil would work its way toward it, thus time became paramount since no one could accurately predict the density of the pool and length of the boom.

Literally overnight the populations of towns doubled or even tripled. In the single span following the Lou Della's strike, the seven hundred-citizened town of Kilgore numbered twenty-five thousand. Of the peripheral industries affected by the strike, none rivaled construction. The demand for stores, housing, and services soared as rates inflated for structures barely capable of preventing the now prevalent rains from seeping inside.

In Henderson its courthouse spilled onto the street where secretaries of abstract companies worked feverishly to offset the demands of lease exchanges precipitated by the frenzy. Cartographers plied their trade to provide maps that sold as fast as they could be duplicated, though they were often outdated as to ownership due to the pace of trading that occurred in front seats of cars, on farmhouse porches, on street corners, and under the folds of the masses of tents tied to every available tree.

As John Earl predicted, the changes were not all for the better. He persuaded the citizens of Brophy to attend a town meeting in which voice voting elected a City Council and a new School Board. For the most part, the two bodies contained the same men, the trusted choices in Brophy being slim. At his suggestion, emergency ordinances went into effect to curb the forewarned influx of undesirables by regulation of new businesses. When the meeting adjourned, John Earl held a councilman's post and the presidency of the School Board. Cale and Hoyt occupied two of the five Council seats, while Hoyt, Elaine, Willie, the Reverend Ezekiel and two stalwarts would oversee the school. Thus an unsuspecting Brophy allowed John Earl to deposit the town in his hip pocket.

The distance between Hoyt's store and town decreased daily. Everywhere the smell of new wood and paint pierced the senses; the residents like to refer to it as "the smell of oil money."

Already in business were two more general merchandise stores, a cafe, a hardware and oil field supply depot, and the offices of several attorneys thus transforming the failing town into a thriving city in the making. To the immediate northeast, a campus with an original cost of one hundred and twenty-five thousand dollars was on its way to the three hundred thousand mark. On what would under normal circumstances be the playground, six oil derricks rose to cast ominous shadows upon the workmen bricking the school. With every pump and foot of new pipe drilled, the wealth of the school it guarded rose.

The morning sunlight caught at just the proper angle to blind those who turned in response to the roar of the v-16 engine of a polished Fleetwood Roadster. From the wire wheels and the gleaming chrome trim, the refracted rays played havoc as pedestrians and drivers fought for a glimpse of Brophy's most colorful citizen. Even those newest to town boasted at least a passing acquaintance with the red-haired woman shamelessly attired in clothing as loud as her voice. Thus, those lined outside the businesses awaiting their turns for admittance chose to endure the squinting pain of the glare for amusement as much as self-preservation. Comments flew across dinner tables after each appearance, inciting verbal disgust and silent envy of one so young and so rich that she could get away with doing and saying whatever came to mind. As for the men, they also craned their necks to admire the chassises of the Fleetwood and its driver.

Mavis McCallister called all one hundred sixty-five horsepowers into service, only to reign them at the latest possible moment to park the Cadillac in the only available spot in town despite the clearly marked, "Reserved for C. Russell." Once stationary, the thick line of mud that covered the car became visible, a common souvenir of the rain-soaked roads which evolved into deeply rutted entrapments. It was not uncommon to come upon abandoned vehicles too deeply mired for rescue.

"Hell's bells, Rosalinda. Get them babies back in the car," she ordered the nanny. Another Mavis inefficacy, she settled for a girl barely out of her teens since the desired English nanny favored by the Northern gentry proved in short supply in the oil fields. "At least," she had explained to Cale, "the girl is a foreigner, and a foreigner raisin' your kids is what the French folks calls 'chick.'"

Settling back into the car, Rosalinda concluded, *Anywhere out of Senora McCallister's reach is a blessing from God. I have learned many things since coming to Brophy. The most important is not to try and stop the Senora when she has made up her mind.* She replaced the silver-plated pacifier into a contented Pearline's mouth. As usual, Earline clamored for attention within the confines of an identical cashmere outdoor wrap. "Por dios," Rosalinda crossed both babies. "This one is just like the mother. Heaven help us all."

Its five tellers barely visible behind lines several customers deep, the Brophy Bank bustled with activity. As most every business, it ran a twenty-four hour schedule. Clyde liked to explain his latest banking innovation to new customers.

"Wheelin' and dealin' refuses to cease at regular hours, and you don't want to keep bulgin' cash drawers to attract the unsavories. Why, there's been days when we've had multiple deposits for single concerns. As for the working man, well, he needs to hot foot it to the bank with his check."

Clyde was nothing if not innovative with his offering of special lines for royalty checks, another for lease exchanges, courting deposits and securing loans under whatever circumstances customers requested, even negotiating loans to leasees in advance of strikes adjacent to producing wells.

A rattling of bangle bracelets mixed with the clicking of pumps announced Mavis' arrival. Indifferent to the khaki-clad workers, the proprietress of the cafe and a parson, Mavis pushed her way to the barred cage.

"I want to see Clyde right now."

Ebbin Chambers devoted his full attention to the wife of one of the bank's richest depositors. "Now Mrs. McCallister, you must have realized Mr. Russell's absence. Just look where you parked." He motioned toward the roadster.

Tapping her foot and looking in every direction, she questioned, "Then where is he?"

"I'm not quite sure, perhaps I can be of some assistance?"

"Not unless he made you assistant mayor of this town and you can do somethin' about that thief Hollis Cooper, the son of ..."

"Calm down, you don't want the Reverend to hear you."

"I don't care who hears about that crook. Just look at my clothes."

Ebbin appraised the wool coat whose royal blue now bore East Texas mud caked in abstract patterns as did the woman's stockings and shoes. *Poor Hollis has done it this time*, he determined. *Still you have to admire the old man's ingenuity. Too old for the rigs and an evicted sharecropper from land that just grows derricks now. Here he is making his way with what he owns, a wagon, chains, and a team of the slowest jacks around while he lives inside that wagon like a pioneer, waiting on vehicles to mire up to their axles.* He chuckled inwardly at the thought of Hollis' usual strategy of waiting until the driver exhausted himself from pushing and cussing before sauntering over to offer his assistance at whatever price he figured Providence had thrown his way. Since the tapering of the rains, some believed that Cooper provided his own rain to keep his pockets full.

"Do you know what he had the nerve to do? He camped his asses out on the end of the street leadin' to my new house. He was a waitin' for me, a mother with precious cargo. There I was, not long out of my confinement, pushin' that Cadillac and him just a sittin' there lickin' his chops. Well, I let him pull me out, and then he tells me it'll be thirty-five dollars."

By now the patrons and employees had forgotten their chores in delight of Mavis' narration. "And if that weren't enough, he scratched up my car with his chain. Eight thousand dollars that car cost. Do you have a notion how long one of them wells has to work to make that kind of money?"

The entrance of Clyde Russell ended Mavis' tale. When she rushed toward Brophy's mayor, Clyde threw up his hands from disgust with her innumerable complaints concerning the city's responsibilities at her house. "My goodness," he swore.

"Now Mavis, I already got power and phone run out to that house of yours, so don't start with me about anything else. Today I'm the one making demands." He half dragged the flabbergasted woman into his office.

"Elaine's not doing so good, and I want you to get her home and off her feet."

"Is she at the school again?" Mavis shook her head in frustration. "Why John Earl don't put his foot down about her workin' herself to death, I'll never know. It was him put her in charge of the construction. Seems to me he could call her off just as easy."

"I've given up trying to figure out that relationship; it's got me a nervous wreck."

Mavis put her arm around Clyde's shoulder, "Ain't no explainin' the affairs of the heart. Besides, she seems happy as a clam with this baby on the way."

"All the more reason she should be at home." He looked down at Mavis. "Though I've got to admit that I'm mighty proud. She's seeing to it that the kids have a showplace of a school."

"It's for sure kids can't keep meetin' in front parlors and tents. But she don't have to keep them men hammerin' night and day. You know, I can't hire carpenters for losin' 'um to her." She headed for the door, "Don't worry; I got a plan to get her away from that school and off for some relaxation, while you're puttin' Hollis Cooper outta business or six feet under. I don't give a tinker's damn which." She winked and charged through the door.

Clyde, consumed with worry, set back in his chair. *She's pale and so much thinner, and her with not an ounce to lose. Why, she's not been herself since... since a couple of weeks after the wedding.* He had one encouragement. *Making sure they live with me until they can get around to building a house let's me at least keep an eye on her. Though John Earl would move out in a minute if he had a place. Not that he's around much.* He began to pace, mulling over his son-in-law's behavior. *There's nights I know he never even made it home.* An unplanned glance at the Regulator sent Clyde out the door in a flurry. Calling to Ebbin, "I'm late to a meeting with the boys. Hold down the fort."

With Bulldog's expertise and connections, he put towers of men to work spudding an average of four wells a week. As John Earl waved his magic wand, equipment appeared, stacking up in fact. The other partners combed the county seats and farmlands for any available leases from original owners and speculators ready for quick profits. Thus, the Brophy Boys emerged as a formidable presence in the oil business, the envy of many and the nemesis of majors like Oklahoma Oil.

At the offices of Brophy Boys, Incorporated, Willie pushed a roller chair back from his desk. He and Arnolia were straining to be heard above the carpentry racket in the recently purchased storefront. Each of the partners, with the exception of Clyde, occupied identical offices which opened to a common reception area and the two stenographers' stations.

Behind the door bearing the name of William Bacon, Esq. "What good is it all?" she demanded, still stinging from the slight paid her at a Kilgore department store.

By this time, Willie reached his wife. "Ain't white folks in Brophy treatin' you decent enough?" She had to agree, though she could perceive the unexpressed hatred of some who were intimidated by blacks with more money in the bank than they.

"Then don't go back to that store no more. If your money ain't no good to them, spend it where it is." Trying with great difficulty not to allow his true feelings to surface, *Not a dime of Brophy Boys' money is ever gonna be spent at that place; I'll sees to it.*

"They was willin' to let me spend my money, all right, just so long as I used the colored entrance at the back," she spit the words.

"Just what you want me to do, Nolia?"

Tugging on her coat in frustration, "Oh, I don't know, but this oil ain't done nothin' for black folks' grief."

"Ain't done nothin'?" the angry edge to his voice and the violence with which he took hold of her shoulders raised her uncomfortably to her toes and nearer to his face. "Tell me, woman, we got expensive, store-bought clothes on our backs?"

Too upset to respond, her silence enraged him all the more.

"Tell me!"

She nodded affirmation.

"Does your neighbors has more money than they ever dared to dream?"

His subsequent questions were answered with identical replies. "Ain't that your boy I see drivin' a fancy automobile and about to be educated down at that college?"

"You're hurtin' me," she somehow mustered the courage to say.

His release allowed Arnolia to slump into a chair.

"But that ain't enough for you, is it?" He caught his reflection in an oval mirror hung near the door. "That's me, a man of respect," he shook his finger toward the image of a slightly graying man in a tailored suit from whose lapel a carnation jutted. "People come to me, black and white, wantin' my time and my help. Me... the black boy that swept up at Mr. Hoyt's store. Willie Bacon is givin' his people royalty money for a good life and jobs to them that didn't have the blessin' of land to lease."

Her courage returning, "What kind of jobs, Mr. Bacon? All I see them doin' is diggin' slush pits, totin' pipe, and any other work won't no white man lower hisself to take."

He towered over her, "At least they got money to spend to put food in their babies' mouths, and that's one hell of a lot more than they had." He paused. "I've give them a chance at a future. Did you drive by the new colored school? No black chile had no school like that before. Won't nothin' never be enough for you?"

"No so long as my babies got to go through the back doors of life." She stormed out.

Willie reclaimed his seat. Strewn upon his desktop were the projected labor needs for the next phase of operation. *She's right; Nolia is always right. Every job for blacks don't demand skill past a strong back and a weak mind.* In a single motion he cleared his desk, sending papers flying to the floor. A tattered photograph of his grandfather housed in a frame that cost more than the casket that bore him to the grave fell atop the clutter.

"You can't change the world but a little bit at the time," he heard himself say. "Won't no man get it all done hisself, but another will rise up to take his place."

I'm takin' your place, and my children gonna go farther from here till it's done. Damn these men and their pride. Think their work is so important can't nobody take their place. Don't matter how much time they take up in meetin', hirin' folks to build storage tanks and arrangin' easements for pipelines. John Earl could let the other Boys take up his slack so he could run this school business and free up Elaine what with a baby on the way. He sighed. Babies is sure miracle workers.

Mavis relived her stay in the hospital. On his first visit she could hardly recognize the voice behind the stuffed bears and double bouquets of flowers. From under his arm, he dropped a box of Hershey's chocolate kisses.

"While I'm at work, you eat one an hour, and consider each a stand in for the real thing."

He was the Cale of old, joking and laughing, leaving her wondering just what turned him into the empty shell she found in Brophy. Unwrapping a foil kiss, she allowed the chocolate to melt, savoring the taste and mulling over the abrupt change in her husband. "Hell's bells, what difference does it make?" she asked one of the bears. "Life's so damn good, it hurts." She then consumed the pound of chocolate until her bed became a mass of silver foils.

Turning the corner, the Brophy School came into view. *I can't believe how much it's come along since last week. Elaine's promise of an openin' by fall just might come true. But that's Elaine for you; nothing she can't do*, a hint of envy escaped.

Examining the steel girders and columns rising above the construction tile, she could pinpoint the centrally located auditorium that would double as the divider between the high school and elementary wings. Parking the Fleetwood outside a small construction headquarters, Mavis walked in to find Elaine on the phone.

Waving enthusiastically, Elaine pointed to a chair while continuing the conversation. "That's correct, right now we are expecting it to take at least seventy-five radiators for the whole campus." She laughed politely. "I realize that's quite an order to fill. Yes, we will send fifty percent down payment." The two women made faces back and forth as Elaine allowed the Memphis supplier to have his say.

"See if he can get you a couple for in here," Mavis complained about the chill. "This wood burnin' antique is useless." She poured herself a cup of coffee from a tin pot atop the stove as Elaine nodded agreement.

"Mr. Blair, I do appreciate your position, but you must understand that we find ourselves in the midst of a boom. People are appearing from everywhere. At our present rate, even this building will be too small within a few years, and I would hate," she emphasized, "for you to lose out on future sales."

A distinctive click signaled the conversation's end. "He's shipping next week, check received or not."

"You been takin' hard-nosed lessons from your husband, or have you been hidin' it behind that sweet, schoolteacher act?"

"I just told him the truth."

Never one to mince words, Mavis dove in head first. "You look terrible."

She took a loud slurp of the dark liquid. "Why ain't you home in bed?"

"You're lookin' lovely yourself."

"I ain't the one teasin'."

"Nor am I." She helped herself to the coffee. "You know perfectly well that the school has to be built by fall. There's a lot of children depending on me."

"So's the one that's here, not to mention the one warmin' in the oven."

With an exasperated look, she replied. "Both are doing equally well. I'll be leaving in time to pick up Jake."

"Who does your job when you're gone?"

"Oh, a new man out of Louisiana, an old buddy of Bulldog's, of course."

"So, this fella could spell you for say three or four days?"

Elaine could see the glimmer in Mavis' eyes. "What have you got up your sleeve?"

Mavis set her cup on the desk then jumped up and grabbed her friend's hands excitedly. "You and me's goin' to Dallas and stay at that A. Dolphus Ho-tel!"

Caught off guard by such an unexpected proposal, Elaine began to find herself caught up in Mavis' animation before dismissing it with a sudden, "Oh, you aren't really serious? We can't take off to Dallas alone, two women in a hotel..."

"The boys will take us."

"And how do you propose to manage that? You may get Cale to agree, but John Earl is another matter entirely. If you just knew how hard it is to get him home for a simple meal or a full night in our bed, you'd be singing a different tune."

Undeterred by Elaine's obstacles, Mavis was all but dancing around the confines of the one-room building. "Listen, you heard John Earl a tellin' how that H. L. Hunt fella and his cronies is always doin' business at that hotel. And I even heard him say at supper the other night how he'd give his right arm to be up there stealin' leases from under Hunt's nose and rubbin' it in his face."

Elaine's face showed traces of belief.

"So even John Earl can't argue that this will be a good sense business opportunity."

Slumping to the desk, Elaine complained, "But I've got..."

"You've got to do it for me."

This uncharacteristic pleading from Mavis stopped Elaine short. "For you?"

"I...I don't know how I can ask you this. Lord knows you done so much bein' my best friend and all, but...I need you to teach me." Now visible were the tears.

"Teach you what?"

A timid voice, "How to be you."

An uneasy silence fell broken by the construction in the background. For Mavis, who groveled to no one, the experience of admitting her inadequacies even to her most trusted confidant left her overwhelmed by her own stupidity for allowing herself to be thus exposed. Searching Elaine's eyes for some sign of comprehension and finding none, she began groping for her handbag.

"How to be me?"

"You know, to be a lady... how to dress...how to talk all elegant like."

"Why? You are a perfectly charming woman, unique, your own person." Elaine fought for tactful words to describe the garish, blunt woman who was her friend.

"But I got the girls to think on. I don't want 'um growin' up like me and Bethel or bein' ashamed of the way their momma acts."

She wiped streaked make up with a tissue. "I know people snicker at me, and" she pleaded with the sad eyes of an abandoned puppy. "I know Cale thinks you're about the most special person around."

She gasped, "He said that?" horrified that Cale had in some way betrayed their past.

"No, not in words, but I seen him look at you."

Elaine blushed deeply as guilt rose to the surface.

"He don't realize it, and neither do you, but what he likes is your ladylike qualities, the way you're so different from me."

Plunging deeply into her own thoughts, Elaine ignored Mavis. *Why can't I just tell her outright that I loved her husband and that his broken promises drove me to marry John Earl to try and substitute for what never could be.* Not until that moment had Elaine acknowledged her reasoning for marrying John Earl.

The realization sent her slowly from a haze into the stark clarity of reality. *I only wanted to hurt Cale, to let him know the pain of seeing the person you love claimed by another. But it was all so very wrong.*

She wanted to bolt from the room, but her resolve was crumbling under the magnitude of her mistake. *And if I tell her, what good would it do? Mavis is so innocent, with a childlike need for Cale, and now it seems for me, as well.*

"Please Elaine," Mavis came to face her. "Please take me to that store and show me how to be a lady like you and all them that shops there."

"What store?" She could not make sense of Mavis' ramblings.

"This one where all the fine women buy their clothes."

From her bag she pulled a wad of clippings, ads collected for weeks from the Dallas paper, all bearing the name of the same store. "This one."

Mavis pointed repeatedly at a sketch of a svelte woman attired in a stylish suit which fell below the knee. A hat, its brim upturned, was being placed atop the model's head in stop action. She read the name with a reverence reserved for holy writ, "Neiman-Marcus."

Chapter 9

March 1931

The wind that swept the stale odor of railway engines down the Dallas street appeared to alter its course when battering against the railway station that blocked its path. For the two East Texas women the battle to force their skirts and hats downward left them with no free hands to move their baggage.

Mavis objected to Elaine's suggestion of a porter. "You don't never know; he could grab our stuff and be gone like that," snapping her fingers in demonstration of the swiftness with which a nefarious redcap might whisk away their belongings. "Once Ethel Faye Simmons got her suitcase stole that way in Memphis. She was on her way to visit her sister that moved there cause her husband worked the barges. Well..."

Elaine listened to the recitation of the girl's victimization before agreeing to move her single valise and hat box, it being the easier task than arguing with Mavis over the honesty of porters. Now she wished the Simmons woman had gotten herself stolen along with her bag. "Mavis," she interrupted with sufficient force to claim the conversation. "We need a taxi."

"We can walk it; couldn't be more than a mile or two, and we can see all the buildings."

"No," Elaine placed her foot firmly. "I will not walk into the Adolphus Hotel." Wisely diverting a discussion, she added. "The grand ladies of any society do not walk into a hotel carrying their bags. Besides, I seem to remember that you were concerned about my health and that of my child."

"Oh, I'm sorry. You know how I get when I'm all stirred up over stuff. I'll get us a taxi." The hand controlling her skirt flew to her mouth. Two fingers deposited inside produced a whistle that pierced the ears of man and beast for the city block occupied by the station. All heads turned in time for a glimpse at a generous amount of leg courtesy of the wind.

Jerking Mavis' skirt, Elaine averted a second summons. "Now you listen to me. Don't you do anything else without my say so."

Quieted but hardly offended, Mavis began to offer an explanation.

"Dammit, you watch me and learn."

Never having heard such talk from Elaine, Mavis allowed her to take control. "Whew, she must be pickin' up a lot from John Earl and none of it good," she muttered.

Composing herself as best she could while fighting the spiraling winds and the urge to throw herself in front of the next train, Elaine approached a doorman. As she placed the money in his hand, she requested the taxi.

"Of course, Ma'am."

"Well, if that's all you had to do, you could have just told me."

"Mavis, I love you like a sister, but there's no telling you a thing. What I want you to do for the time we are in Dallas is to count to twenty before you do or say anything. While you count, give some thought to what's about to happen, and act in a proper fashion. Watch me; ask my opinion." As an afterthought she added, "And if I see or even think that you're about to do the wrong thing, I'm going to pull at my ear. That's the signal for you to stop before you embarrass yourself."

Mavis grinned enormously, convinced that her transformation from ugly duckling to swan would prove as simple as convincing their husbands that a stay in Dallas would be a profitable venture. John Earl, who embraced the idea, fired orders at the secretary concerning reservations and train schedules. An important meeting with the boss man of a tank building crew prevented Cale and him from joining the girls that morning, but they would arrive by evening in time for dinner and dancing.

Elaine could not believe her husband's reaction. He actually wanted to take her to Dallas, to show her off was the way he put it. As if the women no longer remained in the office, he addressed Cale.

"Nothing' like a couple of good-lookin' females to bring out men ready to deal. With a few drinks in 'um and a fine meal, we'll have Hunt and his buddies right where we want 'um. Now, girls, we're settin' you up a line of credit at the Republic National Bank. Buy somethin' pretty so you can gussie up and turn some heads." In a moment of panic, John Earl pictured Mavis in one of her typical get ups. "Elaine, you pick somethin' out for Mavis!" He sat back in his chair with hands clasped behind his head and feet propped on the desk. "We want all of Dallas to see just how much we're worth so that they're beggin' to kiss our asses for a chance to buy, ship, or refine our oil."

As Elaine settled back in the cab, Mavis pushed her face toward the window to absorb every nuance of the city. "It even smells powerful, don't it? Reckon Hoyt, Millie, and Miss Wythel are seein' anything so fine?" Mavis referred to the European tour upon which the three had departed in January.

Closing her eyes, Elaine tried to rest a bit, exhausted by their early outset and the strain of preparations. Unlike her previous pregnancy, this one drained her of every ounce of energy. Fortunately the nausea subsided early on, but the desire to sleep posed a constant battle weighed against the demands of the school, Jake, and the frequent confrontations with her husband. The marriage eased into its downward spiral with a subtlety that left her unable to pinpoint a specific event or argument to mark the moment when she began to dread his homecoming. There was his refusal to interact with Jake, which she now believed to be a blessing, and the way he ignored her requests for his time, day or night.

At first he came to supper and would sit with the family around the radio. Then began the trips to check on one well or another, his returns lengthening. Soon she began to notice the whiskey on his breath, the faint traces of cheap perfumes as she set his clothing out to be cleaned. *I made every excuse I could, our recent success, living with Daddy, and his preoccupation with drilling every possible well for more and more money.*

The first night he failed to come home, she sent Jake with Clyde and waited for John Earl. At the kitchen table, still in her nightclothes, she head his car. His surprise at finding anyone there left him stumbling for excuses.

"I stayed the night at the Mercedes II; tower's short a roughneck."

She threw a coffee mug toward the door that barely missed his head. "I haven't seen enough roughnecking to know a night's tower doesn't leave a man filthy with mud? Look at you; you've bedded up with some whore at Newton Flats."

Elaine burst into tears, as she ran for the bedroom where she locked herself away from the man who calmly poured himself coffee.

If anything, John Earl found his wife's intuition amusing. "Yes, my dear," he shouted through the walls, "I spent the night in the company of a very talented lady. Take my word for it. The Flats can't claim a place alongside Cancre in Seminole, but the booze flows and the chippies spread."

He took a long drink before throwing the rest in the sink. "But given some time, and if the boom holds, it just might give her a run for her money. And that ballroom on the road between Kilgore and Longview, Miss Mattie's, well it livens things up so a man don't have to drive all the way to New Orleans for his sport."

John Earl arrived at the locked door, raised his cowboy boot waist high and kicked it open with little effort. Sitting up at the intrusion, Elaine stiffened. One glance at his wife, hair in disarray, face swollen and streaked, revived memories of his mother that sickened him.

"Don't you have the decency to fix yourself up?"

"For a man who won't even come home?"

He was over her before she could fight back, pressing her arms upon the bed as he straddled her, his face drawn tightly in anger. Elaine could smell the coffee mixed with last night's whiskey and turned her head to the side.

"I don't need your Daddy's bank or your respectability no more. I'm John Earl Terry, and folks shake in their boots at the sound of my name," he lashed out in response to her defiance.

"Let me set you straight, just so as there's no misunderstandin'. There's got to be somethin' for a man to rush home to besides a prudish woman that don't know the first thing about pleasin' her man. Hell, you couldn't even hold on to that Missouri plow boy."

She spit the words in his face.

"He's twice the man you are."

Terry threw back his head at the comparison. "Tried him out did you? I bet that was a sight to see; two cold fish flouncin' around."

Elaine cried out in pain as he placed one hand around her neck. *Let me die, she prayed. Just let me be free of him.*

"There'll be no more bitchin' about where I been or who I was with. You don't like the rules, run yourself over to Kilgore and get you a divorce. I won't put up no fight; I'll be just as happy to be rid of you." He removed his hands, rose from the bed and began to remove his clothes.

As Elaine fought for breath, she managed, 'I hate you."

"That's not how I remember it." His trousers fell to the floor with the thud of his buckle. "Let's see if I can give you a little refresher about whose the better man before you go off divorcin' me and beggin' Cale to do the same."

"I'm pregnant," she blurted.

John Earl stopped in disbelief. A smile slowly replaced vengeance. If that don't beat all, he thought. *Since my beloved daddy-in-law put up fifty percent of his holdins' for Jake, the other half is sure to go to the newest little bundle of joy whose pappy will have to oversee it.*

"But I'll get my divorce just the same."

As Elaine started from the room, her husband called, "If you try it; I'll swear the baby ain't mine. And won't that be a pity for both your kids when I name Cale McCallister as the adulterer who got you pregnant?" He let the magnitude of his threat hit home. "You'll have one hell of a time findin' anybody that knows the history between the two of you that won't believe it's so. And what about sweet, trustin' Mavis? Wouldn't she just love a shot of that in her mornin' coffee?"

Her heart sank. *What kind of monster deliberately ruins the lives of four innocent children?* she asked herself. *He doesn't love me or this baby.* She placed her head against the door facing, suddenly unable to stand. "Why would you even want to hold onto us?"

He passed through the doorway and patted his wife playfully on her behind. "I intend to enjoy the benefits of fatherhood." He left without returning to the bedroom where Elaine spent her day crying and damning his soul to the hell he deserved.

"Elaine, look here," Mavis fell back to reveal the French Renaissance carvings that decorated the Adolphus' facade.

Twenty-one stories of Beaux Arts architecture stretched into the Dallas sky. The red brick and gray granite hotel born of beer baron Adolphus Busch of St. Louis opened October 5th of 1912, attracting an elite clientele of businessmen and politicos to its original two hundred sixty rooms. With its one point eight million dollar price tag, the Adolphus drew accolades from critics who christened it, "The Most Beautiful Building West of Venice." Since its expansion in 1926, the hotel increased its capacity to the present seven hundred rooms.

As the women stood on the Commerce Street side, Mavis counted silently before concentrating on the building's tower. Reaching the specified twenty, no improprieties or other possibilities occurring, she tapped the bellboy unloading their baggage while a distracted Elaine tipped the driver. "Damn, if part of this hotel don't look like a beer bottle."

She is not of the Adolphus caste, he reasoned, *but the desk clerk will tell her the rates and put her on her way soon enough.* In hopes that he might garner a meager tip, he answered with the deference paid all guests. "Yes ma'am, Mr. Busch was a beer magnate."

Pleased with her assessment, Mavis added, "Liked to turn up a brew pretty regular?"

Stifling a laugh, the boy placed the last bag on his cart. "You might say so."

By this time Elaine rejoined her with a tug at her ear as Mavis sought to lend the friendly boy a hand, "It's his job; let him do it. Now, when we get in the room and he's finished setting things right, I want you to thank him the way we practiced and give him a tip," she whispered.

Unable to resist one more look at the Adolphus' exterior, Mavis took notice of the carvings of faces, flowers, and animals, as well as the terra cotta gargoyles. *We're in tall cotton, for sure. What would the folks in Winnie say to all this?* She made a mental note to send as many hateful customers as she could remember and every spiteful biddy in town a postcard.

Elaine put her arm through that of her friend to force her inside the lobby where the Adolphus further spellbound the waitress come to town. Its windows draped in blue velvet, the lobby's primary source of illumination emanated from an enormous chandelier whose brass eagles held hops within their talon rings, lest guests forget the product upon which the capital for the building was raised. Around the expansive lobby, antique gold fixtures added their own light to the black walnut paneling. An Italian marble staircase led to the Mezzanine level and a panoramic view. Everywhere fresh flowers lent their scents to the ambiance.

"Hell's..."

A hand rushed to the lobe of Elaine's ear.

Mavis took a breath. "I mean, isn't it stunnin'?" She looked to Elaine who smiled her endorsement.

"Isn't it though?" Guiding her to the main desk, she accepted the help of the clerk. "I am Mrs. Terry, and this is Mrs. McCallister. I believe our husbands' secretary made reservations.

"Let me see." He excused himself to knock on the door of the hotel's manager, entering at his response. "Sir, the party for which you requested notification has arrived."

The manager pushed back his chair, and as he consulted a mirror asked, "Are the flowers in place?"

"Yes, sir, but..."

"But what?" He caught the strained expression.

"One lady is... well, sir, I think you'd better see."

Pushing the clerk out of his way, the Adolphus' manager peered from the door. Though attired in her most conservative clothing, Mavis still bore the markings of a woman advertising her wares. Once more in possession of her pre-pregnancy figure, the dress hung possessively to her hips and the bosom that jutted from an opened coat.

Closing the door, the manager gasped, "My heavens," unsure of what to do. "I checked with the Republic and have their assurance that the couples can well afford the Adolphus. Left with no alternative but to show them to their rooms, "*Nouveau riche*", he said with distaste. "At times like these I woe the day I allowed Mr. Busch to lure me from New York. Their money passed from generation to generation to those of breeding and taste." He waved the clerk out. "Take them up." A personal oversight no longer held interest.

"Ladies, please accompany me to the elevator."

As he engaged Elaine in conversation, Mavis ignored their guide in favor of the uniformed black man seated upon a small stood that collapsed into the wall. His highly polished shoes reflected the gold buttons of his uniform. With each stop he asked politely for destinations of new passengers. When they arrived at their floor, he opened the door and stood back as they exited, "Enjoy your stay at the Adolphus."

Removing a set of keys, the clerk walked ahead of Elaine and Mavis with the bellboy and luggage trailing. Once unlocked, he pushed open the door, bowing slightly as the women passed.

"The Presidential Suite."

Even Elaine's poise was stolen by the opulence of their surroundings. A private hallway led to the main salon. As they explored the suite, two bedrooms, each with adjoining, private baths; numerous closets; a breakfast area; and a pre-Prohibition bar were among the amenities.

"Excuse me. Where shall I place these bags?"

"Which room you want?"

"The one with the twin beds, I think."

With a wink to the bellboy as they entered the room Elaine had not chosen, "She's pregnant already," Mavis explained. "That brown one there is hers. You can just set mine down too, and I'll move it later."

"But," he raised his objection only to be cut short.

"Hell's bells." Too late, she bit her tongue. "I mean, it don't, that is it doesn't matter because they're empty anyway."

By this time the desk clerk was at the door, he and his employee sharing doubts.

"You see, we're on our way to Neiman-Marcus to buy us all new clothes from the bottom up, so to speak. Our husbands is partners in oil, and we hit a gusher a few months ago. I bet you people even up here in Dallas heard about it; it was on the national radio and made the newsreel. That's just the first of our wells; now we're up to," she paused to address Elaine who was in the bathroom. "Is it thirty or thirty-two wells, Elaine?" With no reply forthcoming, she left the men with a parting, "When you got that many, hell, who can keep good count?"

Mavis had a chair pulled to the window overlooking Commerce Street when Elaine reemerged. "Did you remember to give the bellman a tip?"

"Hell's..."

"Mavis," she scolded.

"Excuse me." She began afresh. "Oh my goodness, I forgot, but I can run on down..."

"Don't bother. I can call the desk and have them take care of him and add it to our bill."

"Haven't we just died and gone to heaven? Imagine, the President's own room! We was damn lucky he wasn't usin' it."

Watching Elaine pick up her gloves and pocketbook, "Where you headed?"

"I thought you and I had a date with Neiman-Marcus?"

As she thrust her feet into pumps, "We're waistin' daylight."

Long before Cale's dream of oil, Mavis devoured the ladies' magazines as a means of escape from the drudgery of Bethel's Cafe and the stagnating town. Somewhere within their pages, she became aware of "The South's Finest Store." Pictured in an article were the founding brothers, Herbert and Theo Marcus, and their brother-in-law and sister, A. L. and Carrie Neiman, amid the quality of merchandise that characterized their establishment and its clientele since 1907. Twenty-four years later, Neiman-Marcus encompassed four stories of select apparel for women, their husbands, and children that brought the world of fashion to the Southwest.

Once inside Mavis paid close attention to Elaine who advised, "I think we need to get a feel for the store before buying anything." From the fourth floor Le Vieux Carre interior decoration and gift shops, the fur salon, millinery shop, past the Antoine Beauty Salon, they settled upon the French Room.

Upon their entrance, a woman in her early thirties approached, "I hope you ladies are having a wonderful afternoon."

"Oh we are," gushed Mavis, instantly envious of the sales lady's dark dress cut to fall in graceful lines with a slight flare at the bottom.

"I don't believe we have met. I'm Caroline Hodges." She offered Elaine and Mavis a seat near a set of full length mirrors away from the traffic of the salon. Listening to Elaine explain their expectations, she promised. "When you leave Neiman-Marcus, you will be the two most striking women on the Adolphus' dance floor this evening. I'll see to it personally."

Under Caroline's guidance, the Brophy women selected wardrobes, some originals and others copies from the designs of Lelong, Chanel, and many others that Mavis could not pronounce. Elaine especially admired a suit Mavis modeled in shades of dark green jersey. Rows of diamond-shaped print carried over to the blouse and the cuffs of the solid jacket that fitted closely but not snugly at the waist to fasten with four vertical buttons and accented by a coordinating belt. Caroline's return with a matching hat completed the ensemble. Mavis pivoted in front of the mirror, pulling the hat closer to her head, adjusting it so that the brim fell near her right eye as Caroline instructed.

"We must hurry along or risk disappointing your hair stylist," she prompted.

At Antoine's the girls were further pampered, their makeup applied and hair restyled. By day's end, Elaine and Mavis had visited every section of the store where their purchases garnered Caroline a position at the top of total sales.
At the main entrance, Caroline assured them, "Your packages will arrive by taxi within the hour."

Mavis threw her arms around the slender sales girl, "You're the sweetest thing I ever met. Thanks so much."

"It was an honor Mrs. McCallister. I do hope we can spend another afternoon together." Until her retirement, Caroline Hodges received a note from Mavis McCallister twice a year to specify the date of her arrival. As she had done on Mavis' original visit, Caroline assisted her and later the twins. What Mrs. Neiman never learned, Mavis always sent a large bouquet of flowers to Caroline's home with an impressive check in sincere gratitude for services rendered.

Much later in the evening, Cale forced his index finger into the confines of his shirt collar again working through an arcing motion meant to expand the stiffened neckpiece or provide a moment's freedom as he waited for John Earl to offer the maitre d' an incentive that would move them a few tables closer to the oil barons sure to be in attendance. "I feel like a damn fool in this get up." Using his right hand to examine the tails of his tuxedo, "Let's go back up and put on somethin' else," he urged.

"Got to dress the part." Pointing toward men and their ladies throughout the rose damask room, "You got to look better than the waiters at least. See anybody in a suit from J. C. Penney?"

John Earl moved on, leaving Cale with his thoughts. *John Earl always knows his stuff,* he relented. Watching the crowd, *This is just like sitting at the back of the balcony of the Show Me back home to watch some fancy Hollywood movie.* Feeling conspicuously out of place, he found his partner. "Where are them girls?" Waiting at the French Room had been another of John Earl's suggestions. "Can't we just sit?" His finger probed the collar in stabbing motions.

"I suppose," he acquiesced. The entrance of Jim Larimore, a Sinclair big shot, ended the discussion. John Earl spotted him and led the man toward a table bearing the "reserved" designation that resulted from Terry's proper placement of a twenty-dollar bill. As most every gentleman in the French Room, Terry removed a Prohibition flask from his coat pocket. "Join us in a drink?"

"I'd enjoy passing the time; the rest of my party seems to be a little late."

Before Larimore knew what hit him, John Earl and he had their heads together. Cale told himself, *It's times like these that you just got to wonder at John Earl, the way he sells a man a bill of goods at a rate better than the going price of East*

Texas crude. He knows exactly how to sweeten the deal with options for the wells we already got scheduled. Convinced that his partner actually played the man square, he sat back. Suddenly remembering their wives, he turned, slowly rising with his mouth agape.

Since their arrival in Dallas, the husbands had only talked to their wives through closed doors. *She left a healthy chunk of my earnins' at Neiman-Marcus, and it was worth every penny*, he decided.

Reacting to Cale's behavior, Terry followed the man's gaze as did Larimore. It was Larimore who spoke first, "Do you boys know those exquisite creatures?" his optimism unconcealed.

"I think they're our wives," Cale concluded.

Draped over an elbow-length glove, Mavis held a satin cape edged with fox meant to shield a lady from the evening chill. Despite the fact that she never planned to leave the Adolphus, she carried the cape, "To let folks know I got one." Even for Mavis the style was provocatively daring, a haltered look exposing her back but sufficient so as not to denude a hint of cleavage. Falling in fluid lines, the skirt's flair began just above the knees and reached the floor. Both cape and dress were of the identical cream colored satin that offset her red hair.

"Her hair?" Cale addressed his partner. "You think Mavis cut her hair?" Though somewhat shorter, the stylists tamed the curls into three waves layered one atop the other. Pulled back to expose her forehead, spirals framed her cheeks at chin level.

Unaware of their audience, Mavis stepped to the side allowing for a full view of Elaine. A double layer of aquamarine chiffon formed a ruffled bodice that disguised her tiny chest. Beginning at the waist, more ruffles flounced at angles to form an inverted "v" that ended half way to the floor. Another "v" began under the bodice ruffles, revealing her back to the waist where a large bow accented the petite frame.

Appraising Elaine with an objective eye, Terry questioned himself, *Would I give that woman a second glance if she weren't my wife?* As he traveled the length of her body, *It'll take more than a twin bed to keep me away tonight.*

Bounding up the stairs, Cale claimed the arms of both women, "May I escort the two most..." he could not call to mind a word to adequately describe them.

"Breath taking?" his wife encouraged.

"Dazzling?" suggested Elaine.

"That and more," Cale agree. "John Earl got us a table right near the dance floor. As they neared, the men rose.

"My wife, Elaine." Terry freed her arm from Cale to seat her between the Sinclair executive and himself.

Taking her gloved hand, Jim raised it in a grand gesture, gently brushing it against his lips. Staring into the blue of eyes deepened by the tint of her gown, he acknowledged, "And I thought you were only lucky in oil." Devoting himself to Elaine, the two were soon conversing like old acquaintances enjoying a reunion.

The old geezer's bustin' a gut to get at her. If I could just get Elaine to play along, he told himself, *I might talk him into a better deal.* He removed the flask. *Good thing her belly's still flat.* Lifting his crystal in a salute toward Cale and Mavis, his heart stuck in his throat. Behind the wrought, bronze balustrade stood Lamar Tate, stuffed sausage tight into his tuxedo, wiping the perspiration form his forehead and blinding couples two tables away with the glare from his signature initialed diamond ring. With boredom permanently etched into her expression, Estelle unclasped a sable opera coat which she allowed to fall seductively from her shoulders to expose the figure he'd so often dreamed about.

"Finally, there's Tate," he heard Larimore saying. He looked at John Earl in explanation of their tardiness. "It's that wife of his; never ready to come when he is."

Unsure of whether to run or simply dive under the tablecloth, Terry opted for a long swig from the flask. The men left their seats in deference to the approaching lady, who stopped short in recognition of her lover. Unaccustomed to meeting John Earl in anything other than oil field mud or jail house sweat, Lamar reacted only upon hearing the name.

"Lamar and Estelle Tate, Mavis and Cale McCallister and Elaine and John Earl Terry."

Mindful of his surroundings, Tate summoned every ounce of reserve to greet first the McCallisters, thankful that Terry failed to offer his hand.

And I thought this would be just another dull evening listening to old men talk crude prices. Aloud she baited her seething husband, "Oh, you remember John Earl, don't you, Sugar?"

"You all have met?" Cale asked innocently.

"A little before the strike, Cale. I helped Mr. Tate here get a hold of some East Texas leases before they got hot. Turned you a pretty profit, just like I promised your scout." Terry flashed a smile of confidence restored by the liquor and the realization that as Tate's business equal, he need fear no longer his nemesis. "Guess your old boy Carmichael redeemed hisself when the Willie B #1 hit?"

~~~~~~

Ignoring Terry's obvious attempt to draw him into a confrontation in front of half of the Dallas oil community, Lamar addressed Larimore. "Our table is ready."

Unwilling to part with Elaine, Larimore lied, "I gave it up; we're joining my new clients and," he draped his arm behind Elaine's chair, "their charming wives."

"Fine with me," Estelle leaped into the seat on John Earl's left. With little choice Tate glided a chair toward the table and occupied the remaining, seat at Cale's right.

At Larimore's insistence he ordered for the table courses Mavis and Cale found to their liking but dared not ask the contents. During the main course a swing band took its place. Whispering into his wife's ear, "Nubbin, you want to dance?"

"That would be wonderful," she answered in the practiced demeanor. As they eased into the crowd, Cale took her into his arms, pulling her close, the scent of Coco Chanel's favorite number coaxing him closer.

"You are so beautiful."

"Really beautiful?"

"Yeah, just like some movie star."

Pleased at his notice, she gave credit where due. "Elaine's been teachin' me."

He looked hurt. "That mean you're gonna go off and leave me for some educated fella out of S. M. U.?"

She slapped his shoulder, "You know better than to think that. Got all I ever wanted; just don't want to lose it."

He fell silent, *It's like Sarah said when I told her I was rich and had bought back the home place for her, "Don't never forget where you come from; it's a sure sign of bein' lost." Well, I ain't a mind to forget nor lose. Mavis is where I been; she'll be where I'm goin'.* And for the moment, he believed it as truth.

At the table it was Jim Larimore who sealed the evening's fate. "Elaine, I am well aware that Lamar gave up dancing years ago, so if you would do me the honor and can talk your husband into taking the floor with Estelle, we can take full advantage of these fine musicians."

Estelle leaned forward to place her elbows on the table and clasped her hands. The cleavage hintingly exposed by the neckline's scoop plunged into fuller view the largest of the pearls at the point of a necklace that beckoned between her breasts with each inviting, pendulous motion.

With Larimore on his feet to draw Mrs. Terry from her seat, Lamar could offer no excuse without exposing himself as the cuckold. Abandoned, he watched as best he could his wife and her ex-lover.

"Been wearin' my pants leg thin," he referred to the tantalizing rise and fall of Estelle's foot during dinner.

"I didn't want your, now how did Jim put it? Your charming little wife to find us out." Using the tip of an enameled nail, she traced an uncertain pattern beneath his chin. "A wife, John Earl, how very, very sweet."

Terry pulled her closer until he could feel her pulse quicken with his desire. "We have the same lovin' relationship as you and the old man."

She pulled back, taunting him with feigned distrust, "Honeymoon over so quickly?"

"Hell, it never even got started."

"Then we can... strengthen old ties?"

John Earl flashed the grin that first unlatched her bedroom door. "Will he go on up early and leave you with Larimore?"

"Not with you around." She shrugged her shoulders in dismissal of the notion that meeting her lover might pose any difficulty. "We have separate bedrooms; I'll just turn the lock and leave out the front door when he starts to snore. It's worked before." Motioning with her head toward Larimore and Elaine. "How are you going to be rid of wifey, or is Larimore takin' care of that little problem?"

"She'd just soon I dropped down a bore hole, and as for Larimore, he's waistin' his time."

As the couples passed, Estelle appraised the woman who finally got John Earl to the altar. *I don't see it. Pretty, if you like her type, and he doesn't. That Mavis I could have understood; John Earl always liked a woman with a lot to show for herself.* She worked caressing hands under her partner's coat. How he does appreciate a woman with something to offer.

"Supervising a school, taking care of a family, Elaine, you are remarkable."

Jim's praise after months of rejection relaxed Elaine's guard. She found Jim Larimore equally special, relating to him their shared experience when he spoke of his deceased wife. He listened intently, complimenting her viewpoint on construction costs, labor, and the oil business. He even agreed with her criticism of the "Battle of Flowers" statuary group that dominated the room.

They had enjoyed several numbers, the last a livelier tempo when she experienced the discomfort. Not quite a pain, but unsettling enough for Jim to notice a slight grimace.

"Are you all right?"

"I think I should rest a bit. Mavis and I shopped all day, and I don't know a more tactful way to broach the subject. Jim, I'm expecting a child."

Larimore apologized profusely after seeing Elaine swiftly to the table where they talked a while longer. As the twinges spread to her lower back, Elaine excused herself, asking Jim to explain her absence as nothing more than a long, exhausting day.

"Let me at least walk you to your room?"

"I can't interrupt your evening. Besides, you'll need to tell the others."

He watched Elaine exit the French Room.

Lamar Tate vainly attempted to gain his wife's attention. *I've watched them cozy up long enough. Everybody in the room is laughin' at me over this tramp.* Pulling himself to his feet, he trudged onto the dance floor.

In response to the unwelcome tap on his shoulder, John Earl spoke to the stranger he supposed to be cutting in. "You're not takin' my girl."

The hand that cut into his coat twisted him to face a raging Lamar Tate. "She's not your girl, you son of a bitch." Snatching Estelle, he led her back to the table. As he pushed his way through the entanglements of tables and guests, Estelle blew Terry a kiss. "We're goin' back to our room; get your bag."

"All right, Sugar," she agreed.

John Earl returned to a confused Larimore.

"What put Tate in such a uproar?"

Shrugging, "Hard to say, but I don't think you can count on him pickin' up the check. Say, is that Hunt over there? How about introducin' us?"

As they relocated, Larimore reminded John Earl of his wife's absence.

"Fine," he muttered, too interested in negotiating with H. L. Hunt to worry about Elaine's complaints.

Larimore took note of John Earl's lack of concern for his wife, so because he was concerned about Elaine, he again mentioned Elaine, this time to Mavis.

"Don't you think you better get yourself up to check on her?" Mavis urged.

With the room clearing and his business prospect exhausted, John Earl welcomed an excuse to leave the French Room before the McCallisters, who would assume him to be in bed when they returned. Stopping by the desk, he engaged another room and asked for a sheet of house stationery. At the writing desk, he quickly jotted the number before folding the paper and asking that it be placed in the Tate's box. A short climb up the stairs placed him on the appropriate floor just as Estelle slipped into the hall and away from her sleeping husband.

Mavis and Cale closed the French Room. At nearly two, they emerged from the elevator, Mavis carrying her pumps. As Cale bent to slip in the key, Mavis draped her arms around his neck and planted kisses up and down his neck.

"Stop it; I can't see to get the key in."

Hearing it slide into place, she swept his hand from the knob and guided it over the bodice of her gown. They embraced like teenagers excited by impending discovery. Finally Cale lifted his wife in his arms to carry her into the suite.

"Damn, you're heavy."

Giddy with Prohibition whiskey and the carefree existence of the good life, they fell into the Presidential hallway in a heap of laughter and flailing limbs. "Shh, we'll wake Elaine and John Earl," Cale warned much louder than he imagined.

From the bedroom floor Elaine tried to pull herself toward the door but collapsed yet again after only a few feet. Behind her a pool of blood smeared by her nightgown sank deeper into the carpeting. The pains had worsened soon after going to bed, progressing with intensity until she could lie to herself no longer.

I'm losing my baby. I need to get dressed and call for Mavis. The floral wallpaper merged into a kaleidoscope of color that prevented her from distinguishing which direction she moved until she felt herself hit the floor. Emerging from the haze she believed the noise to be laughter. Someone is here. She screamed for help, though only a faint whimper escaped. Dragging her hand across the carpet, she mustered all her strength to call again.

In the main salon Mavis detected a scratching.

"You hear that?"

"Can't you be quiet every once in a while?" He went back to the business at hand.

In search of a faint cry Mavis pushed her husband away. "I tell you I can hear it." Investigating the room's perimeter, she paused at the Terry's bedroom.

"It's comin' from in here."

"Leave 'um alone then."

"Elaine... John Earl... you all right in there?"

Cale fell back against the brocade sofa in frustration. "Get over here; you never know what you're gonna interrupt when you go bustin' in somebody's bedroom.

The persistence of what she now recognized as a whimper sent Mavis into the room. She knocked twice upon the door, "Get ready; I'm comin' in."

A momentary adjustment to the darkness prevented her from entering any further. Alarmed by a muffled cry, she groped for the light switch that sent the room into sudden illumination.

"Elaine! Cale, get in her right now! Oh, Elaine."

Cale jumped from the sofa to discover Mavis leaning over Elaine.

"Do somethin'!" she demanded of her husband. "Where the hell's John Earl?"

Sidestepping Elaine to reach the phone, Cale became aware of the blood. Visions of David Carmichael ready to split John Earl like a sack of feed flooded his mind. *My God, somebody from out of your past has killed you both. I'll find you in the bathtub or the closet.*

"Get the hotel doctor up to the Presidential Suite immediately. Hurry!" He slammed the receiver. Bending next to his wife, it seemed that she had lost what little sense she had. Sobbing uncontrollably, she repeatedly asked Elaine to speak.

A loud banging from the hallway door, sent Cale flying.

"The doc's here, Elaine. Everything's gonna be fine."

Her hand moved first, then glassy eyes opened. "Mavis?" her voice barely above a whisper.

"It's me Hon, and the doc's here."

"I'm dying," the hand around Mavis' wrist tightened. "Don't let him raise my son."

"Hell's bells, ain't nobody dyin'."

Her hand rose in a vain attempt to reach her ear then fell as eyes closed. Mavis felt strong hands upon her shoulders, pulling her away; the doctor took her place.

"What has happened here?"

"Her baby," Mavis cried into Cale's chest.

"This woman needs a hospital," he ordered the accompanying clerk who immediately called for an ambulance.

A small contingency of bellmen and the night clerk watched as the woman was carried from the hotel room. At the insistence of the male guest, the woman in the blood smeared gown was taken to a taxi so that she might be at the hospital. Debating whether to notify his manager, the clerk delayed until he could speak privately with his guest. The man appeared dazed, opening the closets, peering into rooms as though searching for something or someone.

"Sir," he showed the man to the sofa. "Shall I arrange for you to be with your wife?"

"She's not my wife."

The clerk thought he might break down.

"Her husband? Perhaps I could reach him for you?" He was in no condition to deliver such news.

"I don't know... I thought he was here."

"I see. Where might I begin inquiring?" Removing a small notebook from his coat, the clerk listed the names with whom Cale recalled having seen John Earl engage in even a passing conversation. "I'll see how many are actually guests and have a bellboy contact each room."

Cale offered his thanks, pulling his wallet from the tuxedo pocket.

"No sir," the clerk refused. "I can't. Please try and think of anyone else." He eased from the suite.

Left to himself, Cale paced the salon. *Where could he be; who else could he have hooked up with? Damn you, you said you was comin' back to check on Elaine!* He reached for the only thing he could find, a crystal vase of flowers, which he sent hurling toward the wall. He watched intently as the water dribbled.

At so late an hour and for so important a guest, the clerk decided to call on the suite occupied by Mr. and Mrs. Tate personally. After several knocks, a disheveled Lamar Tate answered the door while still wrapping his robe.

"Please forgive my intrusion, but I am in urgent need of locating Mr. John Earl Terry."

"What the hell makes you think he's here? Why, I wouldn't give that son of a bitch the time of day, much less invite him to my room."

"My apologies, Mr. Tate. The man's wife has been taken to the hospital, and he must be found. Her condition is grave, and since Mr. McCallister mentioned that you spent the evening together at the French Room..."

"My wife danced with the man. Come in, and I'll see if she heard him mention any plans." He stepped back for the Adolphus employee to enter.

"Sorry to bite your head off; I wake up pretty much an old grouch." Tate added in his own defense. "I had no way of knowin' about the man's wife."

He knocked softly at first, his force increasing as Estelle's door remained closed. "Estelle, honey, I got to check something." Switching on the overhead light, Tate felt assured of the whereabouts of John Earl Terry.

Returning to the clerk, Lamar saved other party-goers their night's sleep. "You need to know where Terry is? He's with my wife!" Pushing the embarrassed employee out the door he added. "You better get there first, cause if I find 'um, I'll kill 'um both."

The door slammed.

A matter such as this most assuredly extended beyond the authority of a late night clerk; it was now time to notify the manager of the Adolphus Hotel.

Having emptied the contents of John Earl's liquor stash, Cale considered his obligation to Terry completed. *You're as guilty of killin' Elaine as if you'd taken out a gun. As far as me waitin' around to break the news all gentle like, hell, you don't deserve the courtesy.* On his way to join Mavis at the hospital, Cale encountered the clerk.

"Any luck?"

With the imaginary headlines of a double murder at the Adolphus, the clerk related his concerns about the volatile Oklahomian. Clearing his throat, "The Adolphus has its good name to consider; should word of the indiscretions of our guests...You must understand that I am not a rumor monger and closely respect the privacy of the Adolphus' clientele..."

"Say what you got to say and cut the bullshit."

"I seem to recall that Mrs. Tate stopped by the desk. She asked for any messages, and I removed the only one, that being the note I placed in her box not thirty minutes before at the request of a gentleman."

"What'd he look like?" Cale inquired, already sure of the reply.

"Dark hair, mustache, wearing a white tie and tails."

"Damn! Do you know what it said?"

"Certainly not, Sir. The Adolphus is not in the practice of invading the privacy of its guests." The indignant clerk started from behind the desk. From one of the decorative ash cans placed throughout the lobby, he retrieved the wadded house stationery which he placed on the desk near Cale. Absolving himself, the clerk left Cale to his own devices.

Unfolding the message, he abandoned the languid elevator to run the five flights to the room number scribbled by a familiar hand. Pounding the door brought no response.

"John Earl, I know you're in there. Open this door before I wake up all of Dallas."

Cale continued his barrage until a drowsy Estelle peered from a small breach. "You're going to have to sober up, Mr. McCallister. You seem to have gotten our room mixed up with the Terry's." In the split second she removed her eyes to close the door, Cale secured a grip and burst into the room. The force of his entry sent Estelle backward onto the bed with a shriek of surprise and fear.

"Where is he?" Cale addressed the scampering woman clad in a one-piece silk undergarment.

"I told you, this is..."

"You under the bed or in the closet?" Cale raised his voice to a level sure to penetrate into the next several rooms. "If you give a damn," Cale appraised the woman who by this time had managed to place the bed between herself and the out-of-control Cale, "and I guess it's pretty clear you don't, your wife's dyin'."

Stopping at the door, his hand upon the brass knob, he added. "I wish to hell I'd let Carmichael slit your throat with that mill file."

Chapter 10

Pup hurried down the aisle for an impromptu meeting of the Brophy Boys, Inc. being held on the front pews of the New Jerusalem Church. Fresh from his triumph over Mr. Donald Mayfield, the attorney for the Texas League, Pup's spikes never touched the ground. He replayed the scene as he drove to the church.

"You can hardly expect," Mayfield's tone bordered on sarcasm, "for established League teams to play against this bunch of oil field hands you have impersonating baseball players."

"Just cause they know what it means to work for a livin' don't mean they can't play with more skill and enthusiasm than any players in the League. Take a look at what I'm proposin'." He pointed to blueprints of a modern ballpark complete with restrooms, concession areas, tiered seating, and lights being built on the site of the new junior college. "All we want is a chance at an abbreviated schedule of exhibition games, then when my stadium's done, we'll meet all franchise requirements."

"I speak for the League when I say that your proposal is impossible. It takes months, if not years, of planning to successfully introduce a new franchise." He rose to leave.

"I hear the Depression's hit the League smack in its hip pocket. You got teams shiftin' cities lookin' for enough support to stay afloat while others are throwin' up floodlights to attract more payin' customers than bugs." Pup pushed a chair toward the League attorney. "You need me, cause I got the one thing the rest of your owners is short on."

"That being?"

"Ready cash, enough to pay the expenses of each team, includin' salaries of the players, to come to Kilgore for a game a piece against my boys. And if we don't make a presentable showin', then I back out with no hard feelins'. If not, the Kilgore Wildcatters get a full franchise in 1932. Now you tell me what the League's got to lose?" He pushed a contract toward the attorney who accepted it begrudgingly. The player/owner was in business.

"When are you gonna quit actin' like a over growed kid?" John Earl asked in reference to Pup's uniform.

"Bout the same time you start actin' like a husband." Pup spit back. As most of East Texas, Pup did little to disguise his disgust for John Earl, tempered only by Elaine's subsequent recovery and Clyde's frequent avowal that Elaine was ending the marriage.

"We ain't got time for this," Bulldog had a firm grip on John Earl to prevent him from initiating a fight right in front of God and everybody. "There's more important fish to fry."

Eyes boring through the driller's son, Terry reclaimed his seat.

"Dagnabbit," Bulldog addressed his complaint to Willie, mindful of his presence in a house of worship. "Can't you talk some sense into these Christians?"

"You don't understands. The Reverend Ezekiel done 'cided that a well smack in front of the new sanctuary is advertisin' that the devil done got hold of our souls by courtin' us with the root of all evil."

Pup's comment amused all but the church's deacon.

"But he don't mind Him supplyin' a little liquid temptation as long as Ole Lucifer does his pumpin' at the back door." Referring to the New Jerusalem #1, the Boys' third well and a tidy producer for the partners and the flock, he stuck his thumb into the air as if begging for a ride in order to call attention to the sounds of it pumps. It was the royalties from the well funding the construction of a new building to replace the clapboard structure in which the Boys now sat. Under the Reverend Mims' auspices, the New Jerusalem would be a modern rival of Solomon's famed tribute.

According to the plans, both wells would be required to keep up with the Israelites of old. Tucked safely behind, the New Jerusalem #1 would not be visible from the street; however, #2, spudded prior to the Reverend's vision of an East Texas temple, sat directly in front of and between the temple gates and the road.

"We're willin' to pay for the loss of what's done invested in #2," Reverend Mims' offered.

"You're damn right." John Earl interrupted. "And just how much are you figurin' for the time lost that could have been used to bring in another well?"

He pointed accusingly at his partners. "Not a one of you can guarantee this field won't be dried up tomorrow and us with it. And with this Proration nonsense, we need every well producin' before our beloved Governor sells our collective asses down the river."

Proration, the government's attempt at limiting the production of individual wells to prevent the rapid drop in oil prices, had East Texas' majors and independents divided as to its wisdom.

"At best," Bulldog mused, "Proration will stabilize the price of crude."

"And at worst, oilmen will have the number of barrels we can pump regulated by tight-assed bureaucrats that don't know nothin' about oil," snapped John Earl.

Clyde interjected, "I read again this mornin' how the Railroad Commission that calls itself overseein' the oil industry might go to strict enforcement of Rule 37."

"That'll mean no drillin' within three hundred feet of existin' wells and one hundred fifty feet of property lines," added Cale.

Currently, Rule 37, for all practical purposes, did not exist in the East Texas Field due to the issuing of "exceptions" originally aimed at boosting the Depression-starved economy.

Among the Boys John Earl stood alone against Proration for his right to pump whatever flowed beneath their leases as rapidly as possible, no matter how low the price. To Terry volume spelled profits. "I still say that if somebody's gonna be makin' money out of this field that we helped discover, it damn sure ought to be our bank accounts takin' on numbers."

Had the Terry marriage been different, perhaps the Boys might have shared John Earl's view. As things stood, the partners, consciously or not, made symbolic stands against John Earl. Still they could not break the strangle hold Terry's drive and forcefulness had on the partnership; such intimidation and dependency kept the Boys from permanently cutting their ties.

"Now who's to say we can get an exception on this lease?" Receiving no answer he pushed on. Then the only choice we got is to skid the derrick just outta sight but still be on the same exception." His booming voice lifted the sagging rafters of the church in a manner even the Reverend Ezekiel failed to achieve. "Come on, Cale, we're gonna hire us a shooter before the Christians take to breakin' any more of their promises."

Cale looked helplessly at his partners before trailing after Terry. "If we're not bringin' her in, what use have we got for a shooter?"

John Earl stopped abruptly, his vexation released on Cale. 'I swear, I keep thinkin' you've got to catch on to this business some day or other, but damn if you don't keep disappointin' me right on down the line. Man, we got casin' cemented in that hole we can salvage for another well, not that I intend on cuttin' the price the holy band is puttin' back in our account."

"I'm savvy enough to know nobody with horse sense is shootin' a well this close to bein' brought in."

"They do wells every day that's dry holes or been wrung sluggish. What's the difference?"

Cale ran ahead of Terry who was almost to his car. "The difference is, a man's puttin' his life on the line, not sure of how much soup to use cause he don't know about what's down there. Only this is East Texas, and there's proof positive that there's oil and gas down that hole close enough to blow him to hell and back."

"He's right," Bulldog's appearance and confirmation of Cale's assessment hit Terry hard.

"Fine. Lose the money, but don't cry to me when your profits are down." From the church's dilapidated porch, the rest of the Boys watched as gravel sprayed.

"Bein' rich ain't mellowed him none," Pup observed. "If anything, he's got worse."

Racing through town, Terry's chosen path took him beside the tent city just outside the posted limits of his recommended restrictions aimed at keeping Brophy free of such settlements. The city teemed with workers, the backbone of the oil boom's labor force, and their families.

Several acres of tents, makeshift structures of cardboard boxes suspended from anything stationary, and vehicles doubling as homes stretched into a neighborhood formed of necessity rather than poverty. In every direction, children of various ages played, blissfully unaware of the hardships they endured in order that their fathers and older brothers could earn their wages.

From the flaps of a patched tent weakened by the rains Melba Aiken peered at the passing line of automobiles. Catching a glimpse of a woman behind the wheel of a brand new roadster, she sighed. *Another lucky farmer's wife whose fortune fell into her lap. Some folks have nothin' but good luck. While some folks,* she looked at her roughened hands, *don't.* As she finished sweeping the mismatched boards rustled up by her man of twenty-five years, *At least I got these to be thankful for, what with folks and animals mirin' up with every step in this ankle-deep mud, these could be lost in the muck like the ones the city keeps puttin' down on what's substitutin' as streets around here. I'd say, given the rain and this mud, East Texas takes top prize as the worst place Ray has drug us. But one thing's to be said in common about oil towns, they educate the kids right, and I've seen enough to know.*

Only the napping Joe Ray, barely three, required her time. At ages eleven and nine, Billy and Violet went to the temporary sites which housed the elementary children while the high schoolers traveled to Kilgore until the Brophy School was ready. She birthed six Aiken youngsters, eight if you counted the two born dead, the oldest scattered across Texas and Oklahoma at towns that once boomed like Kilgore and Brophy. An older daughter lived in California with her Navy husband and a grand boy she never laid eyes on.

Melba turned from the road taking folks to destinations near and far. *At this rate, I won't see that boy until he's in school hisself.* She opened a battered suitcase slid beneath the cot upon which Joe Ray slept. Unknown to her husband, the valise served as the hiding place for her nest egg earmarked for a trip to California. Counting the money, she returned the bills. *If only Ray would just agree to me gettin' a job. There's plenty of women willin' to watch kids, and with what wages are in cafes, I could be on my way to California in no time. But not my Ray, stubborn old goat. Stuck with the first job come his way so's we wouldn't have to live with the folks, knowin' all along that the most dangerous job in a oil field's a shooter.*

Restless, Melba walked to the flap. Loaded from roof to rear, a V-8 Ford passed. Mattresses strapped to the roof with rusty bailing wire and hemp padded the rides of cardboard boxes of dishes and household goods. Fastened to the back end, road-weary suitcases two deep held on for dear life, and from each window a child hung, as a second fought for room and a glimpse of what now would be home.

Shaking her head, Melba donned her shawl and drew a crate to the single step that led to the tent. Lois Ann Warren, her closest friend since arriving in Brophy, maneuvered the few feet of mud that separated their tents.

She's so much like Melba Sue, the older woman thought. Not that you favor, but I can see my girl all that way in California, pregnant and no family to lean on. Maybe that's why I taken to this eighteen-year-old that calls herself a woman. An oil camp's a lonely place with a baby comin', and where a husband's time at home is as scarce as a rent house.

Rising to help her overturn a wash tub, Melba padded the chair with a quilt. Lois Ann was already talking a blue streak.

"Did you see that last car? You know who that was? That was Mrs. Mavis McCallister, the wife of one of them men they call the Brophy Boys. "She's rich as sin, and Lucille told me her family runs one of the finest restaurants in Missouri."

"Now that's a line of bull. She come from no more than the rest of us. Just had the good sense, fortune, or both to marry a man what hit it big."

"Arnell's gonna hit it big someday."

Melba hadn't the heart to speak her thoughts.

If the Good Lord smiles on you, Arnell will keep food on the table and a roof over your heads that don't beat rhythm with every gust that passes. In an oil field a tank cleaner is just one step above nothin', and the step ain't much of a fall. Little girl, it takes a special brand of fool to willingly climb into those fifty-five and eighty thousand barrel storage tanks alive with gas fumes just for the pleasure of removin' the built up sludge and water. Just watchin' men open up and go into tank vents makes my skin crawl when a single spark from a light cord could explode the tank and set everything inside afire. Course good companies furnish lights run on batteries, but can't nobody protect from slippin' in the sludge nor passin' out from the fumes. Either way, he's a dead man. Never mind that the sludge hardly reaches a man's knees, but a fall most naturally gets him to want to wipe his face, knowin' all along the ooze is gonna stick in his nose and mouth. Some of the bigger operations just let one man in at a time and let the tanks air out good. But Arnell's got to hire on for Mr. Terry who wants tanks shut down as little time as possible.

"I said, did you hear what happened?"

Melba returned to her guest.

Lois Ann continued, having regained Melba's attention.

"One of Arnell's buddies slipped in the tank; took all Arnell could do to pull him out before he smothered, and that boy fightin' him every step of the way. Somehow they got air goin' in him, but Arnell says he could end up daft like the one Mr. Terry paid some boys to take back to his home in Nacogdoches with five hundred dollars in his pocket."

Maybe that's what keeps oil field women so close, the fact that the next accident can claim your man as quick as it can your friend's. She began to think about Ray and the danger she gave up frettin' over years before. *The longer a man works with soup, the more respectful of the explosive he gets.*

As Ray explained, "A man on a crew's at the mercy of a boss man, where a shooter, even if he works for a major, nobody messes with nor questions about his reasonin' about what jobs they take or refuse. It's hard to argue with a man totin' nitro."

Melba could still see the padded up car honking its way through a boom town those many years ago, scattering folks like chickens when they saw the red letters "SOUP WAGON." You were a looker back then, struttin' your wages, buyin' drinks and courtin' the girls. How Daddy fought me about you. He liked you well enough, but he couldn't cotton to his daughter marryin' a man most likely to be blowed into too few pieces to bury and no pension to support his kids.

Looking at Lois Ann, "I got to get movin' on supper. Ray says he's gonna be home early; the kids got a little program over to the school. I hope he won't disappoint 'um."

〰〰〰〰〰

Despite a callused life of poker-faced scams and staying two jumps ahead of a mark, the gooseflesh prickled John Earl's arms. Scaling a rig or hopping a freight left a man little time to contemplate the folly; walking toward a shooter's shack afforded more than he could stomach.

Harmless at first notice, the renovated cow shed now tightly enclosed sat isolated on a few acres. For twenty feet on any side, the land was devoid of trees or grass whose potential combustibility might lead to an explosion capable of leveling a goodly portion of the area and result in a domino effect of well fires. The signs facing each direction warned, "DANGER."

Damn, I wish he'd come on out. I don't dare honk or knock. Sudden start like that if he's pourin' nitro into one of them cans... just a single drop fallin'. He shuddered.

After a good half hour, a wirily-built man emerged. About fifty-five, too old and too small for a laborer, spent more time inside than out. *That'd be a shooter.* John Earl watched him. *I knowed plenty of your kind; trusted few. Pourin' nitro wears away at a man's nerves and to seekin' the calm of a whiskey bottle. Old as you are, the hands have to be shaky.* Now obvious were the reddened eyes to confirm Terry's estimation, yet the sureness of speech and the laggard but stable stride sent a contradictory message John Earl failed to attribute to a lack of sleep. *But you're all I got.*

"What's to do for you? Name's Aiken, Ray Aiken."

With the extended hand came, "John Earl Terry."

At the mention of the name Ray took notice like a front-porch dog roused from sleep at an unfamiliar sound. "I've heard of you." He said aloud while his mind added, *Hell, who hasn't? If the stories circulatin' about you are half true, you're as crooked, conivin' a son of a bitch as your partners are straight. I bet it keeps two of 'um workin' full time just keepin' your nose wiped clean.*

"Got a sluggish well?" Ray chided himself for such a blunder. New fields didn't need the sand around the hole blasted so that more oil could fill in and increase the volume. Most likely he needs a production shoot. He's just the type afraid somebody else's well tappin' the same pool will cheat him out of a dollar. Better to blow his own hole larger and pay a shooter for the trouble so that more oil will collect. Either way, it's money in my pocket.

"Need some casin' broke."

Aiken's interest waned as Terry made his offer. "Sorry, Mr. Terry. I been workin' day and night helpin' out over to the Van Field. They got notions their wells is laggin' and want 'um blowed to keep up with you boys. See me in a couple of days, a week maybe. Your pipe ain't goin' nowhere."

"Don't waste my time by tryin' to drive up the price."

Under normal circumstances, Ray might have let Terry's insult slide, but a pot like his calling the kettle black sent Ray nearer his soup wagon.

"Where the hell you goin'? I ain't through talkin' here."

"That's where you're wrong; I'm headed home." As he reached for the door handle, John Earl staked his claim.

"All right, so there's boys standin' in line to ask you to dance. I can pay you double the rate, and don't tell me nobody's offerin' you that."

He's got me there. Time might be days with no offers; and what an extra check could buy. Melba's face appeared wearing that far off look she got each time she gazed at the grand youngun's picture. Extra money ought to be spent like the gift it is.

"Tomorrow then," said Ray.

"Now."

He didn't care what carrot Terry dangled in his face. The irritation seeped into his voice. "I'm dog tired, no good to either one of us." By this time he was in his car, addressing Terry from the opened window. "Tomorrow, I swear."

Somehow the pipe's worth vanished, replaced by an unanswered defiance of John Earl's will. Poor men were put off; rich ones got what they wanted when the mood struck. "Livin' in the tents, I'll wager."

"You can find me here, same time tomorrow."

"Suppose I could locate a rent house?"

Aiken killed the idling motor. "Better not be no dump."

Though he hadn't a clue as to the availability of a house, John Earl refused to allow such triviality to prevent him from having his way.

"You sure no one's workin' on that well to get in my way?"

"Deserted as a saloon on election day."

Slowly, Ray left his car, trudging toward his shed, while John Earl basked in his triumph. A moment later he left to give the watchman the rest of the night off.

Ray removed two separate keys from his khaki pocket. Once inside, he secured the door with the second. *Room still seems cool enough. Come summer, I'll keep less of the stuff around and buy some big fans, or, if the weather gets as hot as locals promise, I'll have to get ice. Nitro just ain't safe when it hits the nineties.*

Going on Terry's say, the shooter calculated his shot. *Small job like this, better use jelly rather than soup.* Packed in cylindrical cartridges, the term "jelly" was a perfect description of the more solidified form of nitroglycerin. *At least I don't have to do no pourin' tired as I am tonight; it's a tough job for a rested man to hit the funnel.*

Raising the lid of the steel box permanently affixed in the back of the soup wagon exposed a red felt lining. Unseen, a layer of asbestos provided more protection, lest the nitro become displeased with its chauffeur's skills on a rough road. Cut into the box were cylindrical "boots" into which the copper soup cans fit. For the jelly, similar inserts awaited. Contents loaded, Ray again locked his shed for the security of residents. In his experience, nobody ever stole nitro.

By the time he arrived at the well, clouds hung low to the ground in the ominous configuration of a Texas thunderstorm. The wind whipped over the drilling floor with sufficient strength to force angry protests from the rig; the smell of rain permeated his nostrils. *Just what we need; more damned mud.* With the hour and the thickening clouds separating the sun from the East Texas Field, Ray strung a series of lamps to illuminate his work area. Normally he shied away from inviting sparks from lighting not already in place, but his self-imposed isolation left him without so much as a watchman to light the rig. *Melba's gonna be so surprised when she hears the news. On her way to California and a house to come back to.*

As he prepared his shooting line, checking and rechecking the firing pin at the top of the jelly's shell, Ray became aware of a sudden change in the weather. An abated wind responsible for the eerie stillness brought him to his feet. Rumblings overhead and the subsequent fire cracking of lightening sent him scrambling to retrieve the jelly and head for the shelter of the soup wagon. Shells in hand he started for the rig steps as the lightning struck the metal rig and traveled downward until it reached his makeshift lighting. As the electricity surged, sparks flew from the lamps, detonating the nitro.

Explosions in the field caused immediate shut downs; roughnecks called for the location to send their off duty tours to prevent or fight well fires. At the Brophy Boys' headquarters, the offices cleared as everyone took to the street in the direction of the flaming New Jerusalem Church.

~~~~~~~~

In the reception area immediately outside the office of the chief executive of Oklahoma Oil, David Carmichael failed to appreciate his aesthetic surroundings. The ash tray brimmed with evidence of his insecurity and the length of his stay. Patience had never been his strong suit, and an extended wait for the ax to fall did little to quiet his nerves. *It's the only reason the Old Man wants to see me. It sure as hell isn't to give me a promotion.*

Thinking back to their last encounter when he had to own up to the purchase of the East Texas leases, he shudderd in anticipation of what would undoubtedly prove a repeat of the same brand of fury. *He can't demote me any further, so why the hell am I staying to take this?* Carmichael grasped the gold-plated knob just as the secretary called.

"Mr. Tate is free now."

Embarrassed to turn tail and run, Carmichael began a slow trek into the lion's den with a nervous smile for the woman who held the oak door. Standing in front of a massive desk, Carmichael shifted from one foot to the other as Lamar Tate hung up the phone.

"Sit down," he ordered. Settled into the leather chair, Carmichael's mouth gaped as he refused the contents of Tate's monogrammed cigar box.

"They're Havana's, boy. You're not likely to get many of these on what I pay you." Confused by what amounted to amiability from Tate, Carmichael twisted uneasily.

"I don't often admit mistakes," began Tate.

As Tate pulled in an effort to light his cigar, the younger man's thoughts raced. *He's giving me my job back. No, the way those leases paid off, I'm going to be right here in the executive offices.* Carmichael's thoughts were interrupted by Tate.

"But this time I got no other choice."

"I truly understood your reaction, Sir. I berated myself pretty strongly when I realized..."

"What the hell you babblin' about? I'm talkin' about that slut I married."*Now he's accusing me of carryin on with his wife!*

Carmichael's face fell. "I didn't...that is to say I don't understand... well, I can understand, but..."

"Shut up!" Tate's voice returned to its usual authority until the desire to see his plan to fruition regained control. "I'm sorry, son, but this whole business has me hog tied." Smoke curled around his head as he leaned back in his overstuffed chair. "Wish I never married her; did my thinkin' from the waist down." He blew a puff of smoke so thick that Carmichael began to cough, pulling in more of the sickening scent and sending his head spinning. "Divorce is out of the question."

"Of course." Carmichael had no idea why.

"Glad you see the folly in it. And hangins' too good. That's why I decided to kill two birds with one stone. Ever done any bird huntin'?"

"Sir?"

"I want you to make a little trip down to East Texas with the misses and me."

Confusion reigned.

Tate smiled. "You and me both got a score to settle with a Mr. John Earl Terry."

Carmichael's hand flew to the scar.

"Now here's what I got planned. Since he and that tramp can't keep their hands off one another, I want you to let me know when and where they're together."

"You want me to follow them?"

"No, boy, I want you to reserve the damn hotel room and charge the champagne to me. Hell yes, I want you to follow 'um."

"But Mr. Tate, why would you want to know that your wife..." his voiced trailed.

"You married?"

"No, Sir."

"Maybe you got the sense to answer. What would you do if you caught your wife in bed with another man?"

"I'd shoot them both, but..."

"Exactly. And the law gives a husband the right so long as they're in the act." Tate was ushering Carmichael out the door.

"Uh, Mr. Tate, if I help you with this, Sir, could I have my old job back?" he asked with hesitation.

A slap on the back sent him reeling. "Son, I'll make you one of my right hand ass kissers."

The explosion brought Melba to the tent flap with the children shoving for a look at the thick cloud of black smoke billowing into the equally dark clouds. Melba knew instinctively that Ray was gone. Sheets of rain splattered her face.

"Get back in, Momma. You're gettin' all wet."

The children no longer mattered, nor the rain, nor the throng of frantic men and women. On her knees she felt the mud inch up her legs and cover her skirt.

What am I gonna do? Bent forward at the waist, she cried into her lap.

Those first at the scene recognized the soup wagon and called themselves searching for the body of the shooter, but abandoned the futile motions for the meaningful task of extinguishing the fire now threatening the New Jerusalem #1.

As the partners arrived, Bulldog took charge, asking questions until he satisfied himself and returned to the Boys soon after the fire was out. "Salvage anything?" he asked Willie.

"Weren't nothin' in that old church worth a man's life to save." He looked into the clearing sky and the now visible stars. "The

Lord's provided us with the means of a new church; we gots no call to be sorry."

"That's not the way I see it. Mother nature helped him along, but a shooter caused this," informed Bulldog.

Cale dismissed the theory. "We didn't agree on no shooter. Don't you remember, we told John Earl... Damn him, he's gone and got one anyway."

Cale looked at the tangled steel and the smoldering church. *A man's lost his life so we can keep a little more money on the Brophy Boys' ledger, and after we told John Earl we were against it. Mavis and I were able to save Elaine, but for this man...I've cleaned up after John Earl for the last time.*

He addressed the partners. "I can't presume to speak for the rest of you, but I can't keep workin' with a man I don't trust, one who throws away lives like they was nothin'. Now, it's no reflection on you. I hope to God you know me better, but I want out. I can't keep makin' money if it has to be done like this." He gestured toward the ruins.

Cale hung his head as he awaited a reply. *Mavis is gonna pitch a fit, but I have some principles left, a pitiful few since I met up with John Earl Terry,* he admitted to himself.

"If you'll have me, I wants to stay with you," Cale raised his eyes gratefully to Willie.

"This is crazy. What's the use of us givin' up when it's John Earl that's to blame?" Pup started for his car. "I'm gettin' Steven's legal butt in gear. I want the papers tonight; we're buyin' John Earl out in the mornin'," taking their lack of argument as a formal partnership vote.

John Earl rolled over for the millionth time. Swinging his feet to the side of the bed, he reached to the night stand and lit a cigarette. He hated being robbed of a good night's sleep, not by a conscience which vanished somewhere outside

Navarro County, but a failure to provide a plausible excuse for coming out of a mess smelling like the proverbial rose.

He could hear Elaine banging around in the kitchen. Living at Clyde's was more than awkward, but finding a decent place to live made the cold shoulders endurable, especially if he stayed out as late as possible. *Think I'll go face the little woman. Likely as not, she'll start in on the divorce. For as much as I'm payin' that hot shot bookkeepin' boy out of San Antonio, he could hurry up disguisin' my above and below board assets. There's no way I can keep her out of some of the Brophy Boys money, but what I made on the side, now, that's mine one hundred percent.*

After putting on yesterday's pants, he walked into a kitchen littered with picnic and laundry baskets brimming with freshly cooked and canned foods.

"What's all this?"

Elaine continued removing chicken from the iron skillet. "I'm taking this to the family of the man who died last night."

"Who said you needed to do that?"

After turning a piece over in a bowl of flour, she placed it in the bubbling grease. "The man died in our employ; it's the very least we can do."

Exasperated, he snapped, "How many times I got to tell folks, he didn't work for us. Hell, I don't know what got him mixed up enough to go to the wrong well."

"Mavis said you sent him out to salvage pipe," she faced him straight on for the first time, "against the votes of the others."

"Mavis don't know nothin' but what Cale tells her, and that means she don't know her ass from a hole in the ground. A man who's been a shooter as long as he had hits the bottle pretty regular to keep up the guts to pour soup. My notion is he drank hisself up and got confused. He ain't been around more than a few weeks. So you do somethin' else with all this. The Brophy Boys got nothin' to do with that man gettin' hisself blowed up."

"I'm going."

Set to throw the whole mess in the backyard, John Earl rethought, aware of Elaine's hands wrapped around a doubled kitchen towel and the handle of the iron skillet. The glare in her eyes told him of her intentions if he pushed too far.

"Do whatever your little heart desires, my love. I'm going to a cafe where a man can get a decent breakfast."

Passing through the parlor, he responded to the knock at the front door. Callers at such an early hour were not unusual given the number of wells and constant breakdowns. John Earl opened the door to face Lone Wolf Gonzaullas, the one man capable of striking a note of fear in Terry's heart.

At the urging of Mayor Malcom Crim, the Texas Ranger came to Kilgore and the surrounding towns to quell the criminal element that migrated toward the boom. A veteran of previous strikes, the Ranger spent a couple of weeks in the guise of a boomer until he became familiar with the vice of Newton Flats, Pistol Hill, and the honkey tonks scattered about the Field.

Ready to make his presence known, Sergeant Manuel T. Gonzaullas rode astride, Tony, his black stallion, arrayed in Ranger regalia from his Stetson down to twin pearl-handled revolvers. A product of a more technological age, his saddle holster housed an automatic rifle. In the tradition of his breed, the one job required only a single Ranger.

John Earl happened to be in the barber shop at the Kilgore Hotel that next morning when the ruckus started. He and the barber hit the street in time to see close to three hundred criminals marched to a Baptist Church turned temporary jail. On-lookers peered in vandalized windows to watch a chain run the length of the sanctuary and bolted to the wall. Smaller versions emanated to encircle the necks of those arrested before a padlock secured their stay on "Lone Wolf's Trotline."

"Makes Sheriff Jake's box car look like Sunday School," Terry was overheard to say.

A few days in the confines of the neck chain and passing a tin cup urinal left a man with no choice than to accept the Ranger's offer of release, provided he left town in four hours.

"Here to check my hands?"

John Earl turned his palms up for the characteristic inspection applied to any man who roused the Ranger's suspicions.

Should the hand not bear the signs of an oil field worker, the stranger became another catch on the trotline until Lone Wolf could verify a purpose in town.

"Come to talk to you about the accident down at New Jerusalem."

Terry moved to allow entrance. Even with his Stetson removed, Gonzaullas monopolized a room. He awaited an offer to sit when Elaine entered.

"Mrs. Terry," he bowed his head slightly in respect of the lady of the house.

"Ranger Gonzaullas, please take a seat. May I get you some coffee?"

"No thank you, Ma'am."

"I'll take a cup."

Elaine ignored the request by sitting in Clyde's chair.

"I talked to the rest of the Boys last night. Noticed you weren't around. Folks tell me that's not usual, you bein' concerned about the wells to a fault."

"I was at home with my wife. She's still recoverin' from our loss."

Infuriated by the use of her miscarriage, "Why, I didn't realize you were here."

"You were already asleep."

The Ranger's sly eye fell upon Elaine.

"I wasn't asleep that early," addressing the Ranger. "Only my son kept me from going to the fire."

"So John Earl was gone, you say?"

"I was in bed, Lone Wolf. Since Elaine lost the baby, I've been spendin' nights in the guest room. I called around the minute I heard; figured one more car and man couldn't help. My partners was there, so I stayed in bed."

"Did you go in to check on him?"

"No," Elaine admitted begrudgingly.

"Are you callin' on every citizen that didn't register at the fire?" Terry said trying to put the sheriff on the defensive.

"Just the ones that had need of a shooter and owned the well where one died."

"I got other partners," he volleyed.

"As I said, talked to them last night. That's how I found out you were the only one wanted a shooter."

"I don't make it a practice to go against the group, part of the reason we're so successful."

"So I hear." The Ranger started toward the door, "Thank you for your time."

Lone Wolf let himself out.

Before getting into the car, he pushed the butt of the mounted automatic rifle that protruded from the windshield.

I seen your kind every day since I put on this badge, Terry. You don't fool me for a minute. You sent that man, but that ain't no crime. You'll get yours some day; I'll see to it personal.

Elaine stowed the last basket into the car when the Boys pulled up. Giving each a hug, she judged the seriousness of their business by a lack of conversation.

"He still here?" asked Bulldog.

"Far as I know. Lone Wolf just left."

The boys stepped onto the porch as Elaine got behind the wheel. Without knocking the Boys entered to face Terry, finally in possession of his sought-after coffee.

"Come right on in," his offer laden with sarcasm.

Cale threw the cashier's check into John Earl's lap.

"What is this?" He searched their faces. "This is a lot of money to be tossin' around."

"We're buyin' you out," Cale declared emphatically.

As the disbelief became reality, Terry glared. "You can't do this. Hoyt ain't due back for a while yet. I read all that legal bullshit even if you boys didn't. Takes a unanimous vote to dissolve this partnership."

Clyde removed a cablegram from his suit pocket and began reading, "I, Hoyt LaGuinn, hereby vote in favor of the dissolution of the partnership known as the Brophy Boys, Inc. Furthermore, I agree to a reorganization under the same name with Willie Bacon; Clyde Russell; Cale McCallister; Norman Schneider, Sr.; and Norman Schneider, Jr. It's signed Hoyt LaGuinn."

"What the hell are you tryin' to do?"

"Work with people we can trust not to go behind our backs and smear our names with the blood of innocent folks."

"So that's it? Well, I didn't send no shooter. Don't know what I got to do to convince the rest of East Texas."

"Just sign," Bulldog pulled a fountain pen out of his overalls.

"You boys are gonna regret this," he vowed. "I made this strike and took you all along for the ride. Remember, it was me who come here with the map? You was all damned lucky I stopped at that two-bit store or you'd still be just what I found the day I rolled into town."

He pointed his finger at each in turn as he hurled his words meant to pierce their collective resolve with the truth he so seldom employed. "A farm boy turned gas pumper with a bastard baby in a waitress' belly, a Depression-starved banker one step shy of closin' the doors, a whiskey-soaked driller on a company payroll with a son destined for Daddy's footsteps, a colored clean up boy, and a fat-assed old bootlegger. You can cable that back to Mr. signed Hoyt LaGuinn."

He signed; the scratching of the pen echoed. Thrusting them at Bulldog, he warned them all. "Don't you never relax your guard, cause John Earl'll be sneakin' up your backsides."

Clyde added as the Boys took their leave, "By the time Elaine returns, I want you out of my home. Don't know what you got over her that's keepin' my daughter from filin' that divorce, but I don't have to house you another day."

"The hell with all of you," he screamed.

Chapter 11

Elaine forced her car through the ruts of the tent city until she came to a tent more crowded than the others. As she killed the motor, she experienced the starkness of rag town life. Clothes lines hung closely to the ground, draped with washing saved for the rare sunny day the sky seemed to promise. Scattered about, oil barrels cut by torches doubled as cradles, storage, and makeshift seating. Stepping from the car, Elaine jumped back with a high-pitched scream escaping as a rat lumbered across the small expanse uncluttered by some element of tent city living. Her resolve mustered, she grasped a basket. A woman whose gray hair fell in errant strands came to her rescue.

"My name is Elaine Terry; I've come to bring some food to the Aiken family."

"Melba will take kindly to that."

Elaine waited for her to claim a hamper before allowing the woman the lead. Balancing herself and the load of food proved tricky as they walked the boards placed over the mud. Their combined weights caused the planks to slide Elaine into the mire several times as they made the trips necessary to unload. The woman motioned toward the tent flap.

"But my shoes are so muddy."

"We all take off our shoes."

Elaine noticed a row of mud-caked shoes lined on a board set inside a barrel trough. Underneath the board a pool of crude confused the outsider.

"Keeps ants out of 'um; them critters don't take to oil."

Elaine placed her shoes alongside the others before entering the tent. Her initial impression was of the cleanliness. Six or seven women sat on the made up cots or cane-bottomed chairs stacked two deep to accommodate those paying respects. She felt immediately uncomfortable, as if on display. Those behind her whispered. Though Elaine could not hear, they discussed her clothing and whatever gossip each knew about the wife of John Earl Terry. A deep flush began at her neck.

Her guide took her to the middle-aged woman on the cot. At her side a noticeably pregnant woman Elaine assumed to be a daughter provided a possessive, comforting arm. Conversations ceased as Elaine stood before them.

"This here's Miz Terry," she spoke as if addressing a child. "She's the one what brung you so many baskets of food stuffs that it put my back plumb out totin'."

Melba Aiken looked at her benefactress. *Such a sweet face, and married to a man like that, she thought.*

"I wish there was more I could do for you. I honestly do," Elaine said.

"Thank you, you done enough if what Reba says is true. You just stoppin' by means a lot." Melba meant what she said. Recalling workers' deaths at other booms, *Never would the girls there believe that a woman like Mrs. Terry would stop by when a man died makin' their money. Even company town folks has always looked down on us, slightin' us to the point we can't even use no libraries for fear we'll move off with the books.*

"Please call on me if I can help." Elaine left to find Reba pulling up boards to reveal a hole lined in sawdust. In it she placed milk and eggs beside other perishables.

"Miz Terry? The pregnant woman stood on the single step, glancing back to assure Melba's distraction. "Can I have a little of your time?"

"Of course," Elaine moved toward the Aiken tent.

"No, over in mine."

The women balanced the planking to the second tent and sat before the woman began. "I'm Lois Ann Warren, Melba's friend, and she'd have my hide if she knowed what I was up to." Lois Ann twisted a handkerchief throughout her request. "Did you really mean what you said to her? Not just sayin' stuff to be nice?"

"I want to do whatever I can."

"Then I'm tellin', well, askin' you for what she needs. Melba's got three kids, none old enough to hold a job. There's an older girl out in California and two boys don't nobody know for sure where they's at to even tell them about their daddy. What's the truth is, she's flat busted."

"The company has no help?" Elaine's disbelief evident.

"Ma'am," Lois Ann leaned on the word until it took on extra syllables while she turned her head from side to side, "Ray was a shooter. He didn't work for no company; he did his soup pourin' independent. No need to tell a smart woman like yourself about what a danger nitro is. Insurance companies won't take on risks like that. Melba told me once that Ray tried to get one to take him on, but they wanted five hundred dollars a year." Lois Ann accentuated the incredulous sum. "Shooters can make good, when they work, but there's no guarantee of it comin' steady."

"She has no home to go to, some people where she grew up?" asked Elaine.

"No ma'am. You see, I wouldn't want Melba to know I told, but she's seein' the downside of her forties." Melba's age received a commensurate awe with the five hundred dollars. "So her kin is all dead and scattered. Besides, with this Depression, folks can't feed themselves, much less extras."

"I just assumed there was a home place."

"We oil field workers move with the jobs. Even if we settled, no banks makes loans to shooters; no guarantee they'll live to make the next mortgage payment. So you see, Miz Terry, if you want to help Melba, she needs a job."

Lois Ann was pleading.

Elaine thought for a moment and then asked.

"When is the funeral?"

"Ain't gonna be one; weren't enough found to put in no box."

"Tell her to come by my house as soon as she's up to it. I can't manage at home and at school no matter how hard I try. Jake, that's my son, can use a regular looking after; Mrs. Aiken can come to work for me. And if she can't find enough to keep her busy there, she can go over and help my friend. The poor woman has twins."

"Oh, thank you, Miz Terry. Melba's a hard worker."

Elaine prepared to leave, but Lois Ann caught her hand. "One more thing, camp folks generally takes up money to help bury the dead. Course Ray don't need no buryin', so we made up some money for Melba to pay off some bills they run up in town. She still needs fifteen dollars to pay off the doctor and the drug store from when Violet had the pneumonia."

"Tell me the names, and I'll see that they're paid."

Lois Ann walked Elaine to her car, throwing her arms around her as she opened the door. "You're an angel sent direct from heaven."

〰〰〰〰〰

"You think this is straight?" Pup asked a rather disinterested office of critics.

"It's just a letter in a frame," observed Hoyt.

Had he not been so euphoric, Pup might have challenged the understatement. "It's way more than a letter; it's a key to the dream I had since first pickin' up a bat and ball." He stepped back in admiration of the letter of approval of his plan. "After that game, we're a shoe in for a franchise."

Pup moved to a set of pictures from the parade he staged before the game against the Houston Buffs and their ace pitcher who called himself Dizzy Dean.

"You can see the excitement in the crowd as my players passed out those free concession coupons. Hell, half of East Texas paid to see my Wildcatters, and what a show they put on. What a show I put on," he corrected, recalling his game-winning home run.

Only one face in the crowd marred his happiness, a minor irritation, but one he could not control as easily as the Texas League's main office.

As if reading his mind, Hoyt teased, "Why don't you put up that one where the Franklin girl in her majorette suit is plantin' the winnin' kiss? Paper thought enough of it to run it front page, and you don't even have the decency to put it on the wall." He laughed deeply.

"This ain't funny. Damn, if she don't have a way of ferretin' me out that's nigh onto uncanny."

"Boy's right," agreed his father. A girl that young ain't nothin' but trouble."

"I told you what Mavis says," Cale added.

The others shook their heads. It was Bulldog who asked, "Exactly what does Mavis say?"

"Teenage girls swoon over athletes; soon as some fullback Senior catches her eye, you'll be a thing of the past."

"Well, it don't appear Kilgore High School's got much of a team. Now, she's gone and asked me to a school dance? Can't you see me, not that thirty is that old, at a high school dance?"

"You didn't accept?" Bulldog was outraged. "You know what kind of man her daddy is."

Even Hoyt was beginning to see Pup's dilemma.

"Edgar Franklin has always had the disposition of a mule, and now that he's got a bank account he don't have to worry none about improvin' it."

"Maybe he'll send his girl off to college," Cale's optimism was short lived.

"That old skinflint? The family is still livin' in that pitiful excuse for a house that's fallin' in around 'um."

"But with three Cadillacs sittin' out front. Still, when he came into my bank with his first royalty check, I watched him stuff it all in the bib of his overalls. So I asked him what he intended to buy in celebration. Know what he said, an extra plug of tobacco. Nope, it ain't likely the girl's goin' off to no finishin' school."

Hoyt finished the conversation with a warning, "The old man's as mean as they come; watch your step, Pup."

Bulldog continued to chew on the butt of an unlit cigar while staring out the window at the bustle of activity on the main street. The driller's laughter distracted the Boys from the paperwork that called them to the office.

"What'd you see," Cale joined the driller in fear that Mavis might be at fault. Try as she might, Elaine's lessons in gentility failed to penetrate the red head.

"Nothin', just thinkin' about the fire yesterday at the theater. The others joined in.

"Wish I could have seen the faces of them folks who ran like rabbits when the smoke drifted in. I told that boy to burn the trash, but I figured he could see the wind blowin' in the direction of the opened back door."

"Mr. Schneider?" All heads turned where the remaining and definitely less attractive of the two secretaries leaned in. "There's a C. L. Styles." She handed Pup an engraved card which traveled the room.

"C. L. Styles, independent drilling contractor." Pup turned the card over in his hand and mind.

"Won't hurt to see what he's about," Hoyt swiveled in his chair, easing his legs for a second with a low moan. Since his return from Europe, his varicose veins kept him in close contact with the Bayer Aspirin. As he told the Boys when he got off the train, "Trapsin' after two women damn near killed me. That and knowin' the old woman fared better than me." He referred to Miss Wythel, who once informed that her rifle would have to remain in Brophy, opted for an ebony walking stick that she claimed belonged to Bat Masterson. No one had seen the antique rifle since and feared any inquiry lest it return to use.

"Let him in," Pup told the secretary.

Her eyes dancing, "Of course." She returned. "C. L. Styles, the Brophy Boys."

One by one the partners left their seats too stunned to speak.

C. L. Styles always enjoyed the effect her presence had on men. She might have been a beauty, had she the inclination, but her goal of being treated as one of the boys prevented her or them from discovering exactly how attractive the lady driller could be. Dressed as now in faded denim, a man's work shirt rolled at the wrists, and seasoned oil field boots, her trim figure escaped notice. Layers of drilling mud served as her cosmetics, its scent her perfume, and the arduous chore of washing one's hair free of both led the lady to crop her brown hair shorter than did most men.

The lady driller broke the silence. "Uncle Bulldog, don't you remember me?"

The elder Schneider searched the face before crossing with outstretched arms. "Babe? Is that you?"

"Sure is." They hugged as the rest of the partners looked to Pup for an unreceived explanation.

"Boys, meet Babe Styles. Her daddy and me drilled many a well together."

Babe shook hands with the Boys. When the introductions ended with Pup, she devoted her attention to Bulldog's son. "I read about you in the newspapers in Dallas; you must be quite a ballplayer."

Pup never tired of adulation. "You'll have to catch our next game. Takin' on the Fort Worth Panthers."

"I suppose they'll send Frank Snyder up against you. If I had the only twenty game winner in the League, that's who I'd bet my money on."

Impressed, Pup inquired, "So you follow the game?"

"Love it," as if to include the rest of the room, "My daddy wanted a boy in the worst way, so I tried not to disappoint him."

"How is Charlie?"

"He passed away about three years ago; the doctor said cancer."

"I'm mighty sorry to hear that; he was as good as they come. So what have you been up to?"

"Just what the card says. I finished the University down in Austin when Daddy died. I spent some time trying to get an oil company to hire me; my degree is in geology. But I couldn't get them to see me as more than a glorified secretary, so I saved my money and bought a portable rig. I've been in Oklahoma, and I managed to get a few jobs, but none to brag about. You boys care if I sit?"

All except Hoyt jumped to their feet. She accepted Pup's offer and continued. When word filtered up about this strike, I kept hearing about the Brophy Boys, but it was J. D. Sorrells, you remember him Uncle Bulldog, that told me that you were the first driller. So that's why I'm here. I want to go to work for you."

In a quandary, Bulldog bit down on the cigar. *I know she can handle the job. Charlie had her on the drillin' floor by the time she turned six. Folks felt sorry for him at the beginnin', losin' his wife to that oil supply salesman and leavin' him with a little girl to raise. But she won her place, totin' loads and helpin' out, but a growed woman on a rig...?*

Babe slapped the knees of her denim pants with the palms of both hands. "I understand." She stood and began to shake the hand of each man. "Thank you for your time."

"Now wait a minute," Bulldog protested. "I didn't say yea nor nay."

"Taking that long to answer said it all. You were trying to think up a way to let me down easy, and I appreciate that. Most just laugh in my face."

The way Hoyt saw it, he owed no such allegiance and proceeded to set her straight. "You got to admit that if women was meant to work rigs, there'd be plenty of 'um out there. You know about any besides yourself?"

"No."

"That's cause the work is tough and the tours long. Women don't stand up under that kinda strain. You better stay home and raise your family."

"I'm not married, Mr. LaGuinn."

"Then get that way."

Cale tried to save Babe from Hoyt's sermonizing. "I haven't had your experience, but I know that roughnecks don't behave themselves in a way that would...well make a lady very comfortable."

"Believe me, I've heard very vulgar comment ever spawned, and I let it roll off my back."

"It's too dangerous," Pup added his two cents. "Too many unsavory types. We couldn't leave you alone for a minute with the most of 'um."

"Do you mean to tell me that there's not a God loving family man working this boom?"

"Well, sure, but..."

"But nothing. You know the character of every man on your payroll, or you should. Unless I miss my guess, you boys can tell what kind of man... or woman a person is just by looking."

"We try our best, but there's nothin' a hundred percent."

"Now, Babe," the driller hated what he was about to say. "Let's us say, just for sake of sayin', that we could find a tour of men that we knew was respectable as a roomful of preachers. What guarantee is there that any of 'um would work with you? Why, they'd walk right off the job."

Listening to the discussion, Willie observed, *She gots that anguish in her eyes and voice of somebody tryin' to scale a wall that's way too high. But she keeps comin' back a tryin' it again until that one day she's gonna realize it won't never be no different. I knows that feelin', lives it every day.*

"I know some men what will work with her."

Babe flashed a gratuitous look toward Willie and then to heaven.

"I been waitin' for the right time to 'proach this, and this is gonna be it. I been wantin' to start up a crew of black roughnecks, but I been like Miss Styles here. I knowed no white men would work with 'um to teach 'um. So I been sittin' back tryin' to come up with a way. If she's as good as she says, then she can run a tour till its goin' good and move on to work with another till we gots several all black crews."

"I ain't no part of this," Hoyt cried. "Folks not gonna take to a colored crew robbin' white men of jobs, and they sure as hell won't cotton to a white woman out there amongst 'um."

Clyde assumed the voice of reason. "Willie, you'd be openin' up a mighty large can of worms."

"It'd be on black folks' land; I can start on mine. Can't nobody object what we does on land we owns."

"When do we start, Mr. Bacon?"

"I gots my boys in mind already. Most done work around rigs and picked up more than I knowed when we spudded the Willie B. #1. Tomorrow too soon?"

"I'm ready now."

"Let's go."

The Boys sat in silence as Willie and Babe left the office.

Hoyt shook his head, "Worse than ice cubes in hot grease. I'm tellin' you right now, ain't nothin' good gonna come of this, I guaran damn tee you."

Clyde looked to Bulldog with the assumption that he could reason with the girl. "What are you gonna do about this?"

"Pup, get out and hire some boys that can handle a rifle. Be up front about what they'll be guardin'."

Pup was out the door, his concerns about Laura Beth Franklin abandoned.

"Cale, go find Lone Wolf; stick with it till you do. Tell him what's happenin'." He'll do as much as anyone can. Just hope it's enough." The driller returned to his office where he pulled a bottle from a desk drawer and began to do some serious drinking.

~~~~~~

"I could sure use a drink." Carmichael considered turning around and heading back to Oklahoma only he lacked the backbone. The young man dressed in a business suit and carrying the obligatory case, drew scant notice from the bustling swarm around the Kilgore Depot. Taking the few unsteady steps down to the gravel, he stood to the side to await his traveling companions. Lamar Tate huffed his way to the opening, twisting slightly to grasp the hand rails and maneuver to ground level. To those unaware, he represented just another figure in the chaos with his only distinctive quality being the privilege of wearing a suit of clothes to do his work.

Not until Estelle appeared did anyone expend a second glance. With the majesty of a queen granting an audience to adoring subjects, Mrs. Tate stood to familiarize herself with the section of Kilgore directly in view before extending her hand to the porter who accepted it in peasant awe. Mindful of the close proximity of her husband and father, men near the tracks emitted low whistles. Descending the stairs in Ziegfeld fashion, she smiled at her subjects, never tilting her head, confident of the devotion of her manservant. Once on the ground, she opened her handbag to remove a gold-plated compact and began dabbing her face with powder. Every motion kept the men at bay awaiting another seductive sway or sultry glance. "Nothin' but oil derricks and clutter," she announced to the old man.

"What'd you expect, New York City?"

"I thought it might have something with a little more," the word she wished to use would set her husband off on a tirade. *I begged him to leave me in Dallas. I swear, bein' a rich man's toy is dull as choir practice. And this dump, like my dear husband, leaves a lot to be desired in what amuses a lady most.* She finally decided upon the word, "with a little more class."

"Well now, you mustn't be too hard on the town. Up until the Daisy Bradford, it was just another farming community."

I wish he'd shut up! Estelle smiled at Carmichael as if his every word held her rapt attention. *Why the hell Lamar had to bring that fool along, I'll never understand. The man can't carry on a conversation worth rememberin' to the next minute. Men like him shouldn't be allowed in the confines of a compartment where the windows aren't big enough to jump out.*

"Could you see to a taxi, if they have them? The wind is mussin' my hair."

Carmichael was off like a racehorse.

"How long do we have to stay in this town?"

Tate regarded his wife. "Judging from experience, I'd say not more than overnight."

"Then you've been here before?"

"Once, just before the Daisy Bradford came in. Joiner and Lloyd wanted me to invest."

"And you didn't, did you? Bet the stockholders loved that."

"Carmichael saw to it we had our leases, a much more profitable arrangement than bein' one of the million and one stockholders in the Daisy Bradford. We were makin' money while those fools stayed tied up in legal squabbles that ended in receivership."

Lamar counted his refusal of the Bradford crew as one of his most astute business decisions. Black deeds, those for leases sold in excess of one hundred percent shares, came out of the woodwork as soon as the gusher was capped. "Hunt had to bail out Dad Joiner by offerin' him thirty thousand in cash, a total of four notes to the tune of forty-five thousand each, and 1.26 million to come out of the production. Then he took the heat from the two hundred and fifty claimants, and if that lucky son of a gun didn't come out on top of 'um all."

He straightened his initialed ring. "At least he fared better than Lloyd, who left here without a trace after some woman appeared claimin' to be his wife and wantin' her share."

Carmichael returned fifteen minutes later with the announcement that he had secured a taxi of sorts. In actuality their transportation amounted to another oil boom entrepreneur operating a jitney. Normally he specialized in field workers going from one lease to another, but the opportunity to make an even quicker buck appealed to his sense of Christian good will.

Estelle balked. "Lord have mercy, they don't even have decent taxis." Lamar opened the door. She bent forward as men who discretely followed took a long look at the rounded portion of a pink jersey skirt so amicably provided. "Look at this seat. It's covered with oil and mud. For what you paid for this dress, you can afford to find me another way to that hotel. This place does have a clean hotel?"

"Carmichael, walk Mrs. Tate to the hotel. Couldn't be more than a few blocks, but I don't want her on these streets alone."

"Yes, Sir."

As the jitney lurched into the street, cutting in front of a truck laden with pipe, Carmichael watched as the two collided. During the ensuing argument the Oklahoma Oil employee forgot about his charge. When the curtain came down on the afternoon's entertainment, he addressed the woman he assumed to be at his side.

"I guess we can go now."

Her silence sent him into a frenzied investigation of the depot. Biting the bullet, he marched up to his boss to deliver the news that he had lost her.

To Carmichael's surprise, Tate grinned enormously. "Couldn't have planned it better. If I know Estelle, she's makin' a bee line to John Earl right now."

"But how are we gonna find them?"

"Damn good thing I don't pay you to think, boy. How's she gonna cover her tracks for the afternoon if she don't show up at the hotel in a reasonable amount of time? No shops to her taste, and I don't see her drinkin' coffee with the locals at the Shanghai Cafe."

Estelle dropped into the first store that held promise of a telephone. The intensity of the cleaning solutions and the steamy heat of its machinery almost forced her back into the throng on the planked sidewalks, but the woman behind the counter already questioned her presence.

"What can I do you for?"

"Actually, I'd like to use the phone."

"I ain't allowed to do that, Ma'am. Mr. Clay don't let nobody use that phone less he puts in the call. Anything else?"

"Where's the nearest phone I can use to call Brophy?"

By now the woman's curiosity was piqued by the expensively clad stranger who kept one eye on the window as if avoiding somebody or in anticipation of the passing of someone of consequence. "Well, if you can tell me who you need in Brophy, maybe they're a customer, and I can make up some excuse to get Mr. Clay to place the call."

What the hell, thought Estelle. "The office of the Brophy Boys will do; I need to speak with Mr. John Earl Terry."

"Then it ain't Brophy you need."

"Excuse me?"

She leaned over the counter. "Everybody in East Texas 'cept you knows that Mr. Terry's partners done give him the boot over that shooter who blowed hisself to kingdom come on their well at the colored church. Oh, they paid him off, some folks would say at fairer than he deserved, so he moved here. Comes in all the time. A gal remembers a man like Mr. Terry. Seems like he told me he was rentin' an office above the First National."

Estelle opened her bag, withdrawing a five-dollar bill. "You have just been so helpful. Now, if I could impose on you a bit more? If a man with a scar down his cheek turns up, say, askin' about a woman dressed like me, you wouldn't let on about me bein' here or our little conversation, would you?"

She smiled, "Ma'am, five dollars can make me forget my own name."

<center>~~~~~~</center>

Before signing his name, John Earl looked at the papers. *Buyin' oil payments can be risky, but a man never got nowhere waitin' for a sure thing. I can triple my ten thousand with this loan to an independent with a rig and no cash to drill. Paid in full three weeks after she produces, now what bank can offer a sweeter deal?* For only a second, the thought of a dry hole occurred. *Then I lose the ten. Hell, there ain't been a dry hole in this field yet.*

The appearance of Faye, his secretary, distracted Terry. *Not much on a typewriter, but she can keep an office full of men waitin' without complaint.*

"There's a woman here."

Unaccustomed to female callers at the office, John Earl assumed the worst. "Tell that Aiken woman my wife hired that I got nothin' to say to Elaine what ain't been said already."

Faye slid in and closed the door. "I don't think she's from around here. You should see her clothes, and the jewelry's real, too."

"Every farmer's wife in East Texas can afford good clothes and jewelry now. You're gonna have to come up with a better description. A name might be a real clue to placin' her."

"Wouldn't give one, fact is..."

The opening of the door ended the dialogue.

"Hi, Sugar."

John Earl was on his feet and round the desk.

"I'll tell your next appointment that you're gone for the day."

"One thing about Faye Sodders, don't never have to tell her when she ain't wanted."

John Earl took Estelle in his arms, and the two shared an ardent kiss.

"What are you doin' here?"

"Now, if those just aren't the words a lady's dyin' to hear."

She walked toward the desk chair and sat down. "No picture of your little wife on the desk? Not a good sign."

"If her daddy's lawyers had of laid off me, she'd be a free woman today."

"We girls have to look out for our own interests."

"How is the old goat? One foot in the grave, I hope."

"The old goat's at the Kilgore Hotel, wonderin' where I am. I don't have time to chat." She raised her eyebrow invitingly.

"How long are you stayin'?"

"Maybe overnight. Believe me, you're the only thing that attracted me to this outpost."

John Earl was bent over the chair, his hands on its arms. Estelle took hold of his tie and drew him toward her. "What time can we meet?"

"I'm livin' at the Kilgore, but takin' into consideration our luck with hotels, you better meet me in back about eleven or so. I got just the place where we can take advantage of some privacy."

As he tried to kiss her, Estelle managed to elude his advance and reach the doorway before blowing him a teasing response. "See you at eleven, Sugar."

David Carmichael paced his employer's room deep in thought. *How can he sit there just readin' that paper? We're about to commit murder for God's sake.* Until he actually boarded the train, Lamar Tate's proposition had been nothing more than a childish fantasy, the kind mulled over for the gratification of revenge with none of the actual consequences. The knock at the door sent him into the air.

"You gonna have to calm down, or you're no use to me at all. Don't just stand there; get the door."

Estelle burst in with packages of the first articles available at the Drug Store. "Just as I thought, not a place in town I'd let touch my hair."

"Your hair looks fine for what you've got to look forward to."

Both wife and employee reacted incredulously.

"I know how you hate business, and that's what the boy and I are here for. Why don't you just order up somethin'? Paper says they've got a movie theater here; you'll be fine if you don't wait for the second feature."

"And where will you be while I'm takin' in the night life?"

"Got a call, they want us to come over to Longview. They're sendin' a car. Don't you wait up; sounds like a long night."

"I'll just freshen up before I go downstairs. Kind of get myself ready for an excitin' evenin'."

Lamar smiled confidently.

Estelle disappeared into the bathroom. Filling the tub with hot water, she doused the rising liquid with the best scented bubble bath at the Kilgore Drug Store.

"I'm leavin'."

"Bye, bye, Sugar." Lamar walked to Carmichael's room while his employee sat behind the wheel of a rented jitney.

~~~~~~

In the Bacon home the freshness of new lumber and paint lingered, faintly disguised by the scent of freshly brewed coffee. Sitting uncomfortably atop the fine furnishings, the eight men hand-picked by Willie were awed by Bacon's promises.

"I wants you to know you wouldn't be here if I didn't believe from the depths of my soul that you was honest, upright men."

Nods of affirmation followed.

Separated from the front room by a closed door, Arnolia and Babe sat at the kitchen table sharing the coffee.

"Do you think they'll accept me?"

Arnolia stared at her cup. "You a brave woman. Not for workin' with no black men, cause them in there's no threat to you. But you goin' against all what this world is built on. White men runs everythin' tellin', women and black folks what they can and can't do. And here you go a tellin' them what you gonna do, darin' 'um to say you can't." Her hands trembled. "Some's gonna take that dare, and what you gonna do then?"

"I'm not afraid."

Willie held open the door. "This here's the person who's gonna teach you to be roughnecks."

"I guess that's my cue." Babe drained her cup.

"Babe Styles, meet the crew."

The men stood, nodding in deference to the lady.

"Keep your seats. Willie tells me you've worked around rigs; mind giving me an idea of what you did?"

Asa Jefferson spoke, "I done dug the slush pits, Ma'am."

Babe had never seen a man with more muscle. "Asa, you're on the monkey board. Takes strength like yours to move those pipes. Don't mind the height?"

"No, Ma'am."

"I think we need to get clear on something. I'm not a ma'am or a Miss. It's Babe. You'll be calling me worse by the end of the first day."

The combined experiences of Babe's crew included more diggers from the pits and pipelines, but all possessed a working knowledge of operations. By the time they parted, Babe had her men at ease.

"You know we're liable to have some unhappy folks breathing down our necks that say a woman and a bunch of coloreds can't drill a well. I want you to realize that I believe in you, and if each of you is man enough to do a day's work, then so am I."

Arnolia stood in the background offering a prayer only those in heaven could hear. *This is what I been a wantin' Willie to do, rode him til he seen it my way. Now I's afraid for them all.* She watched as they left, so full of naive expectation. *Splain to me why's that things in life that's right have to cost so much to get done?*

~~~~~

Estelle exited the Kilgore Hotel and slipped into the alley over which derricks loomed in the evening sky. John Earl started the engine and threw open the door with his free hand.

"Did he ask why you was late gettin' to the hotel?"

"No, come to think of it, he didn't put up a fuss at all. What do you suppose that means?"

"It means we're in for some good luck for a change."

In the jitney, David Carmichael merged into the traffic, cautious not to betray himself. Arguing with his conscience, his hands shook as he clasped the wheel. *If I tell Tate I lost them what's the worst he could do? Fire me, demote me again?... But I know he planned on trapping his wife and Terry...He can't afford to treat me wrong...Can't afford to keep me around, either...What do I care; these two are nothing to me. Terry I hate; Estelle's a waste of a fine lookin' woman...All I have to do is tell him how to get here. I'm not doing anything a friend wouldn't see it his duty, telling a man his wife's cheating.*

John Earl pulled off the main road a little piece out of town at a lot filled with oil tanks mostly owned by the Brophy Boys. A scant few near a small office for the watchman fell under his control in the buyout. As yet he failed to hire a man to keep an eye on the tanks, figuring that the predictable Boys would save him the price of a salary.

"What is this place?"

"Once you're thrown out of the Adolphus, there's no place to go but down."

Jiggling the knob and finding it unlocked, he entered the watchman's shack and felt for the overhead light. Bulb in hand, he turned it until the harsh light illuminated the room.

Carmichael abandoned his car. Hiding behind some trees, he watched as the light came on and the bodies locked in an embrace which assured him of their plans to remain at the shack. Hurriedly, he returned to Tate.

"This the best you could do?"

Estelle examined the close confines of the shack. An ancient stove, coffee pot in place, a well-worn chair, and a makeshift bed accounted for the furnishings.

Scattered about, discarded newspapers and cafe lunch sacks of the variety prepared in advance and set on the counter for the crews to pick up prior to each tour bore the watchman's name. For a dollar and a half, an oil field worker could get a ham or fried egg sandwich, a piece of fruit, and a slice of pie as a standing order.

"I got a half built house in Brophy, if that's more to your likin'."

"When are we gonna stop all this high school foolishness?"

Terry looked hurt.

"Oh, Sugar," she realized his misinterpretation. "That's hardly what I mean. You see," Estelle draped her arms around his neck. "I been thinkin'. Since we just can't seem to stay away from one another, why should we?"

Skeptical, John Earl removed her arms. "Thinkin' can be a mighty dangerous undertakin'."

"Don't be silly," she plunged into her handbag for the cigarette he would light. "There was only one reason why I didn't leave Lamar a long time ago and run off with you."

"What's changed?"

"You have, that is your bank book has. You are still the most excitin' man I ever met. Now you can afford to take care of me in the manner to which I have so easily become accustomed."

"Why would he let you go without puttin' up a fight?"

"He's got nothin' to hold over me but a settlement. He knows I don't give a rat's ass what people think. So he cuts me off without a dime, what do we care? Don't you have enough money to take care of me?"

"We might squeak by," he grinned.

Estelle threw her arms up in surrender. "So what's left, the man's gonna shoot me or somethin'?"

They both laughed heartily as they fell back on some blankets and pillows provided by the Kilgore Hotel.

As the jitney neared, Carmichael again attempted to persuade his boss to allow him to stop the vehicle.

"You've got no more need of me, Mr. Tate. See, there it is. No reason for me to go any further." Carmichael began to veer off the road.

"Get this car the hell back on the road. I told you, you don't have to watch, but you damn sure got to stay to drive me back.

I can't see good at night, least not well enough to drive. You wouldn't want me runnin' over some kid on a bicycle?"

Carmichael guided the jitney to its previous spot. As he busied himself with the process of killing the engine, Lamar removed a revolver from the waist of his suit pants. Examining the chambers, he assure himself of six shots.

"I haven't fired one of these since my eyes went bad, but a man never loses a well-hewn skill."

"We can turn around then."

Tate leaned back. "You don't get this far in life backin' down on what you set your mind on doin'."

His feet were out the door as he issued his last instructions. "Since I got a coward as my partner, let's get the story straight now. You saw her leave with him and decided to protect the interests of your boss. That's when you came for me and brought me back. All right so far?"

"Yes, Sir."

"Then we walked up to the shack, where I called out to my wife. Nobody answered. That's important. You, no I, kicked the door in. When we saw the depths of my wife's betrayal, I pulled the gun I brought along for protection from whatever kind of riff raff roams boom streets at night. And I shot'um both, right in their lovers' nest."

"Yes, Sir."

John Earl and Estelle lay on the makeshift bed with a blanket their only barrier from the wind that picked up shortly after their arrival. It was Terry who heard the approach and placed his hand over Estelle's mouth. As she wiggled in the darkness, he whispered, "Someone's outside."

The woman stiffened.

"When I yell, 'Now,' you roll as fast and as close to the wall as you can." He felt a nod and released Estelle. John Earl crawled to the door opposite its swing, rising to his feet, heels placed to the side of the shack until he reached the door. *I'd trade a prime lease for a weapon of any kind.*

Whoever comes up to a tank shack has to be up to no good, Estelle told herself, *like a Depression vagrant. Oh, God, everybody knows they'd as soon slit your throat as look at you.* As the chill of the spring night filtered through the cracks of the shed, Estelle began to shiver.

When Tate reached the door, he cocked the revolver and took a deep breath. As his foot crashed against the door, he bellowed, "Nobody makes a fool of Lamar Tate!"

Accompanying the splintering of the wood, Terry yelled his signal, and Estelle responded. Only the men witnessed the fire from the revolver as it split the darkness in two quick staccatos. Eyes acclimated to the dimness, Tate observed the vacated bedding. The narrowness of the lighting prevented a view of his wife mouthing what she hoped would suffice as a prayer.

Cautiously, Tate moved forward. Spying Estelle, he raised the gun in preparation to fire. As his finger nursed the trigger, John Earl lunged to send the ensuing shot upward.

Estelle screamed. No longer concerned with John Earl or his insane orders, she scrambled upon hands and knees for the perimeter of the guard shanty in an all-out attempt at freedom. Heart racing, her nails scraped against the wood like a cat's. Aware of the men as they fell onto the bed, she thrust herself through the opening and onto the ground while the final shot discharged. As she continued to crawl toward the trees, a dolorous moan brought her to her feet, and she broke into a faltering run.

He's killed John Earl.

The realization that her sole protector lay dead at the hands of her crazed husband heightened Estelle's panic. *He'll come for me next.* Glancing back toward the shack, she unwittingly plunged into the arms of David Carmichael, who had ventured as far as the trees after the third shot.

Carmichael leered at the naked form. "And what have we here?"

Relieved at what she perceived as a savior, Estelle began to point wildly, oblivious to her state of undress or the absurdity of Carmichael's presence and timing.

"He's killed John Earl! We've got to get out of here!" She tried pulling free of the man by pounding her fists against his chest. "Do you want him to shoot you, too?"

Dragging the hysterical woman, Carmichael fought free of the tree break.

When the last shot reverberated, several seconds elapsed before Terry fully comprehended that Lamar, not he, received the bullet, for during their struggle, the gun's mercuric aim imperiled both. His face distorted by pain and disbelief, Lamar collapsed .

With the shot still ringing, Terry heard nothing of Estelle and Carmichael's arrival, alerted only by the loss of what little light shone on the wooden floor.

"John Earl!" she broke free and embraced her lover.

Disgusted by her sobbing and clinging, he shoved her back. "Get some clothes on, and shut the hell up."

Carmichael was racked with indecision. *If I run, Terry will shoot me down. If I stay, what's to say he won't anyway?* As he began to back from the entrance, he froze in response to the man with the gun.

Though he faced Tate's body, John Earl sensed Carmichael's movements.

"What's your part in all this?" Pulling back the hammer, Terry twisted toward the door while still seated on the planked floor. "Just out for an evenin's drive?"

His hands flew into the air in Old West fashion. "Now I swear, I had nothin' to do with this," the tremble in his voice a betrayal.

"Bull shit. You didn't have the guts to be the old man's back up, or you'd have a gun yourself. But I believe you did your part." He rose unsteadily, "Whatever that may have been is enough to get you killed right along with him." John Earl gestured to the corpse and aimed the gun at the man who was now on his knees.

"Don't kill me!" he shrieked. "All I did was drive him out here. I didn't know he even had that gun. When I heard the shots, I came runnin'."

"Try again, Davey boy. How'd he know where to find us? Hell of a lucky guess?"

"You were supposed to be in Longview," Estelle inched forward. "Lamar told me that," she informed her lover.

"It don't matter," Terry replied, "cause when the watchman that the Boys hired gets over here, we're gonna tell him that our Mr. Carmichael drove the three of you out here, shot his boss, and tried to force himself on you. That's when I come along to check on my tanks, bein' my boy was laid off. Did a damn good job of gettin' the drop on him."

Without thinking he blurted, "Won't be any watchman." Observing the alteration in Terry's face, David slowly made his admission. "I gave him a few bucks before I...we..."

John Earl began to laugh.

"Well, I don't see what's so funny. The man wanted us dead."

Still entertained by the lack of sophistication of Tate and his crony, "I tell you what let's do. I never liked you Carmichael, and that's a fact, but you've been available and damn stupid enough to fall right into place when I need you. You can thank your lucky stars I got use for you now."

He gently allowed the hammer to return to a position of safety. Carmichael, though wary, relaxed somewhat as the gun occupied a position similar to the one in which it made the trip to the tank lot.

"I got a little business deal for you, and unless you want to end up like your boss man, I'm makin' book you're gonna accept it."

"But I..."

"Estelle, darlin', did your lovin' husband there remember you in his will?"

Confused, she admitted, "Sure, I get whatever he had."

"No kids from other marriages or what not?"

"None I ever heard."

The characteristic grin returned. "Then David Carmichael's fixin' to be the new president of Oklahoma Oil," John Earl announced as if bestowing the title provided him the greatest of honor.

"What?" It was difficult to determine which of the two reacted with more surprise.

"Listen up. Ole John Earl's fixin' to turn this whole mess into the best thing that ever happened to any of us," he glanced over his shoulder, "except for that son of a bitch over there. You want to be the future Mrs. Terry?"

"Of course, but..."

"Then for six months, you're the grievenist widow Oklahoma's ever laid eyes on. Given your distress, you are placin' the reins of the controllin' shares of the company so lovingly bequeathed to you by the dearly departed in the hands of the man that assisted you so unselfishly durin' your time of sorrow and need."

"But why are we givin' him a damn thing? He wanted us dead as much as Lamar."

John Earl's face assumed a more serious expression.

"Cause we can explain away one old dead man, but him and his assistant is a stretch even for me. Besides, you heard old Davey, he just drove him out here." John Earl's last remark was laden with sarcasm.

"That's right, Estelle."

Now, as president of the company, you are filterin' information directly to me. What I say goes."

"Wait a minute. If I'm the president, then I..."

"Get to live." John Earl patted the revolver. "Take it or leave it. I'm a resourceful man; I'll come up with a way to cover up your untimely death."

With little hesitation, "All right, all right."

"See how agreeable he is, Darlin'? Then when the lady's tired of widow's weeds, she and I will say our I do's, and you will be my right hand man. Now ain't that just the most mutually satisfyin' way for us to solve this little problem of ours?"

Estelle was kissing the back of his neck. As if the thought suddenly burst into her head, "But what if he decides to double-cross us?"

Placing his arm around her waist and drawing Estelle closer, John Earl reassured his lady. "And admit he was a party to murder?"

"I got too much to lose; don't worry about that."

"And what about Lamar?" the widow inquired.

"The three of us are gonna take a little trip as soon as I send you into town. You got hold of yourself?"

"I think so."

She smoothed hair from her face in an effort to feign composure.

John Earl placed his hands upon Estelle's shoulders, staring down into her face, "Now this is important; you can't mess up on nothin'." She nodded.

"Go back to the hotel and pack up everything of yours, Lamar's, and Carmichael's. Be sure you tell the clerk that your husband's been in touch, and that you're meetin' him and his assistant in Longview. Then get back here as fast as you can so that you and Davey can put miles between you and East Texas before daylight."

Carmichael spoke up.

"We can't go back to Seminole and expect folks to believe he died and we buried him along the way."

"That's the reason you're goin' to Matamoros."

"But what's in Mexico?" wailed Estelle.

"An old buddy of mine who can set you onto a Mexican official who'll fill out a death certificate and his only question will be how much you're willin' to pay him."

Terry's plan was beginning to make sense to his newly recruited ally. "All we have to do is say Mr. Tate died in Mexico, where we buried him."

"Now, you're gettin' smart. Tell the folks back home that Estelle just couldn't bear the anguish of bringin' him back." He addressed Carmichael, "Be sure to buy a casket and a head stone, good ones. We don't want no raised eyebrows. As soon as the will's read, we're in business."

The men watched as Estelle slid into the jitney. "I'm countin' on you to keep her in line. If she can't play her part, you let me know."

"How long do we stay?"

"Wouldn't look right to drive across the border and have him die all in one day."

Terry consulted the sky as if summoning inspiration. "Wait about a week before contactin' my man. That and the time it takes for him to get the paper work done ought to do it. Now help me get Tate wrapped up."

Shrouding the dead man in hotel bedding, his former protégé and his greatest adversary hoisted the corpse on their shoulders and made their way toward the Brophy Boys' tanks. Unsteady footing and the cumbersome load slowed the pace and drew Carmichael's complaints as John Earl passed tank after tank.

"What's wrong with this one?"

"Too old and likely to be cleaned sooner than it will take the oil and sludge to eat up Tate to the point that his own momma wouldn't know him"

When Terry located a tank that met with his satisfaction, he began to tie the rope, which he stored in his trunk for freeing mired wheels, around Tate's body. With the corpse secured at both ends, a second length served as a sling to balance the load.

Terry began his ascent of the metal ladder with Tate's remains dangling. Behind him, pushing against their burden, Carmichael's added strength enabled John Earl to reach the roof of the tank. Exhausted, the men sat atop the storage unit separated by Tate.

"We got to get rid of him before somebody comes along," Carmichael urged. Though the wind blew unchecked across the tank, perspiration beaded upon the man's face.

"You worry too much," he began loosening the knots. "That's the only thing that concerns me about sendin' you to Mexico with Estelle. The blind leadin' the blind." John Earl pried the metal covering off one of the vents before quickly moving down wind of the escaping gases. In reference to Lamar's size, "He's gonna be a tight fit."

Draggin him by the arms, they guided the body toward the cavity. Their combined strengths suspended the dead man over the opening, forcing him into the confines. Spent, the boys all but collapsed.

The awaited splash confirmed that that the oil man had reached his resting place. Had the two been able to peer inside and observe the body as it sank slowly into the murkiness, the confidence that increased with each passing day would have been replaced with the torture of impending discovery.

As it were, the boys descended the ladder with a phase of the plan neatly tucked under their belts, unaware that as Lamar Tate's right ring finger disappeared, the diamond chips that divulged his initials glistened a final time in the moonlight that filtered through the vent.

Chapter 12

July, 1931

Lifting the rusting lid from the metallic water can, Asa Jefferson savored a long, cool drink using the lid as his cup. Asa's back hurt, but in a way that produced a pleasure that superseded the pain. *These past couple a months been tough, but Babe Styles has done kept her word by drivin' us from daylight to dark.*

He looked with pride at the crew hard at work. *Them that quit weren't worth the time took to write their last checks, 'specially now we got a second crew operatin'. Hadn't been for the accident, might even have a third by now.*

He and Babe were just a few feet from the drilling floor when Abel Frederick and Tom Bailey started arguing. *Over what amount to nothin'*, Asa recalled, *just Abel's stubbornness in wantin' to do the job without Tom tellin' him how. Like Abel had been trainin' long enough to know. Abel always did let his temper have hold of his mind; damn fool for jerkin' up a travelin' block that fast.* The loss of control started the block swinging into the pipe lengths already removed, causing them to fall like dominos. *It was like they was movin' slow, but I knows they was goin' fast.* A length crashing into the monkey board left Orel swinging by his safety belt. Derrough screamed just before another section caught the side of his head.

With each passage of the suspended body, drops of blood sprinkled the drilling floor. "Who's going up with me?" Babe asked. Their silence prompted her anger. "You just gonna leave him up there for the buzzards to eat?"

"No Ma'am, but I ain't climbin' that rig to bring down no dead folks," answered Cecil Benton with head bowed.

Babe stormed toward the rig. Behind her, the crew watched unsure of whether to collect their last wages or watch to see what the farm boss planned to do.

"Bunch of damned cowards. White folks is right about you." Asa spat at their feet before following Babe.

"How we gonna do this?" Asa asked as they reached the monkey board.

"Luckily the belts aren't long. If I grab him from one end and you the other, we ought to be able to pull him up." Babe was already on her knees after securing her belt. Drawing on all his strength, Asa knelt beside her and began to draw Orel Derrough closer to the board.

Unbeknownst to the two on the platform, several cars came to abrupt stops at the site. Cale, Willie, Pup, and Bulldog craned their necks to witness the rescue.

"Why the hell is she up there and the lot of you are here on the ground?" screamed Pup.

Before an answer could be mustered, the men saw Babe's mud-slick boots skid and heard her desperate cry. Pup bolted the rig's ladder without seeing Asa drop Derrough's body in time to save Babe from sliding off the monkey board. When Schneider reached the board, Styles sat, knees up and head between her legs.

Pup refused to allow his relief to show, "Damn fool woman! Get down off here and let Asa and me finish."

Babe peered defiantly over crossed arms. "This is my well, and I don't take orders from you."

"Startin' now you do," Pup was at her side, loosening the belt to fit himself. With little effort the two men pulled Derrough's body onto the board. Once on the ground, Babe fired the rest of the crew.

When the next roster was posted, Asa spotted his name at the top of the first tour with the words "Farm Boss."

"Only a man that cares about his crew can be the boss; that's why I'm puttin' you in charge while I train a night tour."

Asa smiled in remembrance. "Here I is, the boss man, earnin' good money, and," he chuckled, "too tired to spend it."

Babe Styles entered the Brophy Cafe followed by Arnolia Bacon, Elaine Terry, and the ever-chattering Mavis. Drawn by the tantalizing aroma of grilling onions, the twenty-four hour cafe's booths, counter space and tables overflowed with the general boom crowd and those there to claim sack lunches for their evening tours. Luckily a table opened soon after the women entered which allowed the girls to seat themselves at the red-checked table.

Eyes of those unable to accept the independence portrayed by the dauntless quartet followed as they took their seats. Some rehashed the scandalous divorce of the Crawford woman; others discussed Mavis' latest escapade or her ostentatious home.

The shameless woman who commandeered her own drilling crew entirely of black men drew conversation, but they all noted the gall of Arnolia Bacon to stroll in the front door. Money gave folks uppity airs, true enough, but even oil field cash could not buy what Arnolia sought by trying to join white people in a cafe-cooked meal.

For Laura Beth Franklin, the presence of Arnolia Bacon drew scant notice. Rather, the object of her ire was the lady driller. I *swear,* she pouted, *since that woman came to town, she and Pup have been joined at the hip.* At first, the teenager rationalized Pup's attention as concern for his investments. *But now I'm not so sure.* She caught her reflection in the stainless steel coffee urn. *What Pup can possibly find attractive about that woman escapes me. Why, she hasn't a shred of femininity.* She looked at Babe with disdain. *Dressing like a common oil field hand. And I don't believe for a minute that hogwash about you having a college degree. Enjoy your little success, Miss Styles, because I intend to have Pup Schneider despite your interference.*

Mavis slid the two menus from their habitual insertion between the glass jars that held salt, pepper, and sugar, passing one to Babe and Arnolia and leaning toward Elaine so that they might share. "What do ya'll figure is safe to eat?" The one-time waitress scrutinized the cafe as only one accustomed to the ins and outs of restaurant ownership might. What she deemed imperative, like a freshly mopped floor and a sparkling kitchen, the Brophy Cafe's clientele merely dismissed in gratitude for a place to eat.

"Pup and I get the chicken fried steak a lot; it's always good."

An auburn eyebrow arched, "You and Pup get by here a right smart, do you?"

If Babe detected Mavis' attempt to ferret information that might indicate a romance, she did not let on. Still intent on the menu, she offered matter-of-factly, "He gets me to help him with the line ups and deciding how to pitch certain batters, stuff like that."

"I didn't realize you were a baseball fan," Elaine commented.

"Sure, love it. Wish there was more time for me to make some practices. Maybe now that I've got Asa running the day tour I can get out to the field. Course, the season's over for the Wildcatters, but Pup's not letting them loose until the first frost."

Arnolia seized the opportunity to put in a word for an old friend. "Asa's a good man."

"They don't come any better."

"Speakin' of good men and how hard they are to come by," Mavis interrupted, "When can you drop John Earl's name and go back to signin' Crawford?"

"Maybe two or three more weeks. All of a sudden John Earl's become unusually cooperative. Why, he's practically begging me to hurry my lawyer along, and we all know he's been the foot dragger through all this."

"I haven't experienced the displeasure of meeting him, but judging from the plenty I've heard, you'd be well served to slow down. That sort of an about face from a snake like John Earl's got to mean's he's up to something that will benefit him and not you," said Mavis.

"You're better off without the man, and the good Lord will see to his punishment for all he done did to you and lots a other folks we ain't never likely to hear of." Arnolia squeezed Elaine's hand.

"Sure is slow in here this evenin'."

Mavis looked around and noticed that several tables where p eople had arrived later than they were already served. "Well, how do you like that?" She shared her findings with the girls. "I'm gonna say somethin'."

Elaine grabbed her arm. "Give them a minute more; just look how busy it is." Reluctantly Mavis spread her skirt and replaced her napkin.

"How's the school business?" Babe inquired.

"We'll make our date; I'm sure. The only thing that has me concerned in the least is the heating."

Having picked up one of the menus with which she now fanned herself, Mavis snapped, still miffed that Elaine would not allow her to complain to the cafe's owner, "I don't guess you'll have to turn it on the first day or two."

"Of course not, silly, I'm thinking of how it's been set up. You see, the decision came from John Earl while I was still in Dallas."

"Enough said; change it all."

"If it were only that simple. To redo the system now would be costly in time and in money that could be better spent."

"Oh, what trouble could it cause?" Mavis posed her question to no one in particular. "Heat's heat."

"But this is gas heat, not the commercial type but directly tapped from gas producing wells on the campus and sent straight into the building. They say it will save the school close to three thousand dollars a year."

"I wouldn't worry," the one of the four with the most oil field experience explained, "Folks have been doing that about as long as there's been the means. Long as it's done right, there's no problem."

"I know; I know. Melba says camp towns and especially tent cities couldn't get along without direct tapping. And the other Board members think it's a grand idea." She admitted rather ashamedly, "Maybe I just don't care much for anything that remotely reminds me of John Earl."

"My, my, now ain't that a surprisin' thang!"

The girls' laughter filtered over to the counter stool where Laura Beth situated herself at an opportune angle to keep watch on the door for Pup to saunter in. *I've got to get them out of here before he comes, or he'll set himself down by that woman. Now, how can I...*

Her eyes fell on Arnolia Bacon. Easing off the stool the smitten schoolgirl approached the cash register located near the entrance. After wading the line of customers, Laura Beth gained the ear of the proprietor, Lemuel Banks, a boomer newly arrived with the intent of moving on as soon as the strike abated.

"Enjoy your dinner?" the graying Banks asked with all the interest of a dime a dance hostess.

"The food was fine, but I won't be comin' back." Laura Beth watched as he looked up from his cash drawer. "And neither will anyone else once word gets around that you're servin' their kind out front instead of in back where they belong."

Momentarily confused, Banks scanned his crowd. Given the hectic pace of business, he failed to notice Arnolia. With genuine surprise, "She been here long?"

"Long enough to ruin my meal and those of most of your customers. You'll be lucky if you have anyone but coloreds by the end of the week."

The proprietor abandoned his register and the Kilgore teenager in search of his wife, Sadie, furious that she had allowed the woman to remain a sufficient amount of time to damage business. Finding her just behind the double swinging doors of the kitchen, he tore into her. "What the hell have you been doin' all this time? Ain't you seen that colored girl a sittin' out there like she was the Queen of Sheba? Why didn't you get her out here?" He gestured toward a shoddy table and chairs near the back door.

"I been up to my eyeballs in orders. You're the one workin' the front."

"And I'm the one tellin' you to get rid of her. Folks is already complainin' and leavin'."

Sadie peered through the crack provided by the ill-fitting doors. "We can't throw her out; look at them women she's with."

"I don't care if she's with the Virgin Mary and a band of angels, she ain't eatin' here. Who's their waitress anyways?"

"Margie!" Sadie Banks leaned out the door and caught the startled waitress. "You taken the order of the table with that colored woman?"

"No ma'am. I been waitin' for Mr. Banks to tell her to leave." She looked rather sheepishly, "I didn't see it was my place."

"Get rid of her," Lemuel pushed his wife through the door.

Sadie wiped her hand upon the soiled apron that tied behind her neck. When she neared the table, Mavis began before Sadie could open her mouth.

"It's about time; folks is eatin' that got here way after us. What do you girls want?"

Mustering all her courage to challenge both the saint of Brophy and her irrepressible friend, Sadie addressed her customers in as polite a voice as remained after twenty years of marriage to Lemuel Banks.

"I got to ask the colored lady to sit in the section with her kind." At first unsure of what had been said amid the din of the cafe, Mavis asked the woman to repeat herself.

"I said we serve colored folks in the back, not here in front."

Fearing Mavis' brand of reprisal, Elaine reacted, "I take it that you haven't had the pleasure of meeting the wife of one of our partners? This is Mrs. Bacon. She's our friend, and we would appreciate you treating her with the respect you afford all you customers."

Sadie snarled inwardly.

That patronizin' little... how dare she think money gives her call to run my cafe?

The proprietress addressed Arnolia, "You folks know the rules. You want to eat here; you eat in the back." To emphasize her resolve, Sadie pulled Arnolia's chair slightly away from the table.

"Now you wait a minute," always the genteel lady Elaine began, her arm noticeably in her lap,

Mavis was on her feet. "You got a hell of a nerve here."

Voices now rising above the cafe clatter, all eyes turned toward the confrontation.

"Mrs. Bacon will eat where I do," added Babe.

"Suit yourself. There's plenty of room in the back. These ladies may feel a bit out of place, but you're well-known for bein' right cozy with the colored folks, especially the men."

Springing to her feet, the lady driller rounded the table and hurled herself at Sadie Banks. Emitting a deep moan, the cafe owner landed on the wood floor, flat of her back. Before she could react, Babe was astride the woman, twisting her left hand into the salt and pepper hair of her victim.

Intent on pulling apart the struggling pair, a couple of roughnecks seated just to the left entered the fracas. Babe threw back her free hand which caught a man off balance, sending him into a third table, and inviting four other diners into the fight. Schooled in the art of brawling in Winnie's more exciting night spots, Mavis swung her chair across the head of the oil field hand who had directed his attention to Babe in retaliation for his partner's embarrassment. The crack of the chair was drowned by the cheering of the crowd that had settled on its favorites. Standing atop the counter, an industrious patron took bets on the outcome from an eager line of risk takers.

Horrified, Elaine fell back into the crowd where she was soon engulfed and forgotten. Arnolia tried to follow Elaine; however, Lemuel Banks' determined hold on her shoulders pulled her toward the kitchen.

"This is all your doins'. I got a good mind to beat the tar out of you, then maybe you can remember your place."

Arnolia began to scream. As they passed the counter, she managed to break free one arm and grab a pot of coffee that she slung toward Banks' head.

The scalding brew sent the man's hands to his face for protection against its blistering effect. On hands and knees, she fled into the kitchen.

The front door flew open to the shouts of Brophy's duly elected Constable. Brady McDade, who since election had been called upon to do little more than remove a few drunken tankies or search for stray children, fancied himself another Lone Wolf Gonzaullas, nevertheless. "I'm haulin' off to the Kilgore jail them that's responsible for this disturbance of the peace," he spouted before investigating.

From behind the damp towel that covered his blistering face, Lemuel rehashed the events leading to the "unjustified attack" on his wife. Margie substantiated his rendition as she saw to a rather large knot which had formed on Sadie's head.

As yet unheard from, Mavis and Babe sat on the dish and food strewn floor. As they examined their scrapes and the tender spots that would eventually turn varying degrees of blue, Elaine emerged from the background. Having grown up with Elaine, the lawman recognized her as the most credible source and listened with a patient respect.

"But I don't see no colored woman," he stated rather perplexed by the widely conflicting tales.

Arnolia Bacon seemed to have vanished. Concealed by the counter, her escape through the kitchen was aided by Negro cooks. Once in her car, she sped to the Brophy Boys' offices.

"Now, Elaine, you and I go way back, but the fact is these folks," he pointed to the Banks, "got every right to say who they serve and who they don't."

A muffled, "Amen," escaped the confines of the towel.

"I got no choice but to take in these two ladies and do my best to find that colored woman, too."

As Elaine pleaded, Pup and Arnolia pushed through the crowd. A delighted Laura Beth began her way toward Pup as

Sadie's accusing tone and pointing finger alerted the Constable to their arrival. Pup was removing his wallet while Arnolia went to the women who fought for her honor.

"I'm payin' the damages, McDade, and we can all go home." Digging into folding money, the young oilman called for a ten-year-old. "Sammy, take this thousand down to the pool hall and get some change from my daddy."

The child took the bill at a run. Sights set on the billiard room a few doors down, the boy narrowly missed Cleve Brandenburg, who caught him by the belt, almost ripping it from the loops.

"Whoa, there, Sammy. Got a bee up your pants leg?"

"No, Sir, Mr. Brandenburg. I got to run a errand for Mr. Pup Schneider that's real important."

"What's Schneider need?"

The farmer turned millionaire listened with interest and a good deal of amusement as the boy retold his version of the goings on at the cafe. Examining his own wallet, Cleve began to thumb through a mass of bills representative of every denomination Clyde kept on hand.

"Save yourself a trip." He peeled off royalty dollars. Passing up several thousand-dollar bills, he arrived at a consecutive string of hundreds. "If Pup needs more, I'll be comin' back to the cafe. I 'spect I better get a hold of his daddy and Cale. You scoot now." Sammy stuffed the bills in his shirt pocket and scampered back.

McDade was having none of Pup's proposal.

"As long as the Banks want to push the matter, I got no choice but to arrest these women. The way I see it, Elaine didn't deliver no blows. That the way you seen it?" he addressed the crowd.

"One's as responsible as the other in my book." Sadie registered the lone objection.

Pup abandoned the Constable and stared into the woman's face as he spoke to a Brophy Boy roughneck in the background. "Steve, you worked your tour?"

"Yes, Sir."

"Then tomorrow, you spread the word to the other boys, hell, to anybody that so much as draws a dime from any Brophy Boys workers, that them or their families step a foot in this dump, they can kiss their jobs good-bye."

"Now you wait a minute," interrupted Margie. "My husband lays pipe for you, and I got my job here."

Without removing his eyes from Sadie, "Then you quit or he's fired; don't make me no never mind which."

Sadie reacted, "This ain't no company town. We got plenty of business without you."

Pup helped the women to their feet. "Can you at least keep them here in Brophy until the judge sets his fine.?"

Elaine spoke up, "Of course he can. Brady McDade is a fair man."

Pup doubted the estimation, but Elaine's avowal saved them a trip into Kilgore.

An exasperated Laura Beth watched Pup leave with a possessive arm around Babe. *I'm going to see to it that you're out of Pup's life for good, she promised* .

Right at a month to the day, the Brophy Cafe closed its doors with the dubious distinction of being the only business in two counties that failed during the boom.

~~~~~~

By the next afternoon the events in Brophy loomed in the headlines. Folding the newspaper, John Earl leaned back in the swivel chair of his new office at the refinery. *The most* *satisfyin' aspect of my ouster from the Brophy Boys is this refinery. It was my baby from the onset; didn't none of them have the foresight to diversify. And now all the big boys are beatin' a path to my door to get their crude refined with as little added cost for transportation as possible.* The thought of the light ends crude pulsating through the veins of pipes in his operation made him giddy. *Just another part of the glory of the East Texas Field; a finer grade can't be found. So far with my marginal investment of twenty thousand, no matter how far prices fall, which they're droppin like lead with this Proration mess hangin' over our heads, this refinery will turn me a profit.* He did some quick arithmetic. *Buyin' cheap, production costs low with so fine a grade, and sellin' sixteen gallons of gasoline for every barrel... I can't lose.*

He returned to the newspaper. *Damn, I wish I'd been at the cafe. What I wouldn't give to see Mavis buttin' heads with roughnecks and that sour-mouthed Sadie Banks.* He laughed aloud as the images came alive in newsprint, but his face fell as he considered the repercussions for the Bacons. *Sendin' Arnolia on a vacation with the kids was a wise move, Willie. If you had more sense, you' join her and make it permanent. Memories last a long time in East Texas.*

"Faye."

The secretary appeared carrying a pad and pencil.

"Send Mavis McCallister some flowers, and make 'um as gaudy as she is... Don't sign my name, or she won't let 'um in the house. Just put, 'I always knew you were a better man than Cale.'"

Faye enjoyed the humor. "Your guests are here," she informed. "Want me to sit in?"

"Nope, fewer witnesses the better."

Ushered in were Warren Ware, a Tyler independent; Leslie Shipp, editor of the Overton newspaper; and Junior Pharr, a

Congressman with considerable clout in Washington. John
Earl waited until they were comfortably ensconced and cigars
lit before pressing his agenda. These boys represented the
leaders of the Anti-Proration League, a group aimed at
repealing Rule 37 and preventing further restrictions on the
production of East Texas crude like the edict issued on April
4th by the Texas Railroad Commission.

Since May 1st when the order took effect, the Field had
been parceled into twenty acre tracts with the legal rate of
production for each of these sections tied to its "potential of
the field."

Of the one hundred sixty thousand barrels allowable per
day, each of the tracts could pump at least one hundred barrels.

Terry referred to the descent of thirteen Pullman cars filled
with both sides of the Proration issue on the state's capital to
plead their respective cases.

"Anybody think that little march on Austin done any good?"
Terry asked.

Ware pointed with his cigar toward the Congressman, "I
thought we all agreed that the Railroad Commission and that
SOB of a governor aren't gonna lift a finger to help
independents? Washington is our best shot at defeatin'
Proration."

"As you are surely aware," the Congressman retorted, "East
Texas' cheap oil is closing some proven producers in and
outside the state and interfering with imported oil."

"The hell with them other countries," John Earl interjected.
"We don't need their oil. Don't the President know that this field
can produce all the oil it takes to keep this country goin'? You
mark my word, that War in Europe didn't decide nothin'. We'll
be back to fightin' them Germans and whoever the hell else is
fool enough to take us on, and the United States will be wishin'
it had more of our oil on the market, not less."

"Which my colleagues on the Hill use as ammunition to shoot down any anti-Proration legislation. All the better that our oil is stored beneath the ground until we need it."

The editor added his views. "Then show them some back issues with pictures of lines of folks waitin' to spend their oil field wages at every business from food to clothing, or railroad and trucking industries operatin' at full speed, and Texas steel mills producin' rigs and pipes when their doors used to be shut tight."

Congressman Pharr surrendered. "Save your spechafyin' for the independents over at the East Texas Counties Proration Advisory Committee backed by your pals, the Brophy Boys. They seem to be gettin' exactly what they want out of Ole Governor Ross. Seems this plan of 'potential of the field' to keep prices up came from their caucusin'."

"At least those Railroad Commission fools didn't put a halt to drillin'. As long as they don't, we can keep spuddin' new wells to up a parcel's output."

"Don't talk so loud; they'll hear you down in Austin. Right now, I'm dependin' on drillers applyin' for them permits to keep little boys like me refinin'."

Warren pleaded with the editor, "Can't you do nothin' in that paper of yours to convince them Country Proration Advisory boys to see the light?"

"I'm afraid all they hear is their own tongues spoutin' market glut. They're not ready to listen to reason. All they can see is dollar a barrel oil down the road. Course, when enough of those farmers who've borrowed against royalties that aren't comin' in get to lightin' fires under their butts, maybe then..."

John Earl interrupted. "They'll still be a bunch of gutless cowards ready to let the government tell them what to do. Hell, I swear, first we let the government tell a man when he can drink, and now it's tellin' us how much of our own damn oil we can take out of the ground. Next they'll be tellin' us when we can take a piss and taxin' us for the privilege."

"Did you read my editorial on the MacMillian decision?" Without waiting for a reply, he continued, "At least there's a judge who recognizes bullshit when he smells it."

Pharr responded, "He can invalidate anything he wants and say all he cares to about physical waste not bein' a direct result of open drillin', but you see your boys down in the Legislature are workin' on a market demand law."

"Sterling says he'll veto."

"No offense, Junior, but," Terry argued, "you ever met a politician yet who wouldn't break a promise?"

"None taken, but the fact remains, you got to get your override votes lined up fast." The Congressman rose. "To coin an old phrase, gentlemen, the shit's gonna fly. This August is gonna be the hottest East Texas has endured in a long time, and only the real players will live through it."

"You take care of Washington, Junior, and we'll see to Austin," John Earl ordered.

After Pharr's exit, Warren posed, "You believe any of that martial law crap?"

Shipp shook his head. "Sterling doesn't have the wherewithal to keep that kind of operation goin'."

John Earl slid open the side drawer of his desk and removed an ivory-handled revolver. "Let those glorified Boy Scouts come; East Texas is ready for 'um."

〰〰〰〰〰

August 17, 1931

East Texans held their collective breaths during the first days of August. By the fourth day, Oklahoma Governor William

"Alfalfa Bill" Murray closed the Oklahoma and Greater Seminole Fields to keep the wells from pumping until the price per barrel returned to one dollar. This after a special Texas Legislative Session ended the proposed restriction of oil production tied to market demand. Tacked onto the legislation were strict prohibitives of physical waste. With tempers flaring, a petition asking for martial law initiated by the East Texas Chamber of Commerce reached Sterling's desk.

The following day when production reached a startling one million barrels of crude per day, the Governor acted by giving the National Guard the task of supervising production and quelling what he termed "insurrection and open rebellion" against the laws meant to prevent the waste of Texas crude and natural gas.

While resentment ran high among the anti-Prorationists, an uneasy welcome evidenced itself in the faces of curtailment sympathizers as the community stood on the sidewalks watching twelve hundred National Guard troops march through Brophy on their way to Kilgore, Overton, and Gladewater. The partners and families, including the recently returned Arnolia, had to shout to be heard above the lumbering convoy.

"This ain't about to stop them pumpin' more than the allowable," Mavis spoke as she held a twin on each hip. "All it's apt to do is get some folks killed."

Taking Earline, Cale agreed, "None of you women need to be out past dusk."

"I'm increasing the guards at the wells," Pup promised.

"I don't see where that's necessary at our rig," Babe challenged.

Pup was adamant. "We got to prepare for the fact that some production cut backs are comin'. That means a loss of jobs and idle men lookin' to put blame on the first scapegoat in sight. You and your men are prime targets."

"No arguin'," Bulldog pronounced. "Stray shots from part time soldier boys can set this whole field afire."

"There's the big man," pointed Clyde at the commander of the Guard, "one Brigadier General Jacob F. Wolters."

Further down the street, John Earl spat toward Wolters. "Damn Texaco front man. As if martial law ain't a sufficient slap in the face of those opposin' Proration, he's got to wave this lawyer on Texaco's payroll in our faces." Had Terry been acquainted with the guardsman second in command, he might have used his sidearm. Colonel Walter Pyron drew his pay from Gulf.

Thus the majors tightened their stranglehold on independents under the auspices of the Governor, and East Texas appeared helpless to stop it.

"I ain't so sure this was such an all-fired good idea," Mavis said. "With pumps idle, we can't afford no payrolls. We might be able to ride it out till prices rise, but what about folks livin' for them paychecks?"

"Everyone's goin' broke," prophesied a shopkeeper privy to the conversation. People you can't pay, ain't spendin' in no stores."

"It's a fact," agreed Bulldog. "Only those with new leases and the permits to drill can keep crews. I plan on askin' workers I don't want the majors pickin' up if they'll sign time sheets as guards and clean up. The rest... "

Drug kicking and screaming into its third week, East Texans stretched the Guard in thin lines by calling them to instances of arson and sporadic outbreaks of violence spawned by idleness, rising debts, and notes payable. Even whiskey runners suffered as eagle-eyed pilots flew over the countryside in search of pumping wells, discovering instead clandestine moonshine. With the supply of whiskey diminishing, the situation bore an added mark of seriousness.

As a preventative of an inevitable armed uprising against Sterling's "toy soldiers," mass gatherings were forbidden. Invitations from Edgar Franklin reached those seated on cotton bales at a gin storehouse between Kilgore and Brophy by closely guarded word of mouth. Distrust ran high in a war where it became increasingly difficult to interpret loyalties.

Franklin took the floor when the last two guests stole past the warehouse's shot gun laden sentries. Resentment seething since his daughter's accounting of how she had been openly insulted by the traitorous Babe Styles fueled the fire in his oratory.

"I guess you boys all feel the same as I do, or you wouldn't be here. You got families to feed and bills to pay on money that ain't a comin' in."

His eyes bore into the audience. "We ain't strong enough yet to take on them part-time soldier boys, but their turn's a comin'." He paused. "What we can put a stop to here and now is the Brophy Boys givin' jobs that rightful belongs to whites to them blacks."

A cheer arose. Only Floyd Wiggins, a roughneck laid off by the Boys, stood to challenge. "It ain't the Boys' wells that's workin' that colored crew. Them leases is on black land and run by that colored partner of theirs."

From the crowd, "What the hell's that got to do with it? Them's jobs that should go to us."

"All the more' the reason," cried Lemuel Banks. "It was Willie Bacon's wife forced her way into my place, demandin' to sit with whites. She scalded me good, and that coward hidin' behind a badge didn't do nothin' but put a fine on her and them women she was with."

Franklin regained the floor, "This ain't goin' unanswered no longer. We'll be splittin' up. Banks is takin' the house, and me and my boys is headed for the well. Don't nobody come back here after we're through nor make no contact for at least a week."

The men mounted horses, a posse of sorts in a camaraderie borne of hatred, deception, and frustration with the controls placed upon them by forces they could not fight. For others whose lives had been irreversibly altered by the boom, an unwillingness to allow further change sent them into the night. As they rode, each harbored a private demon that guided him.

When the thirty men reined their mounts, the Bacon home sat in isolation, protected by dogs now sleeping near the porch. In silent signal, Lemuel swung his leg over his bay and removed from his saddle a white roll. Pulling the sheet over his head, he donned a hood which pointed defiantly toward the sky. Turning to the others, he waited until all that could be seen were glazed eyes behind white shrouded faces.

John Earl jumped from the drilling floor followed by his crew. Under the cover of night, he was rebelliously pumping "hot oil." He was not alone in the practice. Hot oil, so named for a test of storage tanks by state inspectors and troops to determine how recently crude had been piped inside, was rampant. Thus the field resembled the cat and mouse game played by revenuers and moonshiners.

As quickly as those in supposed control of East Texas' production could shut down one hot oil source, more took its place, sheltered by the lack of enforcers, the sheer vastness of the field and the seemingly infinite number of wells to police. Texas ingenuity disguised shipping both by rail and pipeline under the noses and sometimes the feet of the curtailers.

As was his practice, John Earl selected the well right before the tour, ferrying his men to the rig lest any prove disloyal. Recognizing a degree of agitation in a particular roughneck who did an inordinate amount of checking of the time prompted Terry to shut down the well hours earlier than planned.

"Why are we shuttin' her down?" questioned the driller.

Motioning with his head, the boss replied, "Ask Morgan there. He's the one occupied at keepin' up with the time."

The accusatory tone prompted the crew to turn on Morgan. To a man, they all needed the income. If Morgan was a traitor, they were prepared to deal with him on the spot.

Morgan began to step back in response to the cold stares. "I... I ain't worried about no time, no more than the usual wantin' a tour to end so's I can go home to my family. Since when is wantin' to go home a crime?"

"I noticed him, too," charged the second driller.

The first driller came from behind and slipped his arms through Morgan's in a lock from which the smaller man could not escape. "You even asked me last night if I could get another man in your place for tonight."

John Earl walked toward Morgan at a steady pace. At the last second his arm flew back with a quickness that startled everyone as Terry drove his fist into Morgan's stomach.

"I want to know what the hell is goin' on."

Only the first driller's strength kept Morgan somewhat on his feet. Fearing further reprisal, he strained to make himself heard amid the pain. "I just wanted to go to the meetin'."

"What meetin'?" Such an unexpected excuse stayed Terry's hand.

"The one at the gin."

"Who's at the gin?" demanded the captor.

"Ain't nobody there now. Likely they's already gone to see to things."

Tiring of Morgan's evasions, Terry threatened, "You're gonna tell me everything right now, or you'll get a beatin' from which you won't never recover."

"The Klan."

The boys began to talk all at once.

"They're teachin' that uppity Bacon and his wife a lesson." He dared not look Terry in the eye. "And I think they got a mind to do the same over to the well that them black boys and their mistress just spudded in."

John Earl had his hands around the man's throat.

"You better get the hell out of East Texas," he roared, "cause when I get time, I'm gonna take pleasure in killin' you. Jasper!"

"Yes, Sir."

"Go get Lone Wolf and tell him what's about to happen." John Earl called as he sped toward the Bacon house.

〰〰〰〰〰

Propping his feet on the opposite door panel of his car, Pup stifled another yawn. He hadn't slept much in the past weeks.

With the allowable rate, we're barely breakin' even. I don't see what's left but to sell the crude for fifteen cents a barrel to the majors. He shut the tablet upon which he had been figuring. *The only one that's even courtin' us hard is that Carmichael feller. Wantin' us so bad he's even willin' to buy us all out down to the last lease, but things ain't that bad... yet.*

A flickering in the distance disrupted his thoughts as Pup strained his eyes into the night. From the monkey board a cry went up. Above the drilling noise, Pup could detect the fear. Scrambling from the car, he raced to the shack and began to gather rifles and boxes of shells.

Babe met him at the door.

"What's goin' on?"

"Best Lester can tell, it's men on horseback carryin' some sort of torches.

"Is it the Guard?"

"We're drillin' a hundred percent legal; they got no call to raid us."

At the perimeter the watchmen gathered in a single line of defense. Once the riders came in range, a sentry cocked his rifle, causing an echo of imitation. More obvious with each step, the white robes and hoods began to gleam eerily in the flickering light.

"Tony, run warn the well."

Welcoming the change of escape, Tony tore toward the rig.

Two deep the Klansmen stopped within a natural range of voice. "We got no cause against you boys. It's them coloreds workin' white jobs that's brung us."

The seven watchmen kept guns poised in reply as the man in charge called to the torch-bearing riders. "We don't want no trouble, neither."

His words bore no signs of the fear that racked his body.

"You just take yourselves on home and consider your message delivered loud and clear."

"Guess," Lemuel ventured,"there's no accountin' for what some white boys will do, a lowerin' themselves to work for colored money. Is what they're payin' you worth your lives?"

Each guard wrestled with his conscience. Despite Pup's forecast of trouble, none actually expected to encounter anything more dangerous than late-night inspections from the Railroad Commission's hired troops. Wages or not, putting their lives on the line hardly seemed worth the sum handed weekly by the paymaster.

"Any of you boys want to throw down them rifles can walk back behind these horses free and clear. We're men of our word."

First one, then a second let his weapon fall with the force necessary to sound his decision. As those around him deserted, the spokesman cursed the cowardice of those who exchanged their manhood for survival.

At that moment the lights at the well went out, drawing the attention of Klansmen and sentries. From which barrel the shot came would be lost, but the shoulder wound sustained by a Klansman prevented him from showing his face in public until the stiffness disappeared.

"Aim at them torches," he cried. The crisp discharge of the marksmen's rifles hit their targets. Reacting to the unexpected resistance, the riders calmed their mounts and madly reached for weapons which allowed the watchmen to begin a footrace to the well.

As the shots rang out, the crew sought cover before the onslaught. Pup pushed Babe toward the car. "High tail it to town and get us some help."

"I can't leave my men, and you need every shot you've got."

"Dammit, Babe, I'm not gettin' you killed or worse. Those men are crazy so long as they got them robes and hoods hidin' their faces. Who knows what they got planned. One more shot ain't gonna do us the kinda good we need. Now get the hell out of here!" Impulsively, Pup grabbed the woman by the waist and pulled her toward him.

Dizzy from the effects of his kiss, Babe stumbled to the automobile and barreled into the darkness rather than draw attention with headlights.

~~~~~

The frenzied barking of the dogs sent Arnolia straight up in bed. "Willie," she punched her snoring husband. "There's somethin' got them dogs all in a tither."

Willie's unintelligible response prompted her to don a robe thrown carelessly over the foot of the bed. As she reached the parlor, light from the torches danced on the walls. Her screams brought Willie to her side.

Arnolia broke for the children's rooms as the door burst open and the hooded intruders blanketed the parlor in a pallid wave. Fiercely, Willie fought back, kicking and swinging against odds he could not overcome.

Banks himself led the search for Arnolia who huddled in a closet with the children. As Klansmen pulled Elizabeth from her arms, Jeremiah attacked the man who held his mother. With the back side of his hand, Lemuel slapped the boy into the closet with such a force that he lost consciousness.

"Unless you want a taste of what your brother got, you better get inside," ordered the ominous figure in white.

"Do what he say," the mother urged as tears streamed down her face. "Please don't hurt my babies," she begged.

Her pleas for the children and herself went unheeded. To combat her struggles, a man held each arm and leg to bring her into the parlor where Willie lay face down on the floor. Blood from the beating required to subdue him puddled on the rug Arnolia did not even allow the children to walk upon. In response to Arnolia's cries, Willie moaned and attempted to rise, a boot in the back of his head the reward for his efforts.

A Klansman entered. "We got everything ready."

At his words, the disoriented husband was pulled across the floor and down the steps.

They's just gonna burn a cross, she repeatedly told herself. *Just tryin' to scare us. Sweet Jesus, she prayed, you can take my soul to paradise, but save my husband and my children from the wrath of these devils.*

Once on the porch, all questions concerning their fate were answered. In the huge pecan that shaded her home hung two nooses.

Her heart sank, causing her to become limp and a more cumbersome load. Arnolia's mind could not hold a focus, save for the prayers she uttered. When the men coarsely bound her hands, there was no painful response. A numbness controlled her emotions to shield her from reality in an almost trance-like serenity.

Having roused from the blows, Willie's desperate offer further enraged his captors. "I gots money, plenty of money to pay you all to leave right now. My family ain't never done nothin' to nobody. Let us be."

Cold eyes bore through the oval slits in the hood. "Your money ain't buyin' you nothin' 'cept a sooner trip to your maker."

Without warning he loosened his grip on the noose and kicked the dining room chair Arnolia ordered directly from the furniture store the fancy women of Dallas frequented. The pop of his neck prompted another Klansman to follow his lead.

"What about them kids?" called a faceless voice.

"There ain't no time."

The Klansmen remounted and spread themselves in all directions. Once in the darkness they removed the robes and hoods abandoned through the Texas countryside. A gentle evening breeze swayed the bodies of husband and wife as they dangled a few feet from the soil whose wealth provided them with birth and death.

Inside, the children cowered in fear of the return of their tormentors and the incertitude of the unknown. Ripped from them by hatred and bigotry was a childhood innocence and the fairy tale life providentially anointed by the gushing wells. The sound of John Earl's engine sent the smaller girls into the arms of their sister and a renewed sense of foreboding teeming through their bodies.

Terry took on two wheels the last bend of the limestone bedded road, straining for any signs of the trouble forecast by Morgan. *Looks calm enough. Damn that Morgan, got me worked up over nothin.* A multitude of stars and a goodly portion of moon illuminated his approach, though the shade tree near which the house had been purposefully set prevented him a clear view. *Won't hurt none to look around.* Rifle in hand, John Earl left his car some half a mile from the house lest he ride headlong into a maelstrom.

What a lone man could do had yet to enter Terry's mind, his singular thought to save those he held dearer than his own family. John Earl Terry had put his life on the line for a meager few; in this instance, there had been no question.

Falling to his knees, John Earl wretched at the sight. It did not occur often, the determination not to release his feelings a direct defiance of his old man's hand, but Terry allowed his emotions to reign and wept bitterly. Even the harsh commands of the corporal as he held his weapon near the back of his head failed to rouse John Earl from the transfixed posture. A Brophyite conscripted from his porch swing to serve as guide stayed the soldier's hand.

"He ain't the one done this," the codger spat in the direction opposite the most feet. "This here's John Earl Terry. Him and that man a hangin' yonder was partners up till a while back."

The sergeant in charge ordered his men to cut down the bodies. Already they had stiffened, necks bent at unnatural angles, eyes frozen in the split-second of disbelief before violent death. Carried to the Army-issue truck, Willie, then Arnolia were placed uncovered in the opened bed. There they would remain for the curious until the Guard allowed the colored undertaker from Kilgore to perform his task. Many an East Texan passed by the temporary armory for a glimpse. It was, as a youngster grown to manhood would recount years later, "the singularly most gruesome example of hatred I ever hope to witness."

Terry slowly rose, then like a man possessed, he began to run toward the house. "The children!" he called to the Guard. "Help me find them kids." John Earl bounded up the stairs while the soldiers fanned in search of what they assumed to be more victims of the Klan. "Jeremiah, Miriam, it's John Earl. Come on out."

Panic led him to every conceivable hiding place. *Not the kids*, he begged. He could see the girls crawling into his lap in a hide and seek game for the candy he kept. *How can anybody live knowin' he killed innocent children? They got nothin' but love and trust in their hearts even for animals like...* He threw open the closet door.

When her eyes adjusted to the light, Miriam flew into his arms. "They kilt Jeremiah!"

Scooping up Tamara and Elizabeth, Terry ordered the soldiers who followed his lead, "Get your doctor quick. This boy's in bad shape."

He ain't gonna make it, John Earl decided as he watched the irregular rise and fall of the boy's chest. To shield the girls, he quickly left the boy to the field doctor. With the youngest girls in his arms and Miriam by her quivering hand, he walked down the porch steps amid soldiers with heads bowed in a mixture of reverence and shame. A silent path cleared for the stern-faced white man and the orphaned charges dwarfed by his strength and trenchant presence.

John Earl guided the car through the maze of men and vehicles toward Brophy and the sole person to whom he could entrust so delicate a package. The small rise from street to driveway forced his headlights across the porch and into the parlor of the Russell home. From behind the draperies Billy Aiken peered until snatched from behind by the mother who replaced him.

Since the accident, Melba and her brood lived with the Russell's, first cramped in the house and now in a converted garage apartment where she served as housekeeper, nanny, cook, Elaine's most trusted confidant, and now the most avid of John Earl's enemies. Jerking her robe tighter, Melba opened the door to face the man responsible for the collective miseries of each member of the household.

"What do you want?" she demanded, her displeasure unbridled.

"I need to see Elaine."

"Not tonight you don't." Melba began to push the door only to have it fly back with a force that sent her staggering into the parlor.

"Where is she?"

The anger in his voice and carriage inspired Melba's reply. "She spent the night over at Mavis'. One of the babies got the earache. You know, Elaine can't pass up a chance to help somebody."

"You ought to know all about her generous nature."

Melba opened her mouth to respond as Elaine walked into the room. Obviously roused from a sound sleep, she adjusted slowly to the reality of the presence of her ex-husband.

"Bad pennies just keep turnin' up." Melba moved protectively toward her friend. "But this one's a goin' on his way of his own accord or on the arm of the constable."

Something in his stooped shoulders, the downcast expression led her to believe, *He needs me*. To Melba, "It's all right; he can stay if needs be."

"Wake up, honey. This man ever brought anything but grief? Why just think of..."

"Dammit, woman! Hold your tongue!" He raged. "Willie and Arnolia's dead, and I got the girls in the car," he faltered lowering his temperament and body onto the hassock, "And I didn't know nowheres else to bring 'um."

Elaine flew to his side and sank to her knees. "What in the name of heaven happened?" John Earl appeared to stare through Elaine before closing his eyes as if to block the memory's return.

"They was hangin' there like they was no more worth than wolves on a fence post."

Elaine put her arms around his shoulders as he bent forward to cover his face with his massive hands.

"When?" she sobbed.

"Just now. I couldn't have been more than a half hour too late to stop it." He pleaded with Elaine for absolution. "I tried to stop it; soon as I found out about it I come fast as I could...I did..."

Melba handed John Earl the bottle Clyde kept for special occasions. He nursed the bottle as the women transferred the now sleeping children to the guest room. The unanswered ringing of the phone sent him across the room and to the receiver. "Yeah?"

A strained silence followed. "Hell's bells, John Earl. You got nerve, I'll say that for you."

Unwilling to abide yet another querulous female, Terry yanked the phone from his ear, ready to slam it into place when he caught a portion of Mavis' ranting about the shooting at the well.

"The damned least you could do is get your ornery tail out there to help out instead of following your ex-wife around with your tongue hangin' out."

A few seconds later, when she returned from settling the children, Elaine found the phone hanging by its cord and the strident voice of Mavis McCallister's lambastings filling the parlor.

~~~~~~

As his training in Europe's war returned, Pup rallied each of his drillers to position. Most of his crew had been raised to shoot, and he held no doubts as to their skills. The darkness was Pup's idea on a gamble that most of the Klansmen knew their way around a farm better than a drilling rig.

Judging from Lester we're outnumbered about three to one, he estimated. I've faced worse. As the Klansmen neared the well, Pup wanted to give out a yell as he watched them stumble in the semi-darkness over the equipment and their cumbersome robes. *Them robes was a hell of a idea; all's the easier to see 'um while my men got natural coverin' and drillin' mud to boot. I just hope none of the boys fires until they're close enough to spring the trap I learnt from that battle-field promoted lieutenant.*

The hem of a robe caught on an offshoot of pipe to send both man and weapon to the ground. Frightened by what he mistook for an attack, Edgar fired and drew a response in every direction and elevation from Pup's crew.

White robes fell to the muddy ground. As the cries of the wounded echoed, Pup began to relive the battlefield horrors he had banished. Watching a hood rise over a generator, Pup squeezed the trigger. He always marveled at what appeared yet could not be the simultaneous response of the recoil and sound of his weapon as it felled a nameless body. This was his only thought as he pivoted the barrel toward his next victim with the mindless automation of a seasoned veteran.

A roughneck named Jimbo stepped from his protective cover to catch the bullet of a Klansman. Still able to fire, he mustered a return. From behind he felt a slight sting followed by a warm oozing down his back. Pup appeared seemingly from nowhere.

"You all right, Jimbo?"

"I's still shootin', ain't I?"

Pup fired cover as the wounded man eased nearer the slush pit.

Met with such stubborn and unexpected opposition, the Klansman began to scatter in panicked confusion. Only Edgar's persistent outcries prompted some to regroup and position, the result being a statement of sorts marked by sporadic fire that did little but keep men pinned.

From the doorway of the shed Pup relaxed somewhat. *Damnation,* he swore, *there's no tellin' how many's left. Don't see as we got but one sure fire thing in our favor.* His thoughts turned to a spunky little gal burning the road between the well and Kilgore.

~~~~~~

The first miles had been rough going for Babe, who expected to draw fire from Klansmen as she barreled through the East Texas night with her destination the first accessible phone in downtown Brophy.

Rounding the last corner, she braked and turned sharply to avoid the mob of townspeople, boomers, and a smattering of soldiers that lined the main route. Babe abandoned her car in the middle of the street and ran toward the unmistakable vehicle with its front-mounted gun pointing into the crowd to underscore the authority of the man who stood with one leg resting on its front bumper.

The lady driller pushed and shoved through the crowd, calling the lawman's name, only to be heard as she pierced the last layer of people. "The Klan's at the well!" she managed in a sort of breathlessness.

The relay of her announcement further stirred the curious.

"Calm down, Babe," the Ranger advised. "You can't tell nothin' all flustered."

"Out at the Willie B. #6. My man on the monkey board spotted their torches and gave us the time to pass out the guns." Her closed eyes pictured Pup and her crew murdered at the hands of the Klan. The thrill of his parting kiss trickled into her emotions. *I can't lose him*, she thought.

"You got to get out there," she begged. "They can't hold off that many." She tugged at Gonzaullus' arm.

"What do you mean, Klan?" came the voice of Lemuel Banks. "Hell," he scoffed, "everybody knows there ain't no Klan this side of the Sabine. If them coloreds got themselves kilt, it was some of their own set on gettin' a holt of their money. Don't waste your time, Ranger, runnin' after no wild geese."

Babe released the Ranger's arm and lunged toward Banks. An alert soldier intercepted the desperate woman.

"See, the woman's crazy as they come. I'm tellin' you folks, there ain't no Klan."

"Then who's shooting out at the well?" she demanded.

Banks addressed the man holding Babe in check. "Probably some friends of these army boys here firin' at your crew would be my guess. They're runnin' hot oil, and done been found out. Mighty convenient way of coverin' it up."

"Seems to me you're doin' a good bit of sayin', the most of which I don't buy. You heard the lady, boys. Mount up." As the men ran to their cars, the Ranger looked down at Babe. "I don't want to waste time takin' no wrong turns. You up to ridin' shot gun?"

"Hell yes," she answered almost in the car.

On the way, Lone Wolf filled Babe in on the Klan's raid on the Bacons. Uncharacteristic tears streamed down the face of a woman hardened by years of competition in a man's world.

As the derrick became visible in the early-morning sky, the Ranger ordered, "Give 'um a taste of what's comin'." He pointed to the mounted weapon.

Despite the errant rays, the identities of those headed toward the well stayed in question until the rapid retort removed all doubt. The hooded assassins broke for their horses, some managing to reach them unscathed, others felled by the aims of the crew. A meager few would make it home despite the soldiers' efforts.

Realizing that the Klansmen were in flight, Pup eased from the shed, *They're not gettin' away scot free, nor goin' before no jury that's half made up of members and sympathizers, not while I got shots left.*

From behind came a harsh voice. "My girl sets a good deal in store by you, but she and I don't necessarily share opinions, 'specially when it comes to white men desertin' their kind, even if it did make 'um rich. Nope, won't be nobody followin' suit no time soon."

Pup heard the discharge and felt the pain tear through his leg. A second shot echoed as he pivoted and raised his rifle in defense. As a circle of red traveled the white sheet, Franklin fell to reveal the smoking barrel of Babe's weapon.

Babe threw down the gun and ran to Pup. Holding him in her arms and crying, she pushed back the hair from his sweaty face and kissed it repeatedly.

"I just kept praying we'd make it in time," she said.

"Looks like you get the save," he grinned before a stab of pain distorted his face.

Chapter 13

After the opening of the wells on the fifth of September, the Governor began whittling at the allowable rates. From two hundred twenty-five barrels, which was held to be the point at which a driller could break even on his costs, Sterling trimmed to one hundred eighty-five and later to one hundred sixty-five..

John Earl and his fellow hot oilers continued to produce what they deemed rightfully theirs despite the consequences. For the independents, belts tightened one notch at a time until they were squeezed into deals with the majors or outside investors who could provide working capital.

At Mavis' insistence, the Brophy Boys family lunched at a home left unfinished due to Proration's curtailment of funds. Still the home was vintage Mavis. As the society editor of the Kilgore newspaper expressed in confidence to a friend, "Mrs. McCallister possesses a rare talent. Never have I encountered a woman able to spend thousands in Texas' finest stores only to achieve a decor barely on a par with the Sears Catalog."

No fool, the editor printed a glowing account of the McCallister Mansion, posing Mavis in the least tasteless room, that being the kitchen.

"Hell's bells," Mavis' exasperation evident as she passed personal copies to the women. "You think she could have taken that picture somewheres else. I didn't come all this way to end up back in a damn kitchen."

The gathering needed the levity of Mavis' unperceived slight, it being the first since the funerals, and given the circumstances of the company. As Miss Wythel tried to return her copy, Mavis pushed the newspaper back across the massive dining room table.

"That's yours. All of you get a copy for your scrap books. I got at least a hundred more upstairs for Momma to hand out in Winnie."

"What do you hear from Gabriel?" Millie interrupted with a note of solemnity.

Elaine replied, "He says Jeremiah may never come out of the coma."

"I thought they took him to some fancy place down to Galveston?" Mavis questioned.

"They did, but even the best of doctors can't work miracles. One of them said that the boy just didn't seem to want to wake up, like staying asleep was better than facing up to what happened. At least they have Arnolia's sister living there to take care of them all."

Miss Wythel started around the table. "It's a damn shame. A damn shame." Reaching the halfway point of the table, the old woman leaned on her cane in disgust. "Couldn't you find a bigger table? I hear tell they got one up at the White House seats upwards of fifty."

Incensed at the one-uppance, Mavis pleaded with Elaine. "She makin' that up?"

"What the hell does it matter? You ain't got a handful of friends aside us."

Mavis pouted, "When the twins get older and start havin' parties, this house will be full of kids, all of 'um fightin' for a chance to be sittin' up and down this table." Her arms flew out in gesticulation. Suddenly the idea burst through the clutter of Mavis' mind. Running to Babe, she got down on her knees and took the startled girl's hands. "Oh, I know. We'll have the weddin' right here."

She was on her feet, alive with plans for the Styles-Schneider nuptials. "And there's this place over in Longview where they rent out them love birds. Picture this everybody: There'll be cages full all around the parlor. They'll be a tweetin' and a chirpin' all durin' the service."

"And a stinkin'," Miss Wythel scoffed.

Envisioning a wedding at the mercy of Mavis' ghastly taste, Babe did her best to curtail the planning which now centered on the reception. "Hold it!" Babe screamed for the third time. "I thought Cale put you on a Proration budget?"

Her face fell. "Damn you, Sterling. My man's got oil bustin pipe tryin' to turn into money, and..."

"It's awfully sweet of you, really, but Pup and I aren't setting a date until we know where the Boys stand. Their backs are up against a wall. I don't know if the men told you all, but they had to sell some of the unpumped crude to Oklahoma Oil at a price that could make or break us."

Taking her cue from their confused expressions, Babe explained, "In order to stay solvent, independents entered into a speculative game with the majors. We sell the crude but leave it in the ground until our buyer is ready."

"So money's money. That's a sure thing." Mavis scoffed.

"Not when it may cost you more to pump at the time the major wants his oil than what he paid you to start with."

Ever the optimist Elaine added, "But it could cost us less?"

"Not likely." Miss Wythel scowled. "Them majors want us out, so they just leave us a hangin' till they can put us out in one swift blow."

"Now here's what's truly odd." Babe inched forward in her chair and lowered her voice. "That new man, David Carmichael, that took the place of Lamar Tate, presented us a sweetheart of a deal, way over what Humble or Gulf did. Now why do you suppose he'd do that?"

"Maybe he feels sorry for us since we're workin' skeleton crews and movin' 'um to different wells when each allowable's used up?" Mavis speculated.

"Even the majors have to respect us for not flooding the market with hot oil. Did you hear the latest scheme? Burying fire hoses for pipelines under the street! Do people have no scruples where money is concerned?"

~~~~~~~

Since some of the Brophy Boys' tanks sat virtually empty, the men employed one crew of tank cleaners to dispose of the bottom sediment which they christened "BS" for good reason.

Arriving outside town with his tour, Arnell Warren again thanked heaven for Melba's providential hand in his job security and his luck at drawing the third shift into the bowels of the tank, which reduced the fumes and danger at least by some scant degree.

The bottom sheet of steel removed from the vent, mops, brooms, and wooden shovels fell from the opening. As he descended into the hell in which he earned his living, Arnell's mind traveled back to the tiny rent house, also one of Melba's string pullings, and his argument with Lois Ann. Since the birth

of the baby so close on the heels of Ray's death, she wanted
him to quit.

"And just how I am supposed to support us?" he demanded
in a voice so tempered with reality that she went to bed crying.

Thus distracted, Warren drug his broom absently across
the BS until an unusual sensation stole his thoughts.
Reworking the spot, he heard an object hit the side of the tank.
"Hey, boys, there's somethin' goin' on here."

Inching their way toward Arnell with questioning faces, the
crew bent forward with Arnell as he rescued the object before
it could sink too far. Dismissing the sight as the dizzying effects
of the fumes, the tank cleaner looked a second time at the
muck-covered mass.

"Dammit!" he screamed. "It's a skull!"

Elvis Dial, the most senior of the tour, accepted the find
from the trembling Warren.

"Looks like somebody let the steam and sludge do their dirty
work.

Steam alone can cook the flesh clean off in no time."

"Time's up," came a voice from the vent.

As soon as he made the surface, Elvis placed the discovery
in the hands of their boss man while Arnell sat on the roof of
the tank, his malady more the effect of the find that the deadly
gases.

Removing his bandanna, Hagen wiped at the sludge and
announced, "Reminds me of my mother-in-law."

The boys roared.

"Better go get the law," he advised in a more somber tone.

"You think somebody killed him?" a tankie questioned.

With a look of exasperation, "No, I suppose he decided to
crawl in for a warm spot on a cool night. Which one of you
idiots found it?"

"Warren."

"I guess I just snapped his head plumb off with my shovel and sent it a flyin' against the wall." As the words sounded, Arnell's hands covered his mouth as rapidly as he ran to the side of the tank. Included in each man's accounting of the day was Warren's lengthy stay with his head hung over the side of the tank. When he shamefacedly joined the others, he informed Hagen, "I ain't goin' down for the rest."

"You will or you got no job; this ain't all of him to find."

Without further exchange, Arnell Warren started for the ground. *This is as good a time as any,* he told himself. *We're headin' back to where folks cover bodies with at least six feet of good earth.*

"I'll give two dollars for his spot," offered a tankie.

"I'll go three."

From the grimy coveralls appeared a wad of small bills that soon lost their green backs to BS smudges.

Men scampered into the hell hole with record speed in competition for the dubious honor of recovering more of the body.

"Be easy with them shovels," Hagen warned from the vent. "Lone Wolf's gonna want what's left of that poor bastard in as near a whole piece as we can get."

On the ground, boys readied the cables and plank-bottomed bed used in emergencies. Once it reached the floor, the boys tried easing the bones in a single motion, but the brittle condition caused sufficient splitting to result in a jigsaw of mismatched bones.

"Damn," Hagen swore as he examined what he presumed to be part of a leg. "There's gonna be hell to pay when the Ranger gets a look at this. Couldn't you boys do no better?"

By the time the men and remains hit the ground, Lone Wolf Gonzaullas pulled to a stop at the tank yard. "This is the third since the boom got in full swing," he told his audience. "Not a clue to the names of any." Careful not to allow any of the BS to fall on his alligator-skinned boots, he leaned over the blackened bones.

"Got any water to clean this off?"

"What's the use, Ranger?"

"I dunno, maybe an old break. If some lady's missin' her husband, she might be able to tell me he once had a broke arm or..." Gonzaullas stopped cold.

In cleaning what he surmised to be one of the fingers, a brilliance emerged. Pressed against the bone by the heat and pressure, a misshapen diamond ring caught the sun in its facets. The boys crowded more closely with each venturing a guess.

"L. T.," Lone Wolf announced.

Addressing Hagen he ordered, "Stay with these until the constable gets here and the undertaker. I got some calls to make, startin' with the boys that own these tanks."

"You don't think none of them done this?"

"Can't rightly say. You never know about folks when money's concerned." The lanky Ranger strolled back to his car with the ring wrapped in his handkerchief.

~~~~~~

POP! The cork of the champagne bottle flew across the room of a posh New Orleans speak easy to force the jubilant couple for whom the tuxedo-attired waiter opened the now foaming bottle backward in their chairs. A round of applause accompanied the toast to the newlyweds, a handsome couple reeking of money.

As she examined the large diamond on her left hand, the bride approved of the degree of sparkle caught by the chandelier. Not quite the stone as my first trip round the bend, but a damn sight bigger than the ring he stuck on the finger of that prude, I'll wager. Estelle Tate Terry flashed an adoring smile toward the latest man she promised her faithfulness, a vow she fully intended to honor this time around.

Her groom reciprocated, though his thoughts centered on his predecessor. *I figure you're laughin', even with them flames lickin' your ass, just knowin' what I got myself into by marryin' Estelle. Well, Mrs. Terry, you better enjoy this while you can.* He patted her hand lovingly. *Cause the first time you get outta line, I'll cut you loose with what few clothes you'll have on your back, now that I'm in the driver's seat at Oklahoma Oil.*

Taking his affection to heart, Estelle leaned forward to expose the contours of her most noticeable assets. "I can't wait to get you to Oklahoma City. I got friends that will just die when they see how good lookin' you are."

"They'll just have to wait a spell."

"Oh," she inched her chair nearer, "you plan to keep me all to yourself?"

John Earl signaled the waiter of his desire for their bill. In a distracted manner, "You're not lettin' on to nobody that we're married."

Momentarily stunned, Estelle recovered with a lighthearted though somewhat apprehensive chuckle. "You quit jokin' like that. You almost had me believin'..." A steel gaze silenced her.

"In case you've forgot a few tiny details, we got more at stake here than you gettin' to parade me around a bunch of fat biddies like I was your prize stud. I got them ungrateful SOB's around their throats. So long as you keep your pretty mouth shut and those fools in the Capitol keep Proration goin', I'll own most all the crude them Brophy Boys got in them wells."

"But... but I thought you hated Proration?"

Exasperated, Terry fired, "Havin' them politicians tell me what I can and can't do with my oil chaps my ass, but it don't hurt near as much knowin' how it's gonna feel when I walk into those offices and tell them Ole John Earl's got them over every single one of their barrels."

"So where does that leave me?" Beginning to regain her confidence, "I am the majority owner."

John Earl jerked her left hand from her lap to force it only inches from her face. "*We* are the majority owners of Oklahoma Oil, my dear, and not a sane man on that Board is about to take orders from a woman, especially one who made her way in life lookin' up at a ceilin'."

Smiling broadly, he released Estelle, suddenly amiable. "Besides, it won't be for long. As hard as the independents are fightin' and the more those roughnecks go without work, Proration is on its deathbed."

"Excuse me, sir. There is a call for you. Let me escort you to our office."

"I didn't tell nobody where I'd be." He glared at his wife whose expression told of equal bewilderment.

Once inside a cramped but elegantly furnished office, Terry waited for the waiter to leave before taking the receiver. "This is John Earl."

"Thank God."

"Who the hell is this?"

"Carmichael."

A series of epithets ended with a single question. "How'd you find me?"

"Someday you have to stop underestimating me." Wasn't it you that gave me strict orders to keep a close eye on the woman's who's going to be your next wife? Well, I knew she was in New Orleans, even which hotel. Just a matter of checkin' speaks.... Never mind, we're in a hell of a mess."

"What now?"

"Estelle's housekeeper called. It seems Western Union delivered a telegram, and the woman's got no clue to finding Estelle. So I had her read it to me."

Terry's eyes widened as he gripped the edge of the desk. "Act outraged; offer a big reward."

"But if we do that..."

"Then you look like you got no worries. Nobody saw a thing. I'll get the grievin' widow on the next train. Tell folks she was sightseein'." Terry slammed the receiver. Contemplating his next move, he leaned back in the desk chair as his face clouded with doubt and apprehension. Suddenly he was on his feet, strolling confidently toward his wife. *Damn good thing I had the weddin' done in secret; maybe I ain't been givin' Carmichael enough credit after all.*

"Who in the world knew we were here?"

"Carmichael. We got to get you packed and on the next train to Seminole."

"You're crazy; I ain't goin' nowhere."

"Your first husband has just returned from the great beyond."

The stern expression moved Estelle to down the contents of her champagne in a single motion.

∧∧∧∧∧∧

A series of chimes rivaling Big Ben resounded throughout the McCallister home. Mavis left her guests still engaged in Babe's decidedly more accurate rendition of the Brophy Boys' crisis. Swinging open the oak doors, Mavis's eyes traveled upward into the face of Ranger Gonzaullas.

Hat in hand, the lawman stated his mission. "Pardon my interruption, Ma'am. I'm Lone Wolf Gonzaullas, and I got business with your husband and his partners. The girl down to the office says they're all havin' a bite of lunch."

What does the Ranger want with the Boys? It must be bad news... Gabriel. Gabriel's made good on his threats to get even...

"Mrs. McCallister?"

"Yes, of course, forgive my bein' so rude and all. Get in here. You just took me back, that's all. I'll go round 'em up. In a place this size, there's little or no tellin' where they got off to."

Nodding his approval, Lone Wolf began to take in his surroundings. *It's a showplace. Only seen one other with more atmosphere; shame we had to shut down that brothel.* His thoughts were interrupted by the entrance of a woman supporting herself on a cane.

"You're the Ranger, ain't ya?" her words more of an accusation.

"Ma'am," Gonzaullas bowed in respect. "You have the advantage."

"Wythel Sue Wallis. What business you got here? Rangers don't pay no social calls."

Mavis seized the brass knob of what she insisted Cale refer to as his study. "Lone Wolf's here. What the hell have ya'll done now? I knew times was bad, but are we runnin' hot oil or just drillin' on the slant?"

"Stop your frettin'," advised Bulldog. "Likely as not, there's still unfinished business over Willie. This case ain't never gonna be closed, cause you know the scum what did it won't be named."

His son responded, "That Franklin girl and her momma got knowledge of every last one. Damn, I'd like to..."

The Boys reached the parlor where Elaine was serving coffee to the Ranger and the now seated ladies. Lone Wolf sat a china cup upon its saucer, the room's silence allowing the distinctive notes to sound much too loudly. "Have any of your boys from over to the storage tanks called up?"

"Not so that I'm aware," Clyde answered. "Is there some trouble with our waste products?"

"In a manner of speakin'. Seems your crew cleaned up so good that they dug all the way down to a dead man."

"You mean someone dumped a body down one of our tanks?" asked Mavis incredulously.

"You boys got any idea who was doin' the dead man's float in your crude?"

"Certainly not," Clyde was on his feet with his hands speaking more rapidly than his tongue. "Why, our watchman can..."

Embarrassed to confess his role, Pup spoke up. "Since the Governor tied our hands, we been cuttin' back on expenses. All the men we could keep on we have, and those watchin' out for things that ain't easy carted off got moved to other jobs or let go..."

"So it's been a while since you've had a man out there steady?"

"Since the order, I been meanin' to do some switchin', but since Willie and Arnolia, I got to put boys where I think we need 'um most."

"Face it, Lone Wolf," came a father's defense, "you been around oil fields enough to know that tanks is the first place a man wantin' to rid hisself of a corpse is apt to choose. Everybody and his dog knows can't no identification be made."

The Ranger fished into his pocket. "Well, this time our killer was wrong." He showed what was left of the diamond ring to his audience. "This dead man left us a callin' card."

Elaine gasped in recognition. "That ring is just like the one Lamar Tate wore. Don't you remember it, Mavis, from that night at the Adolphus? You and I talked about it."

"But I thought he died down in Mexico somewheres?"

Hoyt entered the conversation. "Yep, the papers said it was his heart. Ask me, it was tryin' to keep up with that alley cat he married."

Lone Wolf delivered the ring to the palm of Elaine's hand. "Then you're certain this belonged to Tate?"

"I'd recognize it anywhere."

Suddenly aware that she was being excluded from the excitement, Mavis grabbed the diamond from Elaine. "Lamar Tate and me was this close," she measured the proximity between herself and Elaine. "He was a wavin' it around like he was mighty proud to be sportin' so many sparkles. It took up most his knuckle."

The Ranger gently reclaimed his clue. Before turning he inquired, "You boys had a goodly amount of dealings with Oklahoma Oil, if the way I hear it is true?"

"That was after he was dead," Pup leaped in defense.

"That so?" The Ranger faced Pup squarely as the younger man bit his tongue over what he now realized reeked of incrimination. "Maybe that new fella runnin' the show cuts a better deal?"

"They came courtin' us, and I got the papers to back it up," snapped Clyde.

"So the gossip mills got this one wrong? I guess the Brophy Boys' oil ain't worth more to Oklahoma Oil than other folks' crude."

The lanky Ranger shook his head. "I can't imagine where I could have got such poor information." Relaxing once again in his chair, Lone Wolf pushed further. "I don't know how the man was to work for, but I bet you could tell me, Bulldog. You're an old Oklahoma Oil hand from way back."

Bulldog shifted uneasily. *If all the cussin's I give that man ever comes to light, no jury in the world will believe I didn't kill him.* Aloud, "I got no call to hurt the man. Me and my boy give him an honest day's labor for every check we drew. Wasn't like we was dinin' up to the mansion every night." His last remark drew nervous laughter. "Besides, all our dealin's is with Carmichael. None of the rest of us had no business with Tate himself."

Faintly, Cale claimed the attention of the parlor. "Except John Earl."

"What's Terry got to do with Lamar Tate?"

"It's not somethin' I should be discussin' around the ladies."

"Hell's bells, Cale, there's nothin' gonna burn our ears."

Cale attempted to quiet his wife, "I just meant that some of us might not want to open old wounds."

Only Elaine seemed to comprehend his intentions. "It's fine. I can't believe Ranger Gonzaullas isn't aware that my... that John Earl was in the company of Mr. Tate's wife the night I nearly died at the Adolphus."

"I do apologize. I was truly ignorant of those circumstances."

Attempting to save Elaine further humiliation, "I never told no one, not even Mavis," Cale stammered, "but John Earl and Estelle Tate went back further than that one night in Dallas. See, he was run out of Seminole for... for being too friendly with her. He was fresh out of town when he showed up at Hoyt's store."

"Does John Earl have any business interest with you boys?"

"None," unisomed several partners.

"We bought him out to the last dot of an 'i.' After what he did to my daughter and the way he got that shooter killed, we couldn't stomach another day."

The Ranger made his way to the foyer. "Any idea where John Earl might be?"

Seeing him to the door Mavis answered for them all.

"None of us give a damn."

As the door closed, Lone Wolf replaced his hat, his mind a myriad of thoughts. *After I send a wire to the Captain for a man to hold reign over the place while I make a run to Seminole, I'll see about havin' a little talk with Mr. Terry.* He tapped his hat into place and slid behind the wheel.

~~~~~~

It was two days filled with phone calls to old friends in Mexico before the Ranger arrived in Seminole. As yet, Lone Wolf had no fast and sure conclusions, save his belief that Lamar Tate's Mexican death was a ruse. Confirmation, he felt sure, could be found in Seminole.

The headquarters of Oklahoma Oil rose five stories and housed a variety of business and professional men. From the drug store situated in its corner, Gonzaullas passed the display windows of both a shoe and flower shops before turning into the main entry which led to the offices located above street level.

Scanning the directory, the Ranger recognized names painted on the street-side windows by the attorneys, doctors, and bookkeepers before realizing his journey would end on the fourth floor.

The Ranger ambled in and removed his Stetson before the desk of a middle-aged woman listening to a Dictaphone.

"May I help you?"

"Yes, Ma'am, you sure can. I'm Ranger Gonzaullas, and I'd like to have a few words with the president of your company."

A faint scowl crossed the secretary's face. "Mr. Carmichael is merely the acting president."

Lone Wolf smiled to himself. *There's no love lost between those two. Play my hand right, and she could be just the trump card I need.* "I do apologize," he responded penitently. "I'm not familiar with the everyday goins' on here. All I know is what I been told, which," he laughed, "must not be all that good."

With a wave of her hand, the woman tried to brush away her loss of decorum.

"I shouldn't have made a fuss. This has just been a bit difficult for me, adjusting to a new boss after all those years with Mr. Tate."

"You thought a lot of the man?"

"Indeed I did." She became intent as she spoke of her former employer. "Mr. Tate hired me right out of the Business College when I was desperate for any job." Her voice became wistful. "He was awfully good to me over the years, helping me with my finances and buying cars, things that a woman on her own can't seem to manage."

"You were his girl Friday?"

Her face brightened at the suggestion. "Well, I guess I am, was. I got him through the death of Mrs. Tate; it hit him really hard."

"But I thought Mrs. Tate was still living?" the Ranger feigned confusion.

Returning to the hateful countenance, the woman replied, "That would be his second marriage. It was not looked upon by those who knew him as a well-thought decision."

As he appraised the lady, Lone Wolf began to piece the signals. *This woman feels more than gratitude for Tate. Never married, worked at his side for years, yep, you expected to be the second Mrs. Tate.*

"She was more suited to a younger, less socially prominent husband. Mr. Tate seldom made mistakes, but when he did... All she did was spend his money and...," she blushed.

"Seems she had the good sense to appoint a trusted colleague to run the business for her late husband."

"Carmichael? Mr. Tate had no use for him. Why, he fired him not so long ago. That would be after he was duped by that Terry man into buying up leases in the East Texas field. Of course, those did turn out to be of value, but at the time, Mr. Tate was mad enough to send him packing."

"Then Mr. Terry does business with Oklahoma Oil?"

"Not at all, and believe me, I'd know. It just proved what kind of business know how Carmichael has, falling for a slick trick, and now that woman has him in Mr. Tate's office. We'll be lucky if this ship can stay afloat."

"I have no doubt that you'll be the anchor. Is it possible for me to see him?"

"Of course, let me set things up."

As she left her desk, Lone Wolf's mind was churning. *So Carmichael's rise to power had nothing to do with business sense. Then, there's the man's connection with Terry. An unpleasant union, but nonetheless a common thread.*

Inside the office, David Carmichael paced its length. Since the discovery of Lamar's body, he had slept or eaten little, sure that any moment would see him led off in chains and destined for execution.

That John Earl's a slick operator, and before he's finished, I'll be labeled the trigger man, while he comes out smellin' like a rose. How stupid could I be, and why did I take this job? It gives me the motive for killing the old man. All Estelle has to do is plant a few hints, and my days will be numbered.

He flopped into his chair just as the knock sounded.

Without waiting for a reply, the secretary entered. "There's a Texas Ranger to see you, Mr. Carmichael. He tells me that it is a professional call."

Carmichael blanched. *They're here for me. Damn John Earl.* To his secretary, "Fine." He was alone for endless seconds.

"Mr. Carmichael? Lone Wolf Gonzaullas." The hand was extended, but Carmichael could not find the strength in his legs to rise, so he reached out and took the hand that Gonzaullas offered.

"What can I do for you?"

"I'm here to clear up a little matter that occurred under my jurisdiction down in Kilgore. Are you familiar with the area?"

He could only nod his recognition.

"I assume that you're aware of the discovery of a ring similar to one belonging to the late Lamar Tate on the finger of a corpse dumped down a storage tank?"

Again the nod.

"Well, sir," the Ranger settled back in his chair and crossed his long legs with a degree of superiority, "I need to find out how it managed to switch fingers."

"How... how could I possibly be of help?" he stammered in a voice an octave above regular pitch.

Smelling the fear, Lone Wolf closed in on his prey. "Oh, I hear you were with Mr. and Mrs. Tate down in Mexico at the time of his untimely death. Seems pretty obvious to me that you would know if he was wearin' a ring that big or if the widow requested that he be buried in it."

"Oh," he squirmed further into his chair.

"Now that you mention it, I don't think Mr. Tate had his ring." The end of the labyrinth loomed. "I seem to recall that he lost it while we were in Kilgore. Yes," he brightened, straightening in his chair with a renewed confidence, "he mentioned something like that."

"I guess a ring like this would be worth a goodly sum." Lone Wolf removed the mangled ring and set it on the desk, watching Carmichael's eyes rivet upon the piece which robbed him of what composure he had managed to claim.

"Of course it is. You can certainly see why it wasn't returned. Whoever found it must have kept it to sell."

"Damned if that ain't probably so." The Ranger eased forward until he was as close to Carmichael as the desk would allow.

"It just beats the hell out of me why whoever killed the man who "found" Mr. Tate's ring would let a prize like that drift into a storage tank."

Hands shaking, Carmichael dug for the handkerchief in his breast pocket and began to wipe the cold sweat from his face.

"I appreciate that this is unpleasant for you, Sir, but I'm gonna need your help in breakin' some news to the man's widow."

"What news?"

"I got some boys down in Mexico doin' some grave diggin'. Only they're takin' out instead of puttin' in. I was in hopes that you, bein' on friendly terms with the Widow Tate, could explain how her husband's body is comin' to the surface, so to speak."

"Why would you dig up Lamar's body?"

The Ranger rose to leave, "Cause I don't believe for one minute that the dead man, assumin' that there's anything in there at all, is Lamar Tate."

"Now see here," Carmichael somehow mustered the ability to stand and fight. "Lamar Tate died in Mexico. Now if some crooked Mexican locals took advantage of trusting Americans and put someone else in his casket, now Mrs. Tate and I can hardly be responsible..."

He had his information, but Lone Wolf decided to play a wild card on the gut instinct that seldom failed him. As his hand turned the knob, he began fishing.

"The folks at the hotel say Mrs. Tate left in a hurry. Something about meetin' you and her husband in Longview where ya'll was doin' business. Strangest thing... can't find a soul in Longview that saw a one of you, and the big boys didn't have dealins' with Lamar Tate planned. But you boys here at Oklahoma Oil do all kinds of business with John Earl Terry. Maybe I better talk with him."

"John who?"

Without further exchange Gonzaullas left the office with eyes set on the road to Texas. Initially his plans called for a visit with Estelle Tate; however, David Carmichael proved such an encounter unnecessary. He admitted to himself his error in judgment.

When that secretary let slip about Carmichael's rise from banished failure to presidential prodigy, I'd have bet my check on hanky panky between the widow and Carmichael. But that outright lie about Terry, I got to reset my sights. That and the fact that Estelle's too much woman for not enough man. Now John Earl, there's where the Estelle Tate's of this world meet their match. John Earl, you and I got some things to discuss about a certain corpse, a late night check out, and the true contents of a grave down Mexico way. I'll bet my star you're in this up to your sweet ass.

Chapter 14

Butts littered the ground, indicative of John Earl's intense desire to see his plan to fruition. *If they tie me to Lamar's death, there's one last piece of business I ain't leavin' unfinished, he promised. John Earl Terry always pays his debts in full. As for this particular obligation, it's been outstandin' way too long.*

A wind gust forced his gloved hand into the pocket of his top coat. Normally beset with temperatures no lower than the eighties this early in September, a second cold snap now gripped East Texas, and while it lasted, thin-blooded Texans winced.

From beyond a pine row the hum of an engine announced the men for whom he waited. Taking one last drag, John Earl threw down his Lucky and ground it with a vengeance.

Just like I told Faye, their kind can't resist the lure of easy money, even if it means meetin' on a back road eight miles outtta Brophy.

"You boys tell anyone you was comin?"

Looking at one another, their replies overlapped.

"No, Sir."

"Nary a soul, like Miss Faye told us."

"Ya'll better be playin' me straight, cause one word leaks out, we all got our tails in the same crack." He paused. "What I need is a couple of boys who can keep their mouths shut and eyes peeled on this here valve." Terry pointed to a by-pass concealed by scrubby brush connecting a pipeline to an oil storage facility some miles away.

"Plannin' on runnin' hot oil?" Banks rhetorically posed. By opening or closing such valves, hot oil ran either to legitimate tanks which Proration enforcers were welcome to inspect or illegal destinations where the crude could be transported to refineries without detection.

"If you are, you got the right men. Ain't no love lost in seein' oil flow. Everythin' was goin' good till the government come in and started..."

Less eager to put himself in jeopardy to line Terry's bulging pockets, Wiggins interrupted.

"How'd you decide on us?"

"Why, I owe you boys."

Banks and Wiggins exchanged cryptic glances.

Head bent and shaking, Banks pawed at the ground with his left boot.

"I don't recollect I done nothin' to warrant such gratitude."

Before the man could raise his head, Terry withdrew a revolver from the deep pocket of his overcoat.

"This is for Willie and his family."

Both men stared at the barrel; Wiggins stepped back with his hands in the air and palms pressing forward to signal his desire for a cooler head.

"Now wait just a minute here. We ain't kilt nobody."

"Where could you have got hold of such a notion?"

With a calm, steady hand, Terry cocked the gun. "Anybody ever says money can't buy everythin', don't know shit. It'll get you all you want and all you ever wanted to know. The same boy that tipped me off to what was goin' on the night you bastards murdered the Bacons turned Judas for less than the price of this coat." He laughed, "But I wouldn't feel so bad, boys; this coat didn't come mail order cheap."

"Now we can work this out if you just put that gun away," Banks pleaded. "I swear you got the wrong men. We don't know nothin' about no Klan. Ain't that so, Floyd?"

"Shut up!" Terry demanded. "Willie was more man than the both of you put together, and if that weren't enough, you put children through the kind of torture that eats up their sleep. Don't nobody that hurts children deserve to draw breath."

Tiring of the exchange, he pulled the trigger, hitting Banks in the chest. The man fell to his knees, looking at the gaping wound, incredulously seeking the eyes of his killer before his own closed in death. Seizing his opportunity for escape, Floyd ran for the car.

John Earl methodically raised his weapon a second time to set aim for the fleeing man's leg. The bullet pierced flesh and felled Wiggins as he cried out. Slowly, the gunman walked toward the writhing form. As he kicked the man onto his back, John Earl lowered the gun until it almost touched Floyd's head. Wiggins' blood- covered hands held his leg in an impotent effort to stay the flow collecting on the ground.

"You gotta stop; this is crazy." In a grimace of pain, "I tell you, we had nothin'..."

"Did they beg for their lives? Did they die knowin' you all but killed their boy?"

John Earl had asked himself those questions time and again. Though his rational side assured that he could have done no more for the Bacons, guilt racked his sleep with dreams in which he arrived seconds too late just as Willie and Arnolia began to swing from the nooses.

As he steadied his aim, "I may rot in hell, but I swear killin' the two of you will make every lap of hell fire worth it."

The discharge blew away the upper portion of the skull which scattered with the acrid smell of gun powder in the wailing wind. Terry drove deeper into the countryside to a stock tank. From the bank he hurled the gun into its center. As for the blood-splattered coat, the burned residue caused as scant notice as did the disappearance of the two men.

Even with Sadie's persistence, it took nearly three weeks for anyone to institute a search for the pair, distractions being what they were. Folks were just too numb. By then what the animals hadn't carried off left little by way of clues as to who lured the men to their deaths.

A gnawing hunger reminded John Earl of the lunch he failed to eat and sent him to his watch.

"Three o'clock," he announced as the earth shook with a force that sent him to the ground.

~~~~~~

As Melba Aiken entered the Tanner Drug Emporium, she hastened her pace. *Don't know why I left myself so little time to run these errands and get them younguns picked up, she muttered. They'll just have to forego their walk home and drug store treat what with the wind a cuttin' and Jake not over his cold. Vicks Vapo Rub. Got to remember that, too.*

On her way to the back of the store, Melba passed the Pangburn's candy display featuring a drawing of a stylish woman in a swimsuit peering into a treasure chest of the chocolate delights. *Didn't get that way eating' them things*, she told herself. The red and black checkerboard flooring crackled under her feet as she passed a cosmetics counter that ran half the length of the store before arriving at a wall of shelves which she searched before spying the Vicks. "Sixty-three cents!"

"Help you out, Melba?" Mr. Tanner the druggist called over the sound of the soda fountain's gush as he filled a clear glass etched with the name of the pause that refreshed. Placing it on the counter, he removed a straw from the silver-topped container by sliding up the pole attached to the knobbed lid. Once in its new surroundings, the straw battled to the top despite the crushed ice that spread over the rim like a wintry glaze. With a towel, he wiped the excess as it traveled over the Coca-Cola inscription.

"You got in any liquid Brilliantine? Clyde made sure I knew he was close to out."

"Sure do," he laughed goodheartedly. "We wouldn't want what hair he has left to lose that Brilliantine sheen."

Melba scanned the six tiers of shelving. *Witch hazel, Unguentine, Tiz tablets. I bet those sell like hot cakes as many sore feet as come out of drillin' boots. Tincture of Arnicca, formaldehyde torches.* The Brilliantine in her hand basket, she searched for one last product: *True Test Beef Wine and Irons. With the new school opened, Elaine is paler and thinner. This oughta help until she gets the kinks outta that buildin'. Just hope that photographer fella from Americana was worth a missed breakfast.* She smiled. *Bein' wrote up in Americana all but assures folks countrywide is gonna know us, a little old oil field school. Well, Brophy owes its renown to Elaine Crawford. Cept for the time she was laid up after losin' the baby, she's all but laid every brick herself.*

A large clock advertised both Doan's Pills and the time of two forty-five. *If I hurry, I can stop by with this letter Clyde wanted and still dose her up before the bell rings at three fifteen.*

Rather than repark the car, Melba walked the block and a half to the bank while a wave of regret traveled up her skirt with each gust of the unmerciful wind. A particularly heavy gust ushered the woman into the bank and closed the door with a resounding thud. Spotting Clyde at the northern wall, she excused herself through the line, swatting an old rancher come to town with her purchases. *Bein' rich ain't sweetened the old cuss' attitude none*, Melba decided as he refused to move an inch to allow passage.

Clyde held a cloth in his right hand to wipe the door of his latest acquisition, a state-of-the-art vault opened and secured by a timing device. Since its installation, for which the entire north wall had been removed, Clyde shined the steel as a ten-year-old would his Christmas bicycle.

"Clyde," a wave of the woman's hand drew him through the swinging door of the half wall that separated the vault from the public. As she handed him the letter, Melba felt a slight discomfort followed by a warm sensation moving the length of her left leg. Instinctively she lowered her hand and looked toward the floor. Blood streamed from a jagged tear just below her knee. Of the deafening noise, she held no recollection. Suddenly the customers and employees began to scream; some lay prostrate on the carpeting. Now she could feel the wind as it blew through the spaces where the picture window panes stood only seconds before the timer on the vault measured three in the afternoon.

~~~~~~

It's kinda like old times, Cale told himself. *Cept there's no thrill no more. We'll hit oil; know just exactly how deep. Cept Willie, Gabriel, and John Earl's not here. Cept we got a female workin' second.* He held his hands over a barrel of fire to warm them one last time before relieving Babe on the drilling floor. *Hell, it ain't nothin' like old times.*

The Boys were back on a rig drilling a legal well but saving the wages of a crew. Only Pup and Babe seemed to enjoy themselves. *Like me and Elaine was before...A man just don't know when life is the best,* he acknowledged as he trudged to the floor, replacing his gloves during the mounting of the steps. *Am I better off? Depends on which side of the fence you're standin'. The company's got its problems, sure enough, but I got a home that would put up most of Winnie, the cutest little girls that ever drew breath, and a wife who loves me. What man has a right to even think of havin' nothin' else?*

At Bulldog's instruction, Cale climbed the rig to the monkey board. From his vantage point, he could see similar rigs stretching as far in every direction as the lay of the land and the tree breaks would allow. His eyes lingered on a tiled roof catching the afternoon sun. *Today's her big day; the Americana Magazine man is interviewin' the lady that heads up the country's richest per student school.* A familiar ache returned to his heart, the longing for what might have been. *A part of me still loves her; I wonder if that's ever gonna change?*

Visually he traveled the "E" shaped building before deciding on the window of what he believed to be the office. *Wonder does she ever think on me the old way?* Involved in his own turmoil, he noticed but failed to comprehend the oddity of windows opened at sporadic intervals along the first floor. *I could leave Mavis; walk right over to that school and tell Elaine right now. We got money for a start somewheres else. Maybe buy a farm, go into cattle raisin'.* Grasping the metal rail that he clinched with a fierceness meant to exorcise the demons. *Damnation, I love Mavis; I truly do. She was my sweetheart and birthed my girls.* The cold steel penetrated his gloves. *But it just ain't the same kind of love.* Suddenly he wanted to shout his realization. *There's two brands of love, the kind that's good and wholesome that you raise a family on. Then there's,* he sighed, *the kind that's hunger that ain't never filled.*

"Let's shut her down," Bulldog called. "It's too damn cold for my old bones."

"You'll get no argument from me." Pup busied himself with the process of dismantling the operation. He could see Babe bending over some pipe and stopped to admire the view.

Here she's worked a full tour, not shirkin' a job for a minute. She ain't the ravin' beauty I spent the better part of my time chasin' or escapin', but Babe Styles, you're the most excitin' female imaginable.

Right about three, he estimated by the sun. *Got time to clean up proper and make a movie before supper.* As Pup watched Babe walk toward him, her pace quickened. She all but fell into his arms with an urgency. Words formed on her lips that a deafening roar prevented hearing. Catching his fiancée, Pup staggered against the platform and fought to maintain his balance against the shuddering ground and the weight of Babe's body lunging against him.

〰〰〰〰〰

Tapping her cane against the floor, Miss Wythel peered from the curtains. "Damn that Mavis. Hirin' a jitney's more dependable than that scatterbrained redhead." Decision made, she began her way through the hall to her telephone when the distinctive rumbling of an approaching automobile gave cause to retrace her steps.

Dust flew like a cattle stampede as Mavis bounced from chug hole to chug hole without a decrease in speed. As she all but fell from the car, she exclaimed, "Hell's bells, with all the money you're worth now, why don't you fix that damn road?"

Miss Wythel bristled, "Cause most of the folks who come a callin' got the good sense to drive around 'um." Hobbling down the steps, the older woman barked orders to her chauffeur. "Get back in that car; I ain't extendin' no hospitalities this afternoon. We're late already."

"I had baby troubles," she defended. "You try takin' care of two the same size a wantin' to eat and makin' messes all the time."

"I'm sure," Miss Wythel's tone colored with sarcasm, "that all the hired help sees to the majority of the baby tendin'."

Called to account, Mavis softened, "That may have been true for a while, but we had to cut back, and there's just the nurse and a maid now."

"Don't this thing have no heat?"

More contrite due to her sudden awareness of the woman's discomfort, "Hurtin' pretty bad, are you?"

"I ain't complainin'."

"Not out right, but you're so ornery I don't see how you live with yourself."

Swelling like a wrinkled toad, Miss Wythel began to brood. Mavis continued to rattle until the turn into the main road where she too became silent. The arthritis that set in her legs years before flared up a few weeks prior. Typically, Miss Wythel stubbornly refused to allow the disease to control her life until the wind and cold aggravated the symptoms beyond even her endurance.

The inertia of Mavis' turn forced the old lady toward the door and the cane which once sat at an angle to fall across an arthritic knee. "Damn walkin' stick," She tossed it into the back seat. "Never had so much trouble when I used my rifle." She addressed the driver. "The metal helps arthritis."

"You still got that old gun?"

"It's right by me most all the time at home."

Hoping to keep her engaged in conversation and her mind off the pain, Mavis pressed for information on which she held not the slightest degree of interest. "You don't think that thing could really fire?"

"And why not?"

"Didn't it come to you left over from the Civil War or somethin'?"

Miffed, "And that's about all you know. If our boys had of had some guns like mine, Pup would have us all standin' for 'Dixie' at the start of them ball games of his. No, it ain't no Civil War relic. And I keep her oiled and cleaned better than you take care of them younguns. At least it," she motioned, "it don't leave no puked milk stains."

The driver took her eyes off the road. "Hell's bells, now I got to go by the house and change."

"You're a lettin' me off first," objected the passenger. "Look at the time; it's three o'clock." Miss Wythel became aware of the change in Mavis' face. They were well into town by now and nearly over the top of a rise in the landscape that afforded a view of several landmarks, the school being the most prominent. Mavis' eyes appeared to cover her entire face, her arms stiffened, and she was almost standing to brake the speeding car.

"Hell's bells," she screamed as the car began to skid in defiance.

~~~~~

With a gloved hand, Elaine Crawford battled the mother of pearl buttons on her dress coat. "It must be in the fifties in here," she muttered. *The heating system has a few glitches, granted. At least this cold snap is freak, and we can have it up to par by the time the real weather rolls around.* She paused to straighten her hair in the reflection of the trophy cases that lined the foyer. *It worked fine during that earlier norther. Maybe a few more complaints of the runny noses and eyes, but we get those whether the heat's on or not. Not that those symptoms aren't common place enough around town what with the fires that burn off and on from the wells. Besides,* she reasoned, *what new building ever came without a problem or two at first?*

She began to travel the lengthy entry in as much of an attempt to warm her feet as to stave off her nervousness. *I deserve this,* she told herself repeatedly since learning of the magazine's desire to feature what it christened "the richest small-town school in the country."

It's only right that they by-passed John Earl and the Board. John Earl. She allowed herself to dwell on the name as she surveyed the school and thought about the prosperity of Brophy and the surrounding towns since the boom. *How could the catalyst for all this happiness be the devil's own spawn? The Lord does work in mysterious ways, using a man like him to lead us to a blessing.* She stopped short. *What if it's not a blessing at all? What if he got us to sell our souls to the devil like Faust, and he's just biding his time until collection?* Absently, she brushed away a tear.

"Gettin' to you, too, Miz Crawford?" Weldon Briles the school's janitor offered a freshly laundered kerchief from his starched khakis. "It's a heap worse down on the lower floor where there ain't no windows open."

"You and I can make a trip down after the photographer leaves. As for now, that area is just storage until we need it for extra classrooms anyway."

He straightened a tie sported for the occasion.

"You look very nice today."

"And you. Guess all of us gussied up; never seen so much Sunday best on a weekday for anythin' but a weddin' or funeral."

"If the elementary choir fidgets through 'Texas Our Texas' the way it has in practice, the service will be mine." Maxine Green, the music teacher rushed by the pair toward the auditorium where the students would gather in a school-wide assembly to greet their guest with a showcase of the special programs Brophy's tax base provided. Besides the rendition of the state song, a band concert and a dramatic production were planned.

"Everything seems to be falling in place otherwise," Elaine's statement received Weldon's reassuring nod. She recognized the selfsame confidence in the members of the band filing past clad in uniforms each costing upwards of one hundred dollars.

An unfamiliar automobile rolled to a stop at the parking slot reserved for visitors. A man in his late thirties fished about the back seat before removing a camera and its flash and approached the building. Matthew Tolleson bowed his head in reverence to the Texas wind. *When I'm wrong, I'm wrong,* he admitted. His editor, a hard man known for impulsive firings, left him little recourse than to accept the assignment he at first mistook for exile. *Those old money aristocrats back home could take a page from East Texas. These common folks in a moneyed delirium, now this is a story worth writing and photographing.* Already in his pocket a roll of exposed film captured both the beauty of the Texas landscape amid the rows of derricks and the bustle of the boom streets. *This story is going to capture America as only a true rags to riches tale can.*

"Good afternoon, Mr. Tolleson. Welcome to Brophy School. I'm Mrs. Crawford the principal." She ushered him through the marble foyer to begin their journey down the hallway. "I thought we might tour the campus. Then the students have prepared a short program in your honor. I hope you won't mind. The children and the faculty, too, are so in awe that a magazine of the stature of *Americana* would pay us a visit. Well, they want the assurance that your readers will long remember Brophy, Texas, and its students."

"I am in your capable hands. But let me say, that from what I have witnessed, it is *Americana* that is in awe of the Brophy School System."

As she opened the door, "This is our home economics laboratory."

A cluster of high school girls assumed their positions with the precision of a battleship crew. The camera snapped in the directions of rows of sewing machines; four equipped kitchens; a living room; and a formal dining room set with china, silver, and freshly cut flowers from the school's own greenhouse.

After sampling an assortment of baked goods, Tolleson followed his guide to a modern chemistry lab where a petroleum engineer on loan from a major oil corporation trained the company's future.

At the library he captured pupils hard at work seated at oak tables and surrounded by shelves brimming with volumes of materials. A visit to the music facilities brought them once again into the open air.

More Spanish arches, their openings spanned by black wrought iron, allowed an unrestricted view of the athletic facilities.

"I wish the weather were more agreeable, Mr. Tolleson. It really is unpredictable here." Hurriedly she designated the swimming pool, grass tennis courts and track still under construction.

Tolleson smiled. "I'd like to interview some of the children."

"Oh, they'll be thrilled to death. I think we can find some of our high school girls during gym class." Walking under the word "GIRLS" etched in stone above the doorway, they entered the gymnasium. The parquet courts still smelled faintly of the varnish that reflected the young women engaged in a volleyball match. To the side, the teacher positioned the wooden dowels of a posture graph on a student in a demonstration of the evils of slumping shoulders.

"Bebe," the principal summoned a slim brunette clad in a maroon gym suit. "This is Mr. Tolleson from *Americana.* He'd like to ask you some questions."

Bebe' face illuminated.

"Tell me, have you lived in Brophy all your life?"

"Oh, no sir. My father brought us here with the boom."

"So he does what in the field?" The reporter's hands scratched furiously through the increasingly cluttered note pad.

"He builds storage tanks."

"And how would you say Brophy compares to your other schools and homes?"

"It's grand," she exuded in teenage fashion. "I've been in schools that were thrown up just like the town, outdoor toilets, wind and dust whipping through cracks in the walls. At one town, we even had a tent for a school till they built a brick one. Of course, it was nothing like this. I sure hope the field holds so that I can stay here a long time."

Elaine dismissed the girl who immediately became the focus of a barrage of classmates.

"Our Miss O'Neil's Senior English students are just around the corner."

As they neared the classroom, a tall, muscular young man who was somewhat green around the gills bolted from the door to narrowly avoid a collision with his principal and her guest.

"James Raburn," she scolded. "where are your manners?"

Shifting nervously, the boy apologized. "I'm dreadful sorry, Mrs. Crawford. It's my stomach, well, my head. I mean Miss O'Neil is sendin' me home before I embarrass myself right there in the classroom."

Elaine softened somewhat. "Then I hope you feel better."

"If it's like the last time, I'll be back in shape by chores this evenin'."

"You have this often?"

"No, ma'am, that is just this school year seems like it hit me a might often." Careful not to appear less than the masculine example, he added abruptly. "It's nothin'. My momma says she thinks I might be needin' eyeglasses, but that's not gonna help my football career none." He smiled awkwardly and darted down the hall as if pursued by would-be tacklers.

Elaine paused longer than necessary as she mulled over the headache malady that seemed to be reaching epidemic proportions.

At the opening of Miss O'Neil's door, she repelled from a blast of colder air. Despite the chill, Elaine felt the fire of embarrassment. Every window pushed to its maximum height bore the winds of the Texas Norther with an even greater strength in the newly created draft. A mixture of fear and humiliation that the photojournalist from New York should discover her shivering students as they battled stiffened fingers in valiant attempts to jot down notes from her lecture on Mark Twain sent Miss O'Neil into a sputtering of apologies and explanations.

"I... I," she stammered as much from her inability to invent a plausible excuse as from the temperature, "... am so sorry Mrs. Crawford. The students complained of being lightheaded again, and their eyes were..."

"And tomorrow they will complain of pneumonia," snapped Elaine. "Some of you boys close those windows."

Every male rushed to comply.

Examining the double radiators adjacent to the now tightly closed windows, the reporter satisfied his curiosity. "Which way do these pipes run?"

"Under the flooring."

The corners of his mouth drew upward as the lower lip protruded signaling the intensity of his thoughts. "I'd say there's gas leaking from your radiators since you have them pumping at what I assume to be the maximum level."

"But they're built to withstand fifty pounds of pressure."

"Curious, nonetheless." Tolleson stared out the window toward the wells which pumped their profits and excess gas into the school.

Her eyes pleading forgiveness, Miss O'Neil ushered the couple to the hallway.

"Old lady O'Neil's gonna get it now," chuckled a dark-haired youth from the back row. The class squirmed with anticipation of what might be transpiring. Calena Duncan shook her head in silence, a message caught by Vincent Mead, her steady boyfriend for the past two years. If Calena had her way, she would be Mrs. Vincent Mead as soon as the graduation ceremony ended. As usual, Vincent assumed his role as class entertainer by amusing everyone with his witty comments and quick responses.

Uninspired by the antics of his classmates, Jacob Redwine remained absorbed in a worn copy of *Gray's Anatomy.* Although he boasted an edition newer than most physicians' in the area, the pages bespoke of his voracious study from dog-eared corners, notations and underlining. *If I can just talk Mother into letting me graduate at semester,* he often thought, *I can enroll at the University of Texas for the spring term.*

To his left, Norma Henry once again consulted her compact. *If the photographer notices my good looks, and how can he help but do so?* she asked herself, *I'll land in that magazine. From there, my success in Hollywood is insured. Everybody knows the tiniest exposure in Americana can launch a career.* She focused her much practiced smile in the reporter's direction only to be disappointed to discover the door already closed. *Not to worry*, the ever self-assured Norma told herself. A stroke of sheer genius caused her to volunteer to be the mistress of ceremonies, even if it does mean, of all things, introducing the elementary choir. *Still, it can be my big break.*

"Hey, Norma," Albert Frost, in another of his attempts to gain the school's most famous beauty's attention, "I got near all the boys ready to vote for you for Class Sweetheart." Usually such talk would grant him a few precious moments of Norma's favor.

"And who else would they elect, Maribelle Sloan?"

Norma's sarcasm was not lost on her admirer. "She can't hold a candle to you."

"She can't hold a candle to my dog," she responded as both stared across the room at the girl for whom plain could be considered a kind description.

I can feel them staring; God I wish the earth would open up and swallow them all, especially all those new folks the boom's brought in. Maribelle turned to the window in a futile attempt to escape the laughter she knew was at her expense. *One hundred wells strung from the front yard across the farm land has put a quarter of a million in trust each for my three sisters and me. And Daddy thinking he can use them to make us the belles of the county.*

The return of the pristine Miss O'Neil produced a pall that remained until the group filed into the auditorium. An energy akin to that which rumbled beneath East Texas neared release in the elementary classrooms and caused a pale hand to reach in desperation for the back of the heavy oak teacher's chair.

The last few steps to this haven were a climb up Everest to Jenny Venable who fought to conceal her first pregnancy.

"Thank heavens," she muttered for the opportunity to sit and the mysterious illness which allowed her to disguise her morning sickness. A gnawing regret of her deception was quickly dismissed by anger at the forces which made what should have been the joy of their lives a closely guarded secret. *If it weren't for Proration, I'd be at home deciding on a layette. Instead, my salary is all that stands between the Venables and the poor house.*

She folded her arms upon her desk as a cushion for her head. *At the very best, I can hope for a couple of more months before mandatory dismissal.*

"Quit grabbin' my pigtails! Miz Venable, make him stop."

The teacher pulled herself up. "Travis Pool, so help me, I'm gonna keep you in this room and as far away from that program as I can if you don't leave Violet alone. You hear me?"

The impish Travis lowered his eyes in feigned remorse.

"It's two forty-five," announced Mrs. Venable. Let's go on. Maybe we can get seats closer to the front."

Thirty nine and ten year-olds raised their seats in a clamor of creaking metal against argumentative wood. When queued perfectly enough to pass muster, the fourth graders emerged into an already crowded passage.

Miss Lettie McClain's stepping in front of Jenny caused a repercussion of obedient chicks bumping into one another in a domino effect. "I believe," the thirty-five year veteran of first grade began in her habitually recriminatory tone, "that the youngest children were to be first."

As did the majority of the adults and children alike, Jenny Venable both hated and admired Miss McClain who epitomized the first grade teacher, able to whip into line the most immature, rowdy, or difficult of children and parents. "I'm sorry. I thought

I might should pass by the restrooms so that the children don't interrupt the assembly."

"In the morning and at lunch," she snapped. "That is the rule." She gestured toward her militarized class. "Bladder control, Mrs. Venable, is a prime example of teaching self discipline. I suggest you cease to mollycoddle these fourth graders."

"Of course." Jenny felt her vulture eyes travel toward her abdomen.

"Putting on a little weight, aren't we?"

Before she could muster a denial, they had reached the elementary entrance to the auditorium. *She knows*, Jenny decided in a mixture of dread and ire. *But how could she?* Jenny glanced at a flattened abdomen. *She couldn't.*

The auditorium of the Brophy School rested between the elementary and secondary wings as a dark, cavernous divider that frightened the smaller children. Fifteen hundred theater seats stained maroon lined the floor level and the balcony. At the end of each aisle, a bronze tab designated a letter of the alphabet. Scrolled metal decorated the chair legs. As the children reached their places, the hinged seats contributed to the din of excited students. A chasm of some ten feet divided the room into two grossly unequal sections utilized as a "No Man's Land" between the high schoolers and the "babies." This main aisle led directly through the room to the wide arched entries of the classroom wings. On the stage, flanked by proscenium pillars, a curtain of maroon velvet prevented the audience from viewing the preparatory activities.

As Jenny scanned her row, she spied Travis just at the precise moment he delivered a dual knuckled blow to Violet's arm. Passing the information down the line, she called for the boy. Travis sulked toward Mrs. Venable, who with her hand tightly around his arm, began escorting the culprit back to the room in a silence which ended only when he was seated at his desk, pencil in hand, and the dictionary opened to the entry word "aardvark."

"Now you will copy every single word on the page before you go home."

Travis watched his teacher return to the assembly.

"Didn't want to go to no dumb old program no ways," he pouted aloud. "Gonna tell my momma, too." he vowed to the echoing walls. The vision of his father's hand around a switch gave him cause to reconsider. "Hope they believe I'm cleanin' them erasers again." He went to work on the page he was beginning to know by heart.

"I want to sit by Ivy," begged Dorcas Kuykendall of Mrs. Sellman, her seventh grade teacher.

"But you'll have the post in your way," she reminded.

"That's fine; I have to sit on my feet anyways," the petite blonde replied.

"Very well," she relented in the tone of voice that adults reserve for those children who refuse to profit from their advice. "Cleon, trade seats with Dorcas."

Quickly the boy leaped to his feet to relocate some twelve seats further and a good distance from the wooden post that helped support the weight of the ceiling. This exchange would haunt his dreams and cause him to question the very reason for his existence for the next forty years.

A hush traveled the length of the assemblage as the principal mounted the winding stage right steps toward the podium. Elaine noticed that the auditorium proved decidedly warmer due to the body heat and her order that the windows should remain closed. "Good afternoon, students and faculty."

When the response died away, Elaine continued. "Today the city of Brophy has welcomed a most distinguished visitor."

A thunderous applause followed.

"If you will direct your attention to the balcony, I would like for you to express our gratitude to Mr. Matthew Tolleson." Elaine closed her remarks when the clapping ceased. "In your honor, Mr. Tolleson, several groups have prepared short presentations. I am sure we will all enjoy the elementary choir, the theater class' production, and the band. I now turn our program over to the mistress of ceremonies, one of our seniors, Norma Henry."

Applause and several stifled whistles urged Norma to the podium. Alive, in her element, Norma flashed a smile in the direction of the photographer. "If you will all stand, the choir will lead us in our state song, 'Texas, Our Texas.'"

The curtain parted to reveal the frightened faces of those survivors of the arduous audition process dictated by Mrs. Maxine Green. In a starched white shirt and dark slacks, Billy Aiken stood at attention on the top row of the risers. A bow tie heaved with each breath.

"Texas, our Texas, all hail the mighty state."

Serving as a backdrop, an enormous Lone Star flag slowly descended, to the delight of the audience.

"Oh empire wide and glorious, you stand supremely blessed."

In the wings the band awaited. Standing in a single line that wove out the stage door and into the hall, the director inspected his troops. Tubas and drums littered the passageway.

"God bless you, Texas, and keep you brave and strong,"

We are blessed. I haven't realized how much since... well, since Mavis came, Elaine admitted to herself. *If I had just trusted my instincts about John Earl, then...but the hurt just got in the way. I had to ease it with something.*

Elaine stiffened with a renewed self confidence. *I've made my mistakes and served my time for them.* Her heart swelled with pride in her school, the children, and her triumph over the tragedies of her short life.

I've beaten you, John Earl Terry. I've taken the worst you could dish out, and I came out the stronger for it.

"That you may grow in power and worth, throughout the ages long."

As the youngsters filed stage left, the theater troop entered from the opposite wing and began its performance following Norma's overly dramatic introduction.

Noticing that they were not destined for the auditorium entrance, Celia Poynor tugged at the arm of Mrs. Green. "You mean we can't watch the rest?"

With a look of surprise, "Oh, I planned on going back to the choir room and letting ya'll go on to the buses or home, like a little reward."

"Sure, let's go home," responded Billy.

"No, let's stay," begged Celia.

Torn by indecision, Mrs. Green finally relented. "We'll stay then. Ease quietly into the auditorium and stand along the walls back where the high school kids sit."

Billy allowed several children to pass in order to be beside his pal, Roger Elkins. "That dumb ole Celia's done talked Miz Green into makin' us stay. What you say we just sneak on off?" His face beamed with the excitement of adventure.

"What if we get caught?"

"We had to throw up. Everybody believes that one; I used it twice already."

Bolstered by the genius of Billy's plan, Roger began to urge others ahead until the two boys were able to edge toward the exit undetected.

On stage the band assumed its semi-circular position with Mr. Baggett atop the wooden square that raised him to a clear view of all his musicians. As he lifted the baton, his wristwatch peaked through the cuff of his shirt. *Three o'clock, we may not get to finish all four pieces.*

Poised for the drop of the baton, Matthew Tolleson's camera captured the Brophy School's place in history. His flash blew with uncharacteristic intensity. At the last notes of the state song, Weldon Briles stole into the bowels of the Brophy School for a smoke that was strictly forbidden by a principal who believed the staff should set an example for the students. Knowing that all were safely in the confines of the assembly, the janitor seized the opportunity and called it square for the few minutes of irritation his eyes would have to endure.

Only a few of the light fixtures held bulbs, another cost-cutting measure, like the tapping of the residue gas line to provide the building's heat. Briles shook his head. For a bunch of rich folks with money to burn, I don't see savin' a few dollars here and there.

As an oil field hand later explained to a newspaperman, "The gas flowin' through the schoolhouse pipes was marked for disposal at well sites after the removin' of liquids such as gasoline. It's on the way back that the gas for the boilers located in the cafeteria complex got their supply. It's a common enough practice; homes and businesses all operate off of excess oil field gas. Wasn't like it was the real flammable stuff like casing head gas that comes when the Woodbine breaks down in the oil seepin' around the casins'. All the experts say residue is more stable and safer. Didn't nobody see no reason to worry."

Briles continued his trek. Before reaching the door, he retrieved his cigarettes and matches. Dragging the head across the penny-box cover produced a flame of incomprehensible brilliance, the last earthly sight visible to Weldon Briles.

Chapter 15

As if time dragged in a motion too slow for complete comprehension, Elaine felt her arms and legs begin to move involuntarily. Instinctively, her eyes traveled to the row where Jake sat with his class. She screamed; at least she thought she did. The roar was drowning every sound save its own; the sky added to the luminous effect.

The sky? she questioned. *I must be crazy.* Then a reflection from the steel beam that ambled downward caught her eye. *Move Jake!* she willed. Elaine tried to reach for her son, but her own limbs failed. Uncannily, she believed herself to be in flight then falling toward the stage, though her eyes never left the child as she witnessed the crash of the girder upon him and his schoolmates. *He's dead;* mothers know these things. Elaine lapsed into unconsciousness.

Had Cale not gripped the rig with every ounce of strength he possessed, he might have plunged to his death when the cataclysmic force shook the derrick. Facing the school as he clung for life, he watched in bewilderment as half the structure's roof traveled into the air only to collapse upon impact with the walls.

Babe's eyes searched those of her lover as she straddled his prostrate form. "This is no soup explosion or well fire. Not even the violence of a gusher...." She felt Pup's strong arms shifting her weight.

"Why did she blow?" the driller asked rhetorically as if vocalizing could produce reason. "We weren't near close to gas or oil."

"Oh no!" Cale cried as he maneuvered the steps. "Get the truck and all the tools we can gather. We got to move fast."

Arriving at their sides, Cale grabbed Bulldog's shoulders to force the man to share the gravity of his news. "Didn't none of ya'll see?"

He traveled from one blank face to another as he pointed repeatedly in the direction of the accident.

"The school's blowed up!"

"How bad?" Babe dreaded the answer already provided by the intensity of the blast.

"Damn near the whole roof went up a good ten feet and crashed back down on the walls."

Bulldog, already on his way to the trucks, cursed orders to those still in the throes of shock to route them toward tool bins and vehicles. "We'll need winch trucks to lift debris. Get on the phone, Pup. Call in every man we know with a torch or a truck."

While Cale ran after the first driller, the thought burst into his consciousness. "Elaine's in there." He stopped cold. "And Jake," he announced to those who had shared so much with the woman and her son.

He stumbled a few steps. "Billy and Violet..." His list lengthened with the names of children of this employee, that friend or spouse. Falling to his knees, he covered his face with mud-caked hands. "Why, God? Why a bunch of innocent kids?"

Miss Wythel, forced back in the seat after her head caught the dash, came up calling upon the Almighty herself. "If I ever live to get to that doctor, this will be the last time I ride with a crazy red-headed female..."

Mavis' expression calmed the tirade. Tears flowed over pursed lips as the woman banged her clinched fists against the steering column which supported her writhing body.

"Mavis, honey, are you hurt?"

Without looking up, "The roof just heaved like the chest of a dyin' man." Several persistent tugs at her right arm incited a dazed reply to the older woman's pleas. "But you saw it, too?" Mavis tried to convince herself that some momentary madness provided the vision rather than an unspeakable reality.

"Saw what, girl?"

"Why, the school blow up."

Stunned, Miss Wythel sought the back of the seat. "I wasn't lookin' straight out..." the voice trailed as the ramification began to form.

"It felt like an earthquake or somebody droppin' a bomb." As if all became clear, "It's them damned Germans, and me without my rifle." She flung her cane into the back seat. "This is the last time I'm caught without out it, that's for damn sure."

"We got to get over there quick. They'll be needin' help." Mavis appraised the spirited old lady. "You up to pitchin' in, or do you want me to take you on to the Doc's?"

"The time I can't do my share is the day I'm six feet under. Besides, Miss Wythel told herself with prophetic accuracy, *won't no doctors be takin' no office calls for many a day.*

At the bank, Clyde informed Melba after a quick inspection, "I'll get you a doctor. That leg of yours is going to need some

stitches." Clyde rushed to the telephone to give the Doc a call
only to be distracted by the chaos in front of his bank.

"What could have happened?" Melba asked in confusion.

A customer reclaimed his feet. "I hadn't heard nothin' like
that since that nitro man blew hisself to hell."

Pushing her way to the street, Melba corrected the man's
error with authority. "Ain't enough soup around to set a charge
like that." She joined the rush of people who appeared certain
of their destination as they fought for road and sidewalk space.
In recognition of a P.T. A. acquaintance, Melba grabbed her
with sufficient strength to cause them both to falter.

"What's goin' on?"

Effie Murdoch jerked Melba's hand away. "We got to get
down there, Miz. Aiken. Our babies may be dead." Effie began
to drag Melba down the street. "The school's done exploded."

It was Melba's turn to break free of a grasp. Effie tried
unsuccessfully to urge Melba on then turned and ran in the
direction of the campus. Melba stood transfixed.

Somehow, Clyde emerged from the rapidly forming mob
of pedestrians. "I'll take you," he offered. Her leg forgotten,
Melba arrived at the school yard not quite aware of how the
bank and the school became one.

John Earl's fingers fumbled at the controls of the radio.
Kilgore now supported its own station of rather pathetic
wattage. Slamming the gas pedal until it became even with
the floorboard, Terry sped into town. *The whole of Brophy's
gone up*, he reasoned. *But there's no smoke from a well fire*.
Abruptly, the swing music stopped to be followed by an eerie
silence. The driver banged his fist on the dash, "Work, damn
you."

As if in response, a voice racked with emotion began, "I
apologize for interrupting 'The Big Band Afternoon Review,'
but I have..." the announcer sobbed between phrases, "terrible,

just terrible news. For reasons known only to God Almighty, the Brophy Schoolhouse exploded just around three this afternoon. Details are very sketchy. City officials are begging for all able-bodied men, heavy equipment, hand tools, and most especially any of you with medical training to respond to this call." Only the crackle of dead air space remained as John Earl raced toward the scene.

Reaching the main road, he saw women with their smaller children standing on the shoulder craning their necks toward town in hopes of catching a glimpse, a glimmer of some hope for the safety of their school-aged youngsters.

"To repeat our earlier announcement," a different voice broke the silence. "An explosion of undetermined origin has occurred at the Brophy School. The full extent of injury and damage is not known, but the appeal of medical assistance, heavy machinery, and man power is urgent. Our prayers are with the families of the Brophy community and with our regular announcer, Odell Kuykendall, whose five children were in attendance."

At the edge of town, the line of cars began to creep. Deafening sirens permeated the air one upon the other yet unwilling to blend into a single lament. Everywhere panic-stricken adults pled for news of anyone who would listen.

Unable to see, though aware that his lids were not closed, Jacob Redwine pushed his second fingers deeply into his eyes and rubbed furiously. Still the gray cloud persisted, dense, choking, impenetrable. *I can feel*, he told himself, *my arms, legs, my face.* A warm sensation from his forehead prompted, *laceration, lengthy but not deep; oozing not spurting. It's minor*, he diagnosed as he began to urge his feet from beneath the weight of unnamed objects. Muffled in the remoteness of the cloud, screams and cries for help reached his ears. *Folks are hurt, lots of them, and they're going to need a doctor.* His work to free himself assumed a greater urgency. From across his feet he managed to elevate a splintered section of what he presumed to be a theater seat. Once on his hands and knees, the young man felt inches ahead for whatever dangers and obstructions might block his path. Something akin to daylight struggled to part the haze, thus affording sufficient illumination to distinguish motionless forms shrouded in gray.

Jacob's hands pressed into the rubble before resting upon an uncharacteristic softness. *It's an arm. Somebody else is alive, too.* "It's me, Jacob... Jacob Redwine." He spoke into the murkiness. "See, I have your arm; let me get you free." Pulling gently, he fell back. No longer weighted, the severed limb now rested in Jacob's hand. Redwine screamed as he threw the arm over his shoulder, only to chastise himself a moment later. *You say you want to be a doctor? Well, act like one. You're alive for a reason. Somebody's doing all that hollering, so they must be hurt real bad.*

Crawling toward a vague luminescence, he touched yet another victim, this time with a reactionary cry of pain.

"It's Jacob Redwine. How badly are you hurt?"

"Jacob?" The voice was strained. "It's Bebe."

"Is anyone else around you?"

Fear began to creep into her response. "I... I don't know." Through the gray shadows, the boy could not see Bebe groping at each side and above her head. "There must be, but..." She moaned. "Oh, Jacob, something's wrong with my leg."

By following the muffled sound of Bebe's voice, Jacob found his way to her side. She felt his hands travel down her torso.

"Right or left?"

"Left."

He felt her become more rigid when he gingerly touched the injured leg.

"What happened to us?"

"Some kind of an explosion." His fingers gently moved over the leg until he determined the break.

"I expect you won't be dancing at the Lodge this weekend. She's broken."

Without a clear view, the frightened girl sensed her rescuer move away.

"I'm going to go and get you some help."

"No! You can't leave me here to die."

Reassuringly, Jacob found her hand and squeezed it tightly.

"You won't die; I promise. But I can only crawl, and I don't even know which way to go."

"Then you won't be able to find your way back," she pleaded. "Just drag me along behind... please, Jacob."

He believed he could see the anguish in the familiar face. Though a year his junior, the size of the Brophy School made it impossible not to know one another with an intimacy foreign to city students. *How can I abandon her?* A new concern seized him. *Suppose there's a second blast?* He tried to make his tone more optimistic. "All right, but it may hurt. So when it gets too much, tell me, and we'll stop and rest. You ready?"

While Jacob and Bebe sought safety, hundreds grappled with the carnage. What had been a majestic presence resembled little more than a heap of rubble straining to sustain itself. It would later be estimated that ninety percent of the school building collapsed during the blast and the ensuing rescue efforts. Twisted steel protruded from the mass of crushed brick and splintered wood. Already men and a few women crawled atop the ruins, ants racing in all directions over the hill, pushing and dragging pieces too large for their normal physical endurance in an unorchestrated swarm.

As one reporter would describe to his readers, "...The building appears crumbled at its center, as though some phantasm of titanic proportions has wielded a crushing blow. Defiantly, the extremities of each wing stand, their roofs declining so sharply into the destruction as to suggest an almost architectural design meant to create a passageway or buffer against the evening sun. To these sections oil field engineers have begun the process of shoring the walls against further collapse."

Tours from wells nearest the site joined parents who witnessed the tragedy inside parked cars as they awaited the school's dismissal bell. Several bore the markings of sprayed glass slivers and shrapnel. Others suffered the effects of shattered windows in town. Houses several miles away cracked, and two deaths from rig accidents would be attributed to the school explosion.

A haze of silt and mortar transported by the pulsating winds settled upon the rescuers until it coated everything living and dead that encircled the school yard. Rumors spread like prairie fire as grieving families on foot and in private vehicles were pushed aside by ambulances from Brophy and its sister cities and towns.

Someone, no one, everyone instructed those with trucks to the forefront to be backed toward the demolished building. Hundreds of men straddled the ruins to pass hand to hand splintered lumber, furniture, bricks, and materials so distorted as to defy precise determination. Incessantly, the wind blew the choking silt across their faces until they assumed the grayish pall that blanketed like a dingy snow.

Numbed parents on their knees dug through the rubble to add their own blood to the sediment. Amid cries of the names of children, a din of anguished shouting and sirens hampered the detection of faint voices separated by inches or feet of ruin so that it became virtually impossible to hear even those who stood next to one another.

Yet amid the perdition, the miracles sheltered by divine providence emerged. Before the throngs converged, smatterings of confused and battered children emerged to respond instinctively to their training.

A few days shy of her eleventh birthday, Joetta Pemberton shoved the flooring which annoyingly hampered her escape. Moving in a somnambulistic state through the nightmare, she bypassed the contorted bodies of playmates and teachers. She, as the other survivors able to extricate themselves, functioned in a surrealistic beneficence.

Her corduroy jumper in little more than shreds, Joetta crawled over whatever blocked her path to the light until she inched out of the school. *Things are different in this dream. I can't tell which way to go.* Then her eyes focused on the yellow image that seemed so far away. I'm going home. Dragging the plaid book satchel her mother purchased only a few weeks before, she climbed the steps of the school bus and trudged down the aisle to the seat she shared with her seven year-old brother Wyatt. Joetta passed ghostly forms of friends. Some were crying, some shivering, some transfixed, all unable to verbalize the experience that shattered their existence.

Not knowing what to do, Zed Nelms, the driver, bolted onto the bus he had exited just after the explosion. The father of three school-aged children, he sought the best avenue of service by digging with a piece of the tile roof until he became aware of Joetta stumbling toward the bus. When his cries to her went without response, he took the three steps to the driver's seat in one leap. *There's six, seven, ten of them all in their places. Their folks will sure be glad when we get.... But my own kids? I got to keep searchin'.* He sank to the steps and stared toward the rubble that shrouded his children. *Their folks got to be frantic, but do I deliver these gifts from God? What God?* he asked in defiance. *What God snatches the lives of children with one blow and delivers up a pitiful few with His other hand?*

Zed rose to face his duty. "Hank, is that you?"

A slight nod.

"Mary Ailene?"

A feeble, "Present."

"Rosalie?" He questioned with uncertainty. *There's so much blood and silt, I can't make out her face.* Addressing the child again, "Leona?"

"It's Rosalie," a voice behind settled the dispute. "Leona's folks can't buy her no Buster Brown saddle oxfords."

"Stoney?"

"Yessir."

Stoney Hartsfield left his seat and fell into the man's arms. Void of tears, he patted the adult's back, "I'm awful sorry, Mr. Nelms. I know you got kin under all that. So we'll understand if the bus runs a little late today."

Several minutes elapsed as the man and child clung to one another. "I got to have your help, son. You're the only one of us with good sense right now." The embrace ended. "Who else we got here?"

"Gene Ed's lyin' down; I had to help him on."

"Is he hurt bad?"

"Don't appear so. But all of us is cut up somewhere. He's pukin' on the floor, too."

Nelms nodded. "The strongest men around are doin' the same."

Stoney pointed his identifications. "Judith Nell, Freda, Myron, Luke."

Now in the driver's seat, Zed started the engine. "Stoney, come stand by me and help get us through all these folks."

"That's against the rules." He referred to the edict painted above the rear view mirror.

"Son," he informed the child, "there ain't no rules when hell breaks loose."

At the back of what had been the auditorium, Jacob Redwine drug Bebe from under the cloud and into the waiting care of one of the many Guardsmen who had abandoned the Proration war.

"Her fibula is broken," he advised the uniformed man. "You'll need a stretcher."

"Her what?"

Piqued by his ignorance, "Her leg, the left one."

Covering his mistake, "Oh, sure."

"Jacob!" Bebe's hand groped to grasp his. "Thank you."

He could only smile as he saw her brown eyes fill with tears that streaked the grime-coated face. He managed, "They'll take care of you till your folks show up." In anticipation of her question, "I have to stay and help the others."

Bebe was gone. Jacob turned his attention to his first real examination of the scene that would appear worldwide in newspapers, magazines, and newsreels. *There's nothing left.* He stood, mouth gaping at the ruins of the school.

"This child needs a doctor!"

Jacob recognized a local merchant despite the silt and tattered suit that bespoke of the intensity of his labors at the site. A winced beam suspended just high enough to free the child cast an eerie shadow across man and boy.

Jacob bent to examine the unconscious child. *Couldn't be more than seven or eight.* "His pulse is barely discernible." He barked orders to the merchant. "Get him to the nearest ambulance; tell them he's bleedin' inside."

He never learned the child's name or if he survived. He was one face, one body among so many he saw in the ensuing twenty-four hours. "The lessons I learned from the Brophy School Disaster served me well throughout my career. Never saw anything that came close to comparing," he told the grandchildren poised on his knees who never tired of his story about how Grandpa Doc rescued Grandma, broken leg and all. On cue Bebe would raise her skirt discretely to furnish the necessary proof.

As Bebe's stretcher bearers passed from view, they maneuvered a gauntlet of parents fighting one another for a glimpse of what might be their daughter. With their free hands the bearers shoved the crowd back.

"Stop! I think that's our girl."

"You got no right to keep me from tryin' to find Carol Sue."

Bebe feared that the force of the people would send her crashing to the ground. Even when the doors of the ambulance slammed shut, they beat upon the vehicle for admittance as it eased forward through the chaos that now included Mavis and Miss Wythel.

At the older woman's insistence, Mavis proceeded alone. "It looks like a scrap bag of quilt workings." Miss Wythel referenced the swatches of clothing that dotted the landscape, hung from trees as eerie decorations, and protruded from the maelstrom as last vestiges of those pulled beneath the whirlpool.

Mavis bent to retrieve a shoe. "God knows if the one wearin' it will ever have use of it." She gently placed the shoe upon the ground before witnessing a woman walking aimlessly through the ravaged school yard. From out of the crowd a man appeared and began shaking her violently as if such force could still her babbling. His failure led him to stop anyone who would listen.

Mavis broke into a run for a destination unknown.

"Help me with this, Mavis." The order stilled her steps.

Babe allowed some of the bed sheets she held to topple into the redhead's arms.

"Where are we goin' with these?"

"They've set up a morgue where the buses are stored." She motioned with her load.

Little more than a glorified shed, the bus garage consisted of a tin roof about fifty feet in length supported by three walls. Its dirt floor contrasted with the stark whiteness of the sheets already in place stretching toward the far wall. Perfectly aligned rows of bodies of varied ages lay in repose too grotesque to be mistaken for sleep.

"The Beckman girl, the Adamson's boy, I know this woman from church," Mavis tried to erase the scene by blinking fiercely at the tears swelling in her eyes.

"Quit standing there, woman' get to coverin' these children."

With anger brewing, Mavis gazed at Babe. Babe's already shortened fuse ignited. "Dammit, you're a mother. Could you come in here looking for your girls and see all this?"

Mavis stared at the rows of mangled bodies, some of which were missing limbs, and all to some degree embedded with varying amounts of debris and the perpetual layer of silt. Stiff-frozen in rank and file, they resembled the macabre mannequins in a traveling show fun house.

A serpentine formation of loved ones bent over each to pray all the while that this would not be the one before trudging to the next to repeat the motions. Some exited with confirmation, leaving the rest to continue down the ghastly midway.

What if my girls had been in the school? Mavis asked herself while she hovered over the corpse of a boy no more than ten. Mavis spread the coverlet. *His face is pox-marked with...these are like cement pellets.* She tried to flick a grayish-red spot from his face only to discover that the coagulated blood held firmly. *What could cause a cut to reach from near the shoulder all the way to the elbow of this poor darling lamb?*

"Your boy?" The voice startled Mavis into what sufficed for reality.

"No, I'm just helpin' some, whatever I can."

"Then have you seen our girl?" His optimism faded as the ludicrously scant description bore no results. "She's twelve, well, she will be her next..." The wife suddenly began to sob and point frantically in the direction of those yet uncovered. "Her coat," she repeated as the pair walked solemnly toward their child.

An intrusion on a moment so private caused Mavis to turn away in shame from a scene like the many others soon to make the world voyeurs in print and film. She busied herself spreading the linens until she reached the corner of the barn. When Babe approached, Mavis declared emphatically, "I can't do this no more; I'm goin' home."

"You're going no such place. The last count I had, Elaine hadn't been found, nor Jake, or Melba's kids, either."

The McCallister woman sighed. "Then I'll stay just long enough to know they're all right, then I'm leavin' this God forsaken place."

∧∧∧∧∧∧

"Elaine! Elaine!" Cale called repeatedly as he clawed through the rubble of the school. With the delivery of a campus blueprint, the workers finally began an accurately gauged search for the future of an entire town.

"Get back," demanded a nameless face.

Cale stumbled to his feet. Like the army of civilians and soldiers commanded by no one leader, he obeyed the orders of anyone foresighted enough to formulate a plan of action. Somehow the distinctive noise of a welder's helmet falling into place penetrated the din. Soon a string of acetylene torches dotted the waning afternoon as their sparks shot in frenzied patterns over the debris. As rapidly as each section of twisted steel gave way, a team fastened chains from winch trucks and directed the removal of girders toward an expanding dumping ground to the east of the campus. After the initial movement, still more oil field hands, parents, and soldiers delved into the newly released ground.

〜〜〜〜〜

In the cavernous darkness, Elaine roused from a sleep so intense that it required every ounce of strength to open her eyes. Several minutes elapsed during which the stupor and the extent of her injuries prevented a sensible explanation as to why the eyes she knew must be open could not pierce the ebony curtain.

The light. I'll turn on the night stand lamp.

Though her range of motion was slight, Elaine's effort triggered pain that shot throughout her body to render her quite incapable of ascertaining one actual source. Instantly, the memories flooded her mind in a deluge of mental and physical anguish.

"Jake," she moaned as the vision of the beam crashing upon her only child appeared as a colored newsreel upon a murky screen of the darkened theater that entrapped her. Frightened children and colleagues tore for exits only to be crushed by the collapsing school.

The captive watched as the event replayed and the reality of her fate replaced the surrealistic tableau.

"I killed them all." Elaine's body began to heave; she choked on the stagnant air, amplifying the intensity of the pain.

My name...in the distance. They're calling my name. She became aware of a constant droning. *If I concentrate on the sounds, then I can leave this place.* The humming grew louder. *I hear my name. No, it's not real. Then... I'm in hell. This is what the preachers meant in their sermons. Everlasting torment is watching those memories that haunt you most over and over...*

The rhythmic grinding became deafening until it seemed to echo her heartbeats. *Dear God, it's happening again.* The light reappeared more brilliantly than before as it displaced the blindness.

I won't open my eyes; I'll have to watch it happen again.

"Here's one; get some more help. This one's full growed."

"Alive or dead?"

"Can't say yet. It's the foot end."

Watching the now familiar signs of discovery, Cale hurried to the spot, for once a body was located, shovels and hands replaced heavier equipment to brush or toss away debris. From the style of shoe, Cale assured himself that a woman, probably a teacher, lay buried. Had he realized the large number of mothers attending the assembly in hopes of a shot at immortality in the pages of *Americana,* he might have been less sure of the woman's reason for being at the Brophy School that fateful afternoon.

As it was, women like Cora Myers never viewed their likeness in the famous magazine the following week, but Cora's husband recognized her among the corpses caught on film by a photographer daring enough to climb onto a fire escape left intact. With his ability to bring time to a standstill, his gruesome portrayal of the cost of the Brophy disaster captured the grim reality and the world's sympathy.

Digging with renewed urgency, Cale unearthed the garnet-ringed hand he had held in the movie theater and on the front porch swing.

"Elaine! Dig faster. It's the principal, Mrs. Crawford."

To the rescuers, one name, one more victim bore no greater significance. Mrs. Crawford, a nameless child, it mattered not.

"She got a pulse?"

He tenuously felt for a sign of life. "She's alive but unconscious. Elaine, Elaine, it's Cale, honey. We're gettin' you out."

Unaware of her freedom, Elaine concentrated on the new drama projected upon the veil. *It's Cale... the Cale before... before Mavis and John Earl, before the strike, before things went so far wrong.*

"I'm gonna get you out," he told Jake.

Jake hung from the tree out in front of the house. He was smaller, up to his old mischief, and a savior in the form of a total stranger was easing their fears. The screen suddenly changed. "The Adolphus suite? No, I want to go back to the happy times, not the day my baby died."

She lay in the floor with Cale hovering over her.

"Everything's gonna be fine, sweetheart. It's Cale. I won't let nothin' happen to you."

Nothing's ever gonna be better. You can't make things right; you never could. No matter how much we wanted it to be so, fate had its mind made up.

〜〜〜〜〜

"I love you, Elaine." The man's lips brushed the powdery coating that covered her face and body.

Hurried to the spot by the rapidly spreading news of their friend's survival, Babe and Mavis pushed through the crowd in time to witness and overhear Cale's profession of love.

Babe wrestled with the impossibility of the situation. *Do I go with Elaine, or do I stay with a friend who's just found out that her marriage is a lie?* Placing her arms around Mavis' shoulders, she supported the woman as her husband held a garnet-ringed hand and walked swiftly toward the first available vehicle. Yet again Hoyt's old grocery wagon accepted a victim; this would be his third passenger.

I can't believe Mavis' reaction. After what she's seen, and to just stand there, silent. I should say something... but what? I told Pup when he let me in on Cale and Elaine's past that Mavis' blissful ignorance would backfire one of these days, but why today of all days?

From the left window, Hoyt noticed the women and called, "You girls get up front with me."

"No!," Mavis declared much too emphatically, before softening, "We can be of more use here."

Babe intercepted the words Mavis whispered under her breath. "Elaine's got all she needs to look after her."

Still glaring at the wagon as it sped from the scene, Mavis began to sob. "How could I have been so blind?"

Built into every being, the capacity to see only what one wishes to be true shields the soul, but when coerced into acceptance, even the Benignant Goddesses relax their grip at the commands of Fate.

*The very day I showed up...Elaine's protective ways...*Mavis' mind whirled in recall. *At the hospital when he got hurt...the times I caught him staring at her just a little too long... Jake... that's why he never wrote me back home... why, he had it set to be that boy's daddy until... until I came along to let him know he was a daddy in his own right.*

Mavis pushed Babe away and walked toward a tree where she buried her face against her left arm.

Hell's bells, they must have laughed...Poor, dense Mavis, too stupid to see Elaine as more than the daughter of a business partner. And Cale, you son of a bitch, too tired to lay a hand on me... and I blamed myself. No wonder it galled you so much when John Earl began payin' her court when you wanted to be the one in her bed instead of him. Well, you can have her, and may the two of you rot in...

"Mavis, Mavis honey." She awoke from the past to become aware of Babe and the maelstrom. Seemingly from nowhere Melba had appeared.

"Did you see Billy and Violet?"

Mavis' reply was tainted with the venom that now engulfed her. "See them where?"

"Anywhere," Melba pleaded.

That Melba should intrude on her thoughts at this, the lowest single point in her life, drew the fury meant for Cale and Elaine. "They're nowheres I been; I got more things on my mind than lookin' for your younguns."

Melba's eyes implored Babe for an explanation.

Why, Babe thought, *am I the only person in three counties with any lick of sense during all this? Destruction and death in every direction, and instead of helping I'm left to look after a mother about to lose control of all her faculties and Mavis primed to tar and feather the world over something she should have been told from the start?*

Babe decided to concentrate on Melba; Mavis could stew in her juices.

"Mavis and I will help you find them, won't we Mavis?"

The biting tone did little to whip the McCallister woman into line. "Now, are you sure they didn't walk home or take a ride with someone?"

Her face brightened with a spark of hope. "Sure, that's the way it is; those kids walked home. I know they did. Billy just can't do without a stop at the store on the way home for candy and Violet..."

"Hell's bells, them kids are spoilt rotten and don't walk nowhere in this kind of weather nor take rides from nobody. I heard you myself a million times tellin 'um not to go with nobody but to wait for you. They're around here somewhere or likely as not still buried."

Melba lost all color hearing her fears confirmed.

Mavis caught the woman as she began to reel, her breakdown routing Mavis from the selfishness of her personal turmoil. "Course today's no regular day'; kids aren't behavin' like they been taught."

"None of us are," Babe added curtly.

"Let's make one last look at the garage and wherever else they set up... places to look. Then we'll drop by the house to check; next there's the hospitals. But I'm sure they walked. What child would stay around all this?" Mavis tried her best, but her last remark hit them all like a blow to the stomach.

The women navigated the unsteady course of the perimeter, stopping what stretcher bearers they could for a glimpse at the identities. Using some shred of evidence, Melba passed on each. "Wrong clothes...too tall...too heavy." Of those beyond recognition, Melba examined the hands of little girls for Violet's bitten fingernails and boys for the souvenir of Billy's broken collarbone.

Suddenly it occurred to Mavis, "Who's got Joe Ray?"

"I done forgot about him. He's with Sara Nell. Oh, them other two must have went over to Sarah Nell's. They know that's where I take Joe Ray when I got to have him minded in a hurry. You all know Sara Nell? She lives behind us." She searched their faces for signs of support.

"That's where we try first," Mavis announced as she silently vowed to purge Cale and Elaine from her thoughts and center on Melba's children. "But I got to get Miss Wythel first. We were on our way to take her to the doctor when it all happened."

"Someone's in your car, Mavis" Babe pointed. "At least we've found one on our list."

Even the crusty Miss Wythel buckled under the magnitude of suffering as evidenced by her tear-stained face.

"They pulled that picture feller out, still a holdin' onto his blamed camera. I seen that thing a sittin' up on the stretcher. You'd have thought it was the one hurt."

"You mean he came out without a scratch?" Melba looked for optimism she could direct toward her children's survival.

"Hard to tell; all he cared about was that camera, like it was worth a million dollars."

And for Matthew Tolleson, the film inside brought him the fame and fortune that accompanied a Pulitzer Prize. Despite two broken legs, Tolleson managed to locate his camera in the abyss. When the first rescuer reached him, the *Americana* reporter snapped one picture after another until a lack of film stilled its shutter.

Writing from the eyes of a victim, coupled with the shot taken at the moment of explosion, earned Tolleson the Prize. Spread across two pages, the image of the crumbling building and those caught in its wake graphically portrayed the last expressions and movements of the trapped children. Readers devoured each detailing.

The beauty of Norma Henry, hands above her head in a dramatic posture worthy of Harlow, flew from the page as did the row of first graders scrambling for the exits. The band members, poised to play, the principal floating in mid air, the intricacies written upon each face were impossible to comprehend in a single look. With each examination, a myriad of observations as yet unnoticed emerged to send readers back in gory repetition.

As for the residents of Brophy, the notoriety they craved assumed the pungent odor of cedar chests where they remained interred with the memories of loved ones, too painful for examination yet too treasured to be discarded.

As Mavis struggled to pull onto the clogged road, the women fell into silence. Much like the day the Willie B. #1 came in, cars inched at a snail's pace. Honking drivers refused to quiet as if those blocking their progress did so in perverse stubbornness. Only the fact that the city contained no hospital allowed vehicles carrying victims some degree of speed once they passed the bottleneck of town where they turned toward Kilgore, Overton, or Tyler on any available expanse of road.

〜〜〜〜〜

A camera flash temporarily blinded Zed Nelms as he stepped from his bus. From nowhere, journalists converged to spit questions in his direction.

"Were you actually able to deliver any children to their parents?"

"Did you witness the actual blast?"

"What do you remember about the sound of the explosion?"

Nelms felt dizzy, but managed to formulate a response that answered no particular query and furnished several newspapers with a feature story that tore at many a heart.

"The bus kept shakin'."

"Before or after?"

"Them parents was just like crazy folk, a poundin' on the bus, tryin' to make me let 'um on. But I couldn't." He pled for absolution. "Them kids has been through enough without them bein' badgered with questions they couldn't answer, and all of 'um hurt in some way or other. So I only stopped when Stoney would recognize a ma or pa that belonged."

"That's Fred's ma. See that one yonder in the blue coat?"

Without pulling off the road, Zed stopped and slid from his green-upholstered seat as the springs expressed their gratitude. He screamed to the group of some six or eight mothers and smaller children crowding around the bus. "I ain't lettin' nary a one of you on what don't have kin in here, and just Mrs. Gaston fits that bill."

Ignoring the angry protests and barrage of obscenities, Freda's mother parted the women and twisted through the tiny opening Zed allowed. By-passing the driver, Mrs. Gaston fell to her knees as she took Stoney by the shoulders.

"Where is she?"

His eyes riveted to those of Freda's mother, while his hand motioned toward Freda.

"I watched that momma grab her girl and rock her like she was a baby. Then," his tone bore personal shame, "she thanks me for what I done. Said she won't never be able to repay me. If she'd just knowed how much I wanted to stay here and look for my own." His shoulders sagged. "That's when I had Stoney make signs from his tablet of the names of the children I had. Stuck 'um on all sides with gum." He smiled wistfully. "That boy did a powerful lot of chewin' in a small time."

Zed seemed to drink in his surroundings for the first time since his return. The magnitude of the rescue operation had intensified two-fold.

"How does word get around so quick? Out on the road, cars full of parents was lined up, and jumped out when I slowed so's they could read the names. But when I got to my real stops and had to see the faces when they figured out what it meant when their kids wasn't comin' home this trip."

When he closed his eyes that night, the images of mothers' hands flying to their faces in realization and anguish appeared. It would be late the next day before Zed learned that two of his three youngsters perished in the Brophy School Disaster. The third, a boy of ten, lay near death for three weeks in Mother Frances Hospital in Tyler where his wife kept vigil. The burial fell on his shoulders.

"Then I guess you're a hero?"

He looked confused. "Not me, Stoney. You mark my words. Without that boy to keep me sane, I wouldn't never have left out on that bus. And the way he helped Gene Ed off the bus with him sick to his stomach. Or how he was the one got Joetta Pemberton to even move. Poor girl wouldn't do nothin' but stare straight ahead even for her ma."

Like many of the newer and a few of the old-time residents of Brophy, the Nelms moved on in a futile effort to leave their shattered past in the ruins of a school building and a cemetery west of town.

～～～～～

Before her startled passengers could complain, Mavis whipped into a vacant parking space.

"We ain't gettin' nowhere fast on the street, so I'm goin' in to call over to Sarah Nell's."

Once inside the grocery store, the sign on the register bespoke of the curtailment of normal business. The storekeeper ignored Mavis as he pulled bandages and other first aid items at a furious rate. To the rear of the building, a line twisted toward the front as those of a similar mind waited for a turn at the telephone. Mavis examined the distressing postures and expressions.

A grandmotherly woman felt obliged to inform the new arrival. "I been here more than a hour hopin' to call my older daughter to tell her to come home to a funeral. Looks like I may be here the rest of the day." She looked questioningly at Mavis before bursting into tears. "But what else is there for an old woman like me to do?"

Returning to the front of the store, Mavis removed a weather-beaten cane-bottomed chair from the space reserved for the perpetual occupation of old men attracted to the store and its constant commotion. Just as the grateful woman seated herself a cry of triumph went up from a man much closer to the phone.

"He got through."

An exuberant cheer erupted. "He's the first; them lines must be jammed terrible."

"Yeah, this is Mike," the voice shouted into the receiver. "Oh, it's much worse than anything we've ever handled...No, hundreds dead, kids, teachers...Send all the doctors and nurses... and," the voice lowered in deference to the feelings of those behind him, "embalmers and caskets...as many children's as you can rustle up. They've set up a headquarters at the railroad station. Have them go there first... Right," he peered over his shoulder, "I can't say right now... Just get every available volunteer we got. Tell them to be ready to relocate. There's not a hospital in the town, and they've had to set up morgues everywhere."

The swelling in Mavis' stomach drove her to the entrance where Sara Nell and two children were squeezing into the car to avoid the abating but still uncomfortable wind.

Babe recapped for Mavis' benefit. "Sarah Nell hasn't heard a word from Melba's kids or her older ones. Oh, Mavis, can you believe any of this? Why, the first I realized anything was wrong more than another gusher out of control was Cara

Settle's boy Raymond come walkin' in my front room covered in blood and cut every place I could see. He was plumb delirious, kept goin' on about the school and how everybody else was dead. That boy thought he was at home when Pine is a good two streets over."

"What'd you do?"

"Put a pallet out and tried to ring Cara. Even then there weren't no use. So I bundled up the kids and went for her. She's at my house now, afraid to move him till a doctor sees him. Lord knows when that'll be."

"Red Cross man in the store says the depot is the place to get any kind of news. Now that Brophy' got one, looks like it's the logical spot for a beginnin' point."

Babe took charge. "I say we send someone home with these," she indicated the confused children. "Then we can head to the depot."

"I'll stay," Miss Wythel volunteered.

"But I was takin' you to the doctor. You don't feel like messin' with no kids."

Miss Wythel waved her hands in dismissal. "I just wanted to get you to the house today. You don't visit enough no more. Besides, I can get Millie to help out. Likely as not, she's at Clyde's waitin' for word."

After leaving the children and Miss Wythel with Millie, Mavis pulled back into traffic with a, "Hold on," that drown amid horns and squealing tires.

As the girls passed the ball park, Babe asked of no one in particular, "I wonder where Pup and the rest of the men were sent?"

~~~~~

The cheers of a raucous crowd? The terrifying sounds of the European front? Pup Schneider placed both hands upon his ears in a futile action he hoped would stop the insanity of it all. When he walked upon the playing field, fear gripped his heart and controlled his feet. It's worse than them nightmares after the War.

A dusky sky clouded his senses.

This is the ball park, reason shouted. But the sounds and stench of death produced the horrifying spectacle of War. Across the infield the dead strewn haphazardly awaited transfer from the freshly cut grass to the dug outs.

Pup scanned his stadium, his source of greatest pride and accomplishment.

How can I, how can any of us come back to this field to sit in the stands and cheer on the boys like this never happened? I meant for this to be the place folks took their families for fun, and now...so many got no families left.

One of the coverings had blown to expose the face of a girl sleeping peacefully on the green. Pup yielded to the urge for an explanation as to the girl's serenity in contrast to the others. Easing back the bed sheet, as if a sudden movement might startle the child, he left without answers to any of his musings.

"I understand that you're the man who owns the field." A man near his own age moved from the dugout.

"That's right."

"Then, can you see that these lights get turned on later?"

A nod.

"I'm afraid that at this rate the embalming will have to go into the night...even longer, maybe. There's a couple of hundred and more coming from the hospitals, not taking into account the ones who may die in the next few days."

He watched as Pup resigned himself to the facts. "I am truly sorry to have to ask you."

"No," his head jerked upward, "I should be thankin' you...and everyone else that we ain't never gonna have the name of for comin' to do what, what nobody ought ever to have to do."

"You in the War?"

"Yeah," Pup stared off into space.

"Where I learned my trade."

Pup faced him. "I was in the worst of it; saw more than most. But I swear, it wasn't nothin' compared to this."

A large hand rested upon his arm. "If it's any consolation, I'm havin' trouble, too. I get called on to prepare children now and again, infants mostly. But I can see my own kids out here, and I wonder how this happened at a school. Kids are supposed to be safe there. Makes me want to run back home and hold them just to make sure they aren't out among all these."

Tentatively, "Do you have children?"

"Nope, not married."

"Then I hope you won't take this in a way it's not intended, but I believe you are truly blessed."

Pup watched the undertaker return to his work only to be stopped by a set of parents supporting each other.

"Our boy's here. We done identified him over to the bank vault, and they said we could claim him here...after they's done."

"Greatly sorry," Schneider muttered. He watched them trudge across the outfield. *Clyde's new vault...a morgue.*

Anywhere a goodly amount of space existed like the newly opened community center and all the churches now housed the dead and injured. Thus the bereaved became unwilling participants in a perverse scavenger hunt complicated by distance and the continuous additions of more casualties which sent them back time and again to the same locations.

~~~~~

Mother Frances Hospital represented the pinnacle of medical facilities in East Texas. Sitting with a degree of majesty on a small rise of Smith County landscape, the news of the explosion arrived via the air waves to afford the precious time to muster additional staff.

Beverly Dodd adjusted the starched white cap that set atop her upswept hair. *That ought to hold, come what may,* she said of the bobby pins. Despite her fifteen years of ministering to the sick, she stood unprepared for the strain on manpower and materials that lay ahead. Some forty-eight hours would pass before she abdicated her duties as head nurse. In that span every emotion and shred of medical knowledge were taxed, and, in her eyes only, found lacking with each patient lost.

In the distance, the cry of an ambulance prompted a "Get ready."

The lamenting vehicle followed by a weather-beaten delivery wagon backed into the indention just in front of the emergency station. Before the driver killed his engine, the doors of the wagon opened. Covered by a blanket soiled with a curious silty substance, a woman, middle thirties by estimation, was wheeled by.

"In here," directed Nurse Dodd. "Doctor Price is waiting."

The man clutching the patient's hand balked at her next demand. "You'll have to wait out here."

"But I can't leave her alone."

"Are you her husband?"

The man strained for every inch of height to follow the woman with his eyes.

"No...yes," he lied. "That's my wife. I've got to get in there." He tried to push the obstacle in white.

"You'll best help her by giving us information. Now sit down and fill in these questions. You do read, because if not I'll..."

"I can read," he lashed at the woman whose attention to detail he mistook for callousness.

A muffled moan escaped the cubicle as a hospital worker emerged, sending Cale to his feet.

"Has your wife spoken since her trauma?" questioned Doctor Daniel Price.

"No, not what you'd say was understandin' words."

"Have you any idea as to what may have struck her?"

Cale closed his eyes on a quest of recollection. "There's bricks, boards, beams just everywhere."

"I see, Mr...?"

"McCallister."

The doctor gently removed the papers from the man's lap.

"Elaine Crawford?" He turned to address the nurse. "I thought he was the husband?"

Cale's head shook slowly in denial. "I'm just a friend," he quickly added. "Her husband's dead. See, I helped get her out, and naturally, her bein' a friend and her daddy my partner..."

"I understand." The doctor retreated toward the examining room.

"Will she...?" Cale groped for the pristine sleeve of the lab coat.

"Mrs. Crawford has suffered a severe blow to the head. Right now, she is comatose. As to further injuries, she's a collection of deep bruises and lacerations...cuts...There don't appear to be any broken bones, a miracle in itself. Internally? Too soon to say; time will tell us about recovery. The longer she sleeps, the more serious it becomes."

"Can I sit with her?" he begged.

"Normally, no, but we're going to need every available person. So, I can use you to observe Mrs. Crawford." His tone changed to that of authority. "Now, I want to know if she moves, even the slightest, and if her eyes open, send someone to get me."

Cale nodded eagerly. When he entered the room, he lost his last reserve of strength. The staff had cleaned away the silt, and the true extent of Elaine's condition became obvious. Her swollen face bore different shades of blue and black as did the slender arms protruding from beneath the sheet. Cuts of varying shapes and lengths crisscrossed the exposed areas.

She's never gonna make it.

From quivering lips, Cale began to mouth his prayer. "I guess it's been way too long since we last talked, and I feel real bad about that. Sarah always told me your Good Book was truth. Funny, I just picked out the verses I wanted to fit. That part about money being the root of all evil? You hit that nail on the head. You gave me money, plenty of it, and I didn't even take time to thank you kindly. I was all wound up in spendin' and buyin' and makin' more. I should have done right by you with it, give more to Sarah and Jerry. Now, I paid off their debts and set them up in good style, but I could have done more.

"As for Mavis and the babies, well, I bought whatever flew into that crazy red head of hers," he paused in reflection of the severity of his actions. "But I left her with none of me that counted." He looked down at Elaine. "See, I couldn't stop lovin' Elaine, but you know all that. You said that a man is what he thinks in his heart. That bein' so, I'm lower than dirt. Anyways I'm here to say that I'm sorry for what I done and for all the trust you put in me that I gone and done flittered away."

He smiled. "You made me a high-powered business man, God, so I'm gonna cut you a deal. If you'll let...if you'll please let Elaine live, I promise to get my life on the right track again, like it was when I was true in every way to my family... and myself, before I was Mr. Big Shot of the Brophy Boys, before I let John Earl show me the easy life on that broad road." He began to pace the limits of the hospital room. "I sure ain't in no position to be the one offerin' deals, huh?"

He looked heavenward in frustration. "Oh, I wasn't never no good at words, God. You know what I tryin' to get out. Just please keep her alive. She's got a boy to raise, and she's suffered a heap more than she's earned a right to, just in the short time I knowed her." Cale went to the woman's bedside. *Maybe that's the problem... I knowed her.*

~~~~~~

With the darkness of night came the merciful calming of the chilling winds. "Thank heavens for that shred of favor," Bulldog told another volunteer. "Looks like the very thing Proration and marital law aimed at has finally happened. The East Texas Field's not pumpin' hot oil nor bad blood."

"What I wouldn't give for a fuller moon," the roughneck sighed.

From another direction a faceless voice complained, "Ain't there no more of them kliegs?"

He referenced the cluster responsible for a giant outpouring of light over the debris of the school. Still some of the ruins remained in shadows that prevented the use of heavy machinery. In comparison to the until now unappreciated speed of the daylight hours, the rescue efforts crawled. In response, Bulldog commandeered an idle truck for a trip to a downtown warehouse. With the assistance of passing guardsmen, he loaded a massive configuration of lights onto the flat bed.

Once on site he parked beside the derricks that sat nearest the school. "Let's get her up, boys."

By nine, the rescuers declared the majority of the auditorium area picked clean of wreckage, thus allowing for the first time a scant few to search the less severely damaged portions. The group followed the stream of kliegs and flashlights into a classroom wing.

"But they was all supposed to been at the program."

"There's still plenty unaccounted for, too many not to check every inch of this place."

"Sure, a few could have got confused tryin' to crawl out."

The men divided the two wings and returned to the tedium of pulling away obstacles. Once inside they conducted a preliminary search by calling out but expecting no response.

"Wait,"James Raburn alerted the man nearest him. "I think I hear somethin'."

Raburn, the senior who left early in the day complaining of the mysterious symptoms, rallied once removed from the gas that stole like a death angel through every crevice of the building.

He raced to the scene when word reached him and began pulling familiar faces from the wreckage. Later he carried the caskets of classmates, saying his good-byes amid the empty words of preachers, silently pleading for his friends' forgiveness of his desertion.

But the self-imposed penance never absolved him of his crimes. The boy that was James Raburn perished alongside his friends, replaced by a man consumed with embittered guilt.

"I hear it, too." The men pushed through overturned cabinets and sagging boards toward a whimpering mass clinging to a desk seat as if waiting for an inevitable second blast.

"You all right, kid?" James questioned a form moving in the pervading dimness.

Tentatively, as if afraid to trust the phantoms emerging from the shadows, "My arm's hurt."

Raburn lifted the boy. "How'd you get so far from the others?"

A rush of tears accentuated the earnestness of his reply.

"I was bad."

"No you weren't." He hugged the boy more closely.

"Yes, I was. I whopped ole Violet, but I was just funnin' her, honest. Miz Venable brung me in here to copy out of the dictionary."

He paused between sobs. "I only got to 'abbreviation,' and she's gonna be real mad. See, I can't go home till I finish the page, but I can't find my papers and my book."

James carried his burden toward the shambles of what had been a hallway. Having seen the lifeless body of Mrs. Venable hours before, he reassured the child. "I bet she's real glad she sent you back."

Travis Pool, Violet's tormentor, was one of five who survived from Mrs. Venable's class. Exhausted, the child fell asleep in the security of rescue in the muscular arms of the star quarterback of a team that could not muster eleven healthy players for the season.

~~~~~~

At the tiny Overton Hospital, Mavis and Babe supported Melba down yet another corridor. As did its Kilgore counterpart, the halls collected the overflow until passages became so restricted that one needed to turn sideways to achieve any degree of maneuverability.

A look at Melba's glazed eyes prompted Mavis to pray, *God, let this be over soon. Just how much more do you think she can take?*

Melba faltered as they approached the next blood-stained bed, only to turn in disappointed relief. A knot tightened within her stomach at each bedside and released for the few seconds necessary to pass to another.

My babies are alive, Melba repeated silently, though each failure chiseled a fraction of her resolve. *Please forgive me for the jealousy I felt when Sarah Nell found Victor when we first stopped in Kilgore, and help them through this all.*

Victor's doctor had been blunt, for no time existed to offer soothing reassurances. "The boy's crushed inside, and I'm not up on how to treat him. If he can hold on, I've given orders to send him to Dallas. That's the best I can do." The country doctor watched as the women consoled one another. Awake most of the previous night delivering a baby, he responded like everyone else to the call.

The boy won't make it through the night, he told himself. *But I've seen my share of miracles in twenty-five years of rural healing.*

At Sarah Nell's insistence, the others continued the search for the Aiken youngsters. Later that evening Victor and Karen Snell would share an ambulance ride to Dallas while their mothers followed in the Snell's car. The three month recuperation of their children forged a lifetime bond between the mothers.

The Brophy women pressed against the wall. Babe felt her head spinning from the stench of ether mixed with the body fluids and the stagnate odor of the silt. "Maybe there's some sort of main listing," she heard herself say.

"Hell's bells, kids don't wear no dog tags. They don't know one from another less the kids can talk."

"But those who can?" Melba grabbed for the thread of hope.

Mavis acquiesced, "All right, all right, I'm goin' down to the desk and ask, but you two keep lookin' cause I'm waistin' time." Mavis twisted and turned until she reached the main entry. *Another line*, she thought with disgust.

Little ladies in street clothes did their best to answer the barrage hurled indelicately in their direction from the panicked and anguished.

"Is my child here? His name's..."

"But we've been to all the other hospitals; this here's the last one..."

"No, I ain't checked there; my girl ain't dead, I told ya."

When the opportunity afforded, Mavis pushed toward a white-haired Daughter of the Confederacy matron holding a stack of note pages.

"Excuse me, Ma'am. I know it's near to impossible, but the child of a friend of mine. She thought just maybe there's some way of keepin' track of who all's here."

Peering over her glasses, the woman patted Mavis' hand. "I understand, dear. What's the name?"

"Aiken, A-I-K-E-N, Billy or Violet."

The older woman expressed sympathy with her eyes. "That poor woman. Come on, we can work faster if you help." She spread the papers scribbled with names, numbers, and partial reports so that both might see. Several were marked with large red "D's."

As Mavis traveled the worn pages, she brushed away tears. Over half the names were familiar. "Wait." She caught the woman's hand. "I think that's it." Mavis pointed to a name partially smudged. "What's the number look like to you?"

The page moved closer to the woman's glasses. "214?"

Throwing her arms around the volunteer, the redhead hugged with a force that left the woman teetering. "I found her," Mavis screamed as she roared down the corridor.

Assured that only Mavis McCallister possessed the dubious talent to be heard above any confusion, Babe and Melba emerged from a room.

"Where?" Melba begged.

"It was kind of hard to read, but I think it's 214. Anyways, it's a place to start."

The flight of stairs proved more difficult than the teeming hallway. At the landing a mattress lay on the floor. Every inch of space by necessity served as a room where loved ones rode a roller coaster of emotions.

Melba stopped a nurse laden with dressings on the second floor. "214. My little Violet is there."

"This way."

With puppy dog allegiance, Melba fell behind. Room 214 was Overton Hospital's version of a ward. Built to house six, perhaps eight beds, a ninth had been moved at the end of the elongated room. Each bed and all but a single mattress contained a patient.

From a concoction of pulleys and braces, a child's leg was suspended in an unnatural posture. A heavy layer of gauze wound around the head, covering the eyes and much of the forehead. Of the visible portion of the face, a crusty red surface replaced what should have been a welcomed sight.

"The doctor done give her somethin' to make her sleep."

Melba jumped.

The woman left the bedside of a little girl and approached. "She yours?"

"I don't know," Melba admitted in shame and frustration.

"Her name's Violet, but that's all I got out of her." As Melba swooned, the woman fought to prevent her from reaching the floor. The arrival of Babe and Mavis provided the assistance to ease Melba onto the vacant mattress where Mavis pressed a dampened handkerchief to her head in hopes of bringing Melba around.

"What's wrong with Violet?" she managed some minutes later.

"She was here when my Becky was brung in."

"What time was that?" urged Babe.

Apologetically, "Time has got right away from me. Couple two or three hours? But she must have been one of the first if they had time to rig her up like that."

"Which doctor is hers?"

"None come to see to her, but one did come around after Becky. She got crushed by somethin'. 'Her pelvis bone is all mashed,' he said."

The four fell silent.

Mavis reached for the chart at the foot of the bed before abandoning the hen scratching. After slamming the metal covered chart against the doweled foot of the bed, "I'm goin' to get somebody to tell us what the hell's goin'..."

"Mrs. McCallister?" a feeble voice inquired.

Melba was on her feet and at her daughter's side.

"Oh, Violet, it's Momma, baby."

The child's hands groped pitifully until they clutched those of her mother.

"Am I gonna die? Everybody else did. It was so awful, Momma. I couldn't see them, but I could feel. I don't wanna die, too." Tears seeped through the gauze.

Overcome, Melba and Mavis stifled their own tears.

"It's Babe Styles, Violet. Mavis and I brought your momma to take care of you." She tried to reassure the child. "Don't worry about the other children; they weren't hurt as bad as you thought. Neither are you. Why in a few days ya'll will be out on the playground trading stores about all this."

"But I can't see, and my leg hurts somethin' awful." She tried to move, but the rigging held tightly. "Momma, take all this stuff off me."

Melba stroked the matted hair. "That's got to stay to make your leg better. Doc says so. Go on back to sleep. You can't get no better less you rest up."

When the child drifted off, Melba turned to her friends. "You two done more than I can repay."

She turned to Violet. "But I got to ask you this...please find Billy for me. I can't leave her like this, but Billy's..."

Mavis snapped the gold clasp of her handbag after extracting fifty dollars. As she thrust it into Melba's hand, "Here, we may be a while gettin' back. When we find Billy and Jake, one of us has to stay on."

"I can't take this," Melba pushed away what represented days of wages.

"Hell's bells, take the damn money." She was already weaving down the hall.

Sighing, Melba returned to Violet's bed. A metal chair commandeered by Mavis in a manner she refused to divulge sat empty. She pulled it as closely as she could, then slumped forward after retaking the pale hand. Exactly when she succumbed to exhaustion, she knew not, but the sun shone brightly through the window before Melba lifted her head from the edge of Violet's bed.

〰〰〰〰〰

The room was vastly different from Violet's as a direct result of two twenty dollar bills paid to a hospital worker. A nudge sent Cale's head into the air and a sharp pain down a stiffened back.

"Elaine," he slapped her hand. "Elaine, wake up."

Slowly eyelids rose. The image of a babbling Cale took shape. Elaine attempted to lift her arm; the ensuing pain roused her senses.

"Jake!" she screamed.

"He'll be fine," Cale cajoled.

"The children," she forced her body upward despite the agony that prompted a cry unlike any he had ever heard. Cale eased Elaine back onto the bed. "Don't try to get up."

Elaine's screams intensified as her fists pounded against Cale's chest. Seemingly from nowhere a doctor appeared to thrust Cale into the background.

"What's wrong with her?" Cale begged.

"She's delirious." The doctor accepted the timely arrival of a vial and syringe. Both men and the nurse restrained Elaine as the medication was administered.

In her hysteria, Elaine believed she spoke. *Don't tie my hands. Stop!* The ceiling fell again, and her body flew through the air. The pervading dust began to obscure her sight until the darkness consumed once more.

Chapter 16

Brophy, Texas, stumbled into another day, a collection of people who functioned in disbelief and bewilderment. Mavis and Babe returned in the early morning. As they mounted the rise on Brophy's outskirts, both women strained for a more accurate understanding of the lights that illuminated the sky.

"M-E-R-R-Y C-H-R-I-S-T-M-A-S?"

"What in the..." Mavis swore at the paradox emblazoned over hell's newest piece of real estate.

"It's Bulldog's lights," Babe explained.

In one of his more civic-minded expenditures, Bulldog urged the Boys to foot the bill for a set of several thousand lights to be strung from adjacent rigs for the holiday season. Before the belt tightening of Proration, the driller oversaw a team of electricians and some payroll welders to spell out the greeting in red and green.

"They must have every klieg for miles aimed at the school," the lady driller estimated the degree of lighting rebuffed by the clouds to transform one small section of town into an eerie type of daylight.

"And Pup's got the lights on at the field. Now, I wonder what he thinks he's doin? That field isn't completed, and as for the lights helpin out, he' too far away. Even if it backed up to the school, I bet it still wouldn't be enough," she sighed.

"Nothin' ever is. You do your damnedest, and still it ain't enough." As it did each time their conversation lulled, Mavis' mind turned to Cale and Elaine and what she should do with her discovery.

"Let's stop by Clyde's. Maybe Jake and Billy have been found by now."

The cars that snarled the streets hours before diminished to a steady but progressive stream even at this early an hour. As houses replaced storefronts, their porch lights revealed home after home for whom sleep remained elusive.

"Oh no," Mavis gasped as the Henry residence came into view. On the front door hung a large black wreath.

"And the Davis house." Babe pointed to an ebony ribbon that drooped limply from a pillar.

Easing her foot from the accelerator, Mavis crept down the once vibrant row of houses resplendent in oil-moneyed finery. "Most every one of them," she moaned. "I didn't know the world held so much black ribbon."

With few exceptions, the homes in Brophy and its rural routes bore the markings of death. Those whose mourning went unmarked grieved over relatives and friends, so that no one escaped the horror of the disaster.

"I can't look no more."

But they were impossible to dismiss. Guiding the automobile into Clyde's driveway, the two sat staring at the porch.

Jake? Elaine? Mavis' heart rose into her throat. God forgive me, but it would be so much simpler if she could just fade into memory. Then I wouldn't never have to let on what I seen; we could go back to things the way they was before he ever met Elaine Crawford.

She bit her lip defiantly in a battle within her heart. *But she loved me like a sister, even with me takin' the man she called hers. Oh, I'm too confused to take hold of any kind of sense.*

At the Tyler and Kilgore radio stations, the more level heads urged a speedy accounting. Since the explosion, the two suspended programming to broadcast only information pertaining to the catastrophe.

The owner of the Tyler station managed a conversation with the governor by way of a hefty contribution toward the election chest of the man making his way to East Texas for a first-hand investigation in the form of a committee of experts he could chair composed of representatives from the United States Bureau of Mines and the Department of Agriculture.

Throughout the night they remained on the air to list confirmed deaths and names of the injured as did the continually arriving newsreel cameras and journalists who linked a sympathetic nation to the grieving community. It was from the Kilgore station that Clyde learned of his daughter and where to claim the body of his grandchild. As the girls would discover, Russell left for Mother Frances soon after placing Jake's casket in the parlor.

By midmorning the curious converged to sample what the newspapers could only provide in small doses. Some claimed pieces of the rubble as souvenirs and probed anyone they encountered for miraculous stories of survival so that they might vicariously experience the horrors by questioning those fortunate few.

On everyone's lips and hearts the question burned. Why?

~~~~~~

"He knows, I tell you!" David Carmichael resumed the incessant pacing which paused for the few seconds required to loom ominously over the back of a seated Estelle and make his pronouncement.

Adjusting a skirt that had risen seductively during their conversation, Estelle tugged at the strained material with a practiced deliberateness sure to divert any man's thoughts into a realm she controlled.

He noticed; they always do.

Estelle lit a cigarette and crossed her legs so methodically that the brush of her nylons lasted long after the act was completed.

"Now David, you got to get a hold of yourself. What does that fool of a Ranger have on us that he can prove?"

"He's got the ring, dammit," he shouted as he inwardly berated himself for his involvement with the scheme. *I can't believe the stupidity of this woman... and me. Here the law holds crucial evidence, and she acts like it don't shed a ray of light on us.*

Carmichael faced a park bench which contributed to the ambiance of the Tate garden and upon which Estelle sat like some carved goddess of love.

In hopes of easing his fears, Estelle feigned indifference though she struggled to stave off her own misgivings. *If only the Ranger had paid me the call. I'd have quieted his suspicions on the spot. Instead, all I have is David's inept recollections. If only I could talk to John Earl about all this.* A fact she kept from her cohort, Estelle had placed repeated calls to her new spouse only to be frustrated by lines too jammed with callers for her own emergency to go through.

"This is life or death," she screamed at the operator. "What do you mean a school accident? What does some bunch of snot-nosed kids got to do with message deliverin'?"

She took a hesitant glance at Carmichael. *John Earl's got to be let know that he's ready to cave in on us all.* Her voice assumed a decided edge. "If you had an ounce of sense, you would have convinced that two-bit tin star that my dearly departed husband's ring was lost or stole." A puff of smoke encircled her head in a contradictory halo.

"That's exactly what I told him, but he's got a way of looking right through you to get to the truth. I swear he's digging up that grave even as we speak. We got days, maybe just hours before he comes to arrest us." He pleaded for Estelle's approval. "Let's us high tail it to Mexico."

Estelle threw her cigarette to the dirt and ground it with a stylish pump. *I wish it was his empty head. His arguments were weakening her resolve. Why hasn't John Earl called me?*

"Shut up!" she screamed.

Carmichael fell back a few steps.

"Now you get this straight once and for all. It won't make a dime's worth of difference what's in that grave. So that crook of a Mexican undertaker charged us plenty for a first-rate coffin, and we got took? I was just too touched in my grief to take a last look at the body of my beloved all laid out for the maggots. And if everything does come out in the open, it was self defense. You and Lamar, you come gunnin' for me and John Earl. And now that we're married the jury will come closer to believin'... Damn!" She bit her lip.

He was turning and slapping his hands upon his head. "What a chump I've been."

Before Estelle could react, his hands were about her slender throat while his body loomed over her in an ominous posture.

"Just how long you two been stringin' me along?"

Estelle squirmed as his grip tightened.

"We're not doin' no such thing," she gasped.

"Then how come you never let on? John Earl ashamed of his missus?"

"No, he thought...that is we thought it best to keep it a secret..."

He released her with a violence that jarred the bench upon which she fell. When she recovered, Estelle watched his head fly back in hysterical laughter.

"I always had you pegged for bein' smarter than that." He pointed mockingly.

"John Earl's picked you clean; all Lamar's money, his company, he's ripped it all right out from between your pretty little fingers by getttin' you to say the I do's. Did he tell you that you were the only one?" His tone dripped with sarcasm. "And where is he?" Carmichael rhetorically posed. "I'll tell you exactly. He's down in Texas livin' the life of a single man, countin' your money, and thinkin' on the best way to let you and me take the fall. It's a sweetheart of a plan and pure John Earl Terry."

He flopped on the bench, exhausted. "At least I got the satisfaction of not bein' the biggest fool in it all."

"You're wrong," she insisted. "He does love me." She pressed her finger repeatedly into her bosom.

"So how long's it been since you two spoke? Wait." He held up his palm in a traffic cop pose. "Let me. He doesn't want you to contact him for some reason like..." he thought... "like diverting suspicion. Hell, he knows you can't get in a witness chair against him; he just doesn't want you around cramping his style with the ladies. And just you wait," he spewed the words at her face. "He'll find a way to get rid of you and me like he did Lamar."

David Carmichael was gone, leaving Estelle trembling in the garden. *John Earl wouldn't do that to me, to us.* Carmichael's words whirled through her mind with staggering, convincing speed. She ran into the house where the contents of a leather handbag fell onto her bed with the tinkle and jingle of feminine trifles. Tearing through the jumble, she grabbed the card with the number she promised not to use.

After completing the necessary steps to place the call, she waited an intolerable amount of time during which each second took its toll on her trust in the con man she married as David's pronouncement played like a Victrola record. "He'll find a way to get rid of you and me like he did Lamar."

No wonder he was so easy to get to the altar. Now he has half or more of my money and stands to get it all when I ... The ringing began.

Faye Sodders had spent the night at John Earl's, like all of East Texas, unsure of what to do exactly. When he never made it to the office nor home that night, the loyal secretary decided to camp out at his place with the sheaf of messages too important to leave on his desk to the off chance he might run by.

Half of Texas has a mind to talk to him. These calls and papers from the office that need his once over can hold, but that grapevine gossip that Lone Wolf's askin' lots of questions about John Earl's part in Lamar Tate's strange reappearance, that and the Governor's man showin' up with a summons for everyone connected with the buildin' of the school. There's no tellin' what they'd do to a man who'd miss that.

Roused from a deep sleep, she stumbled to the phone into which she responded instinctively without regard for her surroundings.

"Hello."

Estelle bristled at the sound of a woman's voice.

"Hello," an irritated Faye demanded.

"Who are you, and what the hell are you doin' answerin' this phone?" a virulent woman blared over the wire.

The secretary answered by driving the receiver into its cradle and falling immediately back to sleep on the sofa.

"I'll kill that bastard," Estelle vowed to the buzzing in her ear.

The road to East Texas became more crowded by two cars on similar missions to see that Brophy would bury yet another of its citizens.

~~~~~

One unending funeral procession wound through town from its five churches to culminate at the Rosemont Cemetery. From nine o'clock the first morning until the evening of the third day, services were recited over victims that changed with the hours.

For many families, double or even triple funerals laid to rest siblings and cousins and trimmed what would have been an overflow of mourners at each service to a small lot of decimated families and friends trying to take solace in shared losses.

At times the audience remained seated as another casket occupied the space beneath the pulpit while at Rosemont the bereaved traveled from grave to grave listening to the parting words of ministers that more often than not were unsure of the exact names of those whose spirits they commended to the Lord.

The McCallisters rode the mile and a quarter to Rosemont with little exchange during this, their first moments of privacy since his return from Tyler. Somewhere during their continued search for Billy, Mavis decided to keep her wits.

Confrontin' him after Elaine's come so close to death will only force his hand and most likely spell the end of my marriage when nothins' to be gained by rakin' him over the coals as tired and dim-witted as we all are. When Elaine's better, if that ever comes, then I'll speak my piece. That's if I can work up the nerve even then. I got the twins to think on. Hell's bells, who'm I foolin'? Ain't nothin' ever gonna make me stop lovin' Cale. Not pride, nor...nor him yearnin' for my best friend. She closed her eyes in deep concentration.

Cale parked behind the last car. The roads, paths really, between the plots barely allowed a single lane, thus drivers pulled onto the grassy areas to either side to balance their cars precariously in the ditches.

Scattered groups of old-time residents gathered at family plots. With the majority of the newly dug graves located in close proximity, the section furthest from the iron-barred gate teemed with relatives and friends due to the Cemetery Committee's offer of grave sites to those unable to afford burial of their dead. The result being that scriptures read over the coffin at one burial mingled with those in progress in any direction.

Among the symmetrical divisions of earth a small group of singers progressed to provide hymns.

Joined by the rest of the Brophy Boys' inner circle, Mavis and Cale stood over the grave of little Jake. A preacher left a burial just concluded a few steps to the west to talk with God about a child whose name he had to inquire to begin anew the words spoken minutes before and repeated throughout the days until they became rote.

"It is not for mere mortals to question the will of God. We cannot comprehend the wisdom in this tragedy," he gestured toward the mounds of new earth being shoveled behind them and toward those in the forefront staked or spaded. "But by faith fulfilled we will, in our own victories over death, learn the answer to this and every human question."

"Why?" the voice emerged from Cale's past to blend with the words of the minister. They were seated on the wooden benches as the Reverend Ezekiel pounded the podium to underscore his rage. Flowers covered identical caskets which flanked either side of the area separating the preacher from his audience.

"Why do the Lord Almighty allows the devil to touch the just as well as the unjust, the guilty alongside the innocent? Hatred, jealousy, and greed. Them is the devil's tools to deceive men to his will. And I says to all of you, since the Lord done allowed us to reap from His bounty, we, all of us, done been guilty of one if not all them sins. And the innocent has shed their blood to cleanse us yet again."

"Amen!"

Mavis tugged at his arm to signal the conclusion of the brief memorial. Once at their cars, the friends waited for Clyde in one last show of respect. Bent and looking older than Mavis remembered, Clyde placed both palms on the roof of the car.

"They want me to bring Elaine home," he announced with dread.

Mavis interjected, "So soon?"

Clyde forced himself from the car.

"They need the bed, and according to her doctors, she's not hurt nearly so bad as some so that she can't be looked after at home with a doctor stoppin' by each day."

He looked solemnly at those who over a few short months had become closer than blood kin.

"So, I'll need some help to look after her. She's..." he stared down at this hands, "They're givin' her medicine for the pain we can see, but her mind's not quite right." He looked up at Hoyt. "Can we use the wagon?"

"Normally, I'd drive, but I got to make a showin' at the Governor's meetin', but Cale can have the wagon."

"He's got to look for Billy," snapped the scorned wife, desperate to keep her husband from Elaine. "Let Pup or Bulldog drive you over."

"You and me will get her home," the driller promised.

"I don't understand at all about Billy," said Miss Wythel. "Ain't they covered every damned inch of dirt with a fine-toothed comb already?"

"Some can't be identified by face. They got a list of bodies and another of missin' kids they can't match up. I hear they even put one name to a corpse, buried it, and found out this mornin' they was wrong. Now the family's got it all to do over...Billy's bound to be amongst them, but with Melba refusin' to leave Violet." Pup' estimation of their circumstance trailed.

"I ain't givin' up," Cale announced. "Maybe there's someplace nobody's thought of."

The somber group split for the women's return to the house to accommodate callers and prepare for Elaine's homecoming.

In the car, Miss Wythel spoke with disdain, "Didn't bother to show his face."

"Who?" Babe naively questioned.

"The one who really deserves the blame for all this. And he don't even remember he was the boy's step-daddy there for a while, not that he ever took the job serious."

"As if any of us would let him within ten feet of the house," Millie reminded.

As an afterthought Miss Wythel requested, "Drive me out to the farm after you let them off, Babe. Looks like I'll be extendin' my stay in town. And," she rubbed her arthritic joints, "I'm gettin' my rifle." She stared out the window at the pallbearers supporting yet another coffin. "It's all I can depend on to ease the pain."

"Yes Ma'am."

Driving by the City Hall, Babe commented on the people gathered outside. "You think they'll ever really know what caused it?"

The women stared at the scene as traffic slowed to a snail's pace. The crowd of late arrivals unable to secure seats inched closer to the opened doors and windows.

The Governor's Board of Inquiry into the Brophy School Disaster was about to convene.

A large table normally home to the City Council awaited the men who would require its services. At either end, the men rushed to East Texas as representatives of Sterling, sat scanning the papers which held their findings. All members faced the audience to some degree in order to leave the fourth side open to demanding residents and an inquisitive press.

Between them, a hand-picked sampling of Governor Ross Sterling's political cronies flanked the state's chief executive. The white-haired Sterling adjusted his glasses before pounding a gavel commandeered from the local J.P.'s court. As he raised the wooden hammer, the throng of press poised its pencils.

"I want to say that I come with both regret and appreciation. That we find ourselves amid such a tragedy defies mere words. For those who have worked tirelessly to rescue the victims and minister to the injured, the city of Brophy and every citizen of this great state offers his profound thanks. And to the grieving families, we extend our sincere condolences. To the survivors, our wishes for a speedy recovery."

He drank from a glass of water at his side. Texas had returned to its normal weather pattern, and coupled with the tightly seated mass of people, the room became uncomfortably warm.

"As most of you are aware, I took it upon myself to assemble this Board of Inquiry in full belief that all of us, but most especially the families touched by this catastrophic event, are owed a speedy explanation."

"Damn right," a voice underscored.

"For those parents who send their children to the hundreds of schools across the vastness that is Texas, there must be a confidence that such a tragedy can and will be prevented from reoccurring."

Applause.

"Sounds more like a politician's forum to me," scoffed a dissatisfied member of the crowd.

"I would like to introduce Misters Patrick Allred from the Bureau of Mines and Lee Shivers from the Department of Agriculture."

The men nodded acknowledgment.

The audience craned to ascertain those seated in the front row of chairs. At the far end, John Earl Terry fingered his hat. From the moment he felt the shock of the explosion, he labored at the site. Only the Governor's summons brought him from the search.

Oscar Culberson sat to his right, the depth of loss over his own two sons evident in dark circles and deep lines beneath his eyes. Martin Fanthrop; the Reverend Ezekiel; and Hoyt LaGuinn, who entered after the Governor's call to order, finished out the row. Two seats remained vacant for Elaine Crawford, the other an oversight in counting Willie Bacon among the living.

Allred rose and addressed the sea of faces.

"Governor, Members of the Board, citizens of Brophy, visitors, I must preface my remarks by saying that the findings today are preliminary. So few hours of investigation can hardly be considered conclusive, yet as Governor Sterling so aptly stated, we feel a solemn obligation to quell the numerous rumors that arbitrarily attribute blame. It is our consensus," he awaited gestures of confirmation from those seated at the table, "that no malicious intent existed to harm any individuals or sabotage the operation of the city's school."

When none of the expected comments arose from the stunned gathering, he proceeded.

"We base our findings upon interviews with the survivors and exhaustive examination of the ruins. To a one, those questioned referred to symptoms of an illness producing headaches, watery eyes, and nausea that plagued the school occupants. These complaints existed to a slight degree from the opening day, intensifying with the cold snap and the necessity of heating the building. While more extensive research will be forthcoming, and recognizing that the true culprit may be found to exist in the heating system itself, it is our belief that the opened windows of early fall released a lethal gas which became trapped when this means of ventilation ceased as the weather turned inclimate."

Afraid to express either dissatisfaction or agreement lest they miss a key phrase, the room sat in rapt silence.

"Most likely the gas had been seeping through the pipes throughout the school since it came on line until a large amount collected in an unventilated space, that being the basement, judging from the explosion pattern."

"Natural gas?" someone asked.

The audience broke into a myriad of small conversations voicing disbelief and anger.

"Please," the Governor rapped his request for order, which he regained after a several minute lapse. "Let the man finish," the snowy-haired Governor pleaded.

"But we all use Brophy Gas, and ain't nothin' blowed up before?" a father who lost two of his five school-aged children shouted.

"The school," Allred replied, "did not receive its gas from a company. Rather, you gentlemen correct any error, it tapped the wells on campus for what is commonly called residue gas."

The room again erupted as accusations flew.

"That Crawford woman?"

John Earl bolted from his seat to seize Sterling's coveted gavel. "Everything Elaine Ter...Elaine Crawford did was above board." He met the ensuing disclaimers head on. "I brought up that we tap the residue gas while she was in the hospital up in Dallas. By the time she got out, things had gone too far to change. But I want it said for all to hear, and you boys from the newspapers get it straight, she never liked the idea and told us so in no uncertain terms."

Terry looked to the Board for support.

As if it required every ounce of strength, Oscar Culberson rose to join John Earl. Tears that required frequent brushing with his sleeve streamed.

"Residue gas," the back of the room strained to hear the man unable to speak much above a whisper. "Residue gas never caused no more trouble than the casing head a good many of us got in our houses."

There was a pitiful urgency for belief. "We didn't see no danger in it, and it saved us maybe thirty-five hundred a year."

Culberson broke under the reality that the lives of so many had been sold for so little. Both Fanthrop and the Reverend helped him back to his seat as he pleaded, "How were we to know?"

The constant scratching of the journalists' pencils echoed as they wrote with a fierce intent to preserve the dialogue. Allred, himself consumed with emotion, assumed control.

"It is our opinion that the Brophy School disaster was an act of God, which no one could have foreseen or for which no single individual bears the totality of the blame."

Recognizing that the crowd bore signs of becoming a mob, Sterling slammed his fists on the table.

"This Court of Inquiry stands adjourned until such time as the final conclusion can be released."

With Guardsmen buffeting his exit, the Governor brushed through the East Texans shouting questions and their collective dissatisfaction with the findings.

"Somebody's to blame; let us know who.."

"If you don't have the backbone to see justice done, we do."

"What about the builder?"

"Pipe was the cause."

"It's Terry, I tell you."

"The Crawford woman."

The shouts grew in intensity as did the onslaught of people pushing toward the door. On the steps of the meeting hall, the overflow which had now received the news with equal response, pushed nearer the initialed microphones overlapping the impromptu podium from which Sterling was obliged to speak.

"Now boys, I can't hear everyone at once."

"Is it true, Sir, that so called residue gas caused the school to blow up?"

"Right now it appears the most likely source."

"And your committee affixed no direct blame?"

"An act of God, gentlemen. The gas accumulated somewhere, the basement we think, and somehow ignited."

"How many deaths are confirmed?"

Sterling looked to an assistant who handed a sheet of paper.

"This is the most accurate information as of..." Again the reference to his assistant, "ten this morning, three hundred fifty dead. Of this three hundred fifty, nineteen were adults, either faculty members or parents there for the program. An additional one hundred seventy-three can be considered serious injuries. We pray to God that they will recover."

A respectful moan and a reverent silence followed as the impact of the numbers changed from mere figures to lives of children by loved ones left behind to spend lifetimes remembering what occurred and what might have been if...The consummate politico's presence took on an air of optimism.

"You keep forgetting about the survivors. Bear in mind that fifty, maybe as high as seventy walked away virtually unscathed."

"Fifty to seventy? That's some leap."

"No accurate means of accounting exists. Some children simply went home, and," his countenance fell, "forty-one children are missing, either unidentified as yet or, and this possibility is so remote as to defy mention, are still buried somehow."

A clamor arose for men to return to the site and begin digging anew.

Sterling held up his hands for quiet.

"Please, rest assured that every square inch of the Brophy campus has been searched and searched again. Absolutely, and you can take this to the bank, absolutely no dead or injured remain buried."

∧∧∧∧∧

"You still there, Roger?" Billy Aiken pleaded.

A feeble, "Yeah."

"Wish I could see my watch Momma got me with them cereal boxes."

The darkness imposed by debris blocked the faintest rays of light.

"How long we been here?"

"Not more than a few hours," Billy lied.

During the eternity of entrapment, Billy asked forgiveness for his lies meant to bolster his friend. *I know he's hurt bad the way he comes around and goes out. Maybe it bein' dark so long has made me think wrong on the time? I bet it's just been a few hours.* But Billy could not construct a lie convincing enough to obscure the reality of their circumstance. *It's been a day, more likely two. I keep expectin' to get hungry or thirsty. Guess we're like bears hibernatin' out the winter.* Whenever he could muster the strength, the child tried to push away unseen weights from around him.

Were the two able to observe their surroundings, the boys would have appreciated the stroke of Providence that allowed them to survive the blast. As the duo sneaked down the hallway during the program, they reached one of the small foyers that architecturally accentuated each exit. When the earth began to give way, the boys fell against the outer wall which collapsed over the children to form a life-saving arc bolstered by the rubble of the main structure. Though it saved their lives, the formation obscured them from the constant barrage of rescuers' tools.

If only my arm weren't broke, he imagined, *I could push all this old stuff outta my way. At least I could get to Roger.* Though he could not touch his pal, Billy sensed he lay no more than a foot to one side. What remained hidden to Billy was the large wound to Roger's temple which resulted in the boy's bouts with consciousness.

"Why's it so quiet?"

"I dunno, Rog." But the Aiken boy resigned himself when first aware of the quiet. *They've stopped lookin'.* With the roar of the machinery, the hope of rescue loomed, but the silence underscored their abandonment and Billy's great fear that they might die undiscovered.

My momma won't let 'um stop lookin', he told himself. *She's out there this very minute, I bet.* He wanted to scream her name, for anyone to hear. *But that'll upset Roger more; he's awful scared already. It's all my fault we're in this mess, talkin' him into sneakin' out of that dumb old program.* What Billy would later discover, the majority of the choir that lined the back wall of the auditorium perished.

Cale joined the handful of people stumbling over the rugged landscape of the school. Sightseers, parents denying the inevitable, folks simply struggling to understand walked over the debris while conversing in reverent tones. Like some appearing in town, a man hawking sodas saw an opportunity to turn a profit from the misfortunes of others. Cale was on his way to run the man out of the area when he stopped short *Gonna be a hell of climb outta this mess, even for you John Earl.* Cale had to wonder at the paradox. *Just when you'd bet your last dime that you got no heart, care about nobody but yourself, if you don't let down that guard and surprise the hell outta me. Just like with Willie and Arnolia; you took it worse than the rest, even swearin' with Gabriel that you'd see their killers dead if you had to do it yourself. Now, you're here long after folks has give up.*

It was Terry who sought out his former partner to ask with genuine concern. "How is she?"

"Clyde's gone to go get her; he wanted to wait until after Jake's burial."

John Earl fixed his eyes toward town and away from Cale. "I'm sorry about that boy."

Cale scrutinized Terry's face, detecting the single emotion unobserved during their tumultuous relationship. Disguised at Willie and Arnolia's funeral by the mask of rage and desire for revenge, and overshadowed by self-satisfaction at the culmination of his underhanded schemes, Cale now detected the pain of remorse.

"She's bunged up pretty bad. Nothin's broke but some ribs, but she won't talk. Cries mostly and looks through folks like they ain't there."

Terry dislodged a brick with his foot. "Why are you still here?"

"Melba's boy, Billy, they can't account for him. She's in Overton with Violet, so I'm still lookin' in her place."

He nodded.

"Then I'll lend you a hand. I stayed here till they called off the search, and I know pretty well what went on where."

He pointed to various portions of the building still standing or in ruins.

"Best anyone could tell, the whole of the school was at the program over here. A few managed to get out into the halls, about there, and close to the same number on the opposite side. The band was on the stage, not many of them made it, though. That heavy lightin' stuff fell awful hard. Found a few scattered outside the actual buildin', force of the blast and all. Saw a girl myself lodged in that tree; dead. You remember Slim Cravitt? His boy was on that section of roof that's standin'. Hardly a scratch; you go and figure it."

"Anywhere they didn't look?"

A few spots they figured no one got to. Given how quick it happened, no kids nor grown folks could have traveled farther than a few feet, lest..." Terry's voice rose with optimism as the men reached almost a simultaneous conclusion. "Ever know that scamp to be where he was supposta?"

Cale grinned, "Nowhere near."

Partners once again, the men laid off the most unlikely sections. Picking up discarded shovels, John Earl and Cale began a dig that lasted for most of the day.

Dirt fell across the bridge of his nose to be wiped away involuntarily. A second, a third until Billy roused at the annoyance. Now striking him with a regularity of sorts, the boy's face broadened with realization.

"We're here! Get us out."

On the surface, the men pitched their shovels with a clamor that solidified the child's belief. "Momma, it's Billy," he cried to the darkness.

On hands and knees, the remnants of a school flying, Cale and John Earl answered, "That you, Billy boy?"

"We're here, son. gonna get to you right soon. Keep talkin' us to you."

"Roger, Roger, they're here for us. Roger, wake up."

Despite the pleas, his pal failed to respond.

"It's Mr. McCallister and Mr. Terry. They come to dig us outta here." Billy concentrated on their rescuers.

"Me and my friend Roger is here. He's hurt real bad."

"They can't be more than a couple of feet down. Dammit, why'd we give up so soon?" A bit of light broke through as the men scooped away silt and bricks.

"I told you somebody was a comin'," Billy addressed his silent companion.

"Our mommas wouldn't never give up on us."

"I see somethin'," John Earl announced. Crusted trousers peaked through the hole. "How bad off are you, boy?"

"Arm's broke; my legs can't move none, but don't worry over me. Roger's the one hurt. I can't get him to answer no more; guess he passed plumb out."

His face now bathed in sunlight, the boy smiled at his deliverers. "I ain't never been so happy to see nobody."

Terry tweaked the child's nose. "Even if it's the likes of me?"

"Ah, I don't set stock in the half of what my momma says about you. No man alive can be that mean and still be left livin'," stated the happy boy.

John Earl could only laugh. "Who knows, Cale, maybe Melba will invite me to supper now that I helped bring her boy back?"

"Stop," Billy ordered. "Dig for Roger. He's that way." The child motioned with his good arm.

"Hey," John Earl stood signaling frantically to those milling around. "We found two more children."

Without a moment's hesitation, men joined the effort to free Roger. A woman scraped debris from around the Aiken child while cooing in maternal tones that momentarily distracted Billy from his friend.

Calling Roger's name, the men unearthed an arm, then a head. As John Earl thrust himself downward into a newly dug hole, he touched the child's face before looking back to the others. "You can slow down."

"How's Roger? He's gotta be fine. It was all my doin' that he got hisself trapped." Billy broke down. "I talked him into sneakin' off like we done. Roger didn't want to do bad, honest." Billy managed to grasp Terry's leg. "You can help him. There's nothin' you can't finagle; Momma swears it's the God's truth."

John Earl brushed the tears from Billy's face. "The man upstairs don't trick so easy as a bunch of men with an eye for quick money and a greed for oil."

As the mass of bricks dropped away, Billy eyes fell upon the suit coat that covered Roger.

"Does the feelin' ever go away?" he asked of the man with first-hand knowledge. "The one when you know you're the one what done the bad, but someone else done the payin' instead of you?"

Terry choked on his reply.

"Billy, that's somethin' I ain't never considered," he panned the ruins of the school, "...till now."

"Let's get you to Overton. Will your momma ever be proud to lay eyes on you." Cale carried the child toward his car.

Left alone, John Earl took only a few steps before deciding that even the deliverance of her son would do little to soften Melba Aiken's resentment. Hers or anyone else's. He closed his eyes, only to visualize the hundreds of pallid faces.

All of 'um paid instead of me.

Terry stumbled to the car, still tormented by the apparition. From under his seat he extracted a flask. Several long drinks preceded the start of the engine, and by the time he pulled into his driveway, the emptied container lay discarded on the seat.

Before killing the motor, he listened to the broadcaster on the Tyler station conclude his report.

"Based on their findings, the Governor's committee declared the Brophy School disaster an act of God, singling no individual governing body or private enterprise responsible."

~~~~~~

Click. Truman Macon muted the radio and allowed his hand to slide gently down the cabinet as if caressing the woman who saved her egg money to purchase it.

"Never thinkin' of yourself; always me and the kids come first. No fancy clothes from your earnins'. How many evenins' we all sat around this radio a listenin' to the music and enjoyin' the serials." He sank to the floor on which his children once sprawled. A smile of recollection momentarily drifted by. "And many's the time I told you all to quiet down." He strained for some inkling of sound in a home so tomblike that his own heartbeats echoed.

Macon buried his whole family side by side at Rosemont. Patsy, his wife who decided to watch the elementary choir; little Delmarie; Teddy; John Mark; and Gladys, "All gone," he muttered. "And the Governor's college educated fools can't place no blame?"

His voice rose. "Damn politicians speakin' outta both sides of their faces while they take big money in their outstretched hands. There's somebody to blame, all right. The sorry bastard admitted as much, and he goes on livin' while everythin' I loved rots in the ground. Where's the justice in that?" he asked the framed portrait of Jesus shepherding His flock. "Got money to buy anythin' he wants said."

Macon continued to sit and stroke the cabinet until his course of action became clear.

"If no one else can get up the nerve to dole the punishment due, hell fire, I can."

He rose and went to the rifle he kept loaded to shoot wolves. After checking the shells, he vengefully snapped the weapon into position.

"John Earl Terry," the radio in Elaine's bedroom announced, "informed the standing-room-only crowd that he, not Mrs. Crawford, his former wife and the school's principal who supervised the construction project, ordered the use of residue gas to save money. Now you folks out there are only too aware of the wealth of the Brophy School District, the self-same body that spared no expense on the least details and costliest fixtures. I feel compelled to question where the logic resides in scrimping on something as lethal as gas? The answer we must demand is whether Mr. Terry is telling us the truth or protecting Mrs. Crawford in the time-honored practice of Southern gentility?"

"Bull," Miss Wythel spit the words toward the radio as she eased herself upward with her rifle. Plodding to the set, she snapped the room into a silence broken only by the barrel tapping on the hardwood floor. Tenderly she adjusted the quilt around Elaine.

"There's nothin' wrong with you a few more days in the bed won't cure. Just had too much shock to your system. So don't you worry none." She paused at the door. "I'm goin' to bed down in the guest room, sweetie. If you need anything, just give a..."

Elaine's   fixed   gaze   revealed   no   discernible acknowledgment, and the old woman disappeared into the hall.

She thinks I can't hear or think, just like Daddy and the rest of them. But that's all I can do is think. Since regaining consciousness, Elaine battled to keep her mind focused for any great length of time before it began darting in all directions. At that moment John Earl broke her concentration. *It's always been about money,* she decided. *All he wanted, make it, save it, spending. Nothin' mattered, not a human soul. How dare he defend my honor. He never gave a damn about me...* The school burst into the forefront preceded by a pounding in her head. *If I had...*echoed until she tried to scream it away, but the sound refused to come. *There's only one way to peace.*

Elaine lay in bed until no sounds could be heard from Clyde's or Miss Wythel's rooms. An urging back of the covers allowed Elaine to pull herself upward and to a position where she could dangle her feet over the side. Several minutes elapsed before the dizziness and pain subsided to allow a degree of maneuverability. *If I'm going to make it, I'll need more of this.* Without regard to the amount, she drank liberally from the bitter pain medication administered by her aged nurse not minutes before. As a welcomed numbness eased over her, she rose and tottered to the bureau. A tug at the middle drawer revealed neatly stacked silk undergarments through which she thrashed to uncover a revolver. *You wanted me to protect myself from John Earl, so we'll see if those shooting lessons paid off, Melba. Here it's been waitn' all this time. If I'd only used it sooner...*

~~~~~~

Sooner or later, John Earl. You can't keep avoidin' me. I checked the Flats and every known establishment where a man can buy himself a drink, a woman, or a game, and nothing. As a last resort he drove past the house. *I'll be damned.* A sudden thought struck. *If he's at home this early, he' plannin' on leavin' out. I got no time to waste.*

He drove undetected down a block where under normal circumstances an unfamiliar car would have drawn attention from curious residents. Even his turn into an alley was attributed to a relative's arrival to mourn the dead. *What I don't want is another fight..* Fear drove Carmichael to construct erratic scenarios. *First, I'll get him to talkin' about, oh, closin' out the Brophy Boys. Yeah, that always drives him to distraction. Then, when the opportunity presents itself, I'll shoot the son of a bitch in the back.* As if some Wild West ethic reminded him of the cowardliness of his plan, *Deserves no better; probably what he's got laid out for me.* Then in dismissal, *No, he wouldn't plan on that in his own house...Way too incriminatin' for a smart man like him. Out in the country, at a pump site. Now that's John Earl Terry's style.*

With the glow of the sporadic rigs back in operation serving as his only light, Carmichael left his car in the alley and walked toward the Terry house. As he rounded the front, he plunged behind a row of waist-high shrubbery. *Damnation,* he swore at a tottering woman approaching the porch. *Got women makin' house calls. And you a married man,* he added sarcastically. *She'll be here all night. That's all I need is a witness.*

He slumped against the house in defeat until a spark of optimism brightened his spirits. *But a witness that's dead drunk. Maybe she's the scapegoat I need to cover my tracks?* He looked into the starlit sky. *Why, thank you kindly for providing the necessary materials to finish off John Earl Terry for good.*

In a parked car across from a home, that although she owned half, she had yet to step foot inside, Estelle's cigarette traveled from her lips to the window. The wait had done little to improve her disposition, though after the passage of an hour, she could not as yet bring herself to face her husband head on, for to do so would surely end a relationship with the man whose touch she craved like a back-alley drug. During the long trip from Seminole, the argument raged within. *There's got to be a good reason for that woman on the phone. Operator could have plugged me into the wrong number. Or more likely, it's his way of discouragin' unwanted callers.* Somewhere around the Texas border it occurred, *Did I even bother to say who I was?* Still the lingering shred of doubt clung to her resolve, strengthening and waning by the moment until...her persistence paid off.

"You bastard!" The old fire blazed in Estelle's eyes as rage boiled. *"Just keep the whores rollin' in. She'll wish she hadn't been so anxious to crawl in bed with you."* Estelle flipped the cigarette into the street and watched it bounce. *Lamar had it right; guess the old coot knew a thing or two after all. Waitin' till they're under the sheets makes it easy as pickin' birds off a fence post. But I,* she stated with an insolence formed during a lifetime of self-preservation, *don't need a bunglin' idiot to back me up.*

A light breeze which blew through the screened porch rattled the swing to break the silence of an anesthetized town. Elaine contributed to the clatter as she beat her fist against the frame. "Open this door," demanded a voice so altered by disuse that even its owner failed to recognize.

Slumped deeply into an overstuffed chair, John Earl lowered the glass of whiskey from his lips. "Damn newsmen," he swore under his breath. When the caller refused to leave, "Get the hell away from here," echoed. As he struggled to extract himself from the chair and grasp his rifle, Terry vowed, "You'll leave when my rifle sends buckshot up your ass."

The room crossed with some difficulty, he groped for the molding of the large expanse that allowed entry to the room from the foyer so that he might steady a form swaying from the drink that blurred his senses.

Resting against one of the embedded wooden doors that could be drawn together for privacy, he slammed it into the crevice with a slurred, "I'm comin."

Terry blinked, then squinted at the impossibility of the apparition. The face is swole and bruised up. *God Almighty, I never seen a man alive or dead look that bad after no kind of lickin'.*

Enough sense penetrated the fog to prompt, "Elaine?"

"I need to come in." The pause between words resulted in a gasping effect which lasted for seconds.

"Sure." He set the weapon aside and threw back the door. Then as reality took hold, "How in the hell did you get over here? You're supposta be..."

"On my deathbed?" She glared at eyes glazed by drink.

"No." He measured his words. "Just meant that Cale said you wasn't yourself."

He quickly attempted to soften the sting. "That you was awful weak and needed as much bed rest as you..."

She covered the few feet to the entrance of the parlor with an unsteadiness that drove John Earl into a bungled attempt at assisting Elaine but that sent him staggering into the wall with a heavy thud.

"You still talk about me? How touching to know you care." The sarcasm failed to penetrate the veil of liquor. Too confused to formulate sensible questions or actions, he followed her into the room.

"A gentleman would offer me a seat," each word a labor, "but we both know that's one of the few things no one's ever accused you of bein.'"

With an unsteady hand, he began knocking newspapers onto the floor. "Sit on down."

The room, tastefully done though decidedly male, needed a thorough cleaning. The end tables that supported china-based lamps bore a grayish haze. Doilies and upholstery protectors were dotted with stains, and a pervading smell of mustiness offended the senses.

A sudden wave of dizziness caused Elaine to claim a settee that faced his chair and put her back to the entry of the house they planned together. The room and her mind spun. *Walking that few blocks took more out of me than I expected. If I'd only brought that bottle of medicine. Oh, how will I get home?*

She looks worse than Dallas. He focused on the exposed arms and legs. *I can't see a place that ain't bruised or cut. Why, she's got to be outta her mind, like Cale said, to traipse over here in the dead of night to see me of all people.*

He addressed his former wife in genuine concern, "Why don't I call Clyde, and he can come pick you up?"

"But we have unfinished business, you and I."

"What about?" He began nursing his drink.

Elaine fought the effects of the drug in answer to the voice of her entrapment. *You're here.* She could feel the cold metal of the gun through the folds of cloth. *And you can't back down. Think of Jake... of all the children... the mothers and fathers that don't want to go on living... the people you worked with who had full lives to lead until he snuffed them out for a few dollars.*

Somehow the image of Mrs. Venable appeared in the mirror above the fire place. *I knew about your baby,* Elaine silently told the vision. *Miss McClain came to me with suspicions, but I saw you needed the money and let you stay on. Oh God,* only a moan audible, *if I'd made you leave, you and your baby would be alive. Why didn't I have the strength to stop him before he...*

"Destroyed everything that was good in my life and theirs. You cost me my son." The words fell to a whisper.

John Earl remained quiet, as if formulating another of his self-serving excuses.

If you let him live, the voice spoke, *He'll come out smelling like a rose. The man is charmed.*

What Terry meant as a penitent confession became engulfed with the false mettle of the liquor. "You want me to deny it?"

He tried to place his glass on the table, but his clouded judgment sent it to rest with a force that scattered droplets onto the doily.

Elaine winced.

"Well, I can't; you're right a hundred and ten percent. Hell, you was always right about everything when it come to my character. Had me pegged from the get go." He took stock of the shell what remained of a once beautiful, vibrant woman.

"Should have paid more attention to your instincts and less to your hurt over Cale McCallister. Only reason you married me was cause you found out your saint stood on clay feet.

Course there was that prickle of excitement you just couldn't resist when it came to me."

He laughed mockingly. "That was pretty good, you got to admit, Mavis showin' up with his bun already a toastin' in the oven. Drove you right into my waitin' arms. And I was waitin', don't never believe otherwise. I had my sights on you, and would have broke the two of you up, but Mavis saved me the trouble. And when she did, hell, it didn't take no work to unfasten your garters, Miss Prim and Proper."

He put his hand in the air in surrender. "So if you come to fight, I give up. I'm a cad and a general good for nothin' son of a bitch. Guilty as charged." He saluted her with his retrieved glass. "That what you come for, to hear that? Well, I already admitted it to myself. You think I don't see the blood of them kids on my hands? I'll go to my grave carryin' the blame."

She saw him reach for the phone. Suddenly the room appeared distorted in a constant motion.

"I'm callin' Clyde to come get you before you give plumb out," Terry said.

Elaine methodically withdrew the revolver. A floor lamp by the settee caught its reflection.

John Earl's dulled senses wasted precious moments before reacting to the threat. "Damn fool woman. You'll hurt yourself with that thing." A wave of pity stayed his anger and tempered his movements. *Clyde's got no choice but to commit her over to Terrell to that state hospital.*

A creaking of the floor in the foyer betrayed the presence of a second caller.

"Well, ain't that just dandy? Another visitor, and you without the manners to knock."

Her concentration on the gun and her rage, Elaine assumed he spoke into the receiver in his right hand.

"You can get the hell out of my house till I'm through seein' to my wife. She ain't well, you know." As the familiar con man's grin formed, John Earl lifted himself from the chair. "Lower that thang."

That self-assured smirk. Talkin' to me like I don't have good sense. Elaine felt the gun discharge with a sound lasting longer and far louder than the times she and Melba practiced knocking tin cans from fence posts.

"That's good, Elaine," she heard Melba say. "You got him."

Terry looked down in astonishment at the hole in his chest.

Elaine could see the blood spurting onto the floor, and lowered the revolver in stunned silence. Within seconds, John Earl's knees buckled, and he fell face down. A pool of red collected about him; a gurgling noise ceased.

With the grace and poise of royalty, Elaine placed the gun on the settee. The room whirled; the smell of blood and powder further sickened her. Backing around John Earl, as if she feared his rising in retaliation, she stumbled to the decanter of whiskey. *I'll need some of this to get back home.* Elaine reeled in the euphoria of the moment and the soothing bronze liquid which she took back to the settee and continued to swallow from the sculpted glassware. The ensuing numbness inched over her body to disguise the horror of what she had done.

"May you rot in hell." She fixated on the dead man, steadily drinking his liquor and enjoying her handiwork in the serenity of suspended time.

The floor in the entry hall again complained before the door closed.

I'm so sleepy. Elaine succumbed to the inviting comfort of the settee. *There's no hurry; everything's fine now. I've seen to it.* A real sleep came, free of the tormenting demons. This time when the blinding light returned, it offered solace.

"Jake!"

The little boy ran toward her and into the outstretched arms of maternal embrace. The light intermingled with the first rays of morning sun only to be shattered by the piercing screams of Faye Sodders.

Chapter 17

By the time the gangly Ranger pulled into the drive, a sizable crowd of gawkers, gossiping neighbors, and a representative of the newspaper mingled outside the oilman's house. Lone Wolf recognized many of the folks draped in bathrobes and the women with bobbie-pinned hair. Yet, one man dressed for the day in khaki stood out.

Now what do you suppose brought Truman Macon to town so early? the Ranger asked himself.

Gonzaullas had used the farmer on a couple of posses when he required a man with a working knowledge of the lay of the land. *That smug attitude and a day's growth of beard is curious. Probably nothing, but in this business every detail has the potential to lead somewhere. Anyways, might be a thought worth holdin' onto.*

"What do we have, McDade?"

"Well, John Earl Terry's been murdered by his wife, that is, she's Mrs. Crawford again."

"And what have you done about findin' her?" The two men walked up the steps to the screened porch.

"Oh, she's in there, but she's dead, too."

Lone Wolf stopped abruptly and stared at the fool on his left. A gasp went up among the bystanders who welcomed the tidbit of information to validate their appearing in public at so early an hour and in such a state of dress.

"So it's true," a woman turned to a neighbor. "The both of them."

"Why would she kill him now?" a man posed. "Too much water's done run under that bridge."

The crowd erupted with speculation concerning whether John Earl or Elaine fired first.

"Surely he killed her. Elaine Crawford isn't capable of shooting anyone, even him," someone opined.

Macon interrupted loudly enough for the Ranger to take a second note of his behavior. "Don't matter who done what to who. The both of them got just a samplin' of what was deserved. No matter what that slick talkin' Governor and his paid experts got to say, ain't nobody ever gonna make me believe that them two ain't to blame for the deaths of our kin, especially John Earl."

He spit the words with a vehemence that startled those who knew him as a meek family man who kept to himself and worked his land. He mocked Sterling's interview outside the committee proceedings. "Who, gentlemen, could have foreseen this calamity?" He crossed his arms defiantly.

One woman, an old friend of Elaine's mother, started to wage a protest of Truman's assessment before changing her mind. *I guess he's got a right if anyone does to point the finger of blame. And maybe,* she reconsidered, *a certain part of what he says rings true to all those feelin' loss. Maybe I'd offer an amen if my children weren't growed and livin' away.*

The Ranger addressed McDade, "How did you know Mrs. Crawford killed John Earl, she make a deathbed confession?"

McDade bristled at the challenge. "Not in so many words, but she's got the .22 beside her."

"Ever hear of somebody movin' a gun for a little scent throwin'?" Lone Wolf turned from the Constable without further comment. *Be a damn sight easier if they'd called me first. Lawmen like him who see their badges as chances to throw their weight around always do more harm than good. With any luck he won't have done enough damage to keep the truth from bein' found out.*

They entered the foyer where Lone Wolf deposited his hat on the claw-footed hall tree and nodded greetings to the Justice of the Peace and one of the visiting doctors on loan to the disaster. *Couldn't be more than thirty,* the Ranger estimated of the physician who deferred his position to allow the lawman access to the body atop the rug. *Looks like I'm gettin' no help at all, but a skunk don't come around what he don't leave a stink.*

"Now, ain't that interestin'?" He remarked after examining the corpse from the front and rolling him over in search of the exit wound. "Let me borrow your scalpel, Doc." Feeling in Terry's back, the Ranger skillfully extracted expended metal that was dulled by time.

"Investigated many murders, Doc?"

"No, Sir. This is a first."

"Lost count myself. But I guess you could be safe in sayin' I've borne witness to most every way one human can think up to kill another."

For the first time the Ranger focused his expertise on Elaine. "Sleepin' like she is with her hands clasped for a pillow, I'd say our killer was content enough to take a nap. Only problem, she just forgot to wake up." The Ranger picked up the lady's .22.

"It's been fired," McDade promised.   "Single chamber's empty."

Lone Wolf consulted the doctor. "What happened to this woman?"

"I can't accurately say without a more thorough postmortem." He walked to the side of the settee. "Obviously these cuts and bruises aren't fresh. The men informed me that she was in the school explosion where she undoubtedly sustained them and perhaps others that are not as evident to us until we delve further, so to speak." He pointed to the cut-glass piece that had fallen to the floor. "Though more than likely her death can be linked to the contents of the decanter."

"Poison?" McDade incredulously questioned.

The doctor saved Lone Wolf the trouble of lambasting the constable. "Of course not. You see, a person with, and a check with her attending physician will bear me out I believe, recent trauma of this magnitude must have been in a great deal of pain. My point being that she was most likely taking medication to ease that discomfort, and if she consumed very much of this," he picked up the empty container.

After bringing it to his nose, he offered it to Lone Wolf who nodded his confirmation. "One look at her posture will tell you, this was by no means a woman who suffered a violent death or was in fear of her life."

"Doin' mighty fine for your first time out, there Doc." The Ranger, now on hands and knees crawling the area between the settee and the body congratulated. At intervals Lone Wolf moved furniture, the rug, whatever might hide from view that which he sought. Dissatisfied, he moved his hands along the floral wall paper in so intense a scrutiny that McDade could no longer allow this challenge to his investigative skills.

"Just what do you think there's left to find? Don't you believe nothin' I tole you? We done looked this place over."

The Ranger fingered the tear in the base of Terry's chair. "What I believe," he dug through the upholstery and into the wood with his pocket knife, "is that somebody has to show you your ass so's you'll know where to scratch."

He jerked free the bullet fired by Elaine Crawford and held it out for the humiliated constable to see. "People of Brophy better get them a new man if you can't tell the difference in a man shot by a rifle blast and one hit with a little lady's .22."

"Who found them?" he asked of anyone other than McDade.

"I did," a timid Faye emerged from the opposite end of the hallway where she had hidden so as not have to see John Earl. "I'm Mr. Terry's secretary."

After questioning Faye as to her arrival time, the Ranger remarked, "Always work so late into the night?" A scrutiny of the svelte secretary left Lone Wolf little doubt.

"John Earl never could tell time; his clock worked twenty-four hours. Any of the neighbors will vouch for that. Why, he's just as liable to call me at three in the mornin' to come over and type a letter, not thinkin' it any different from three in the afternoon."

"He call you in ?"

"No, Ranger," she hemmed and hawed. "I was worried about him. Ever since the school...it's just that I haven't knowed him to take anything so hard. He stayed up there pullin' kids out nonstop till they was done."

Faye could see no changes in the expressions of the men in the room. *I'm gettin' nowhere,* she decided. *Why couldn't there be another woman around? Any female would understand that men like John Earl has some good qualities that he has to keep buried deep so's there's no mistakin' how much man he is.*

She decided to offer proof. "You heard, I guess, how him and Mr. McCallister found two more boys yesterday? So when he didn't come in the office, normally I wouldn't have worried none, but he wasn't hisself, with the hearin' and answerin' to folks about his part and all."

A massive hand went up to quell the loquacious Faye. "Know anybody who'd want to see Mr. Terry dead?"

McDade scoffed. "Let's us see, there's a goodly portion of East Texas, folks swindled in Oklahoma, and now there's the entire town of Brophy. I'd say you got a list of suspects only a Ranger could handle."

Lone Wolf chose to ignore McDade since the constable finally made a sound observation. "Miss Sodders, I spect you better make arrangements for the body and notify his next of kin. He does have some kin?"

"I can't rightly say as I heard him refer to any, but I guess his lawyer might have heard tell, maybe for his will?"

"Anyone call Clyde Russell about his daughter?" Lone Wolf appraised the faces gathered about the room. "Surely he's missed her by now."

"I sent a man over to the McCallister's," the constable answered. "This is liable to break ole Clyde, Elaine bein' his only child and the grandson gone in the school. So, I thought it best comin' from a friend."

Little else remained; the Ranger walked into the sunlight of what promised to be a beautiful fall day. Pulling the telegram from his pocket he stared again at the words and wondered about their significance given this unexpected change of events. "Corpse interred was not, repeat not, Anglo male in sixties." Lone Wolf refolded the paper before stuffing it into a worn billfold.

He decided to walk a bit. Something about the beauty of Texas gives a man a more distinctive view of things. *I love it here. Hell, I liked every part of Texas I been; even the dust storms of the Panhandle have an awe-inspirin' appeal. But*

East Texas is as close to paradise as the good Lord meant for a man to get to.

As he passed one black creped house after another, his thoughts turned to the school disaster. I ought to be dodgin' kids on their way to school all excited about the football game tonight. McDade hit the nail on the head. Every house holds a suspect, if not two, with a grudge the size of Truman Macon's.

The Ranger returned to the telegram. *John Earl, Estelle Tate, and Carmichael, they're all in cahoots, but provin' it... I can work on Carmichael. Hell, he nearly confessed that day in the office, and he'll sell Mrs. Tate down the river. Course with John Earl dead, a smart lawyer can convince a jury that Terry pulled the trigger and forced them into the Mexican cover up.* He reached his car. *Still ten to twenty in one of Texas' finest facilities will take the starch out of Carmichael's dress shirt and the swing out of Estelle's infamous hips. But can I prove they killed Terry and planted the gun on a helpless Elaine Crawford? The two might have teamed up for a double-cross?*

Years of lawman instinct cried out against the theory. *But that would have them gettin' the ex wife over to set her up. Elaine Crawford fired her gun, sure as I'm standin' here, but the rifle shot that killed him wasn't no Oklahoma import. If I'm right, this can be tidied up with one more visit before I go after Estelle and Carmichael. And if I'm wrong, this thing might never get solved.*

~~~~~~

Lone Wolf stared at the house from Estelle's vantage point, unaware of the significance. Following Elaine's arrival, Estelle sneaked up to the opened window of the parlor in hopes of catching her husband with his newest paramour. Instead, she watched as she became a widow for the second time at the hands of an assassin obscured by the sliding wooden doors. The shooting sent her running to the car where once inside she lay in the floorboard for over an hour before working up the courage to drive away.

On the road back to Seminole, she formulated her escape. I got two choices. *A smart woman would be headin' south. There won't be no convincin' Carmichael I wasn't the one what shot John Earl; he'll run scared rabbit to the Ranger with the whole mess start to finish.* She pounded the steering wheel.

A fiercer grip of her senses and the wheel brought her back. *You got to look out for yourself now. It's prison or the poor house. Ain't never spent a night in jail, but I growed up in the other. It's a risk, but hell, what's life if it ain't a risk?*

By the time she reached Seminole, Estelle had not slept in nearly two days. Hell bent on self preservation, she eased herself in the back way to avoid her staff. After cleaning out her jewelry box, she opened Lamar's safe. *A sight more than most folks will make in a couple of years of work, but not nearly enough to keep me from a future of slingin' hash or workin' flat of my back.*

A quick change of clothes and a little make up prepared Mrs. Tate for a trip to the Seminole Bank where she emptied most of her personal accounts. "I'm goin' to Illinois to see to my sick sister. Her medical bills are my responsibility, you see."

On a train for New York, Estelle Tate Terry spied a filler article in newspaper. "Oil Executive Confesses Role in Predecessors' Death," she read to the walls of her compartment. "Oklahoma Oil President David Carmichael turned himself in to a Texas Ranger for his part in the disappearance and subsequent cover up of the death of the man he succeeded, Lamar Tate. Authorities are searching for his accomplice and paramour, Tate's widow, Estelle." She pressed the paper into her lap. "That spineless weasel. Don't he just wish that was true!" Under another name and in a less conspicuous second class accommodation, Estelle sailed to Europe where a string of rich Continental men later, East Texas and Oklahoma were traceable only in her accent.

~~~~~~

Lone Wolf headed out of town when the oddity of a truck pulled up under the abandoned LaGuinn Grocery, Gas and Feed covering pulled him from the road for a look see. At the sound of the Ranger's car, Truman Macon emerged from under the hood, wiping his hands on a rag.

"Got troubles?" the Ranger asked before killing his motor.

"Almost got it fixed now. Where was you last night when I had to leave her here and walk on in?" Macon peered through the opposite window at Lone Wolf. "I was sleepin' out front of the store, waitin' for Marshall to open up when all the commotion over to the Terry place first broke."

"You mean no do-gooders come by and fixed her for you while you was gone?" he laughed.

Truman shook his head, "Nope, sure didn't, but then that's the way my luck's been runnin'. Still, it's that every once in a while that a Good Samaritan does come along and takes care of your dirty work for you that makes you believe there's some justice hidin' out there somewheres."

"You still got that old rifle, the one your daddy left you?"

"Wouldn't never part with that, not even for the price you offered me." He pointed with the soiled rag. "Over in the truck if you got a mind to see it again."

In response to the offer, Lone Wolf twisted the key and left his car. Macon had removed the rifle from under the seat and extended it to the Ranger.

"You've taken mighty good care of her," he praised as he opened the weapon to satisfy his professional curiosity.

"Needs some cleanin', I know."

"Hadn't had no wolves in a while, I see." Lone Wolf's expert eyes drank in the ammunition that sealed his suspicions. "I'll be seein you then, if you're sure you don't need my help."

Taking back the rifle, "I got no hurries to get home."

"No, I guess you don't at that." He patted Macon's back sympathetically before moving toward the car. The Ranger lingered over the boarded up LaGuinn store.

I wonder what it must have been like when it all began? A bunch of oil-fevered men riskin' everythin' on a chance of slim to none. Course, to hear Hoyt tell, Proration will have him openin' back up just to make ends meet. He won't be the only one glad to see the end of Proration. Them soldier boys was God sent for the school disaster, but their bein' around waves a red flag in front of frustrated folks.

Gonzaullas checked to his right and left before taking the road out into the country. Rigs and storage tanks dotted the landscape, broken by houses old and new, family farms transformed to family fortunes by the Brophy Boys' lone discovery well.

I would've liked to seen this road all packed tight with car loads of believers and naysayers. Maybe if times hadn't been so bad, things might not have gotten so outta hand. Well, martial law and Proration's on borrowed time; reelections gonna sound their death knells. Every laid off roughneck or falterin' businessman will get in line twice to send 'um back to Austin if no other way than with a ballot.

His turn onto the stretch of road leading to the house caused him to remark. "With or without, this job don't never get no easier."

Before his feet touched the ground, Miss Wythel appeared on her porch with the stalwart rifle poised.

"Excuse me, Ma'am," accompanied the tipping of his hat.

Skeptically, she inched closer to the steps. Slowly the firearm lowered.

"What brings you way out here?"

"You know what happened in town last night?" The two entered the parlor dominated by the dated furnishings Mavis begged her to discard.

"Why waste my money on furniture ain't nobody gonna sit on?" she had asked.

"What else are you gonna do with that money? Saint Peter won't let you in with no pocketbook."

"Leavin' it to them twins and Jake."

The Ranger stopped to admire the pictures grouped on the south wall. A pose of Rubenesque twins and the hopeful enthusiasm captured at the Willie B.'s spudding in flanked a single photograph of a gap-toothed Jake. Lone Wolf lingered on the likeness of the dead boy.

"His death must have hit you pretty hard, Miss Wallis."

The old lady fell into her rocker with a whoosh of weight against ancient padding.

"Loved him like he was my own grandson. Never had no kids of my own, you know." She stared pensively out the window toward the original well that brought her the happiness of a family. "Just like his ma and Mavis was the daughters the Lord never let me bear."

Lone Wolf accepted her offer of a seat.

"You spent last night at the Russell house to take care of Mrs. Crawford, so they tell me."

"Did for a fact," she looked him squarely in the eye. "Guess I didn't do the job I was meant to." Then in her own defense. "Now mind you, Elaine hadn't spoke to no one since the explosion, and she sure wasn't makin' no attempts to be up and about." She shrugged. "Who could have figured she'd get outta bed and drag herself over to John Earl's like that? Her bein' there surprised the hell outta me."

"I'm sure it did." Lone Wolf dug into his pocket and produced the spent ammunition. "You musta been real shocked to see Elaine Crawford in John Earl's parlor when you got there."

A smile crossed the wrinkled face. "Folks always said you Rangers was smart ones."

Appraising the feisty old maid, the Ranger could not quite bring himself to picture Miss Wythel as a woman who did not own up to her own actions. "Why did you leave her there, a woman so sickly?"

A cat-like bristle accompanied the indignant delivery. "I didn't have no idea that she would..." Leaning forward on her rifle, she bore into the Ranger. "Let me tell you this the one time. John Earl Terry was scum. Why, he used that girl from the get go; married her for Clyde's share." She waved her hands, "And tossed her away, just like so much rubbish. Cheated on her, too, with that floozy Tate woman. That caused her to lose the baby. Then just when Elaine got to feelin' like she was worth somethin' again, his interferin' caused the school to blow up, killin' her boy to boot. Elaine was mighty proud of that school."

She eased back and began to rock. "Now, I left Clyde's with every intention of shootin' that son of a bitch myself, but when I got there, Elaine done had the gun pointed. That's when I realized that she needed to be the one. Course," she laughed, "Elaine couldn't hit a bull in the butt with a bass fiddle, even if she had been the picture of health. Hell, I bet she missed him by a mile." She looked to the Ranger for confirmation.

"Hit the base of his chair."

She smiled broadly. "See what I'm sayin'? So I waited, and when she shot, so did I." She patted the rifle. "Wouldn't want this to get around, but that was the only time I ever fired at any livin' thing. Just glad I didn't waste my shell."

The rocking motion ceased. "Made her feel like she got even with him." Their eyes met. "And I just couldn't take that away from her, too. I headed home to tell Clyde I checked on her and found her missin', but before I could get him to check with John Earl, the daylight come and with it the crowd. She had to be fine with all them folks around."

A creaking motion dominated the room once again. "What I didn't think of was that she'd downed so much of that pain concoction; damn near the whole bottle was gone. Elaine weren't no drinker. What on earth possessed her to have that whiskey..." She paused before returning to her original train of thought. "Never guessed they'd call you in, neither. With that jackass McDade on the job, I would have bet my next royalty check he'd have bumbled the whole mess."

"You'd have let her go to jail for you?"

"Hell no. I may be old, but I have a holt of my mind with a firm grip. Now who," she asked the Ranger, "was gonna send the girl to prison? Hadn't spoke for days, lost her boy, and bound to be feelin' responsible for the whole shebang. A jury convict her? That old dog won't hunt, no siree. Outta her mind, pure and simple."

"But the difference in a rifle wound and a revolver's?"

She looked up at the giant of a man. "I said I had a good grip, never claimed to be no genius." The smile returned. "It's your turn to do some of this confessin. McDade didn't know no better? Did he?"

Lone Wolf allowed his face to answer.

She slapped her knee in triumph before her face fell. "Hadn't been for you, I'd be spendin' what time I got left here on my land, waitin' to shake hands with the Maker. But I ain't sorrowful for what I done." She began the difficult process of standing. "I'll get me a bag together." A glance downward, "Guess I won't get to take my rifle?" Her eyes sparkled. "Helps with the arthritis, you know."

Every lawman's instinct cried out within Lone Wolf Gonzaullas. No excuses, no circumstances exist that dismiss a criminal's behavior. *But what's to be served sendin' a crippled up old woman to jail? Hell, if Miss Wallis hadn't meddled, I was within days, hours maybe of chargin' John Earl with Lamar Tate's murder. Saved the taxpayers of the state the price of a trial, if a person had a mind to look on it that way.*

"Won't be necessary, Ma'am. My job is to see justice is done." He tapped his hat in place. "There's folks out there blame John Earl for the disaster; just as many say the same of Mrs. Crawford. You keep somethin' like this in the newspapers and throwin' it in their faces, well either way, now the wound don't have to keep festerin' with the constant attention of no trial and side choosin'. Maybe this way the town can start to heal itself."

No more words exchanged; the Ranger let himself out without looking back on his decision with any regret. At the main road a car driven by Pup Schneider barreled past.

～～～～～

"**Y**ou sure this is where you think he might be?" he glanced skeptically at Babe before looking in the rear mirror at Mavis McCallister.

"What's to be sure of? After McDade's man come and told us about Elaine and John Earl and wantin' Cale to go and break the news to Clyde, I ain't heard a word from him."

"Is Clyde gonna make it through this?"

Pup never received his answer for Mavis, lost in her own thoughts, focused on her missing husband. When she tried to comfort him, he pulled away at her touch and pulled himself to his feet. "I gotta get to Clyde before someone else does."

I wish I could read his mind, though his reaction at Elaine's rescue gave her a pretty clear idea of what prompted his tears as he left for Clyde's. What would have surprised her was the portion shed for John Earl.

His wife nor anyone else would understand his feelings for the man. Every vile thing ever uttered about Terry was the gospel truth, yet Cale had seen him that day at the school. *There was some good come through,* he told himself on his way to the Russell home. *Maybe if Elaine hadn't shot him, John Earl might have brung hisself around. Sorrows got ways of wakin' folks up. But it's too late now.*

Watching Clyde break under the strain of the news left Cale frantic to get away, away from the memories of the house, away from all the reminders of Elaine. Bulldog's appearance afforded him the chance to exit through the back and begin a drive that drew him like a magnet out of town and toward the Willie B. #1.

Cale pulled his jacket tighter against the morning chill that would disappear as the sun rose higher and transformed the day with rays so hot that a roughneck would wonder why he bothered to bring it in the first place. He spent his time at the makeshift memorial the Boys set up after the lynching. Not that passers-by stopped at the replaced derrick for a glimpse of history or even to pay respects, but for the Boys, the site served as a reminder which allowed Willie and Arnolia to live on. And now, he held the picture removed from the tool shed wall. *You was so beautiful and happy. We both were. This picture was your idea, remember? Wanted to be able to remember just what everyone looked like. Elaine in her new hat with the drooping brim, fighting the wind, and everyone laughing with the surety of success in the well and the anticipation of wealth and prosperity. Why did it have to end up like this?*

As if in answer, a shadow fell across the frame. Without checking the identity, Cale asked, "How'd you know I'd be here?"

"Only place made any real sense."

"Look at all of us, Nubbin." He slapped the glass framed photograph, "So damn stupid and full of hope. So sure that bringin' in this well would make life perfect." Pensively he stared toward the rigs that penetrated the blue Texas sky. "If we'd only realized what it would cost us, we would have..."

"Wouldn't have changed a damn thing. Men with their hearts set don't listen to no amount of reason, even if it stares 'um in the face." She sat beside him and took his hand.

Back in the car, Pup squirmed for a better view. "What do you suppose they're talkin' about?"

"If and when she does tell him what she saw, it'll be the end of that marriage, pure and simple."

Pup looked over to the woman he loved. "I don't believe that for a minute."

"Oh, and you think a woman can be happy living with a man she knows is pining away for someone else? Elaine being dead makes it all the worse. Women don't share their men, even if the woman is only a memory, Mr. Schneider. Let's get that straight before our knot gets tied."

Pup looked frustrated. "Cale didn't really love Elaine."

Babe was about to argue the point when Pup cut her short.

"Just hear me out. I could see it all along. Elaine and Cale was just like Daddy and Momma." He could tell by Babe's expression that his explanation was most certainly lacking in clarity.

"It goes like this. When my folks married, they didn't have souls that was kin. That's exactly the way Cale loved Elaine. Oh yeah, he loved her ways, her looks, kind of a fairy princess type of love, but with Mavis things was different. Mavis and Cale loved from the inside out, not the outside in. So when it came time for him to leave and look for a dream that probably didn't even exist, she let him do what was important to him. They had the spirit joined in the way that one person understands what the other one has to do, even to the point of havin' to give up bein' together."

He moved forward on the seat, intent in the validity of his words. "Now Momma, she never understood Daddy when it come to oil. She never saw how it gets in a man's blood and drives him off for ungodly hours, riskin' his life most of the time, just to see it rain black gold."

His intensity softened. "She always saw it as interferin', what with the movin', the time he never spent with us kids, until she couldn't live with him no more and took us back to Louisiana."

"Oil is not another woman," Babe reminded.

"Not in flesh and blood, no, but in commitment, there's not a difference in the world."

"And which way do we love, outside or in?"

"Inside, of course, or we wouldn't be sittin' here solvin' everybody else's problems. I knew you was the one I'd been searchin' my life for the very day you come walkin' into the office all sassy and ready to take on the lot of us men."

Babe laughed in recollection.

"You understand me, what drives me, cause the same things drive you."

"And Mavis?"

"You just wait. We'll be ridin' in privacy." He pinched her leg playfully.

Cale released Mavis' hand. "I can't stay in Texas; the oil business costs a man too much." He looked down at his wife. "It's cost me everything."

"What are you talkin' about? You still got it all, Cale: a big house, more money than we keep count of, two kids, and a woman who loves you." She paused as her tone bespoke of her disappointment in him, "Just what makes everything to you?"

He turned away, unwilling to admit to his wife the true source of his depression.

But for Mavis, the answer to her question loomed ominously. This wedge has got to be pulled out from betwixt us if there's any more goin' on from here.

She blurted, "I know you loved her more than you do me."

Cale's face registered his astonishment.

"Hell yes, I know. Heard your tender scene when you pulled her out of the school and saw," her voice broke. Mavis began choking on her words.

Shame tempered his response.

"She was your friend. Elaine never did nothin'; it was me done the betrayin'."

"Go and figure it. My one and only true friend, and she's the woman my husband takes to bed in his mind." The pent up rage escaped.

"I want you to know that I never, that is we never."

"I said in your mind; you're too upright a man to actually cheat on your wife. But you wanted to just the same." Another possibility burst into Mavis' mind. "Or was your idea to hold off until you could send me and the babies packin' after a decent length of time?"

Coming to their defense, "No, now that wasn't never in the cards. You got to believe me when I swear that I married you believin' that I'd put a stop to my feelin's for Elaine."

"Same way you put an end to your feelins' for me while I sat in Winnie waitin' for the mail to be posted every day and makin' up excuses when nary a word come."

"I'm not proud of what I done, Mavis."

"My showin' sure shut down the drillin' floor. Course, she might still of had you except for the twins."

"Elaine didn't want to let on to you that we was plannin' on marryin'. She was too good a person to..."

"Too good a person? Well, she married that bastard John Earl quick enough. Let me tell you somethin', Cale, so that when you think back on the saint you stuck up on one of them pedestal things you get the right picture. Women share things, personal things that men keep shut up tight. And John Earl made her feel the way every woman dreams. There was a... a," she searched for a word. "I don't know, a passion like is wrote up in them sleazy stories I like to read."

"You sayin' she didn't want that divorce, cause if you are..."

"Hell's bells, sure she did, but only after one thing piled on another."

An awkward silence ensued during which the red-haired temperament of Mavis McCallister mellowed.

"I done this all wrong, dammit. Let my mouth get me in trouble again. I should of taken what I saw to the grave." She became apologetic. "My gettin' all riled up and self-righteous wasn't never what I had set in mind to do."

Cale drifted along the drilling floor in deep contemplation. Finally he stood over his wife and addressed her back. "So why ain't you taken the girls and high tailed it back home to Bethel?"

The rise and fall of her shoulders accompanied the response. "I love you too much, always have," she turned and looked upward, the tears sparkling in the sunlight, "always will."

"I'm not good enough for you, not by no long shot, and not just about Elaine. I've lied, cheated, and stole to bring in this well. Maybe not outright at first, but I, we all, let John Earl do it for us, like our hands was still clean as long as he was the one done it."

He spit the words in disdain. "Never askin' him no questions, never believin' what folks said about him, still lettin' him do whatever he wanted, however he liked so long as we got results." He pointed to the photograph once again. "Look what it got us. Sold our souls for a mess of potash." He sat beside her on the edge of the drilling floor.

Mavis dabbed her eyes with the hem of her skirt.

"After the husband and father I been, you ought to tell me to go straight to hell for what I'm about to say." He inhaled deeply. "I want to make things right... if you think I still can."

Her back straightened; she spoke without the bitterness.

"I believed ever since I was a little girl that there's somebody upstairs decidin' what's right and what's wrong, what's meant and what ain't. And when He sees folks a goin' off in the wrong direction, he gives the old bit a jerk," she demonstrated the motion, "just like you used to that old mule when she went to strayin' and the rows took to gettin' crooked."

She looked up into the sky and shouted. "And we felt it, felt it good. So, you can stop your tuggin' now."

Offering Cale her hand for help in the climb to face him, she added softly, "We're back plowin' straight rows."

As she rose, their eyes met with love renewed.

The length and passion of their embrace did not go unnoticed in the parked car.

Sporting an "I told you so" grin, Pup started the engine.

"Where do you think you're going?"

"Mavis got her a ride, besides all that's gone on the last few days has me to thinkin'. We're on our way to Louisiana to see my momma. First town over the line," he said with authority, "we're gettin' married."

Babe threw her arms around Pup.

"Wave to 'um honey." He pointed to Mavis and Cale. The redhead was signaling frantically for them to go on without her.

The car jerked into gear. Babe turned around once more, watching Cale lift Mavis high in the air under the crisscross shadow of the Willie B. #1.

In Memorium

My uncle, H.R. Burden, left the "bootheel" of Missouri for the oilfields of East Texas circa 1936. After establishing his wildcat drilling company, he sent for his young brother (my father), Harry, to come and roughneck for him.

My dad finished Kilgore High School and began what was Kilgore Junior College before WWII. He went to school by day and roughnecked by night.

This book is not their story; however, their struggles inspired me.